First Novel
(over 90,000
words)

PHOENIX PEOPLE

BY
JAN PAUW

Cover design by Joleen Naylor

Published by Jan Pauw

PHOENIX PEOPLE

Contents

INTRODUCTION

Mark Kauffman was a self-made man. Embarrassed about being poor, he vowed to get rich by his tenth high school reunion. Over forty years he built a multibillion-dollar real estate empire. He and his wife became noted philanthropists. After the 2008 financial crisis, he was convicted of securities fraud, losing his reputation, wealth, marriage and freedom.

We discussed his case in one of my graduate courses in forensic psychology. The professor suggested that an in-depth study of his career and downfall might provide interesting insights into the thinking patterns of white-collar criminals. Some months later we agreed that I would do my PhD dissertation on this.

I interviewed Mr. Kauffman in prison eleven times from June 12, 2011, through October 23, 2013, and we exchanged letters more frequently. Also, I met with some of his friends, colleagues and family. I kept notes, tape recordings and transcripts of the meetings with him and others.

I had no idea that our relationship would change my life in many ways. But rather than try to explain it, I will let our correspondence, my meeting notes, and parts of my meeting transcripts speak for themselves, adding a few comments to help clarify our story.

Dr. K.T. Alvarez
October 17, 2018

Chapter 1

GETTING STARTED

Ms. K.T. Alvarez
Department of Psychology
UW Box 351525
Seattle, WA 98195

May 15, 2011

Mr. Mark Kauffman (Inmate)
Federal Correction Institution-Sheridan
27072 SW Ballston Rd.
Sheridan, OR 97378

Dear Mr. Kauffman:

I am a PhD student in forensic psychology at the University of Washington. We discussed some aspects of your case in one of my graduate courses. I would like to do a research project involving your case and would like to meet with you. Please put me on your approved visitor list. I can explain what this is about when I see you in person.

Very truly yours,

Ms. K. T. Alvarez

# # # #

First meeting

I met with Mr. Kauffman on June 12, 2011, at the Federal Correctional Institute in Sheridan, Oregon. It was nearly a five-hour drive and, although they were expecting me, it took forty minutes to get through security. By the time we met, I was tired and tense. What if he refused to cooperate?

A guard led me to a small drab meeting room, beige walls, vinyl floor, fluorescent lights, down a long drab hall in a large boring brown building, one of several clustered at the edge of town. It was not noisy like the jails I had been in, but it was sterile and soulless.

Another guard brought Mr. Kauffman in. I stood. We shook hands. We sat down. He seemed a man of great dignity, charisma even, like you might expect in a retired general, someone who was used to being listened to. He was dressed in clean khaki pants and a long-sleeved khaki shirt, neatly tucked in, like he was modeling the prison uniform for a fashion magazine. He examined me with an amused and quizzical look.

I explained that I wanted to do a case study of his situation for my PhD dissertation. I did not try to explain the more technical aspects of that; he probably would not have understood them and that might made him even more skittish. I said I would like to meet every few months but, since it is such a long drive, most of our communications would have to be in writing. His reaction, per a transcript of my tape recording:

Mark Kauffman: Write you say? Right. Not gonna happen. I'm a billionaire, right? Billionaires don't write. We have people do that for us. I haven't written anything since college.

K.T. Alvarez: It would not have to be formal or fancy. You could just write down what you would say if we were meeting in person.

MK: And why would I want to do that?

KTA: An in-depth study of your situation could be of value to forensic psychologists.

MK: But what's in it for me?

KTA: To be honest, I haven't thought much about that.

MK: Well, being honest, that's good. But the rest of it sounds like a crock of shit.

KTA: I'm sure there could be some benefits for you, but I want to think about that from your perspective. I don't want to say something stupid and make you mad. Let's both think about it.

He didn't say anything more. I left, feeling quite discouraged.

# # # #

[Handwritten]
June 18, 2011

Ms. K.T. Alvarez
Department of Psychology
UW Box 351525
Seattle, WA 98195

Sorry I was rude to you. Let's talk again. Not promising anything but willing to listen.

Mark Kauffman

# # # #

Second meeting

I met with Mr. Kauffman again on June 25, 2011. It was a beautiful early summer day, a few puffy clouds, everything green and lush. The Willamette Valley is beautiful this time of year. I felt more optimistic than when I drove down the first time, and certainly more optimistic than when I left. After all, he had initiated this meeting. That was a good sign.

I tried again to explain what I wanted, but he seemed to want to start with some small talk.

> MK: Wait, before we get down to business, I'm curious about your name. You introduced yourself as "Katy," but your letters say "Ms. K.T. Alvarez." What's ....

KTA: [Laughing] My mom named me Katherine Teresa but always called me K.T., or maybe Kay-Tee, I never saw it written it down. The first day of kindergarten the teacher kept asking for Katherine, but I didn't know that was me. When she finally asked me my name, I said it was K.T. She started calling me Katy and then the kids did too. I have gone by that ever since, but the UW records show me as Katherine Teresa, so it seems easier to go by K.T. when I'm there."

MK: Did your friends already know you as Katy?

KTA: I didn't have any friends. It was a new school. I didn't know anybody.

We talked a little about being kids and how the first day of school can be scary, but I wanted to get back to the subject of my research.

KTA: I am sorry about our last meeting. I should have been more sensitive about your feelings. It must be hard to fall from being a successful and respected businessman to a disgraced prisoner. Do you think it might be therapeutic to talk and write about that?

MK: Yeah, I've been brought low. Does that fascinate you? It seems to fascinate a lot of people. But I try not to be angry about it. Anger isn't good for you, you know. So, I try to stay positive. I'm doing the best I can. I don't want any therapy.

KTA: I didn't mean I would try to be your therapist. I'm a research psychologist, not a clinical one. But I could be a good listener. After all you have been through, wouldn't it feel good to have somebody try to understand you?

MK: How could you hope to understand me? What are you, 25 or 26? I'm 67. What have you done? Gone to school, maybe worked a few part-time jobs, been an officer in a sorority or something? I've been an entrepreneur, a financier, a philanthropist, for over forty years, since long before you were born. And a husband and father too. My "fall" as you call it, well, I don't understand it myself, so how could I explain it to you?

KTA: Maybe working together we might both come to understand what you did wrong.

MK: But I didn't do anything wrong. Nothing in me or my case could teach you about real criminals, people who lie and cheat and defraud people. I was an honest businessman, or businessperson to be politically correct. Maybe too honest for my own good sometimes.

KTA: OK, "wrong" was a poor choice of words. What I meant was, from your point of view, something must have gone wrong to cause your fall.

MK: You got that right. But, look, how many people did you send that letter to? A hundred? Two hundred? More? Gathering data on hundreds of cases and pretending you've got the mathematical chops do a meaningful statistical analysis, that's not going to teach you a thing about me and my situation.

KTA: Just you. I want to do an in-depth study of you and your situation.

> MK: Why me? How'd you pick me? How'd you even get in here? I bet one of your professors knows the warden or something. People can't just walk into a federal prison with a tape recorder and start talking to people. You've got some kind of connections. What's really going on here?

I should have answered his question, but I was flustered and afraid I might say the wrong thing, set him off, kill any chance of getting him to cooperate. So, I thanked him for his time, said I hoped to see him again soon, and left.

Mr. Kauffman says he did nothing wrong, but twelve people agreed that he was guilty beyond a reasonable doubt, so how credible could he be?

# # # #

June 29, 2011

Dear Mr. Kauffman:

I'm sorry I left our last meeting so abruptly without answering your question. Yes, I do have connections. The assistant warden at FCI Sheridan was a student of the professor who is supervising my dissertation, Dr. Jacqueline DeProulx. I should have told you that when you asked. I got flustered, worried that you might not be willing to cooperate on my project.

Perhaps I have been too focused on my hopes for how this would unfold. I should have been more sensitive to your feelings.

FYI, I am 25.

I would like to continue along the lines we discussed, but I understand you may want to establish some boundaries. I hope we can agree on that.

I promise to be more candid in the future, give you honest answers whenever I can, and be very clear if I am unable or unwilling to answer any of your questions. Likewise, you may refuse to answer any of my questions that you consider intrusive or inappropriate.

Katy

# # # #

[Handwritten]
July 6, 2011

Ms. K.T. Alvarez

I figured you must have connections. Like I said, I know how things work.

But, wait, I don't want to talk about that. What I want to do is say I'm sorry too. I've been grouchy and rude. That's not like me. My mother often said, "It doesn't cost anything to be nice." She was right, of course. I've got a lot to be grouchy about but, still, that's no excuse. Normally I'm a kind and gentle person. I try to be nice to people, always have. That's how I got rich, being nice to people.

I know Dr. DeProulx and I'm quite fond of her. Jackie must have told you a lot about me.

Again, I'm sorry. I'm willing to help on your project. Let's pretend these last few weeks never happened. I'll be a much different person, open, honest, cooperative. You'll see.

Like you said, I've got the time. They try to give us stuff to do, but being a prisoner isn't much fun. I'm trying to be more positive. I try to think up good things about being a prisoner, which isn't easy. It's boring, mainly. The only good thing I've come up with so far is that there's no wife to make you put the toilet seat down. Actually, there's no seat on the toilet.

Mark

# # # #

July 13, 2011

Dear Mr. Kauffman:

I very much appreciate your willingness to cooperate. I am curious about one thing, though. Why the sudden change? Frankly, I had gotten discouraged, thinking you might not be willing to help me. I am very glad you changed your mind, but can you explain how that happened?

Dr. DeProulx talked about your case in class but has not said much about you. I did not know you were on a first name basis with her. I am not. Our relationship has just been professional, but she did encourage me to make your case the subject of my dissertation.

Do you know how to keyboard? I'm having trouble with your handwriting, and maybe it would be easier for you to use a computer.

Again, thank you so much for agreeing to cooperate.

Katy

# # # #

[Handwritten]

July 20, 2011

Ms. K.T. Alvarez

Keyboard? Is that a verb now? I know how to type, or at least I used to. I typed a lot in college, over 45 years ago. They didn't have computers back then. But I hear you about my handwriting. My mom said the same thing. That's part of why she made me take typing. There's a funny story about that but, well, not now.

You seem surprised that I'm willing to cooperate. "Why the sudden change?"

Well, for one thing, I'm fond of Jackie and wouldn't want to disappoint her. Also, I got to thinking about what kind of person I am. That angry, hostile guy you've been seeing, that's not me. I haven't been myself these last few weeks. I'm really a kind, gentle, caring person.

I don't have a lot of friends in here. My friends on the outside seldom come. I tried to be a mentor or father figure or something for some of the other prisoners, but they weren't interested. When you came along, I treated you like dirt. I don't know why I did that. I should have seen it as an opportunity.

And, being so grouchy, I should have seen that as a warning. I need to manage my moods better. I can't get out of here until my appeal is decided, so I need to stay strong until then. I can't risk falling apart. Helping you might help me stay focused, positive, optimistic.

I've said many times the first step toward happiness is to be thankful for what you've got. Focusing on what you wish you had, that's a recipe for misery. I still believe that, but I've got to work harder at it now.

So, I've made up my mind: I'm going to be thankful for you, treat you better, and try to turn this into something good for both of us.

We'll focus on my business career. This isn't some kind of therapy. Like I said, I don't need that.

I've thought of another good thing about being in prison, at least for us older guys who have to get up at night to pee. It's not far from the bed to the toilet. Most of the inmates are too young to appreciate that, though.

Mark

# # # #

July 28, 2011

Dear Mr. Kauffman:

I also hope this turns out to be a good experience for both of us.

I appreciate you explaining your change of heart. Now I would like to move into your career, how you got started in real estate.

I have permission from the warden's office to send you a laptop. You will not be allowed to connect to the internet, but it has a word processing program with tutorials. Your typing skills should come back with a little practice. You can correct mistakes and move words and sentences and paragraphs around or delete them, so it is much easier than typing was in the old days. Also, I have arranged for you to use a printer in the library there. The librarian will teach you how to use it. I am sending some pre-addressed, stamped envelopes.

Thanks again for being willing to cooperate.

Katy

# # # #

[First computer-generated letter]

Aug. 4, 2011

Ms. K.T. Alvarez

I got the computer and have been practicing my typing—or keyboarding. I'm getting the hang of word processing. If you got this, somebody must have showed me how to use the printer. It's a big come-down, though, from being a billionaire financier to learning your basic secretary skills. I know, they're called Administrative Assistants now. Another good thing about being in prison: you don't have to be politically correct all the time.

So, you want to know how I became a real estate developer? I think the best place to start is with Sputnik. Then the I-5 bridge over Lake Union. Then flat feet.

In October 1957, the Soviets launched Sputnik. It shocked the whole country. The Russians had a satellite! How could they be ahead of us? This was in the height of the cold war. We needed to catch up, fast. So, the space race was on when I started High School in 1959. For my sophomore year I had honors English, honors history, intensive chemistry, intensive physics, advanced math, orchestra and PE. I never asked for those advanced classes, and neither did my parents. I got picked. How'd they pick me? I'd been bored in school but hadn't done all that well. Teachers kept telling me I wasn't working up to my potential. Why'd they think I had so much "potential"?

A few years later I found out: a letter inviting me to join MENSA. I'd never heard of it. It's some kind of club for people with high IQs. I didn't remember ever taking an IQ test and I thought having a club for smart people was a dumb idea. I didn't join. But by then I knew I was smart. Of 560 people in my high school class, twenty-two were in honors English and history, twenty-two were in intensive science and advanced math, nine of us were in both.

I loved the classes. We had the best teachers, the latest editions of college textbooks. The kids were smart and worked hard. We were on a mission: we had to learn enough to beat the Russians and save the world. We had all kinds of special stuff. Extra chem labs before school, college professors as guest speakers, tours of modern factories. One time they took us over the mountains to see where they made atomic bombs at Hanford. It was challenging and exciting and fun. Those advanced classes were the best thing that had ever happened to me: a taste of success that I'd never had before.

I did well academically. Socially, not so much. We had a lot of group study times and group projects. We met in other student's homes, but never in mine. My classmates' parents were doctors, lawyers—no Indian chiefs, but professors, engineers, bankers, business owners. I was the only poor kid with uneducated parents. I was ashamed of our house, my clothes, my parents. I didn't fit in.

So, long before I got out of high school, I had a secret goal. Not to beat the Russians or save the world. Much more practical. I wanted to be the richest person at our ten-year high school reunion.

What does the I-5 bridge have to do with it? When I was at the University of Washington, it was the biggest, coolest construction project going on. Huge, high, long spans being pieced together with no supports from the ground—an amazing piece of engineering. It was a few blocks from Terry Hall, the dorm where I lived. Some friends and I walked over every week or so see the progress. Stephen was shy, kind of a nerd, like me. Maybe I was the first person to figure out how smart he was. He was an architecture major. Jonathon, a journalism major, was more outgoing, more extraverted. They were the first new friends I'd made since my brother died. We were just starting our senior year.

Sometimes we walked along the waterfront by some houseboats. Back then houseboats were the slums of Seattle, just shacks on big cedar logs. Seattle has really changed since then. I had a lot to do with that, of course. Sometimes we walked high on a hill to look down at the bridge construction. Going that way, we passed a boarded-up, partly burned house. One day one of the guys said it would be cool to buy it, fix it up, live in it, and not have to pay rent. Stephen said, "You'd make more money fixing it up and selling it."

"What do you mean?" I asked.

"Modernize it, make it bigger and nicer, turn it to take advantage of the view."

"So how much money are we talking about, how much profit?"

"Oh, I don't know, six thousand dollars, maybe more."

Several nights I tossed and turned, thinking about that. Could this be the answer to what had been bugging me? I was a senior. I was supposed to know what I'd do with my life, but none of the options looked good. Becoming a doctor or lawyer was very expensive and would take a long time, and they didn't make much money the first few years. Two professors suggested I apply for a Fulbright scholarship, which could jump-start me onto a tenured professor track, but that would take a long time too and I'd never make much money at that. So, how could I get rich by my ten-year high school reunion?

And flat feet? I got called in for my draft physical. I told the draft board that I had a student deferment. They told me to bring in transcripts for my last quarter and registration documents to prove I was a full-time student in good standing. Seemed easy enough. But Fall Quarter I'd failed one course and got an incomplete in another. I'd been down, not sleeping well. I thought of myself as a star student but now I was on academic probation. I could get my student deferment back in time to avoid being drafted but the draft board made me take the physical. They wanted me ready to go if I wasn't in good standing by the end of Winter Quarter.

Back then getting drafted meant going to Viet Nam. I didn't want to go, but I wasn't going to move to Canada or become a CO—that's a Conscientious Objector, Katy, if you've never heard the term. Kids in your generation don't seem to know much about the draft.

On January 6, 1966, I flunked the physical. Flat feet. 4-F. Four for fortunate. F for free. No need to worry about having my ass hauled off to the jungle to be shot at. As I said, I was not sure what I wanted to do, and down because my grandma died and my dad was sick. But now I didn't have to stay in school for the draft deferment. I could do whatever I wanted. I could buy a half-burned house, maybe.

Mark

# # # #

Aug. 11, 2011

Dear Mr. Kauffman:

Thank you for your August 4 letter. It was very helpful. I have a couple of questions. Why were you ashamed of your house, clothes, parents? Also, you mentioned a brother and grandmother who died. I would like to know more about how their deaths affected you.

But we're off to a good start. I look forward to learning more about the burned-out house.

Katy

# # # #

Aug. 18, 2011

Ms. K.T. Alvarez

By the time I got your letter I was almost done with this one. Maybe I'll get to your questions later, but they seem kind of personal. Our deal was that I would tell you about my career, not get into personal stuff.

The idea of buying the burned-out building and fixing it up kind of got a hold on me. One day I said let's not just talk about it; let's see if we could really do it. The other guys thought I was crazy, but Stephen said, "Why not? You gonna do it?"

I went to see the real estate agent named on the "For Sale" sign. He frowned when he saw how young I was and how I was dressed. The first thing I learned was to wear a suit and tie when you want to do business. Anything goes now, but back then dressing up was important. Must have been a slow day, though; he didn't seem to have anything else to do and was willing to talk to me. I asked how much they wanted for the burned place. He said, "$3,000."

"How'd you come up with that?"

"Lot's worth about $6,000 with the building gone and debris removed. That would cost about $2,500 and take some time, so the owner will take $3,000 for a quick sale."

"Well, your sign has been up for more than two months. How quick is quick?"

"These things take time. Not a lot of people looking for half-burned buildings these days."

"I am. I'd like to talk to the owner."

"No can do. That's why they hire brokers like us."

"Who's the owner?"

"Can't tell you that."

"Sure you can. Maybe off the record as they say."

"Well, the ownership is a matter of record. You can look it up yourself."

"How do I do that?"

It took another hour to get the information I needed. The owner was United American Insurance Company. The guy to talk to was James Hawthorne, downtown on 3rd Avenue near Pine, and his room number was on a directory in the lobby. I promised not to mention the real estate guy.

He said, "By the way, I get—my firm gets—a commission even if you deal directly with them. Don't think you're cutting me out or saving them any money by going to them direct."

"I'm not trying to cut you out. I want to buy that building and fix it up. If I can get in the door and talk to them, maybe I've got a chance. If you took them an offer from me, with no money and no job, they'd laugh you out of their office."

"That's right."

"And I'm going to offer more than $3,000. You're on commission, right? You'll get more if I buy it than if you sell it to somebody else. And, after I get it fixed and ready to sell, I'll be looking for a broker. You'll be at the top of my list."

"Actually, I'm not a broker, just an agent who works for one. But if you come to me, we can take the listing and I'll get credit for that even if some other broker sells it."

"Nice to see we're on the same page. It's been nice talking to you."

"Don't get your hopes up. I don't think Mr. Hawthorne will see you. You probably won't get in the door."

I went to Mr. Hawthorne's office the next afternoon. Wore the suit that Dad bought me for my grandma's funeral. I told his receptionist, "No, I don't have an appointment, but I want to see him for just a few minutes. Can't I wait and see if he'll see me?"

The receptionist left at 5:00. About 5:30 Mr. Hawthorne came out and asked what I wanted. I explained that I was willing to pay 25% more than the asking price for the burned-out house, would fix the place up and sell it. I said I was working with an architect, OK, an architecture student, who'd made some preliminary plans and thought it was quite doable. We talked about getting permits, how long the work would take, how much it would cost, how long it might take to sell the rehabbed building. Things seemed to be going well until he said, "So, this will be a cash purchase?"

"No, but I could pay some down and the rest when we sell the building."

"I was afraid of that. Then the price would be higher, and you'd have to have a bank loan and a licensed contractor. And how old are you?"

"Twenty, almost twenty-one."

"Problem. You gotta be twenty-one to sign contracts to buy real estate and get bank loans."

"Well, I'll be twenty-one in a month or so. Won't it take a while to work out all the details? Won't there be a lot of paperwork that will take some time?"

"How long is 'a month or so,' really?"

"More like six weeks. My birthday is the 20th, March 20th."

"More like seven weeks. But I like your spirit. You've got guts, if nothing else."

"Can I get back to you in two weeks, in case you forget?"

"I won't forget. But yes, call me in two weeks."

After two weeks I called Mr. Hawthorne. "Remember me?"

He laughed. "I won't forget you." I think he kind of liked me, liked my spirit, like he said.

I brought new drawings, material lists, cost estimates and a critical path for permitting and construction. Stephen had arranged for this to be his senior project, with ten credits for Winter and Spring quarters.

Mr. Hawthorne seemed impressed. He took off his suit jacket. I kept mine on. We talked for a couple of hours. Finally, he said, "This is a bit unorthodox, but we don't have any other offers and the city wants the place cleaned up. I'll have to clear it with my boss, but if we can come up with something, I'll take it to him and see what he says."

Mr. Hawthorne introduced me to a loan officer at Seafirst Bank, Mr. Frank Wilson, and explained that the insurance company wanted to help solve a blight, a half-burned house in a neighborhood where both companies had interests. The insurance company would appreciate it if the bank would give me a construction loan so it could be rehabilitated, become an asset to the neighborhood, maybe a catalyst for other improvements in the community.

Mr. Wilson asked how much "equity" I'd have and where it would come from. I said, "I'm working on that." I could come up with $1,500, more if I dropped out of school and used the tuition money for next quarter. I had a job stocking shelves at the IGA that paid $1.85 an hour, and maybe Stephen and I could borrow some from our folks.

He sighed. "Doesn't sound good. But show me what you've got."

I showed Mr. Wilson the plans, materials list and cost estimates. There was a lot of talk about my limited income, zero assets, zero experience. Mr. Hawthorne said the insurance company had given this a lot of thought and wanted to take a chance on "this impressive young man."

"Well," Mr. Wilson said, "we have an exception process we can use for special circumstances. I could take this to the committee that runs it."

When we left, Mr. Hawthorne slapped my back and said "Well, Son, it looks like we may have pulled that off. Kind of fun, huh?"

"I wouldn't call it fun. I nearly lost my lunch. But you think we might make this work?"

"Can't tell yet, but it looks better than it did a couple of hours ago."

There were more meetings over several weeks. Finally, we agreed on a construction loan, but I'd have to come up with nearly four thousand dollars for the down payment, permits, materials and labor before I got any money from the bank.

Mark

# # # #

Aug. 25, 2011

Dear Mr. Kauffman:

Thank you so much for your August 17 letter. Your explanation of how you got into the real estate business is very helpful.

I am sorry you considered my questions too personal. As we agreed, you do not have to answer any questions you consider inappropriate.

Katy

# # # #

Sept. 3, 2011

Ms. K.T. Alvarez

No, I don't think your questions were inappropriate. I'm not ashamed about that stuff anymore.

We lived in a converted A-frame chicken coop with an old rusty Quonset hut attached. Mom, Dad and Grandma lived downstairs; my brother and sister and me slept in the attic. The only bathroom was downstairs. One night when I was about nine, I woke up and really had to pee. I didn't make it all the way to the bathroom and wet my pajamas. My father gave me a coffee can. I was supposed to pee in it at night and bring it down in the morning. I was so mad and embarrassed that I poured the pee out my bedroom window every morning. After a couple of years there was a big stain on the roof of the Quonset hut below.

There was no bathtub. When we were little my mom bathed my brother and me in a double concrete laundry tub. After my sister got too big to wash in the kitchen sink, Mom would put her in with one of us. That embarrassed me. Dad took showers at the store. When I was about ten, Dad converted a broom closet to a shower. Mom said, "Thank God for the shower; ten years of sponge baths was enough."

Most of my clothes came from Goodwill or were hand-me-downs from other families, except my school clothes and they were too dressy. My father was German. To him school was serious business requiring serious, businesslike clothes. Wool slacks, no jeans, shirts with collars, not what the other kids wore.

My grandmother made boxer shorts for my dad, my brother and me out of old chicken feed sacks. In seventh grade when we had our first gym classes, I saw everybody else had white briefs. I'd slide out of my pants and underwear together so my friends wouldn't see those awful boxers. Then one day we had to line up in our underwear to get weighed and measured. My boxers had a flower pattern. I'd never been so embarrassed.

And dating. The only vehicle we had was an old Studebaker pickup. I couldn't take a girl out in that. I always had to double date with somebody who could use their parents' car. Kids didn't have their own cars back then, especially not honors kids. The only kids with their own cars took auto shop. My friends and I never hung around with them.

Mark

# # # #

Sept. 10, 2011

Dear Mr. Kauffman:

How poor was your family? You had a house, so you weren't homeless. You mentioned that your dad worked at a store. Was that a steady job? You were a university student. Were you on a scholarship?

Also, I still would like to know how the deaths of your brother and grandmother affected you.

I am not trying to pry into anything embarrassing and, as I said, you do not have to answer any questions that make you uncomfortable.

Katy

# # # #

Sept. 15, 2011

Ms. K.T. Alvarez

Those terrorist attacks last week are so awful, so, so shocking. What is going to happen to this country? I feel so bad for all the families that lost loved ones. It's hard to think about anything else. I'll get to your questions later, maybe.

Before 9/11 I had been working on the next installment of my history. Here is what I had written.

I asked Stephen, "Isn't your birthday in August? You'll be 21 then?"

"Yeah, August 4."

"Problem. You've got to be 21 to sign real estate contracts and get bank loans."

"No problem. I don't want to sign those anyway. This is your project but I want to help. My dad will loan us a thousand dollars and I can loan you some more, seven or eight hundred maybe."

The burned-out house thing seemed to be coming together but I'd need more money. I put up 3 X 5 cards on bulletin boards in the business school lounge and the

Suzzallo library: "Typing—$0.35/page." Some foreign MBA students gave me typing jobs that needed a lot of editing because their English was poor. That slowed down my typing but got me great recommendations and more work than I could handle. I raised my price to $0.50 a page and made over three hundred dollars typing papers the last month of Winter Quarter.

I told you there's a funny story about me learning to type. In seventh grade I asked Mom to type a paper for me and a friend—he did most of the writing, so I told him I'd have her type it for us. She said, "Just this once, but then you've got to learn to type. You're going to college. You'll need to type, especially since nobody can read your writing."

"You've got to be kidding, Mom. Only girls take typing. And I've got orchestra for my elective. No time for typing class."

"It'll have to be summer school then."

"No way, Mom. I can't do that." But she made me to do it. I was the only boy in the class. And I had zits, acne. I didn't want to be with a bunch of girls with my face all broken out, but Mom didn't care about that.

One day I got a hard-on in typing class, you know, an erection. In typing class you've got to keep both hands on the keyboard; you can't put your hands in your pants to arrange things to get more comfortable. And you've got to keep your eyes on the page. I looked around to see if anybody noticed my problem, lost my place, lost my rhythm, turned very red. But concentrating on my typing helped the problem go away. From then on, I concentrated on typing and tried not to think about the girls around me. My typing got a lot better. By the end of the course I was one of the better typists, or keyboarders I guess you'd say today. This surprised everybody, especially the teacher. Of course, I never told her how that happened.

Back to the project. At first, I thought my friends and I could do a lot of work ourselves, maybe hire an electrician and plumber for a few days. I'd worked construction jobs two summers, mainly ditch digging, hod-carrying, general labor, no-brains grunt-work. Framing and stuff like that: how hard could it be? But Mr. Hawthorne said I needed a licensed contractor.

Stephen and I met at the Northlake Tavern. I wasn't 21 but my buds and I'd been drinking beer there for a year or so. I said I can't go back to Mr. Hawthorne without a contractor lined up.

Stephen said, "My Uncle Vinny, he's a contractor. He's not really my uncle but he married my oldest sister and likes me to call him Uncle Vinny."

"Think he might do it?"

"I don't know, but I'll talk to my dad and my sister and see if they'll help talk to him."

Stephen, his dad, his mom and I had dinner with Vinny and his two brothers and their wives. After dinner the women stayed in the kitchen and the men moved to the living room. Stephen's dad said, "So, this is Mark, the friend of Stephen's we told you about."

I started out pretty ragged, but after a while I got fired up, told them about our plans and my meetings with Mr. Hawthorne and Mr. Wilson. "So, this may sound a little crazy, but we might be able to do it: get the property, fix it up like Stephen's drawings here, and sell it and make some money."

"And it would be my senior project, and get me in with my favorite prof, Dr. Piccolo."

I thought maybe they'd make Stephen and me leave so they could talk about it among themselves, but Stephen's dad said, "What about it, Vinny, could you fit this in your schedule?"

"Well, I've got some bids out but haven't heard back. Might be very busy. Or there might be nothing else going on."

"So, Son," Stephen's dad said to me, "when do you have to have a contractor lined up?"

"I'll see Mr. Hawthorne in two weeks. The property might be sold by then. They want to sell it as is, take their losses, wash their hands of it. We're just a fallback for them, something to look at if they don't get a quick sale. But I'm hoping, you know …."

Vinny laughed. "Hey, Kid, you're not my first choice either. Doing business with family is bad business. I'd rather not do this job, but if nothing better comes along …."

"Well then," said Stephen's dad, "you're not tied down on those other projects, are you? There's a lot of inflation. You might have to raise your prices. There's lots of ways to not get contracts."

"Lots of ways to go broke too," said Vinny. "Lots of ways. I'll keep my schedule clear enough to do the work, but none of my hard-earned money goes into this. And I don't give 'friends and family discounts'—if I do it, I've got to make money too."

Two nights later we started serious negotiations. It was intense. Since then I've been in lots of tough negotiations. When I get stressed about them, I look back and remember what I learned about myself in this one.

By 10:30 there were strips of adding machine paper all over the floor. The numbers weren't working out; we needed to get the cost down. "Lookit," I said, "Stephen and me and some of our friends could do a lot work ourselves. Not skilled stuff like electrical and plumbing, but general labor, things like that."

"No way," said Vinny. "I don't want a bunch of no-experience no-skill college kids on my jobsite."

"Well, OK, but what if it's just me? I've got experience. Two summers in construction. General laborer. Experienced."

Eventually, we agreed that I would get a credit against the contract price for working forty hours a week at $1.85 per hour.

Traditional payment terms for construction materials were "2%10/net 30," meaning a 2% discount if you pay in ten days, full price due in thirty. We needed those discounts, so I agreed to pay for materials within ten days of delivery. Stephen's dad agreed to loan me another thousand dollars to help pay for materials until I could start getting money from the construction loan. Vinny agreed that I didn't have to pay for labor until the project was done, so he did put some of his "hard earned money" at risk, which he'd said he'd never do.

Vinny wouldn't come to my meeting with Mr. Hawthorne, but he let me bring his "portfolio," some 8x10 glossy pictures of his projects, recommendations from satisfied customers, and a balance sheet—the first I'd ever seen—showing his assets and liabilities. I said, "It's really nice of you to put this together for us."

He laughed. "I didn't put it together for you, Kid. I did it for the bank for another project. But I made extra copies for you and my nephew."

Mr. Hawthorne went through the portfolio and Stephen's drawings, material lists, cost estimates and critical path. Then he said, "Look, I can't promise anything. But we haven't got any other offers so we're lowering the price by 10%. If anybody takes it off our hands for $2700, my boss will grab that."

I almost choked. "But, if nobody does, my offer stands and now it's $1050 more than you're asking. What percentage is that? I can't do it in my head."

"Almost "39%. I used a calculator." I grinned. His boss wanted a quick cash sale, but Mr. Hawthorne wanted to show his boss he could get a better result by thinking out of the box.

Stephen and I came back in a week with a construction contract, bank loan agreement, and work schedule. Mr. Hawthorne went over all of it and said, "Not bad, not bad at all. I see you guys worked hard on this."

"Thanks," we said.

"How's school? Keeping up on that other homework too?"

"I'm OK," Stephen said, "I'm tired but I'm juiced. I'm gonna make it."

"You?" Mr. Hawthorne said to me.

"Uh, I won't lie to you. It looks like an incomplete in one course and maybe a D in another. I've been typing a lot of papers to make money, so I haven't had time to study."

Kind of a long silence after that. "Well, at least you won't lie to me. That's good. So, let's see what we can do."

I had to let the price go up to $4,000 to get the terms I needed: $500 down and the rest due in fifty-two weeks, with interest accruing after the 26th week.

Mr. Hawthorne asked if I had a lawyer to review the paperwork. I said, "No, I'll just have to trust you."

"You should get a lawyer."

"Can't afford one, But, then, I can't afford anything if you sue me either, so we'll have to work things out if any problems come up." He laughed.

In the early years I did lots of deals without lawyers, but it's harder when the numbers get bigger. Sometimes they do some good. I've got nothing against lawyers, most lawyers, except maybe prosecutors. Prosecutors can be very nasty. Their job should be to help find the truth, but they see it as putting people away. They don't care if you're really guilty—once they get in battle mode they just want to win. I don't want to jump ahead here, but I could tell you a thing or two about prosecutors. They're not my favorite people. But my big legal problems were more than forty years later. At the time I was just a kid. A gutsy kid, kind of a cute one, I think.

Hey, Katy, when are you going to come see me again? Writing all this down is OK, I guess, but it's kind of, I don't know, one-sided. It would be nice to see you again and talk in person.

Mark

# # # #

Third meeting

I met with Mr. Kauffman on September 25, 2011. We reviewed what he had written so far. We talked about the delays in sending letters by snail mail. Email would be faster, but the Bureau of Prisons would not allow that. I explained that they usually censor outgoing and incoming mail, but they had agreed not to open any mail between us. They logged the dates our letters going out and in and I had agreed to keep them so they could be subpoenaed if it ever looked like we were doing or planning something illegal, like smuggling contraband. Mr. Kauffman seemed comfortable with that.

> MK: Fine, fine. Hard to imagine us getting into anything nefarious like that. But hey, you sure look nice. New hairdo? New clothes?
>
> KTA: Thanks. Mr. Kauffman, there is not a lot of advice in fashion magazines about what to wear to visit a prisoner. You think I did OK?
>
> MK: Call me Mark. You always look nice, very poised, well-groomed, professional. Like you just came out of a slightly old-fashioned charm school.
>
> KTA: Thanks, I guess. It is hard, being a woman trying to break into an all-male profession and dressing to come to a place like this, well, it is a challenge.

Then I moved into more sensitive subjects.

KTA: I appreciate your efforts to be positive, to find good things about being in prison. But you seem think a lot about toilets.

MK [laughing]: No, I don't have a hang-up about toilets. Those were supposed to be jokes. But a lot of the time I sit on the bed and stare at the toilet or sit on the toilet and stare at the bed. Nothing to look at in my cell except a few magazines from the rec room, years old, nothing I'd normally read, worse than a doctor's waiting room.

KTA: I don't know what to say about your typing class story. I guess it's a guy thing, not something I can relate to very well.

MK: I'm sorry you didn't think it was funny. Any half-way good comedian could have turned that into a funny story. I guess I'm not much good at comedy. But you ought to lighten up a little. Terrible, terrible things happened to me at the end, but I had a lot of fun along the way. We should have some fun with this stuff too. You seem so serious. I'd like to see you laugh.

KTA: About those honors classes. I read about them for a Black History class. Do you know what we were taught about them?

MK: No, what?

KTA: They weren't just because of Sputnik. They were partly, maybe mainly, to keep upper crust white kids separated from black kids after the Supreme Court ordered school integration. You might have to have black kids in the same buildings but not in the same classrooms.

MK: Jeeze, Katy. Something's wrong with this country. We're raising a whole generation of young cynics. Maybe race had something to do with it in Alabama and Georgia, places like that, but not at Shoreline. There weren't any black kids in my high school.

Things went downhill when I tried to probe into his family finances.

KTA: So, Mr. Kauffman, Mark, did you have a bike when you were a kid?

MK: Yeah, but it was an old beater.

KTA: Other toys?

MK: Yeah, TinkerToys, an Erector Set, but Dad got them at yard sales and pieces were broken or bent or missing.

KTA: Clothes? How about clothes?

MK: Yeah but, except for my school clothes, they were mostly old, hand-me-downs or stuff from Goodwill, and I told you about those awful boxers made from chicken-feed sacks.

KTA: Food? Did you always have enough to eat?

MK: Yeah, but we didn't eat out much and there was a lot of your basic meat and potatoes, well, lots of potatoes and a little meat, lots of times just liver or tongue or soup bones, whatever was cheapest.

KTA: And housing? Did you always have a house?

MK: Yeah, but like I said, I was ashamed of it.

KTA: Yeah but, yeah but, yeah but. Jesus, you don't know shit about being poor.

MK: What? Where'd that come from, Ms. Hoity Toity Sorority Girl?

KTA: Sorry, sorry. I kind of lost it for a minute, but I'm not a sorority girl.

I was afraid I might have killed any chance of finishing my dissertation project, but Mr. Kauffman was not angry with me. He seemed more curious and puzzled.

MK: You don't really trust me, do you? You think I'm, I don't know, manipulative, maybe, a liar, sleazy, don't you?

KTA: Ah, well, what can I say about that? I won't lie to you. You're in here for securities fraud. Wouldn't most people assume you are untrustworthy?

MK: You won't lie to me? That's good, if it's true.

####

Oct. 4, 2011

Katy

I've been thinking about our last meeting. You seem to have an angry streak in you. Where did that come from? You're not who you seem to be, are you?

We worked hard on the burned-out house project, but I don't want you to think that was all we did. We were normal kids. We went to classes, most of them. We drank beer. We listened to popular music. Sometimes, we sang along on hit songs like "Pretty Woman" by Roy Orbison, "Do Wah Diddy Diddy" by Manfred Mann, and some Beach Boys and Beatles songs that were big that year. We listened to KJR. That would be AM; FM didn't come along until later.

I dated some but not much came of it. I tried to make out with girls, but I always got turned on faster than they did. That seemed to scare them off. Frankly, it scared me too. A lot of kids today get sexually active earlier, but my experience—or lack of it—was common back then. It was like there was a big conspiracy to keep kids clueless. For example, when Elvis Presley came on the Ed Sullivan show in 1956, the network didn't show anything below his waist but there still was a big controversy. Us kids couldn't figure out what it was all about. The news people couldn't say the way he moved his hips was "suggestive." That might cause curious kids to wonder his moves might be suggesting. I knew the TV couldn't show Elvis below his waist, but I had no clue why not.

The only time I remember either of my parents saying anything remotely involving sex was one time in 1957 when my mom heard me singing that old Jerry Lee Lewis song, "Great Balls of Fire." Mom said, "Mark, you can't sing that."

"What? It's on the radio. It's a big hit. Everybody's singing it."

"Well, think about the words."

So, I did. They went like this:

You shake my nerves, you rattle my brain
Too much love drives a man insane
You broke my will, Oh what a thrill
Goodness, gracious, great balls of fire.

"Mom, what's wrong with it? What's the problem?"

She turned red. "Balls," she said, "like, you know, like, like your balls."

I thought about that for a minute or so, finally figured it out, and started laughing. "Mom, every kid in the country is singing that song and I bet not one in a million thought of it that way."

For years I thought I'd make sure my kids had good information about sex, not think it was so mysterious, confusing, scary. Turns out that's not easy. How much should kids know, and when? How much do they already know? It's baffling. Now kids have sex education in school, see a lot of raunchy stuff on TV, know about the president getting a blow job from an intern. If you believe the media, lots of kids still in high school have had more sexual partners than I've had my whole life.

Sorry, I got a little side-tracked. The point is I kept living an ordinary student-type life even though the house project took a lot of time and energy.

But, Katy, I do want you to understand what it was like in the '50s and '60s. You want to understand me? Well, I'm a product of my times. Did your parents talk to you about the world back then? Things have changed so much. Times are so different now.

Back to the project. I signed contracts with the insurance company, the bank and Vinny on March 21, 1966, one day after my 21st birthday. The next day we applied for the building permit. Four days later, the city ordered the building demolished within 60 days.

It looked like I was screwed, about to lose the property and my $500 down payment, money my parents had sent for Spring quarter tuition and books.

I went to the building department, trying hard not to lose my temper. "We're not tearing it down. We filed for a permit to rehabilitate and modernize it."

"Well that's a different department," the man said. "We didn't know about that."

"So, can you please make your order go away?"

"No can do. But you can appeal and that will suspend it until the appeal is over."

"How do I do that? And can't we just fix this—get the permit issued so we can fix up the building and drop this thing about demolishing it?"

"It doesn't work like that. That's a different department. They may never issue your permit."

I was stunned but kept my cool. "How long before I have to appeal?"

"10 days."

"And if they issue my permit before then?"

"It supersedes our order—but they don't move that fast."

Stephen and I met with our friend Jonathon. I said, "We're in trouble. Less than a week into this thing and it's about to blow up." We came up with a plan.

Jonathon and I went to the building department and asked to see whoever was in charge of our permit application. "This is an emergency," I said. "We need to see him right away."

"Well, you can't just do that. You need an appointment."

"Does he have any time available this afternoon?"

"He's pretty busy," the receptionist said without even looking at his calendar.

"OK. We'll just sit here and hope he has a cancellation. If he doesn't, we'll be back tomorrow, and the next day and the next until he sees us. Like I said, this is an emergency."

We sat there for three hours. She glared at us and went in to see her boss several times. About 4:30 she said, "You're lucky. Mr. Watanabe has a cancellation. He can see you now."

I introduced myself and explained our problem as calmly as I could. "You see, sir, if your department doesn't issue our permit in nine days, I could lose all the money I have, or had, $500, a lot for a poor student."

"And who is this gentleman?"

"Oh, I'm sorry, I forgot to introduce him. This is Jonathon Starke, a friend of mine, a journalism student and an intern at the Post Intelligencer. He's working on an article about how we are restoring and modernizing the fire-damaged building."

"Any relation to Herbert Starke at the PI?"

"My dad."

We got our permit 4 days later. I took it over to the guy who issued the demolition order. "I don't know how you got it done so fast, but you must be one gutsy hombre." He got out the demolition order, tore it up, and said, "Go for it, Boy."

We started work a few days later. I was the first one on the job every morning and the last one to leave every night. I did whatever the foreman told me and was careful to be just a laborer, not the owner.

The foreman came around with paychecks but there wasn't one for me. I asked Vinny, "What's up with my pay?"

"You're not on the payroll. You get your hours times $1.85 as a credit against the cost of the job. Saves both of us money. You don't have to pay Social Security and L&I taxes, and I don't either. Didn't we talk about that when we worked up the budget?"

"Yikes!" I said. "Gotta eat. Gotta pay the rent."

"You're still stocking shelves at the IGA, right?"

"Yeah, but I was going to quit. I'm getting tired working both jobs."

"Your problem. But better get enough sleep. Don't come on my job sleepy. Sleepy causes accidents. You ain't got L&I, like I said, so don't get hurt."

Hungry causes accidents too, I thought to myself, but I stayed cool, didn't mouth off to Vinny like I wanted to. I was learning that if you want to get rich, sometimes you've got to keep your mouth shut.

Vinny was sending me bills for materials but no paychecks. I was desperate for cash. I sold my bike, my books and the portable electric typewriter my parents had given me. I'd heard in some places you could sell blood, but the local blood bank didn't pay. I'd heard you could get $25 for being a sperm donor, but I was too embarrassed to ask where you go to do that. I thought about selling my car, a 1956 Chevy, ten years old but already a classic. When my father gave it to me, he said, "I'm putting this in your name so if you wreck it, it doesn't go on my insurance." But I needed the car, and how could I tell my parents it was gone? I was going to take out a title loan on it, but Jonathon said, "Don't be stupid. The interest would be way high. I'll loan you the money, no interest." I hated borrowing from him but what choice did I have?

To save rent I moved out of my room and slept on an air mattress in an undamaged part of the house. At first, I used the Sanikan we had for the job and took showers in friends' places. After a while I had the city turn the water back on.

One evening a cop found me there. "You can't sleep here," he said. "This building isn't habitable. Not 'til the work's done and you have a certificate of occupancy."

"Well, we've got valuable tools and supplies here. I'm like a night watchman."

"So, are you hired by the owner or the contractor? Can you prove it?"

"Well, ah, you see sir, I'm the owner. I mean I'm buying it from the insurance company. I can prove that." The contract was out at my parents' house but, luckily, he didn't ask to see it.

"So, you claim to be a self-employed security guard? I'll talk to my boss, but I don't think that's gonna fly. It would be better if you weren't here, if I couldn't find you."

"I'm on guard duty a lot, sir. I don't want any trouble, but I can't afford to lose a bunch of stuff. Hope you understand."

Every morning I hid my sleeping bag and air mattress in a closet until well after dark when I was pretty sure the cop wouldn't come back. I had to blow up the air mattress every night and squeeze the air out of it every morning and keep the lights off. A bit of a pain but I didn't want him to find me sleeping there.

A few days later the cop came back. He seemed in a good mood. "I guess you're a security guard. Now some security guards do nap on the job a little, but I don't want to see any beds or stuff like that around here. Might find a sleeping bag or something if I had a warrant. Don't give me probable cause to ask for one, OK?" He grinned. I hadn't fooled him, but he didn't want to bust me. A lucky break.

Jonathon wrote an article published in the PI: "Phoenix House Rises From Ashes." When we were getting the building permit it was just a joke: give us the permit or Jonathon will write a nasty article about how screwed up the bureaucracy is. But as progress got more visible, he started taking the idea more seriously. It had been an ordinary 1920s house, facing east on a corner lot with only two small windows on the south side where the fire damage was. We took out that wall and extended the building twenty-two feet farther south, adding two floors of new living space, light and airy with tall narrow windows looking toward Lake Union, the Space Needle and the downtown skyline, and a two-car garage below.

Jonathon wanted to tell how we got the building permit. Stephen and I said no: "We'll be dealing with building department people for years. If you embarrass them, they'll never give us another break." Jonathon argued something about journalistic integrity but I said, "Look, if you tell that story you'll have to say who your dad is; people will think you got the internship just because he pulled strings at the paper, so you'll embarrass yourself and your dad too." He dropped that part of the article. Apparently journalistic integrity is a somewhat flexible concept.

The article focused on Stephen's design but mentioned me too. My parents saw it. I hadn't told them about the building. Dad called, we talked about it for a while, and then he asked, "How's school?"

There was a long silence. "Um, this building thing has taken a huge amount of time, so I dropped my classes."

"I see, but I sent you money for tuition and books."

"Well, I was going to talk to you about that. I paid the tuition but if you drop your classes in the first two weeks you get most of it back, so I did that. I never bought the books. I was going to tell you about all this but, ah, well, things have been really hectic around here."

"Well, at least you didn't lie about it."

"Look, I'm learning a lot. And I haven't dropped out of school. I'm still admitted. I can sign up for classes just like usual Winter quarter."

"What about Fall quarter?"

"Uh, no, I'll still be too busy with the building then."

He was disappointed that I never went back to college. Forty years later the UW gave me an honorary doctorate after I endowed a chair in the department of Architecture and Urban Planning. It cost me five million bucks, but by then it was easy to give that much away. Back in 1966 I needed the tuition refund to have enough to eat.

Stephen came up with a new idea: "We should upgrade the plans: have hardwood floors in the living room, better carpet in the bedrooms, slate in the entryway, higher quality appliances."

"And we'll pay for this how?"

"Professor Piccolo thinks it's a good idea. Ah, actually it's his idea, but Jonathon agrees. When we show this place to the news media, people will see what a high-quality product we can produce. Professor Piccolo and Vinny think you could raise the price by more than the extra cost, so your profit would go up."

"And pay for this how?"

"I knew you'd ask that. My dad says he'll loan you another two thousand dollars to make it happen." We did the upgrades.

Jonathon wrote a follow-on article about the "Phoenix House". This was before things "went viral" but we were getting a following among PI readers. We planned on another article coming out just before we listed the property for sale, but that wasn't necessary. Professor Piccolo asked if he could buy it. I told him how much I was going to ask. He said, "Fine. I'll take it."

We were ecstatic about that, but there was a problem. I'd promised to "give the listing" to the real estate guy I first talked to about the property. I wanted to be ethical, but I didn't want to pay a big commission for nothing. After losing some sleep over this, I talked to him about it. He said, "No problem. We deal with this all the time. We carve out Professor Piccolo as someone who expressed interest in the property before the listing; then if he buys it you pay only a small fee for our help with the closing." The $500 fee didn't seem small, but it was a lot less than a seven percent commission.

I sold the house for $32,950. Construction costs were a little over our revised budget, but after paying the insurance company, the bank, the money borrowed from Stephen's dad and Jonathon and Stephen, and a few other costs, I made almost $12,000. Not bad for a college drop-out in 1966. My parents had never made that much in a year.

My friendships with Stephen and Jonathon went through a lot of twists and turns over the next forty years. Jim Hawthorne and Frank Wilson were important people in my career too.

Mark

CHAPTER 2

GETTING TO KNOW EACH OTHER

Oct. 11, 2011

Dear Mark,

No, my mom never talked about how life was in the 1950s and 1960s. She was born in 1973. But I have learned a little about those times in history classes.

Katy

# # # #

Fourth meeting

I met with Mr. Kauffman again on October 18, 2011. I did not want more conflict, so I thought about our relationship a lot and wrote up specific goals for this meeting.

One, Mr. Kauffman had been willing to write and talk about his first business deal, but not anything "personal". However, my research plan required gathering information about his behaviors in non-business contexts. I wanted him to talk about his family, friends, leisure pursuits and other non-business activities, as well as his business career.

Two, I had tried to avoid preconceptions about Mr. Kauffman but had tried to put myself in his place, to imagine how he must feel. I thought his initial anger, hostility and rudeness were caused by the losses he had suffered, going from rich and powerful to poor and imprisoned. Knowing that emotions tend to reflect, I had been careful not to react to his behaviors by seeming angry or hostile or rude. Looking back, I realized this probably made me seem cold and distant.

Three, Mr. Kauffman seemed pretty perceptive about how I was approaching my project and that seemed to put him off. Instead of seeing him as a unique person, I had been focused on how to assign him to particular clinical boxes, archetypes commonly used in my profession.

Fourth, as Mr. Kauffman pointed out, I was young and inexperienced. He got some things wrong: I hadn't been in a sorority, I had "mathematics chops" he didn't know about, and much of my life had not been in the well-educated affluent class. He seemed puzzled about me, and not likely to open up until he had a clearer idea who I was.

So, if I was ever going to establish a rapport with him, I needed to be less distant and more open. He was right: I should loosen up a little.

After greetings and some small-talk, I started talking about my family.

KTA: You asked about my dad. There wasn't any.

MK: No dad? Or stepdad? Any kind of father figure?

KTA: No, none.

MK: Brothers and sisters?

KTA: No, I never had any of them either.

MK: Grandparents?

KTA: No, just my mom.

MK: It's hard to believe your mom was born in 1973. And you're 25? She was only thirteen when you were born? I'd like to talk about your family, what it was like for you growing up.

KTA: Speaking of dads, did you ever pay your dad back for the tuition and book money you, ah, diverted into your burned-out house project?

MK: No, it never occurred to me to pay it back. He never asked for it back. It was a gift. And if I'd offered to pay it back, he'd have told me to use it for the next quarter of school. For him the issue was that I'd dropped out of school. I didn't want to talk about that.

KTA: And the typewriter your parents gave you. Wasn't selling it kind of like stealing?

MK: No, that wasn't stealing. It was a gift. I could do what I wanted with it. I've always had very strong ethics. I'm disappointed that you'd question me on that.

KTA: OK, let's get off that. You also talked about dating and sex.

MK: What about it? Guys just talked; none of us really did much. Like I said, my lack of experience was common back then. Kids get into sex earlier these days. How about you?

KTA: Not me. I didn't date in junior high, or senior high, or college. Still don't.

MK: You changed the subject when we were talking about your family, or lack of one. Any connection between that and your, ah, what should I call it, celibacy?

KTA: Well, this project is about you, not me. I don't think it's appropriate to go into my personal stuff.

MK: Well, but I'd like to know more about you. There's something, I don't know, off or odd, not in a bad way, just different about you that I can't figure out. You're not really what you seem to be, are you?

KTA: I think we need to keep focusing on you, not get into my personal things.

MK: OK. I felt that way too. But, you know, I've been thinking about that. If you're ever going to understand me, maybe I need to explain some personal stuff. It wasn't just business that made me the way I am. There's more to me than just the business stuff.

KTA: Yes, I know that. Could you tell me more about your brother and grandmother, how their deaths affected you? And more about your parents? But, you know, in your own way, whenever you're ready.

So, Mr. Kauffman seemed to think I was "off" or "odd" in some way, not what I appeared to be. But even if he was right, that had nothing to do with my research. And why did he care?

# # # #

Oct. 25, 2011

Katy

You got a little emotional last week, for the first time, and changed the subject twice. You're usually so cool and focused and professional. I thought maybe you were having your period or something. Then I thought maybe you had a brother or sister who'd died, but you said you never had any. Something about your family triggered strong feelings. What was it?

You asked about my brother. Jimmy was about three years younger than me. Funnier, cuter, livelier, more loveable. Everybody loved Jimmy. He had this funny way of dancing. It was supposed to be the bop, but nobody did it like him. He was so loose jointed, so smooth and so, I don't know, graceful maybe, but funny-looking too. Like Michael Jackson's moonwalk, but long before Michael Jackson's time.

Jimmy cracked jokes. He cracked his knuckles. He cracked everybody up. Then he died. He was riding his bike, crossing Bothell Way to get to the beach. He thought he saw a hole in the traffic but there was a big truck in the close lane and he never saw the car passing it in the next lane over. That was it. He died right there, just like that. He was thirteen. I was seventeen.

We all were shaken, of course, but it hit Mom and me the worst. Dad just kept on working, didn't say much. Lucy, my sister, was sad for a long time but she'd talk about Jimmy and say how much she missed him and tell stories about funny things he'd done. Now, of course, I know that was healthy. At the time, though, I hated it. I didn't want to hear his name or think about him. I tried to pretend he'd never existed. Mostly, I tried to pretend I didn't care.

I had this theory. I'd loved him and got really hurt. So, if you don't want to get hurt like that, don't care about anybody. Love equals risk and hurt. No love, no risk, no hurt. It seemed logical at the time, but how stupid was that? For a guy who was supposed to have a sky-high IQ, it wasn't very smart. I got over it eventually, but that took a couple of years.

Mom was depressed. Nobody used that word but that's what it was. She slept a lot. She managed to get something on the table most evenings, but she lost interest in cooking. We had a lot of macaroni and cheese, bologna sandwiches, Campbell's soup. Before that she'd loved to cook. After Jimmy died, she didn't enjoy much of anything. She even let us eat dinner in front of the TV. That's how we knew she was messed up. Before, she'd never let us watch TV during dinner. Dinner was family time. Did your mom ever suffer from depression?

As I said, Dad was stoic. He'd ask about my grades but as long as I did well in school, he assumed everything was OK. That's what I wanted him to think. But he got what he wanted. My good grades got me into the UW Honors Program. Like the honors program in high school, it got me small classes with the smartest kids and the best professors. That set me up for success. And that's how I met Stephen and Jonathon.

I stayed home my first year of college, carpooled to the U with a neighbor. It didn't do much for my social life, but I didn't care about that. I pretty much stayed in my room. Near the end of the school year Mom said, "Mark, maybe next year you should live on campus with people your own age."

My sister said, "You don't play with me anymore." She stomped her foot. "Don't like being here." Stomp. "Don't like me." Stomp.

"Oh, Lucy, we're still friends, aren't we? You're still my favorite sister." (She's my only sister; that was an old joke between us.)

"No, we're not. It's like you're not even here. You just hide in your room."

"That's another thing," Mom said. "It's been almost two years. It's not good for you to be in there all the time when it's just like it was when, you know, you shared it with, with him. You need to move on, start living again. We'll start by redoing your room. Then in the Fall you can live on campus, and maybe you'll like coming back and being part of the family again. We'll get you a car so you can get back and forth."

"Well, that won't be cheap," Dad said. "And living on campus, how much does that cost?"

"Doesn't matter," Mom said. "We've got to do what's best for Mark, and I think that's it."

Lucy and I were stunned. We'd never seen Mom stand up to Dad like that, especially since Jimmy died. It was like, I don't know, maybe like a hungry bear coming out of hibernation. Dad was surprised too, but he must have felt like a big cloud had lifted. Mom had come back to life. After a minute or so he said, "OK, we can make it happen."

That summer I worked in construction: ditch digging, hod-carrying, general labor, sometimes helping with framing or roofs. At first, I tried to be a tough, macho construction worker. I swore a lot until I noticed most guys on the crew didn't swear. I kept to myself. Most of the guys left me alone, but a couple of painters went out of their way to be kind to me. Slowly I started talking to them. After a few weeks I told them about my brother and what his death had done to our family.

They said they'd pray for me and my family. I don't know why, but that seemed comforting. Or maybe it was just good for me to be talking about my brother after two years of pretending it hadn't happened or, really, pretending he'd never existed.

Later we talked about my theory that no love means no risk, no pain. They didn't tell me I was wrong, but they said they would pray about that too.

One of the painters, Raul, said he had a handicapped daughter, in a wheelchair with cerebral palsy, what used to be called "spastic," back when that meant a medical condition, not a nasty name bullies use to tease weaker kids. "We love her," he said. "God loves her. So, loving her gives us something we share with God, something that helps us know Him better. Does that make sense?"

Before I could answer, his brother, Ricardo, said, "Well, even if you don't believe in God it still makes sense. I care about my niece too, and that helps me care more about my brother and his wife, and about my wife and our kids, and about a lot of other people, including you, Mark."

"Yeah, that's right," Raul said. "It's like you've got caring muscles that need exercise. Some heavy intense caring, some repetitive light caring, some stretching, some balancing. The more you care about people the stronger you get. That's why we worry about you. It's like you aren't using your caring abilities, so you're kind of wasting away, shriveling up."

Isn't that a great story, Katy? Well, it didn't happen like that, all in one conversation, all at one time. But over the summer, in little bits and pieces, they said things like that. They cared about me and were comfortable with that. They weren't afraid that caring was dangerous. Then one day driving home from work I had this big, strong feeling that it's better to care about people than be afraid to. It was a, what do you call it, a catharsis. Caring about people is good. It's that simple. I'd been so wrong. I pulled into a parking lot, sat in my car and cried for the first time since Jimmy's funeral. A cop came by, knocked on my window and asked if I was OK. "Yeah," I said, "I'm gonna be fine."

Driving home, I started singing along with the radio, a catchy little popular song: "Happy days are here again, the skies above are clear again ...." I didn't sound much like Barbra Streisand, but I felt good. When I got home, I hugged my sister and my mom. I didn't hug my dad—we just didn't do that in our family—but I said, "I love you." I'd never said that to him before but, then, he'd never said it to me either.

So, a lot of things contributed to my recovery. My mom and sister telling me I should move away from home so I might be "really there" when I came back to visit. A couple of months of hard, physical work; I'd lost twenty pounds and was in great shape. And I was tan from working outside with my shirt off; I'd gotten a lot of vitamin D for sure. But I kept coming back to the idea that guys I worked with cared about me. They didn't try to convert me or anything, but they'd worried about my grieving and let me know they cared about me. So, I give Raul and Ricardo most of the credit for pulling me out of my great blue funk.

It isn't like I never felt sad about Jimmy after that but, when I did, I could talk about it. I'd tell stories about fun things we'd done, practical jokes on our sister, little lies to our parents, times he'd spied on me and my friends. Ordinary big brother/little brother stuff. Loving Jimmy was OK after that. Loving other people was OK too.

I moved into the dorms in September. I greeted the other guys, asked them about their summer, listened to them, got to know them, and got to know people in my classes. The year before I'd been pretty much a recluse, studying on campus, avoiding my classmates, not making any friends. Several people from my classes then said they didn't recognize me at first, I was so different. Living on campus was good for me. Where did you live when you were an undergrad?

That year several troubled kids came to talk to me about their problems. I listened and tried to comfort them. People seemed to see me as good listener and a caring person. After a while I started to see myself that way too. I've cared about a lot of people since then. A few times it hurt, but I never again questioned whether caring about people was worth it. And, that had a lot to do with how I got rich.

Mark

# # # #

Nov. 3, 2011

Dear Mark,

Thank you for your letter. I am sorry about the loss of your brother and your "great blue funk," but I'm thankful you were willing to write about them.

I have a question: Were you ever diagnosed as clinically depressed or bipolar? If not, do you think you may have had an undiagnosed depression or bipolar disorder? You don't have to answer if you don't want to, but your letter made me wonder.

Also, your story about your Mexican friends was interesting, moving, really. I understand that caring about other people helped you pull out of your depression and succeed in business. But don't you think it helped too that you opened up, made it easier for them to care about you?

I enjoyed our last meeting and I feel that we are making real progress on my dissertation project.

Katy

# # # #

Nov. 10, 2011

Katy

No, it wasn't that I opened up; the important thing is that Raul and Ricardo helped me learn to care about other people. That's what I believed at the time and have believed all these years.

I was never diagnosed as depressed or bipolar. Could I have been? No, I don't think so, at least not bad enough to need treatment. My brother's death hit me hard. The thought of graduating from college with no way to get rich fast, that was tough and triggered a second but milder funk. I pulled out of that by getting involved in the house project. It was so energizing. It was like the last piece of my life puzzle. You've got to care about other people, yes, but you need something that you care about doing too. At least I did. My career was that puzzle piece for over forty years. I loved my work. I got a lot of satisfaction from it. It's a big part of who I was and who I am.

In February 1967, we had a house-warming party for Professor Piccolo. Stephen's parents and Jonathon's and mine came, and Vinny and his brothers and their wives. Professor Piccolo didn't have a wife but some of his friends came. Everybody was impressed with the house.

I'd never had hard liquor before, but I took it easy on the booze. Stephen and I were the star attractions. People were astounded at what we'd done.

My parents seemed uncomfortable. They weren't used to being around so many educated people. Neither had gone to college. My dad worked in a hardware store and my mom was a part-time secretary/bookkeeper. Maybe it was because I'd dropped out of school. My education was very important to them; I would have been the first college graduate in the family. Maybe it was because I'd borrowed money for the project; they grew up in the Great Depression and were terribly afraid of debt. They'd been hurt and scared when I dropped out of school and borrowed money for the project. Anyway, for some reason they left early.

The party was just getting started when Vinny and his wife and brothers and their wives started to leave. I followed them, saying, "I want to thank you again for doing this, the project I mean."

Vinny didn't say anything at first. Then he said, "I got paid. Made some money. But, you're a user, not a giver. You charm people and then take advantage of them."

I was stunned. "What do you mean?"

"Well, take my nephew. Stephen did a huge amount of work for you. Did you ever pay him or give him any credit for making 'your project' possible?"

"I, ah ..., I never thought that was necessary. Everybody knew the design ideas were his. He loved doing the work, he got school credit, got an 'A' and got to know his favorite professor better. He didn't do it for money. He got everything he wanted."

"And maybe more." Vinny spat on the sidewalk, turned and walked away.

Vinny's comments gnawed at me. Was I really a "user"? Sure, I'd worked hard getting people to come together for the project. I thought I'd done a brilliant job of that. It was the biggest achievement of my life. Did people really think I'd been selfish?

I went to see Stephen's dad and told him about my conversation with Vinny. "You're right," he said, "Stephen didn't expect to get paid. And having such a success gave him a lot of confidence. It's the best thing that ever happened to him. You don't owe him a thing. Vinny made more than he expected. You paid me and Vinny's family back. You don't owe any of us anything more."

"Vinny's family?"

"You didn't know? The money I loaned you came from Vinny's brothers. They did it for Stephen, the project meant so much to him."

"Is that what Vinny meant when he said Stephen got 'maybe more than he wanted'?"

"No." Stephen's dad looked at me for a long time. He looked troubled. I must have looked puzzled, which I was. "No, he meant Stephen's relationship with the professor."

"What do you mean?"

He didn't say anything more. It slowly dawned on me. Stephen had moved into the house when the professor bought it, but there were three bedrooms. We'd lived in dorms with roommates and rented rooms in a house. Nothing sexual ever happened among the guys in those places. My stomach started to churn. "You mean they're—?"

"Yes, they sleep together. Have sex." I didn't know what to do. What could I say? After a while he sighed. "I thought you knew," he said. "Want a drink?"

He got us drinks and we sat there for a long time, neither of us saying anything. Finally, he said, "Can you still be friends with him? He's still my son and of course I still love him, but he's avoiding me right now."

"Yes, I think I can."

I avoided Stephen for a couple of weeks, but we resumed our friendship and did projects together for many years. I should have told him about that conversation with his dad right away, which could have saved them a lot of grief, but we didn't talk about that until years later.

Katy, you probably can't understand why this was so hard for Stephen's dad and me. Kids today think a "gay lifestyle" is perfectly OK, but it was different back in 1967.

People didn't talk about this kind of thing. Kids called other kids names like queer or cocksucker or buttfucker, but those were just nasty names. Nobody thought about what they might mean, or at least I didn't. Nobody in my honors classes used those words and I didn't either.

After talking with Stephen's dad, I went to see mine. I told him I was sorry he'd been uncomfortable at the housewarming. "Uncomfortable?" he said. "Hell, I was just bursting, so proud. You're getting things I never got a chance to have."

"What do you mean?"

"Oh, it's a long, sad story. I never wanted to burden you kids with it."

"Well, I'm an adult now, old enough to know whatever it is, aren't I?"

After a while he started talking about his life, how he came from Germany in 1934 at age 18, speaking little English and having no family in the U.S. Hitler had come to power and his family, Jewish on his dad's side, worried about his safety and got him to the U.S. "Your family was Jewish? I never knew that."

"Not really. My mother was Gentile, a big-boned blond-haired German hausfrau type. My parents weren't practicing Jews. As far as Jews are concerned, being Jewish comes from your mother, but that didn't make any difference to the Nazis. My name sounded Jewish. I'd been circumcised. Nazis would pull guys' pants down to check, although that never happened to me. My parents wanted to get me out of there."

He'd studied English in school and could read it some, but he hadn't learned to speak it well. In the US he listened to the radio and tried to imitate the newscasters' accents. Later, after the war, he got a tape recorder, recorded newscasts and then his own voice repeating them again and again, trying to sound like Edward R. Murrow.

In the late nineteen thirties he worked in a steel fabricating plant in Pittsburgh and later a shipyard in Seattle. He went to night school to get an American GED and started college, but he could only take correspondence and night classes because he worked full time, making money to get his parents and sisters out of Germany. He got his mother and his sisters out but not his father.

"What happened to your dad?"

"We don't know for sure, but we think he died in the camps or maybe on the way there."

"I never knew. You, Mom, Grandma, the aunts, nobody ever talked about this. Why not?"

"Well, for a long time you were too young to understand and then, I don't know, it just never seemed the 'right' time to tell you."

"But shouldn't you have told us? Wasn't it hard, not talking about it all these years?"

"No, I never wanted to talk about it. And when should I have told you? I couldn't tell you and not your brother and sister, could I? And when were they old enough to understand?"

"I'm sorry. I guess it's more complicated than I realized."

After Pearl Harbor, the shipyard was commandeered for the war effort. Being German wasn't that much better than being Japanese. They didn't ship Germans to internment camps, but he couldn't work in the shipyard anymore. He got part time jobs for a few months and then a full-time job as a janitor. He married my mom. They had me in 1944, my brother in 1947 and my sister in 1950. Then he got a job in a hardware store, stocking shelves, putting price tags on, running the cash register. He became a naturalized citizen in 1956, but the store owner still took advantage of him. He didn't have a lot of job options at age forty, with his German accent, not being a veteran, not having much formal education.

"I know you hated being poor," he said. "You tried to cover it up, but you didn't fool your mother or me. We tried to give you kids as much as we could." And they had. I didn't appreciate it at the time. (But how many kids appreciate their parents?) They gave us music lessons, Boy Scout uniforms, whatever we needed for school, and serviceable used bikes. They didn't spend much on toys or entertainment and we didn't have a TV until 1958 or 59, but lots of other families didn't either. If it hadn't been for Sputnik and those honors classes, I might have been satisfied, never knowing how richer kids lived.

"I know, and I appreciate it now. I'm sorry I didn't at the time."

This was the only time I felt close to my dad. It seemed like a big breakthrough, but it wasn't. The same cool distance came back, no matter how hard I tried to get close again. And many years later when he died, it triggered one of the things that got me locked up in here.

Mark

# # # #

Nov. 17, 2011

Dear Mark,

I understand how you loved your work and got a lot of satisfaction from it. My studies, and now my dissertation, have been a big part of who I am, so we have something in common there.

Your friend being gay? Well, you are right, that is not a big deal anymore. But there still is some discrimination. Because I never had a boyfriend, some people say I must be a lesbian, suggesting that this is bad somehow.

Your dad sounds like a good dad. You were not so poor after all, I was right about that, but I feel bad about saying you didn't know what poor was. I shouldn't have said that.

Katy

# # # #

Nov. 25, 2011

Katy

Speaking of dads, I was surprised when you said you never had one. Most kids have dads or stepdads or father-figures of some kind. I'd like to know more about your family. There's no reason you couldn't talk about it. It's not like we're in a counseling relationship where that might raise ethical issues. It wouldn't hurt to let me know more about you.

Stephen graduated and got a good job with a regional architecture and urban planning firm. I didn't graduate. I got a contractor's license and was my own general contractor for a few years, but I found the real money was in being a developer, hiring contractors rather than being one.

Another good thing that came out of Jonathon's "Phoenix House" articles was people started offering to invest in my projects. I could use money from strangers, not just friends and their families. The next few years were building years, as they say in sports, making small deals, building up a roster of contractors, experts and, most important, investors.

I worked hard but played hard too. I got to know Jonathon better, bar hopping with him and his friends, sometimes double dating. Jonathon was much more into the party scene than I was. I didn't like getting drunk and definitely didn't like being hung over. Jonathon was wilder, but heavy drinking seems to be a tradition in the newspaper business. In the movies, at least, most newspaper reporters are heavy drinkers. I started seeing him only on Friday or Saturday nights. We laughed about that. When I was a kid, I never liked having to go to bed early on school nights, so I thought the best part of being a "grownup" would be staying up as long as I wanted. I was only twenty-two and already I treated "work nights" just like school nights. On the weekends, though, we were kids again. We did some stupid stuff, dangerous stuff, but we were lucky and never got in much trouble.

Mark

Fifth meeting

Mr. Kauffman and I met again on Nov. 29, 2011. After we reviewed our correspondence, I asked if there was anything he could add to fill in missing pieces, but he wanted to talk about me:

MK: I'd like to know more about your mom.

KTA: Well, what I meant was any missing pieces in your story.

MK: Yes, but I'm curious about you too.

KTA: But this has to be about you, not me. And I have a feeling there may be something important about the Phoenix House project that you left out. Are you holding something back for some reason?

MK: No, nothing important.

KTA: Are you sure? Maybe it would seem important to me, even if it doesn't to you.

MK: I don't want to talk about it.

KTA: Well, of course you don't have to talk about it if you don't want to. But it sounds like my instincts were right—there must be something here you don't want to talk about.

MK: That's right, so back off, dammit. Just drop it.

KTA: I'm sorry. I didn't mean to pry. Well, to be honest, maybe I was trying to pry. I'm sorry. You don't have to talk about whatever it is.

MK: Let's not argue. I want this to be a good experience for both of us, but there's something about you I can't figure out yet.

Neither of us seemed like argumentative people. Was there something about him, or me, or the chemistry between us, that so often caused flare-ups like that?

# # # #

Dec. 7, 2011

Katy

You're right. I did leave something out. It's not a big deal, nothing illegal or unethical or immoral or anything. This must be a psychologist thing; you assume that what I didn't say must be more important that what I did. It isn't a key to my life, or how I got rich, or how I fell into disgrace. You're blowing it out of proportion. But maybe if I tell you about it, that might help you be more willing to talk about your personal stuff. So, I'll try to model the kind of openness I want to encourage. Here goes.

I told you I slept in the Phoenix House during the construction, to save rent and be a security guard. Sometimes Stephen brought a sleeping bag and slept there too. One night we were in our sleeping bags and he rolled over and kind of spooned up next to me. He didn't really touch me, you understand, and we were in our sleeping bags. Still, it made me uncomfortable. "Hold it," I said. "Back off."

He moved a few feet away. "Sorry, sorry. I shouldn't have done that." We just lay there for a while. When he'd moved over against me, I had a hard-on, an erection.

Back then, most nights I, ah, jacked off, masturbated, to help get to sleep. Having him there disrupted that routine. I wasn't going to do that with anybody around.

After a while he said, "You still awake?"

"Yeah."

"Do you ever think about what it will be like, you know, after we're married, having a girl lying next to us all night?"

"Well, I, ah, I think about sleeping with girls, you know, having sex, but I haven't thought much about what happens after. But, hey, this isn't a good time to be thinking about that."

"No, I guess not. I'm pretty horny right now, but I wasn't thinking about the sex part, just having somebody close, somebody to cuddle with."

"Well, I'm horny too. If you weren't here, I would have jacked off by now." There was quite a long silence. I thought about leaving or asking him to leave, and maybe I should have, but I felt sorry for him. He was my best friend and I needed his help on the project. And his dad's money. Finally, I said, "Lookit, maybe we should both relieve this, ah, horniness problem so we can get to sleep."

"You mean together?"

"No, no, by ourselves. One of us should go in another room or something."

"OK." He kind of wiggled out the door and into the hall in his sleeping bag. We both did it.

He fell asleep right away but I tossed and turned for a long time. Had I messed up our friendship? He didn't come to the project at night anymore; I guess neither of us wanted to risk having another incident like that. I avoided him for a week or so, and he seemed to be avoiding me, but I needed his help on the project and I still wanted be friends. Finally, I went to him and said, "Hey, I need your help on some stuff that's come up." Neither of us said anything about what happened that night. I've never told anybody about it.

So, there you have it, the big mystery you were so curious about. It never was a big deal. You must have imagined something much worse. We were young, both virgins and, like I said, pretty clueless about sex. Was he was trying to seduce me? No, I don't think so. Even after I found out about him and Professor Piccolo, I didn't think that. I didn't think about this for a long time, but thirty-five years later, something came up that made me look at it again. My answer was the same—he hadn't tried to seduce me.

Could our relationship have turned into something sexual? Maybe. We'd become close in other ways. We'd let each other see things we never showed anybody else, like how much I wanted to make a lot of money and how much he wanted to be a great architect. Sometimes one form of intimacy morphs into another. When you share really personal stuff, sometimes things twist into sexual feelings, don't you think? Isn't that part of why people keep some distance from others? Why people find it hard to share things that are important to them? Well, that's my theory anyway.

Mark

# # # #

Dec. 15, 2011

Dear Mark,

What you wrote about mentoring and leading by example seems very manipulative. You tell me an embarrassing story and now I owe you one, like a couple of kids agreeing to expose themselves: you showed me yours and now I'm supposed to show you mine.

And all that about being afraid to share because I might get attracted to you? Mark, you are old enough to be my father, no, my grandfather, and I told you I don't date. I'm not worried about that, for Christsake.

You probably expected a different reaction. I understand that incident with Stephen feels important to you, although I do not understand why. But I want to be honest with you about my feelings. What you wrote seemed manipulative to me.

Still, I appreciate your willingness to share something that you consider very personal. I hope you are OK with me sharing my feelings.

Katy

# # # #

Dec. 22, 2011

Katy

Just because I shared something personal doesn't mean you have to. You don't "owe" me that. And I didn't mean to suggest that you won't talk about your family because you're afraid you might get attracted to me. Good grief! That's not what I meant at all. When I talked about shared confidences morphing into sexual feelings, I wasn't thinking of you. I was talking about people in general, or maybe just me.

At first, I was hurt that you thought I was manipulating you, but this seems like a case of the pot calling the kettle black. You've manipulated me to keep your project going. But I understand your dissertation is important to you and I'm going to help you with it. You don't need to worry about me getting spooked and refusing to keep going.

The Phoenix House was the first chapter in my long career. Bigger and bigger things came later. That was a thirty-thousand-dollar project. Then came hundred-thousand-dollar projects, million-dollar projects, ten-million-dollar projects, hundred-million-dollar deals. I did a lot of good stuff, employed a lot of people, gave lots to good causes. Now everybody wants to talk about how it fell apart and how people got hurt. I got hurt too, probably worse than anybody, and nobody else ended up locked in here with me.

In 1967 I did several smaller projects and made $32,000. Doesn't sound like much now, but in Seattle that year top law school graduates started at $7,000. Making over four times that much was very good for a 22-year-old college drop-out. It was fun. Energizing. I was still just a kid, really, but wheeling and dealing, buying properties, organizing construction projects, borrowing money, selling properties, all grownup kinds of stuff.

My next big project was a run-down apartment house near the hospitals in Seattle, a classic brick building, two stories, with inlaid wood floors and stained-glass windows. Cheap to buy and not too expensive to fix up. Stephen had seen it on a field trip for a class on Frank Lloyd Wright and art deco buildings.

Stephen had graduated and become an associate at an architectural firm when he told me it was up for sale. I wanted him to do the architectural work, but he said he had to bring in one of the partners. "The partner said, "Usually partners bring in work and associates work under their direction."

"I suppose that's true, but Stephen and I have worked together before. I want him to do the work."

"Well, he'll have to be supervised by a partner."

"He's a genius. He doesn't need any supervision. What value are you going to add?"

"It's OK," Stephen said to me. "It's their company, their license, their reputation on the line, and two heads are better than one. I'll do most of the work. He'll check it out and help if I run into problems. His help won't cost you much and it will make it a better project."

The partner looked relieved. I felt stupid. Here I was, a master at getting people to work together, and Stephen had to take on that role for me. "You're right," I said to Stephen, "and I apologize," I said to the partner.

My investors and I put up twenty percent of the cost. Frank Wilson helped arrange Seafirst Bank loans for the purchase and construction. Jim Hawthorne arranged for a United American take-out loan for when the work was done.

The building had 32 one-bedroom units on two floors with hallways down the middle. Stephen had the key ideas: combine the outer two units at each corner of each floor to create eight two-bedroom two-bath units, leaving 16 one-bedroom units in between, add decks for each unit and convert windows to glass doors for access to them. We kept the classic art deco features but updated floor coverings, appliances and landscaping, and put a couple of modern sculptures by the entryway for curb appeal.

Jonathon had graduated and become a reporter with the PI, focusing on local business and political issues. He did a nice article and photo spread that helped get all the units rented in less than a week. The building sold for $498,900. I made about $92,000.

I had a couple of small projects going on, but I was looking for a bigger one. That turned out to be Pier 57 on the downtown waterfront. That's where I made my first big money. It's an important part of the history of Seattle. And it's how I met my wife, Cindy.

The ocean shipping business was changing. Container ships were coming in. Exports of lumber, seafood, and other traditional Northwest products were falling off. Grains were moving through big new elevators, not the downtown docks. There was a lot of empty dock and warehouse space along the central waterfront. It wasn't a tourist area like it is now. There were seamen, prostitutes, drunks, homeless and crazy people, but people who worked in nice office buildings or shopped in nice stores a few blocks away never went there. There weren't expensive high-rise condos like now, only cheap hotels and slums. People dressed up to go downtown. Not just professional people, but secretaries and shoppers. My mom wouldn't go downtown without wearing a dress and stockings and gloves. Downtown was worlds away from the docks, just a few blocks away.

The Port of Seattle owned Sea-Tac airport, a fast-growing container port, profitable grain elevators, marinas for pleasure boats and fishing fleets—and old obsolete break-bulk cargo docks along the downtown waterfront that weren't fully used anymore.

Once more, Stephen saw potential where others saw blight: he saw the central waterfront becoming a retail, restaurant and recreational area. Port officials couldn't grasp that. The docks were in a "harbor area," which the state Constitution "reserves" for "commerce and navigation." They thought that meant ocean shipping only.

Stephen had a friend whose older brother, Brett Jamison, was a lawyer, just a few years out of law school and very smart. Stephen got him interested in the idea of redeveloping the waterfront for retail, restaurants and hotels. After a few weeks of legal research, Brett said, "From a legal standpoint, I think it's doable. Some people won't agree at first, but I think we can bring them around. Here's what I propose: Mark, you go to my partner, Branson Stackhouse, and say you'll retain him on this if he'll give most of the behind the scenes work to me. I'll tell him you're coming and that I've already done a lot of the work on my own time."

Mr. Stackhouse helped Brett and me prepare a presentation to the Port's management. I would organize a company to lease a pier for a "Maritime Mart" featuring retail sales of imported goods and a restaurant featuring local seafood. Stephen and I told Jonathon about the project. He agreed to keep it secret, but we promised him an exclusive when we were ready to make a public announcement.

The main problems were getting all the different interests on board, all the egos soothed, all the issues documented in the right ways for different audiences. We had to convince skeptics that people would come to the urban waterfront to eat and spend money, that the old piers were millstones around the Port's neck, and that redeveloping the downtown waterfront wouldn't cost the longshoremen jobs. Professor Piccolo helped us put together an economic team, professors from the schools of economics and business, and graduate students who did most of the work. We paid the professors something, but back then professors weren't so aggressive about consulting jobs. Today, lots of them make more from consulting than from the university. The graduate students still do most of the work and still don't get paid—they pay tuition for the privilege of helping their professors make money as consultants.

You can't do this kind of project without consultants. Bureaucrats and politicians need to have their asses covered. I don't mean to sound cynical. I'm just schooling you on how things work. People pay good money to go to Trump University. I don't know what they teach there, but it's probably exactly what I'm teaching you.

What's that phrase? Herding cats. This project was a big cat-herding challenge. I worked hard to bring people together, but I was honorable too. I never lied or cheated or bribed anybody.

On October 30, 1969, we finally signed the contracts for the Maritime Mart. It was the biggest, coolest, most challenging project I'd done yet. I was twenty-five.

So, Katy, I'm trying to teach you about real estate, and business and politics and the real world in general.

You're a smart woman. You could go far in business if you wanted. You should give up psychology and go into real estate. You'd make more money and have more fun.

Mark

# # # #

Jan. 3, 2012

Dear Mark,

Thanks for the compliments but, just like your career was important to you, my profession is important to me. I am not interested in switching to a business career.

And about me trying to manipulate you, maybe I am guilty of that. My main focus is on your career, but I envision my research including information about your relationships with friends, family, employees, and others, what you did for recreation, etc. Don't get me wrong: I do not want to probe into your sex life or other things that are embarrassing or personal in that sense. Some more general things like at what age you became sexually active might be helpful, but we do not have to get into that if it makes you uncomfortable.

About that apartment house remodel: you must have gotten all the previous tenants out of it. Did you help them find other places to live? There always are shortages of low-cost housing.

Katy

# # # #

Jan. 10, 2012

Katy

Times have changed. If you refurbish old buildings now, you might have to help low income residents relocate, but requirements like that drive up costs and make it more difficult to improve aging neighborhoods.

When did I became "sexually active"? That's a rather personal question. It's not like having sex made me a better businessman or caused my downfall. But, if you think I started sleeping with women because of that incident with Stephen or his relationship with Professor Piccolo, you're wrong. It's a lot simpler than that.

Suddenly women were available. I'd made out with girls in high school and college, but always ran into resistance somewhere around the light petting stage. After Jonathon's articles describing me as "a rapidly rising entrepreneur" or "future tycoon," with some women there was no more resistance and sometimes it seemed like having sex was mostly their idea.

Back in the '60s, every few years there'd be a popular song about how great it was the first time. I especially remember that bouncy one by the Four Seasons, you know:

"Oh, what a night …

"What a very special time for me …

"Sweet surrender,

"What a night."

Well, it wasn't like that for me. I thought things were going fine, and I wondered if this would be it, the first time for me, and then, you know, it looked like it could be, and then it would be, and then it was. But as soon as I got inside her I felt it coming too fast. I stopped moving. I tried to think about something else. I tried to hold back but it just squirted out. It was embarrassing.

Nothing much had happened with her yet and I still had a hard-on, so I started slowly moving again, more from a sense of duty than any great desire. After a while, though, I started to come around again, and after a few minutes I did come again. I didn't think I'd performed too badly, but it wasn't what I'd hoped for. Actually, it was a disappointment.

Premature ejaculation. I'd never heard that term. Maybe the first time is like that for lots of guys, I don't know. Now there are ads offering help for it, but they didn't have ads like that back then and, even if they had, I couldn't have walked into some building to ask some stranger for help with this.

Over the next few months I slept with several other women. There weren't a lot. I wasn't a big playboy or anything like that. I wasn't all that serious about them, but I was looking for someone to get serious about, kind of auditioning my dates, and they seemed to be checking me out too.

This was pretty early on in the "sexual revolution." Lots of young people were sexually active in earlier generations too, of course, but it used to be hushed up. I was coming of age just when "the pill" came along and premarital sex was just starting to be socially acceptable.

I'd moved back into the rooming house. I didn't like having to sneak girls in and out, and I sure didn't want my housemates hearing what we were doing at night. That led to what one girl called the "belts in the bedsprings fiasco." My bedsprings squeaked. I tried to stop it by using a belt to put tension on them. One wasn't enough, so I added another. Still not enough, so I bought three more and added them. One day she said we ought to wash the sheets. I said, "Oh, no, I'll do it tomorrow." But she pulled the sheets off, saw the belts and started laughing. I was embarrassed but then I started laughing too. My housemates came in to see what was so funny.

So, I moved into an apartment. I owned the building and leased the unit to myself, which helped get the building fully occupied and sold. I lived there for years. I could've moved to a nicer place after my one-year lease expired, but girls didn't seem to mind the place. Of course, they knew I could afford something nicer if our relationship turned into something permanent. And I didn't have to spend money on belts. I had enough for a lifetime, except a few years later I put on some weight, so they all went to Goodwill.

I never talked about my love life but, after I started dating a secretary in his office, Mr. Stackhouse said, "Look, Mark, let me give you some advice that could save you a lot of money and grief down the road."

"What's that?"

"You're sending women the wrong message. They know you're available. Some of them are predators. It's fine to be friendly and flirt, but you've got to send signals that you're not available, at least not now. Even if you're not in another relationship, you need know how to send those signals. Otherwise you'll end up in bed with the wrong women and make a mess of your life."

It was good advice. I got pretty good at sending those signals.

Mark

# # # #

Jan. 19, 2012

Dear Mark,

I laughed about your premature ejaculation problem and the "belts in the bedsprings" thing. I know guys don't think premature ejaculation is funny, but it seemed funny to me that, after looking forward to it for so long, your first time was disappointing.

Sometimes it seems that you think about sex a lot, but maybe that is just because you are incarcerated.

In the spirit of openness and candor that I have been trying to cultivate, I admit that I have wondered if you might be a homosexual, or at least what used to be called a latent homosexual. I would not think any less of you if that were true, but it seems you are not.

Finally, about sending signals that you are not available, I too have become a master at that. So, there is another thing we have in common.

Katy

# # # #

Jan. 26, 2012

Katy

It's OK that you laughed about my premature ejaculation problem and the belts in the bedsprings. You didn't have to apologize. I would love to hear you laugh. Whenever we're together, you seem so focused and serious, so tightly controlled.

No, I don't think about sex all the time. It's just that you get me thinking about when I was young. Young guys think about it all the time. I'm over sixty-five now, on Social Security and Medicare. So, I don't think about it so much anymore except when I'm writing this stuff for you.

Why did you think I might be a homosexual, or maybe a homo-wanna-be, what was the term, a "latent homosexual"? I may not be the most macho guy around but I was never like that. This is another generational thing: you kids seem to think about gays a lot, but we didn't back when they all were in the closet.

I was working on the Maritime Mart when I met my wife, Cindy. She was a student at the UW. President of her sorority. I hadn't dated any sorority girls until I got known as a "future tycoon." She wasn't spoiled or stuck-up; she was smart and fun. She volunteered for a new group, the Washington Environmental Council. Environmental issues and "ecology" were new, leading-edge terms at the time.

Her father was a Port Commissioner. They got to talking about my project. She was down on developers, maybe rebelling against her dad and his friends. He argued that it was better to redevelop polluted, decrepit urban areas than plow under farmland or cut down forests for more urban sprawl. We'd been making that argument. It was good to hear that at least one Port Commissioner bought it.

Cindy and I started dating. I was looking for someone to settle down with, but also practicing my "signal sending" techniques. She was cautious too. And I couldn't risk getting crosswise with her dad. I needed his vote as a Port

Commissioner for the biggest project I had going on. We didn't kiss until the fifth or sixth date. Our "dates" were mainly outdoor walks or group events with friends.

Eventually things got a little more serious. We started making out. "Hey, Speedster," she said, "we're not going all that far tonight. Go slow, make it last."

Several dates later she said, "Hold it. Time to back off. I don't want to make you sore."

"What?"

"You know, lover's nuts."

She was right, we were getting to the point where stopping might be painful.

We talked about what we wanted out of life, having kids sometime, what kinds of people we admired, what we hoped to do in our careers. I think most people used to do that, before the so-called sexual revolution. People my age thought we were smarter than our parents. Why not make sure you're sexually compatible before you get serious? Well, maybe we weren't as smart as we thought. My advice, for whatever it's worth, is be old fashioned as long as you can.

Eventually, after the Maritime Mart project was approved, we did become "sexually active" as you call it. After the first few times she said, "You're not very good at this, are you?"

"What do you mean? I've done this before."

"Maybe you haven't had the right teachers. Whatever women you've been with haven't taught you much."

It was embarrassing. "OK, teach me. But before we get to the hands-on part, tell me how to pronounce it. Is it 'kly-TORUS' like Taurus the bull or 'CLIT-eris' like, I don't know, flit or something?"

She laughed. "I don't know about you, you're something else."

She taught me a lot over the next few months. Guys like to think it all comes naturally, no pun intended. Well, it doesn't take much to satisfy us guys. Women, that's something else. I had no idea what's involved. I didn't always get it right, but I did get better.

One day she said, "Now that I've taught you how to satisfy a woman, I don't want you doing this with anybody else."

"I won't. In fact, I've been practicing just the opposite." I told her about the advice Mr. Stackhouse gave me and my efforts to follow it.

"You're a good listener and a quick study. I think we'll be alright."

I think I did satisfy her a lot of the time. Some guys claim they satisfy their wives or girlfriends every time, but they're lying or deluding themselves. Cindy probably faked it some of the time, but that's a way to express love too. Nothing wrong with a woman faking it sometimes, but it should work right some of the time too. There you have it. Kauffman on sex in a nutshell.

She took me to meet her parents. I'd already met her dad, but that was business. Going to their house for dinner was quite another thing. I'd never been in such a nice place. It was on a hill looking down on Lake Washington, Seward Park and the Stan Sayres "pits" where they kept the hydroplanes during the Seafair races, with a view across the lake to Mercer Island and the mountains beyond, a classic old house with white columns, many-paned windows, hardwood floors, a big curved staircase, elegantly furnished. At dinner I was overwhelmed by all the silverware and cloth napkins and napkin rings and stuff. I tried to copy what Cindy's parents did. They must have seen how awkward I felt, but they were gracious and kind. After a while I relaxed. The cocktail before dinner and wine may have helped.

On the way home I said, "So I suppose it's my turn—I should take you to meet my parents."

"I'd like that."

"Well, it would be a lot different."

"So, what would be different?"

"Ah, um, the house isn't nearly as nice, but it's a lot nicer than where I grew up. And my dad, well, he's different. And my sister."

"It's OK. But are you ashamed of them?"

"No, not really. I used to be ashamed of our house, the old one. My dad, he's foreign, German, kind of gruff, not very educated, but a good dad in his way. My sister? She's special, a special needs kid they call them now."

"Tell me about your sister."

"Lucy? Well, she's six years younger and has Down Syndrome, what they used to call Mongoloid. She's retarded. Now they say 'developmentally delayed' but that's bullshit. She isn't just delayed; she's never going to get better. But she's fun and loving and funny sometimes. You just have to get used to her."

"Were you ashamed of her when you were growing up?"

"No, not really. The only time I ever fought was when some bullies teased her, called her names, you know, like 'retard' and 'little kid from the short bus'."

"How old were you then?"

"Eighth grade, maybe."

"What happened?"

"I got a cut lip and a black eye. One guy got a broken nose and the other lost a tooth, and there was blood all over. All three of us got suspended. My parents were pissed. 'It's OK to stand up for your sister,' Dad said, 'but you can't get into fights. Don't ever get suspended again. Your education is too important to mess up by fighting or anything else'."

"Did they punish you?"

"No. But having them mad at me was enough."

We went to my parents' place one Sunday afternoon. Cindy seemed pretty relaxed, but my parents and Lucy and I were nervous. "Are you Markie's special girl?" Lucy asked.

"Well, I hope so!" Cindy laughed.

"I mean good-special," Lucy said. "Good-special like favorite, really neat, you know. Not bad special like special-ed."

"Lucy ...," Mom tried to interrupt.

"Yes, good-special," Cindy said.

"Are you guys going to get married?" Lucy asked.

"Lucy ...." Mom tried to interrupt again.

"I hope so," Cindy said, "but right now we're just friends, just getting to know each other."

"Friends are good," Lucy said. "I have friends."

"Tell me about your friends," Cindy said.

"Lucy, maybe you should go to your room and let the grownups talk," Mom said.

"It's OK, Mom, I'd like for Lucy and Cindy to get to know each other a little."

Mom said, "Umm, this may be more serious than I realized."

"You're the first girl Markie ever brought home," Lucy said.

"Lucy ...."

"It's OK, Mom." I said to Cindy, "She's right, you are the first girl I wanted to bring home."

We talked for a couple of hours. Lucy talked about her friends and her part time job at a local pet store. She loved animals and was proud about working and having her own spending money. Cindy and Mom talked about how the neighborhood had changed since I was a kid. Dad didn't say much.

A couple of weeks later Cindy and I talked about getting married. I didn't get down on one knee or anything like that. We just assumed it was going to happen. We were ready in a lot of ways. I was surprised, though, when she said, "I want to get married in a church. Not for us or my parents but for my grandmother. She used to take me to Sunday school when I was a kid. It's, well, it would be important to her."

"OK. What kind of church?"

"Well, grandma goes to a Presbyterian church, so if you don't have any preference, that would be it."

"I don't have any preference. Actually, I've never been in a church."

"Does anybody in your family go?"

"Well, Dad once said that my grandma went a few times after she came to America. She'd gone to a Lutheran—he pronounced it 'Luterin'—church in Germany, so she went to a Lutheran church in Ballard, but it was Norwegian Lutheran and they weren't very kind to her, probably because she was German."

We got married a few weeks later in her grandmother's church. It was just family and a few close friends. When we planned it, we thought Cindy might be pregnant. By the time we knew she wasn't, it was too late to have a big wedding.

I've been faithful to her ever since. I think she was faithful too except—well, maybe we'll get to that at some point.

Jonathon was best man. I would have had Stephen, but I thought he and Professor Piccolo might be uncomfortable since marriage wasn't an option for them. Stephen was a groomsman. A PI photographer friend of Jonathon took pictures.

We had a short honeymoon out at the coast, a place called Iron Springs. After the publicity about how much money I'd made, people probably thought I had lots, but I had very little cash. And I owed the two professors for consulting work on the Maritime Mart.

We moved to a nicer apartment, one I owned of course. I set the rent a little above market which helped sell the building for a good price.

Those were great times, Katy. Young, in love, married to a fun, smart, beautiful woman, successful in business, successful in life. There were lots more good years too, but this time was special. I felt like an adult. I felt like I was going to make it.

Mark

# # # #

Feb. 3, 2012

Dear Mark,

I found it interesting that Cindy taught you about sex. I've heard girls, women, talk about how to turn guys on, but I avoid conversations like that. I don't remember any women talking about teaching guys how to satisfy them. It probably is more common than I realized, but it is not something I ever thought about.

Cindy sounds like a very kind, caring and smart woman. I look forward to learning more about your marriage and family.

Katy

# # # #

Feb. 10, 2012

Katy

Cindy went to work as an accountant for an insurance company, not the career path you'd expect for a sorority girl or environmental activist. Our money was tied up in the Maritime Mart and some smaller projects. We lived on her salary.

Jonathon started dating one of Cindy's sorority sisters. They met at our wedding and moved in together a few weeks later. It seemed wrong. Was I getting old all of a sudden? Or more conservative just because I was married? I'd never questioned my friends' relationships before. I said to Cindy, "It just seems like it happened too quick."

"Well, everybody always said she was fast."

"Did you mean what I think you meant?"

"Yeah, but I shouldn't have said it. It was a catty thing to say."

1970 was the first year we lost money. The Maritime Mart and other projects were eating money and not bringing any in. We'd made a lot of money in 1969, so we had to pay taxes on that. I saw that we couldn't make all the payments coming due. I called a meeting with Frank Wilson, Jim Hawthorne and our other creditors and investors, showed them our expected expenses and income for each of the next twelve months, explained that I wanted to treat all creditors fairly, and asked them to agree to an extended payment plan.

Frank said, "Thanks for laying this all out so clearly. I appreciate your honesty."

Jim said, "Yes, you've got integrity. And smarts, and guts. We can work with you."

The others nodded. Eventually we agreed on a plan, giving us less relief than I'd hoped for but a fair shot at getting through the recession. Lots of other developers tried to bluff their way through, avoided their creditors, and went under.

We couldn't sell the Maritime Mart until we had a good track record on rents. Tenants hadn't been sure people would come to the downtown waterfront to shop and eat, so we'd agreed to low base rents but with generous shares of their revenues and profits. I took over a year to get our cash flow up, but over time the project became a huge success. All our creditors got paid and my reputation got better.

Well, Katy, I made that look simple and easy. It wasn't. It was hard, very hard, scary, terrifying. What if I lost it all? What if let everybody down? What if I had to tell my dad that I'd borrowed too much, lost everything, and now had no money, no degree, no job, no future? It was awful. And it dragged on for months and months.

But I never gave up hope and never quit working on new things. I was already working on one of my coolest, most amazing, most profitable projects. Early in 1971 we had our annual reunion of people who'd worked on the Phoenix House. The big news was that Stephen was leaving his firm and returning to the UW as an associate professor. I was surprised. He was the youngest partner in his firm and had a great future there. "How come?" I asked.

"Computers, the wave of the future." This was before computers became common. Now almost everybody, even students who've never earned a buck, carry around smart phones with more computing power than most Fortune 500 firms had back then.

Professor Piccolo explained, "The UW is getting two big GE mainframe computers. We'll be able to run more complex calculations than we ever could before. New ways to calculate stresses and mathematically test design alternatives. It'll revolutionize engineering and building design."

"Yes, Mario's right," said Stephen, "we can get more strength and stability from smaller amounts of materials, design better projects that can be built cheaper and faster."

"Wow!" I said. "Good thing I sell my projects as fast as we finish them. Don't want to get stuck with a bunch of obsolete buildings." I was just joking but they took me seriously.

"No," said Mario, "the value of existing buildings probably won't go down. Rents will still go up, but maybe more slowly."

"That's right," said Stephen. "If computers can help you build better buildings cheaper, you can pocket most of the savings. If you stay on the leading edge, you'll be fine, make more money than ever."

"Well, that's good news!" I laughed.

Stephen and I met a few weeks later. He was excited about a new idea he called the parabolic suspended building concept. "What's that?" I asked.

"Most buildings start with big, heavy, expensive foundations, and then the useable parts are stacked on top, pressing down, each level supporting all the layers above it. What if you could hang a building from the top, with downward tension instead of compression?"

He began drawing on a napkin. Four tall towers, two toward each end of a long building. Two large cables anchored in the ground beyond the ends of the building, draped over the tops of the towers, hanging down in a parabola between them, and large parabolic arches on each side, their ends butted into the bases of the towers and their tops rising above the building. The floors were suspended from the big cables and arches and cantilevered out beyond the four towers. Only the four towers touched the ground.

A week or so later, Stephen and I had lunch with Jim Hawthorne. He was bursting to tell us two things. First, he'd become one of the youngest vice presidents at United American. Second, he would chair a committee to plan a new headquarters for his company. There'd be a nationwide design competition.

We wanted to submit a plan using Stephen's suspended building concept. Mario, who was dean by then, agreed to reduce Stephen's teaching load, let him consult on the project, and have graduate students help work on it. The firm Stephen had left was happy to have him back part time for this project.

We felt Stephen's firm might not have the "heft" for a national competition, so we asked for help from a prestigious national firm, Skidmore, Owings & Merrill. I was getting ready to fly to San Francisco for my first meeting with them. Cindy said, "You seem nervous. Is it because this deal is so big?"

"No, that's just numbers. This, ah, is kind of embarrassing, but I'm uncomfortable flying and staying in a nice hotel and all that."

"You're afraid of flying?"

"No, no, not the flying. It's the, I don't know, the etiquette maybe. I've never been in an airplane before. I've never been in a nice hotel. I've never .... Well, I can figure it out, but I might make a fool of myself. How do you get your ticket? Find your plane? Get a taxi? Check in to a hotel? Who do you tip? How much? It seems silly, but I just don't know what you are supposed to do, how you're supposed to act on a business trip."

Cindy gave me a big hug. "You know, a lot of guys would never admit they didn't know about those things."

"Well, most guys probably do know about them. Here I am, a 'future tycoon,' flying off to do a big deal and I'm worried about how much to tip the doorman."

"You have no idea how loveable you are, do you?"

"Well, I wouldn't try to pick up girls by telling 'em how insecure I am."

"I won't teach you how to pick up girls. But, if you want, I'll come along and teach you about business travel etiquette."

"Would you? It would help so much, let me concentrate on making a good deal."

"Sure. Can I go to the stores while you're in your meetings?"

"OK." I didn't know anything about San Francisco shopping. It might have been cheaper to hire a life coach, but I don't think they had life coaches back then. It cost about a thousand bucks, which we couldn't afford at that point, but she came back with some nice clothes.

On the plane she pulled a book out of her purse, Emily Post on Etiquette. "Is it going to be embarrassing to read this? I thought about putting it in a plain brown wrapper for you."

"No, nobody is going to notice. And a plain brown wrapper? People would notice that."

"That was supposed to be a joke. Relax and read your book."

Cindy (and the book) helped me navigate through the airport, the taxis, the hotel. It seems silly now, but that did let me concentrate on business.

Meanwhile, our relationship with Jonathon and his girlfriend was getting strained. They'd always been wilder than us. It started with smoking pot at parties. I said, "I'm not doing that"

"It's no big deal," Jonathon said. "Everybody does it."

"Not me. Too risky. It's illegal."

"Nobody ever gets caught."

"Yes, they do and, if I got caught, I might never be able to get another loan."

"Ah, you're just being paranoid."

"Maybe so, but I'm not doing it and I don't want to be there when people are doing it." Cindy nodded. That was a big relief. I was glad we were on the same page on that.

Then they got into harder drugs. Lots of people just do pot and never get into harder stuff. I'm not claiming pot always leads to hard drugs. But it happened to them and it scared me. Cindy and I worried about them getting caught, destroying their careers, damaging their brains, maybe even getting killed. But there wasn't anything we could do, so we started to avoid them.

The last straw was wife-swapping. It mostly happened at parties where people were doing drugs, and we didn't go to those. They asked if we'd join them and two other couples in a swap party if no drugs were involved. "No, no way." I tried to laugh about it, but Cindy and I didn't think it was funny.

"Don't you want some variety?" Jonathon asked.

"Nope. One woman is enough for me."

Cindy gave me a big hug and said, "I can be." We laughed, but it was sad that our friends were so out of tune with how we felt.

A week or so later Cindy's Grandma Olsen said, "Mark, you seem more serious than usual. Is something on your mind? Something about your work, maybe?"

"Oh, it's not work. That's been great. But I've been thinking about two friends of ours, a long-time friend of mine and a sorority sister of Cindy's. We've grown apart."

"Why is that?"

"Lifestyle stuff, I guess. Drinking, drugs, sleeping around. The stuff they're doing, it makes me, makes us, uncomfortable."

"Yes," she said. "I understand. The old problem of sin."

"Well, you know, most people don't use that word anymore, but ...."

"You're right, Mark, the word is out of fashion, but the idea is very old and never goes away. It's just, well, just the way people are."

"But what do you do about it, I mean when your friends get into it?"

"Oh," she smiled, "there must be thousands of sermons about that."

"Probably, but you know we don't go to church. What do they say?"

"Some emphasize loving the sinner. Some are more into hating the sin."

"I don't think I 'hate' it. I don't like what they're doing, and I wish it didn't mess up our friendship, but 'hate' is a pretty strong word."

"And you care about the sinners, don't you?"

"Yeah, sure I do. But it's hard. They're hurting themselves and there's nothing we can do to help. I want them to quit but I'm afraid to talk to them about it. They'd get mad. It would just drive us farther apart."

"Yes, it probably would at this point." There was a pretty long silence. "Maybe you just need to be on stand-by for a while, waiting for a time when they need you."

"You're probably right. Still, it's hard. But it has been good talking to you about it. Thanks."

"Mark," she said, "for somebody who doesn't go to church you're a very spiritual person. In a lot of ways you're more 'Christian' than many people who go every Sunday."

On the way home Cindy said, "You and Grandma O have a cool thing going, don't you?"

"Yeah. She is so kind and caring, but she must think I'm a lost soul, going to hell for sure."

"No, I don't know if she believes in hell, but she thinks, if it does exist, it's none of her business whether you're going there or not. She believes her job is to love us."

Mark

# # # #

Sixth meeting

Mr. Kauffman and I met again on February 18, 2012. Among other things, we talked about Jonathon and his girlfriend. Again, the transcript shows how he tried to turn things around to talk about me:

> MK: So, Katy, does all this business stuff bore you?
>
> KTA: No, but it is a very different world that what I am used to. I can relate to what you said about your friends, though. I hate it when my friends do drugs and sleep with people they hardly know.
>
> MK: Well, you're better off staying away from all that stuff.

KTA: I do, now. Have for years.

MK: What do you mean? You said you haven't had boyfriends. Did you do drugs when you were younger?

KTA: No, not me, but my mom did.

MK: Jeeze. Even when you were around?

KTA: Yes, but it was a long time ago.

MK: That's just not right. Drugs are risky, not just for users but everybody around them.

KTA: Heavy users, addicts, don't care. They feel like they have nothing to lose.

MK: But they do. Not just risks of getting physically hurt, or brain damaged, or losing friends, or losing jobs or, but going to jail too. Let me tell you, that sure can screw up your life. But let's not talk about me. I want to know more about your family, your life growing up.

I wasn't ready to talk about that, so I changed the subject.

KTA: I haven't been on a plane yet either.

MK: You will. Once you get your PhD and start teaching, you'll probably fly to conferences all over the country. It's a good life, being a professor; I've known a lot of them. You'll enjoy it. But Katy, there is something I can't figure out about you. You seem so prim and proper and controlled but, now and then, something seems off. Who are you, really?

# # # #

Feb. 25, 2012

Katy

The Skidmore Owings people didn't want to be involved in a project using new ideas they hadn't thought up themselves. Stephen made a great presentation on his suspended building idea. Then he said, "We really need your help on this. You can't get anything built with just a concept. You've got to get permits and be able to build it at a reasonable cost. You guys have so much experience with innovative designs. We need your help." It was an important lesson for me: flattery is a great way to disarm big egos.

Of course, he was right. Brilliant concepts don't mean a thing if you can't implement them; lots of architects have designed buildings that couldn't be built. But this kind of blunder isn't unique to architects. Back in the '80s GM built some Camaros with a design screw-up so you couldn't change the back two spark plugs without jacking the engine up out of its mounts. Unbelievably stupid. Back then you had to change plugs every twelve thousand miles or so. I suppose you don't know much about cars, so that may not be a good example for you.

My point is that Stephen wasn't just a visionary. He could work with people to get things done.

Skidmore Owings insisted on being the lead firm, but we wanted Stephen's firm and the UW to have important roles too. We gave the Skidmore Owings folks two weeks to review our proposal. If they opted in, they'd be the lead firm, check all Stephen's work, have veto over the design, and take the lead in all client meetings.

I worried that Stephen might feel bad about Skidmore Owings wanting all the credit, but what he wanted was access to the best computers and programmers and a budget that let him work on the very leading edge of his profession. He got that and I got a chance to make a lot of money.

We looked for a site for the United American headquarters. You probably don't want to hear about our selection criteria and all the properties we looked at. Cutting to the chase, as they say, we found a site farther out than we wanted but much larger and cheaper. Weyerhaeuser Company was offering 2800 acres along both sides of the Green River upstream from Flaming Geyser State Park, over three and a half miles of riverfront, crossed by State Route 169. Most of it was recently logged and looked more like a war zone than a forest.

I met with a couple of Weyerhaeuser people, asked a lot of questions, and came home stoked about the property. Cindy said, "For years the state, the county and every conservation group around has wanted that property for a park. Didn't you know that?"

"Ah, no, I didn't." That raised problems. We'd need zoning changes and permits from the county and things from the state like water rights and widening the highway. How could we get a lot of different interest groups to support our development?

Stephen, Jim Hawthorne, Brett Jamison and I came up with a plan. First, we'd give 450 acres, the gorge and land along the top of the bluff on both rims, to the state for a new state park, reserving the airspace over a small piece of it, and small parcels on both sides of the river for the United American building. Second, we'd construct about seven miles of trails for hikers, runners, and horses along the rims on both sides of the gorge and underneath the building. Third, we'd reserve spaces for new schools and county parks, with easements for branch trails connecting them to the rim trails. Fourth, we'd give the state an easement to use 200 parking spaces for public parking in the future United American parking lots, from 6:00 PM to an hour after sundown on weekdays and an hour before dawn to an hour after sundown on weekends and holidays, and United American would provide restrooms for the public. Finally, we'd give the county planning department and the State Department of Economic Development a grant to study the public benefits of the project.

This package gave all major "players" incentives to want the United American headquarters built. There were long and difficult negotiations, but this "everybody wins" approach made the project possible.

Tax deductions were a key to our plan. If we could value the 450-acre park donation at $400 per acre, the deduction would be worth $126,000 to someone in the top income tax bracket, 70% back then. United American would get deductions for donating use of its parking facilities and restrooms. At its 52.8% tax rate, a million-dollar deduction would be worth over a half million dollars to the company. Those deductions were worth more than the price of the property. If we could pull this off, we'd get most of the property for little or nothing.

Jim Hawthorne briefed their board chairman about our ideas, and he became our lead investor. The park was named for him and his wife.

Could we persuade the IRS that the donated land was worth at least $400 an acre? Let's just leave it that we did some brilliant tax planning. Later, the IRS challenged deductions United American and its chairman took for the donations, but it settled on terms quite favorable to them. Now you can't take tax deductions if you keep any significant use of donated assets or get any financial benefits from a donation. Maybe we should get credit for this change in tax policy. Another public service we never get any credit for.

Mark

# # # #

Mar. 2, 2012

Dear Mark,

You are right that I don't know much about cars, except how to break in with a Slim-Jim or coat hanger, and hotwire them, and get the stereos out in three minutes or less. Mom taught me that when I was nine or ten, but that's a long story we probably shouldn't get into.

Some of that about taxes was over my head, but I get the general idea. Your career is very interesting so far.

Katy

# # # #

Mar. 9, 2012

Katy

What I wrote about cars, it was supposed to be a joke. I can't believe your mom taught you how to hot-wire and burglarize them. Don't you know how dangerous it is to steal car stereos? If the cops caught you, your mom could have gone to jail and you could have gone to the juvie or, more likely, a foster home. What if the owners caught you? A lot of guys really care about their cars and their sound systems. You could have been shot or knifed or something.

You may find the tax stuff rather boring, but it's interesting to some people. For years, business schools used a textbook with a long chapter on our Green River project, "Case Studies on Modern American Management". It's out of print now, but you might find a used copy on Amazon. That was a joke, Katy. I don't expect you to go looking for it.

I'll skip the rest of the Weyerhaeuser negotiations. (OK, I wrote ten or twelve pages on that, but deleted them because I knew they'd bore you.) The main point is we got a terrific deal, over two thousand acres of development land for practically nothing.

I signed the contract with Weyerhaeuser in June 1972. I felt good. I kept humming that old James Brown song: "Whoa, I feel good, like I knew I would ...." I was 28.

Jonathon got married. Stephen was his best man. The groomsmen were Jonathon's drinking and drugging buddies. Cindy and I had a good time at the reception for a while, but it got noisy and we left early. When we got home, I said, "They'll go on for hours and hours and here we are, home at ten o'clock. Maybe I'm becoming an old fuddy-duddy before my time."

"Oh, a little fuddy-duddyism is OK. And when we get into our eighties, I bet you'll be the cutest old fuddy-duddy around."

"Not something to look forward to."

The Maritime Mart was a huge success. Lots of politicians came to the grand opening, and they all wanted credit for the project. That was OK. The people I cared about knew it was Stephen's idea and that I was the driving force behind getting it done.

My 10-year high school reunion was in July 1972. I didn't want to wear a suit but didn't want to be too casual either, so I bought a bright blue polyester bell-bottom leisure suit. Years later my kids looked at a picture and laughed. "Dad," they said, "were you trying to look like a rock star or what?" I tried to explain that people wore clothes like that in the 1970s. I never wore it again, though; it was too flashy for me. That style never really caught on or didn't last long. Kind of like Mao jackets.

Was I as rich as I'd hoped to be? No, but I was successful and was getting known, mainly because of Jonathon's articles in the PI. At the reunion some people stared at me, or sneaked looks at me, or whispered to others who turned around to look for me. Lots of people knew who I was.

Our Green River deal and the United American headquarters hadn't been announced, so I couldn't talk about them. But I knew I'd make a lot of money soon. Maybe knowing that was enough. Maybe I'd matured a little since high school. Anyway, I mingled with my honors classmates, feeling like their equal for the first time. I asked about their lives and wives and kids and what they did at work and for fun. I'd become a good listener. Having a beautiful wife by my side helped boost my self-confidence too.

When we got home, I told Cindy how important this reunion had been to me for all those years, how much I'd wanted to be the richest, most successful person there. I'd never admitted that to anybody and I was afraid she might make fun of me, but she gave me a big hug and said, "You're the most wonderful person I know, and would be even if you were broke."

In September 1972, Cindy had a miscarriage. She was devastated. We wanted a baby. We'd been relieved to find out she wasn't pregnant when we got married, but it had been nearly three years and now we were ready. Cindy was hurting and I hurt because she hurt. To be honest, I didn't grieve much over losing the baby. Don't get me wrong. I got very, very attached to my kids after they were born, but I couldn't really relate to an unborn kid.

I did get horny, though. Hope that doesn't offend you, Katy. It's a guy thing, Horniness is like anger. You've got to understand that it's normal and natural and happens sometimes, but not let it push you into doing stupid things. Don't be afraid of it. Face it, but don't act on it. That's my philosophy, and it's helped keep me faithful to Cindy all these years.

I wanted some new outlet beyond work, so I joined the "Y" and started exercising, running on treadmills, lifting weights, using exercise machines. Getting back in shape was good for me. I'd gotten flabby working 60, 70,

80-hour weeks. It gave me more energy. Getting worn out helped take my mind off sex some of the time.

After a few weeks we resumed our love life. Nothing kinky or exotic, just normal stuff. We made love often enough to satisfy me, considering I was working long hours and exhausted a lot of the time.

There wasn't much for me to do on the United American project. I had some smaller projects going. I made sure everything ran smoothly at the Maritime Mart and reassured our creditors that everything would be OK.

The president of United American held a press conference to announce that Stephen's design won the competition for its new headquarters. Someone from Skidmore Owings spoke for the winning team and mentioned the "contributions" of Stephen and the UW. Nobody mentioned me, but Jonathon's article in the next day's PI did.

We sold the Maritime Mart in October 1973. My share of the profits was about $560,000. We caught up on all of our payments. Our financial crisis was over.

It would be months before construction started on the United American headquarters. I could go on for hours about all the permits and approvals we still needed. Sound like a threat? We can skip all that.

The local and regional economy was still a mess. Boeing had laid off tens of thousands. There was a billboard: "Will the last person leaving Seattle please turn off the lights?" Unemployment was high and rising; tax revenues were falling. We couldn't have had a better political climate for getting support from elected officials.

We tried to get support from environmental groups. We had good arguments about the project's environmental benefits. Their executive directors and boards listened, asked questions, "took it under advisement," and never got back to us. They wouldn't support us publicly but none of them sued to stop the project.

We got the last permits in March 1974 and purchased the Weyerhaeuser property on April 10. The park donation had grown to four hundred ninety acres, but the bigger the donation the less I paid for the land outside the park, so I came out ahead by giving away land that United American's chairman was paying for. After what he paid for the park lands and his company paid for its headquarter site, the rest of the Green River property, over two thousand acres worth about four million dollars, cost me less than $34 an acre. I'd just turned thirty and felt like I'd finally made it.

But I still had zits. I asked Cindy, "You think I'm the only self-made millionaire with zits?"

"Probably not," she said, "but you'll outgrow them."

Mark

# # # #

Mar. 16, 2012

Dear Mark,

I probably should not have written about the car stuff. I just wanted to lighten things up a little. But eventually we did get caught stealing stereos, not by the cops but by the car owner. Mom played it cool. She got down on her knees, rubbed his crotch, said she would "make it up to him," and sent me home.

I liked learning about your 10-year high school reunion. I do not remember the 1970s, of course, but I have seen pictures of those bell-bottom leisure suits.

I'm sorry about the miscarriage. I have never had to go through that. I understand it can be devastating for women but never thought about how it might affect men.

So, what happened next, after you got such a good deal on all that land?

Katy

# # # #

Mar. 23, 2012

Dear Katy

Jeeze, Katy, the thing with your mom and the stereo guy really bothers me. It was dangerous. You could have been really hurt or even killed. What kind of mother would subject a kid to that? What happened after you left? And how old were you?

I was only a couple of years older than you are now, Katy, and I had four million dollars of land and half a million in cash. Like I said, you could switch to real estate and make that kind of money too. Don't get me wrong. I'm sure you'll be a fine professor. I'm not putting you down for choosing a low-income career. I'm just saying the other option is there.

Cindy and I took our first real vacation, two weeks camping in the Cascades. Much of the time we just relaxed, enjoyed each other, enjoyed the outdoors between rainstorms, but we also we talked about "What next?"

We wouldn't build homes on the Green River property until the United American building was nearly done. We had several small urban redevelopment projects going on in Seattle. We'd finish them, sell them, and do some more. We owned a construction company but I'd made more money as a developer. We'd shut down the construction company to free up my time to scout out new deals. I still didn't have an office except the second bedroom in our apartment. To take our business to higher levels, we'd need an office and staff.

We'd start looking at houses. We'd been trying to have a baby for over a year, so we thought we had plenty of time for that, but a month later Cindy was pregnant. By the fourth or fifth month the pregnancy was getting more real and the search for a house got more urgent.

In June 1974, Cindy and I formed a corporation. We named it Inova Development. Stephen said, "Is that for 'In Over Your Head'?" I laughed. "Well no. We were thinking 'Innovation' and maybe 'In an Ova', like in an egg or embryo, waiting to be born kind of thing. But your version works too."

I was Chairman of the Board, President and Chief Operating Officer. Cindy was corporate Secretary. We rented office space near the UW and hired our first four key employees. Gretchen Jaeger, office manager, was great at organizing our files and finding stuff. We had boxes of documents, some labeled by project, some by year, and all were a mess. Harriko Watanabe—"call me

Eeko, my grandkids started it and now everybody calls me that"—Vice President for Permits and Compliance, responsible for getting permits and making sure that we and our contractors complied with permit terms and government regulations. He was the Seattle building department official who'd approved the permit for our Phoenix House project back in 1966; I hadn't forgotten him, and he said he hadn't forgotten me. Sharon O'Reilly, Vice President for Strategic Planning, had been a graduate student on the economic team for the Maritime Mart project. Heinz Vandenhof, Construction Manager, had owned a construction company for over twenty years but got into financial trouble in the recession, never fully recovered, and had gone into bankruptcy.

That was our core team. Sharon, Eeko, Heinz and I worked together for over thirty years.

Now we had a real company with offices and employees. We did more and more projects. At first, I lined up investors for each one. Later we organized a limited partnership with Inova as the general partner, so the same group of investors shared in many projects. Later the limited partnership was merged into a REIT, a Real Estate Investment Trust.

I learned a lot about team building. We had regular weekly meetings, Sharon, Eeko, Heinz and I, sometimes Cindy, sometimes others, to talk about possible new projects and how best to sell projects we were finishing.

Did we ever make mistakes? Sure. Were there some lean years? Sure. But we got bigger and bigger and made a lot of money.

All that took another fifteen years or so. How much do you want to know about this period? Some things happened in those years that helped shape who I am and what happened to me. I didn't peak-out at thirty-one and never mature after that. I got better, more confident, more secure, more comfortable with myself. You think I've always been confident? Not true. Mostly I faked it in the early years.

Mark

# # # #

Mar. 30, 2012

Dear Mr. Kauffman,

Mom and the stereo guy had some kind of sex. She never said exactly what they did, and I never asked, but I knew sex was how she kept him from calling the cops.

He must have liked what he got because we moved in with him a few days later. The guy we had been living with left without paying the rent, so we needed a new place to live. Maybe that was her plan all along. Anyway, it kept us from being homeless again. I was ten.

I would like to know more about your family.

Katy

# # # #

Apr. 8, 2012

Katy

You were ten? I didn't know about sex at that age and my kids didn't either. And then your mom and you moved in with him? Maybe it was better than being homeless but, really, that was very irresponsible of your mom, don't you think? And what was that about being homeless "again"? Had you been homeless before?

Our daughter Julia was born on February 14, Valentine's Day, 1974. We called her Julie.

I started coming home earlier to spend time with her, walking her around the house or the neighborhood, making funny noises. I was excited about being a father.

We were still in our two-bedroom apartment. We'd moved the business files to my new office and converted the second bedroom to a nursery. We hadn't found a house we liked. I'd always wanted a waterfront house, but they were expensive in Seattle, even back then—nothing compared to what they are now of course. We looked at the East side, Meyedenbauer Bay, Hunts Point, Kirkland, but Sharon said, "No, you and your family wouldn't be happy there."

"Why not?"

"People your age can't afford to live there. It would be like living in an old folks' home. Well, there'd be a few middle-aged folks with grown kids, maybe a few still in high school, but nobody near your age or your kids' ages." She was right, of course. Ten years later, after Microsoft went public, lots of rich young people bought waterfront homes on the East side, but not in 1974.

We bought a five-year-old four-bedroom home in Somerset, with views across Lake Washington to Seattle and the Olympic mountains, near the community recreation center and an elementary school. The neighborhood had lots of growing families with young kids. Frank Wilson helped us get a loan from Seafirst. We settled into life in suburbia.

We invited Mom and Dad over. Mom said, "It's lovely, so spacious, room for more kids, and the view, I love the view." Dad didn't say anything until they were leaving, and then he said, "You borrowed a ton of money to get this, didn't you?"

"Well, Dad, we put twenty percent down. We didn't borrow it all. And we can afford it."

"Son, I don't like borrowing. Don't like you borrowing."

I felt like saying, "How about keeping your mouth shut, for a change?" But I didn't. I was trying to be a good son. He didn't make it easy.

Lucy moved into a group home. She was twenty-three. She wanted to live in an apartment but Mom and Dad said she couldn't live on her own. She couldn't manage money; she'd give it away or buy stuff for her "friends" or people she hardly knew. They worried that she'd sleep with any guy who paid attention to her. So, they put her in a group home. It was a good decision. She made new friends. The house mother watched out for her, helped manage her money, made sure she got healthy meals, enough sleep, home on time.

"It's been really good for her," Mom said, "and you know we won't be around forever."

I said, "Hey, you guys are still pretty young, too young to be talking about that."

"Your dad was born in '16. That makes him, what, 59. Not real old, but still ...."

"OK, well, it's good to plan ahead for Lucy. And the group home is good for her."

"But it's not cheap," Dad said.

"We could help with the cost," Cindy said.

"No, she's our daughter, it's our cost. It's just cutting into saving for retirement."

"But Dad, you should be saving for retirement. It's only six years 'til you're 65."

"You should be saving. I know you've made big money, but you did it by borrowing. I don't like that. I don't like you borrowing."

"Dad, it's not like you think. It's the way real estate is done. I know you remember the thirties, in Germany and here too. But it's different now."

"That's how people get in trouble, thinking this time it's different. It's never different. Things never really change."

"Dad, that's about the most I ever heard you say at one time. But we're millionaires now and I'm being careful to keep it that way. So, here's my plan: as long as Cindy and I are millionaires, we'll pay for the group home and you save the money you would have spent on that. If things go crazy and we're not millionaires anymore, then you pay for the group home 'til we get back on our feet. Fair?"

"I don't like it, but I guess it's fair."

Cindy got pregnant again in mid-1976. We were more relaxed about it this time. On March 10, 1977, she delivered a healthy baby boy. We named him David and called him Davie when he was little. He was a great baby. Bright-eyed, alert, good natured. His sister had been an easy baby too. We liked to think they were good babies because we were good parents, but that's probably delusional. Some kids are more difficult no matter what you do. We got lucky.

At first, Julie was enthusiastic about having a baby brother. She was fascinated with his tiny fingers and toes, nursing and diaper changes, especially poopy diapers. Those caused great drama: holding her nose, rolling her eyes, gagging, carrying on. After a few months she realized that he was taking a lot of Cindy's time and mine. She was three. We'd heard about the "terrible twos," but she sailed happily along until after her brother was born. We never figured out how much of her new behavior was a delayed version of the terrible twos and how much was jealousy over having to share us with Davie.

One day when he was about six months old, she pulled down her pants and panties and pooped in front of his crib while he was taking a nap. Luckily Cindy saw it before she stepped in it. It was hard to discipline her with a straight face. She was too little to clean it up herself, but we tried to make it clear that we weren't happy about it.

After that I came home earlier to play with Julie and give Cindy a break. After dinner I'd play with both kids until Davie's bedtime and then read Julie a book while Cindy put him to bed. It probably didn't reduce her jealousy much, but me spending extra time with Julie was good for all of us.

Cindy seemed tired and down. I thought maybe it was post-partum depression, but she didn't think anything was "wrong"—she was just tired from living with two small kids. I think the women's magazines made it worse. I didn't read them, but they were lying around with headlines suggesting women couldn't be happy without a career.

We came up with a plan: two nights a week would be adult time. Monday nights, dinner and a movie or play or concert with me. Friday nights, social events with other adults. We kept that up for years. I tried hard to be a good husband. We tried to find a balance between work, kids and a social life. Did we always get it right? Of course not, nobody does, but we tried.

Mark

# # # #

April 15, 2012

Dear Mark,

I understand that you are curious about my childhood, but I do not think we should go further into that. It would be best to continue with your life without the distractions of delving further into mine.

Please tell me more about how you built your business.

Katy

# # # #

April 22, 2012

Katy

There was a dedication party for the United American headquarters in March 1976. Lots of politicians came. I'd developed relationships with most of them, but I was only one of their many supporters. I wanted some politicians of my own, ones who would be more thankful for my support and more willing to help me on future projects.

Late in the event I talked to a young man from the County planning staff, Olaf Johansson. He said his degree was in political science. I asked how he liked his job.

"It's OK, but not all projects are as interesting as yours."

"Is your political science education helpful or is the work pretty much technical?"

"Just technical. Someday I'd like to get into politics, elective politics. Maybe it'll be helpful then."

"I'm interested in politics too. I'd never run myself, but I'd like to see more smart young people running. Nearly everybody who gets elected is old enough to be my dad. Or granddad. Maybe we should talk about this someday."

"I'd like that."

I called him a week or so later. "I'm Mark Kauffman. Remember me?"

He laughed. "It would be hard to forget you."

We met in a coffee shop near his office. He was shy at first. "I've never talked to anybody about my, er, political ambitions."

"I understand. But if you've got a dream you should go for it. That's my experience anyway."

We talked for an hour or so. He was tall, muscular, soft-spoken, smart and thoughtful, quietly confident, solid in a military sort of way. He didn't seem to have a big ego, at least for a would-be politician. I invited him and his wife, Carol, to dinner.

The dinner went well. Cindy liked him and Carol. After dinner, I said, "I'd like you to meet Sharon O'Reilly. She knows a lot about public opinion and a lot of people in the real estate business."

Olaf and I met with Sharon. After an hour or so, she asked, "So, if you run, would you run as a Democrat or Republican?"

"Hard question. The eastside is mostly Republican, so it would be easier to get elected here as a Republican. The rest of western Washington elects mostly Democrats, so it might be easier to move up as a Democrat. Dan Evans has done OK as a liberal Republican, but a conservative Democrat might do just as well. I'm a middle of the road kind of guy. I want to get stuff done but I don't care about the partisan stuff. Both extremes scare me. What do you think?"

I said, "Both extremes scare me too. I want government that works well at reasonable costs. What does that make me? Independent, I guess. Cindy is a Democrat, though."

"So, you could support me either way?" Olaf asked.

"Yes, you decide."

A few weeks later Olaf said he'd like to buy a house before he quit working for the county. "My salary and benefits are pretty good now, but my credit rating will go down if I go into politics."

"Good point. Let me introduce to a banker friend." I introduced him to Frank Wilson and told Frank that Olaf was a friend who might want to move into our neighborhood.

"Well, not exactly your neighborhood," Olaf laughed. "Somewhere farther down the hill where the views aren't as good but the prices are lower." Neither of us mentioned that Olaf might run for political office. The bank didn't need to know that. Olaf and Carol bought a house a little way down the hill from us.

We talked again about his possible political career. "Well," he said, "County Commissioner would be a fulltime job, but I think that's out of reach for now. I'd like to start with the Legislature. It's easier to get into but it's only part time. I'd need a job where I could get time off when it's in session and for committee meetings and, of course, to campaign."

"I've given that some thought. Didn't you say once that you had some classes in public finance, government bonds, that kind of thing?"

"Yes. To make things happen in government, you've got to find ways to pay for them, so I've always been interested in tax policy and government finance."

"That's good. I'd like to introduce you to another friend of mine, Jim Hawthorne at United American. He works on the investment side. Their bond traders and municipal finance folks report to him. They could give you the time off you'd need, and they encourage their employees to be politically active."

"I suppose so. They've got lots of political problems in Olympia."

Olaf quit his County job to work for United American. Four months later he announced he was running for the Legislature as a Republican. I introduced him to a lot of my friends, said I supported him, and asked them to support him too. Sharon brought him to meetings of the Chamber of Commerce, Association of Washington Businesses, and several building industry trade associations. Cindy brought him to board meetings of several environmental groups and introduced him to some of their major contributors. The incumbent Republican was rather old and seldom sober, but so entrenched the Party hadn't groomed a successor. The Democrats viewed the district as a "lost cause." Olaf was young, vigorous, smart and good-humored. He won by a landslide.

Would he have run without our encouragement and help? Maybe. But he was grateful. We became friends. Our wives became friends. Carol and Cindy shopped together, walked together, went to aerobics together, had their fingernails and toenails done together. His daughter Sarah and our Julie spent a lot of time together. His son Kevin and our Davie were almost inseparable, often in the same classes at school, same T-ball team, soccer team, later the same high school tennis and swim teams. Sometimes both families camped together, had dinner together, went skiing or to plays or movies or concerts together.

After Olaf was elected to Congress and spent most of his time in D.C., our wives and kids got even closer because his family missed him. I was working long hours, so my family may have missed me sometimes too.

It wasn't just politics and business, no matter what people say now. I supported him his whole career and helped him become one of the most powerful people in the U. S. Senate. But when my time of need came, where was he? Gone. AWOL. Avoiding me. He could have helped when the SEC came after me, or with my sentencing. It hurts. Sometimes I try to be rational and put myself in his place, but that just makes me sad and weary. Still, he's my ace in the hole: if I lose my appeal, he'll support me on a petition for pardon or clemency.

Another politician I helped get started was Buddy Graves. His real name is Robert but everybody calls him Buddy. His father owned car dealerships in Pierce County and invested in some of our Tacoma projects. Buddy was quite different than Olaf. He was a troublemaker in high school, president of his fraternity in college, wild and irresponsible, an extrovert. Not my kind of guy.

Still, I wanted to keep a good relationship with his dad and felt like I owed him something because he'd invested in some of my projects that were not very profitable. So, when he asked me to meet with him and Buddy, I said OK.

Buddy was selling used cars for his dad but didn't like it. His dad probably hoped he'd come work for me but, fortunately, Buddy had no interest in that. I wouldn't have hired him. I talked about real estate, getting permits, number-crunching for cost estimates and revenue projections, paperwork for loans. He started to fidget.

"So," I asked, "what are you interested in? What would you like to do?"

"Oh, I don't know. Maybe a rock band or politician or something."

"Do you play in a band? What instruments do you play? Or are you a singer?" This was not going well. His father was fidgeting now.

"No, I don't play and don't sing. I like music but I'm no good at it. That was mostly a joke."

"So, we're down to 'a politician or something'?"

"Look," he said. "I know Dad and you are trying to help me, but I don't know what help I need. I'll have to figure it out myself someday."

His dad was about to explode, so I tried to head that off. "You're right, of course. You'll have to figure it out. But when you do, you'll need help. When the time comes, I hope you'll let us and others help you. It's hard to ask for help, and sometimes hard to accept it, but we've learned to do that. A lot of people have helped us. When you know what you want, you'll attract people who want to help you. Don't be afraid to ask for help or to accept it."

He looked at me for a long time. Finally, he said, "You know, that may be the most honest thing anybody ever said to me. And maybe the most helpful." They left, certainly not arm in arm. I expected hear the dad yell at the kid as they walked down the hall.

I saw the dad several weeks later. He took me aside. "Thanks," he said. "He's changed, comes to work on time, works harder, treats people better. But he seems more distant, like he's pondering something. Maybe nothing will come of it, but thanks for trying."

I ran into Buddy a few months later. "How's it going?"

"Still selling cars, but I've joined SoundKeepers and the Audubon Society and I'm volunteering for the Environmental Council. I want to make a difference. We need to clean up our air and water and protect more habitat."

"That's good. It's good to care about causes and other people. But please don't be too hard on us businesspeople. We need restraints sometimes, but we do a lot of good too."

"Yeah, you're a good person. Even my dad isn't all bad."

I wanted to say he was growing up but held my tongue. "Well, tell him I said 'Hi'."

Cindy began running into him at environmental group meetings and fundraisers. He began asking her for donations. She usually gave a few hundred dollars. A couple of years later he asked to meet with me. "Sure," I said. "Anything in particular you want to talk about?"

"I'll explain it when I get there."

He wanted to run for the Tacoma City Council and wanted my support. "Your wife has supported my causes and I think she'll support me in this city council thing, but I'm not asking just for that. I want you to publicly support me and chair my fundraising committee."

"A lot of your liberal friends might not like that. Can you explain your thinking?"

"Sure. Lots of my friends are anti-business. I don't want people to think I'm like that just because I support environmental causes. I want to see big things happen, like a waterfront park from Point Defiance to downtown and another on the other side of the bay from eleventh street to Browns Point. It'll take decades, but I want to get a long-term plan in place and get started. For this to happen, we'll need business support and a healthy local economy."

"Wow! I like your vision and enthusiasm. I'm glad you found something to be passionate about. I hope your dad is proud of you."

"He's not. He thinks I've been smoking too much pot."

"Have you?"

"That's a personal question. It's illegal. I'm not stupid. I'm not going to jeopardize my dreams by getting caught. Until it's legal I won't be using in the U.S. Maybe I'll take some foreign vacations, but don't worry about me embarrassing you by getting busted."

"Are you going to be that honest if it comes up in the campaign?"

"Well, I can't lie about my past use. Too many people know about that. I'll try to convince people I'm clean and sober now and have been since before I decided to run."

"That might fly with younger voters, if you can get them to turn out. If only older folks vote you're probably screwed anyway." This was in 1977, before Bill Clinton admitted he'd tried it (but didn't inhale, he says).

Buddy was elected to the Tacoma City Council, then the Legislature for several terms and then Congress. I supported his political career for years. Then we had a falling out. He hurt me badly, but I've forgiven him. If my appeals are denied and Obama gets reelected, it would be good to have a powerful Democrat on my team. Would he help me after all we've been through? Hard to say, but you'd think he'd still be grateful for all I did for him.

Mark

# # # #

April 29, 2012

Dear Mark,

It seems that you used a lot of people to help you get rich: your political proteges, Olaf and Buddy, but also Stephen and Jonathon, and others. Did you just see them as tools to help you make money, or did you have real relationships with them?

Also, I would like to know more about your relationships with your wife and kids.

Katy

# # # #

May 6, 2012

Katy

I'm hurt that you think I "used" people. These weren't one-sided relationships. I helped them and they helped me. But it wasn't just business: these were good friends, especially Stephen, Jonathon and Olaf. We had fun together, shared joys and sorrows, supported each other in many ways. I cared about them and they cared about me. You are much too cynical.

My wife and kids? I've got lots of stories about them. Maybe sharing them will help you see what a kind and loving person I am.

Julie taught herself to read. We didn't want her to get too far ahead and be bored in school but, by the end of kindergarten, she was reading at a fourth-grade level. We wanted to keep her with kids her own age, but in the middle of first grade we let her jump into second. She was smart but a little unruly at times.

Davie, three years younger, also was a bright, cheerful, energetic, athletic kid. But raising kids can be a challenge sometimes. When he had just started first grade, at dinner one night he said he'd called one of his classmates "a little asshole." His sister said, "Davie said a dirty word!"

Davie looked at Cindy and me, wondering what we would do. I said, "That's not a nice word. But what I want to talk about is calling people names. We shouldn't call people bad names. Understand, Davie?"

"Yeah."

"Now I want to talk about assholes. You know what they are, right? The hole your poop comes out of. What I want you to understand is, if there's a reason to talk about them, like if they hurt or blood comes out or somebody tries to touch it, you should talk to Mom or me about it. OK? If you want to use that word to tell us what's wrong, then it's OK."

Julie jumped in. "Look, Davie, it's simple. If something goes wrong with your asshole, talk to Mom or Dad about it. But don't call people names, especially body parts in your underwear or stuff that comes out of them, like 'piss' or 'shit' or 'prick' or 'cunt'."

Davie said, "Prick or what—what are you talking about?"

"You know," Julie said, "a penis like you have or a vagina like I have."

"Thank you, teacher," I said. "That's enough education for tonight. How about some ice cream?"

Both kids said, "Yeah, yeah!" I served everybody a big bowl of ice cream.

That night I asked Cindy if I'd handled that OK. "I think so. Some of it may have been a little over Davie's head, but I agree with what you said." Later it turned out that Julie didn't know as much about sex as we thought she did.

The next night at dinner Davie said, "Know what? I told Jimmy I was sorry I called him an asshole and I wouldn't call him bad names anymore. He said then he wouldn't call me bad names either. We traded stuff from our lunches and played at recess. We're friends now."

"Wow. I'm proud of you." I looked at Cindy and grinned. I was proud of myself too.

In the spring of 1984, we signed Julie up for Little League baseball, which was just starting to accept girls, and signed Davie up for T-ball. One advantage of being self-employed was that I could go to many of their games and cheer for the kids, especially our own of course but also their friends, particularly Sarah and Kevin Johansson, Olaf and Carol's kids. Olaf usually was too busy to come.

T-ball wasn't bad but Little League was awful. The coaches were great, the kids were fine, but the parents were terrible. A lot of dads yelled at their kids. I'd never yell at my kids in private, leave alone in front of their friends. One time we had an umpire, just a high school kid, who stopped a game to ask the dads to please not yell at their kids, just let them have fun and learn the game. The dads were better for a little while but started yelling at their kids again. The ump warned them that he would end the game if they did it again. The dads behaved themselves for an inning or so but then started up again. The ump took off his mask, said "Game over," and started walking off. I clapped and said, "Thank you." The other dads glared at me. Clearly, I wouldn't be welcome at the games anymore.

I asked Julie if she wanted to quit the team. She said no, she and Sarah were the only girls and she didn't want to make her friend be the only one. "I understand," I said, "That's very kind. I'm proud of you for that."

Our kids didn't play baseball after that season. We got them into soccer, swimming, gymnastics, pickleball and then tennis. Cindy and I would hit balls to them and try to help them develop basic racquet skills. Later we got them tennis lessons. Cindy and I took lessons too. The kids seemed to enjoy watching us have our lessons almost as much as we enjoyed watching them have theirs.

One day when Julie was ten, must have been 1985, she came in our bathroom as I was getting out of the shower. We'd weren't particularly modest in our family, but this was unexpected. I wrapped a towel around myself. Cindy came in and said, "Julie, I think you're getting a little too old to come in here when Daddy's taking a shower."

"Yeah, I know, but I was, well, um, curious about something."

"What's that?" Cindy asked.

"It's kind of embarrassing, but I wanted to see how big Daddy's, ah, you know, his penis is."

"Well," I said, "I guess it's normal to be curious about things like that."

"I wasn't until yesterday. My friend Amy and me, we were going home from school, cutting through the woods to her house, and this boy, a seventh grader I think, showed us his, his penis."

"And then what happened?" Cindy asked.

"He said, look how big it is, did you ever see a bigger one?"

"What did you say?"

"I said, well, no, except on horses." Cindy and I couldn't keep from laughing.

"Good answer," Cindy said. "Then what happened?"

"He wanted us to show him ours, you know, pull our pants down too, but we ran away."

"Good. So that got you thinking about penises and you came in here to see how Dad's compared with his?" said Cindy.

"Yeah."

Cindy said, "Mark, do you want to explain about penises?"

"Well, OK. Julie, the thing is they get bigger and smaller all the time. Like if you go swimming in cold water, they shrink up. If you're nice and warm they get bigger. And sometimes .... Well, the point is they keep getting bigger and smaller. So, you can't tell much by comparing what you saw yesterday with what you saw today, like maybe mine was smaller today but his could be smaller sometimes too."

Cindy laughed. "That's a good point, Mark, but not exactly what I had in mind. Let's focus here. Now, Julie, you know where babies come from, right?"

"Sure. From their mommies' tummies. They come out of their mommies' vaginas."

"That's right. So, do you know how they start growing in there?"

"Ah, maybe this should be a mother-daughter talk," I said. "I'll just leave you two alone to talk about this."

"No, you stay. So, Julie, how do babies start growing in their mommies' tummies?"

"Well, their parents get married. Or, sometimes they aren't married but they live together."

"Yes, but there's something else," Cindy said. "Do you know what that is?"

"No, what are you asking?" I was a little surprised. I hadn't known when I was ten, but I thought modern kids know about these things.

"OK," Cindy said. "You're old enough to know this. The man, the father, puts his penis in the woman's vagina, and some stuff called semen squirts out, and it has little things called sperm that join with little eggs in the woman, and then a baby starts to grow."

Julie thought about that for a while. "That's gross, Mom, yucky."

"Well, that's how you got started, and me and Dad and everybody else."

Julie thought about this. "So, you and Dad have done that twice?"

Cindy laughed. "Oh, we've done it a lot more than that. It's really fun when you get old enough. People don't do it just to make babies. But Julie, you should wait until you're grown up. Boys will want to do it with you, and try to get you to do it, but please, please wait until you're older."

"How much older?"

"Oh, that's hard to say. You don't need to decide today. When you think you're getting ready, come talk to us, either of us. We can help you get on birth control, make sure you don't get pregnant."

"But when will that be? How much older?"

"Waiting until you're married is best, or at least until you're ready to get married. Out of college anyway. Maybe in your twenties. Some of your friends will do it sooner, but we hope you'll wait, don't we Mark?"

"Yeah, and wait for a really, really special guy. Don't do it with just because you're curious or your friends are doing it."

"Yes, that's right. I should have said that too. See, Mark, you do have good things to contribute."

"Yeah, well, whatever." It still seemed like this should be a mother-daughter conversation. But, at some point, I should sit down with Davie and explain sex to him. He was only seven, so I had some time.

"One more thing," Cindy said. "We should talk about whether to report this incident, the boy exposing himself, to the school and the police."

"No, no, please, no, don't do that, Mom."

"Why not?"

"It would be too embarrassing. I don't want to talk to the principal about it, or the cops, or anybody, and I'm sure Amy doesn't either."

"OK," Cindy said, "I guess we can leave it up to you and Amy. But if you change your mind and want us to tell someone at the school or the police, we will. And if you hear about that kid, or anybody else, doing something like that again, I think we should."

Cindy and I tried to be good parents. Sometimes the kids didn't make that easy. But, you know, Katy, we did pretty well. We raised two good, good kids.

Mark

# # # #

May 13, 2012

Dear Mark,

Why did you not tell the school and police about that boy exposing himself? This should have been an adult decision, not left to a ten-year old kid.

But I do enjoy reading about your kids. Such normal childhoods. So different from mine.

Katy

# # # #

May 20, 2012

Katy

About that kid exposing himself, if it had been an adult flasher of course we would have called the school and police. We offered to call them, but Julie said she didn't want us to and her friend didn't either. Should we have gone against her wishes? Her answer to the kid—"except on horses"—was hilarious, so it didn't sound like she was traumatized. You say we adults should have made the decision, but it's not that simple.

Maybe it's a generational thing. Young people are quicker to call in the government than us older folks. Or maybe it's because you haven't had kids yet, so you haven't had to cope with problems of when to do what your kids want and when you need to do things they don't want. Anyway, I'll go on with my story.

One day Jonathon called, seeming quite upset, so I asked, "You want to get together for a drink?"

"I'd like to see you but I'm not drinking now."

"OK, that's good, that's good, but it sounds serious."

We met at Seward Park and walked the waterfront trail. After a half mile or so he said, "My wife and me, we've separated. It's over."

"Maybe you could work things out?"

"Probably not. Stuff was said. Stuff was done."

"But sometimes, in the heat of the moment, people say things they don't really mean."

"No, it wasn't like that. We meant what we said. It just isn't working."

"I'm so sorry, really sorry. What else can I say?"

"You could say 'I told you so'."

"No, I wouldn't do that."

"But you saw it coming, didn't you? That's why you and Cindy kind of pulled away this last year or so."

"No, that's not it. It was, just, I don't know, lifestyle differences, I guess. We couldn't keep up with the partying. At least we didn't want to. We worried about you, but we couldn't figure out how to help."

We walked on for quite a while. Finally, he said, "Mark, all I wanted was what you and Cindy have. You are so, so, I don't know, not just happy but comfortable, so at ease with each other, secure, maybe that's the word.

You made it look so easy. I thought, man, if we get married, we could have what you've got, but we messed it up."

I didn't know what to say. I thought about saying at least there were no kids, but that seemed cold, or something like "Time heals all wounds" or some other crap like that. Finally, I just said, "Lookit, I'm sorry." I'd already said that, but what else can you say?

Cindy and I talked about it that night. "Did I say the right thing? Is there something I could have said that might have helped him feel better?"

"No, I don't think so."

"Oh, God, if it happened to us I, I, I just ...."

"But it won't. He was right. We've got something everybody wants but few people find."

"Yes, what did he call it? Comfort, ease, security? I've felt it but I never knew what to call it."

It's always hard when friends go through divorces. You never know what to say. I never thought it could happen to us, our marriage seemed so solid.

Katy, isn't it time we met again? It's been over two months.

Mark

Seventh meeting

I had put off meeting with Mr.Kauffman, knowing I had opened a can of worms by disclosing too much about my childhood and my mom. But I could not avoid him forever, so we met again on May 26, 2012. I tried to talk about other things but that was nearly impossible.

KTA: Let's talk about your sister.

MK: No, I want to talk about your mom.

KTA: Well, Mark, we only have a limited amount of time here and I think we should stay on task, talk about you and your family. This should not be about me and my mom.

MK: But she was so, so, irresponsible. How often were you homeless?

KTA: Quite a bit, off and on.

MK: But your mom usually could find some guy to take you in, if she slept with him?

KTA: Well, yes, that's how it worked.

MK: So, how many of them were there?

KTA: I don't know. I was just a kid. I didn't keep track.

MK: How long did they last? Take the stereo guy. How long did that last?

KTA: The stereo guy? I don't remember. Maybe a couple of months. With some guys it was just few days. With others, several months or more.

MK: Why such a turnover? Why did they leave? Or did they kick you guys out?

KTA: Different things. Sometimes one or the other got a better offer. Mom was always willing to "upgrade" to better guys. Sometimes the guy went to jail. Sometimes they caught Mom stealing from them.

> MK: And with your mom having so much sex, why no brothers or sisters?
>
> KTA: Mom had some kind of VD before I was born, so she couldn't have more children. That was something of a blessing. It saved the cost of birth control.
>
> MK: Jeeze. I can't believe it.
>
> KTA: And back to that flasher kid. You are so naïve. Guys who walk around with no clothes on, after a while they want you to touch them or they try to touch you. You think they are harmless, but you should have reported him to the school and the police.
>
> MK: I never thought about it that way. But he was just a kid. I hope he didn't grow up to be a pervert. It's interesting, though, that after all these months, this is the first time you've been critical about anything I've said or done. Maybe you've felt this way before and just covered it up, I don't know. But, let's not blow this up all out of proportion. Let's not argue.

I had thought about using this meeting to explain my dissertation research. It probably is just as well we did not get into that.

A common way to conduct a forensic psychological analysis is for the psychologist to gather information about the crime, the events surrounding it, the defendant's behavior and demeanor during and after the crime (especially when in custody and in court appearances), any prior encounters with law enforcement and the legal system, and any prior acts and relationships reported in pre-sentencing reports, social service agency files, news media or other sources. The psychologist then considers possible diagnoses of mental illness and personality disorder as defined in the DSM, the Diagnostic and Statistical Manual of Mental Disorders published by the American Psychiatric Association. The next step is to select one or more diagnoses and document the presence of specific criteria listed for that diagnosis in the DSM. For violent crimes, often the primary diagnosis is a mental illness, sometimes accompanied by one or more personality disorders. For white-collar crimes, the primary diagnosis more often is one or more personality disorders. Since most mental illnesses and personality disorders are believed to be lifelong, or at least long-lived, and to drive behavior, the crimes then are attributed to the illness or disorder.

There are several potential problems with this approach. Reaching such a diagnosis is more an art than a science, so there are risks that it may be affected by various cognitive biases, such as: anchoring, the tendency to overweight the first information received on a subject; recency bias, the tendency to overweight more recent data and discount information more remote in time; confirmation bias, the tendency to overweight information that confirms what people already believe or suspect. These and other biases, alone or in combinations, may contribute to excessive confidence in a diagnosis. Further, since the diagnosis often is based largely on behaviors involved in the crime or closely related to it in time and context, the crime may cause the diagnosis rather than characteristics associated with the diagnosis cause the crime.

The objective of my dissertation was is to test these hypotheses as applied to Mr. Kauffman's case.

First, I intended to gather data on his behaviors and demeanor over long periods of time, as much of his adult life as possible, in a variety of contexts, both business and non-business, and code them to the defining criteria for a number of possible personality disorders and mental illnesses as defined in the DSM-IV, the fourth edition which was then in use. This would include both positive indications that particular criteria might be met and contra-indications suggesting that a particular diagnosis was inapplicable or a particular criterion was not met. From this, I hoped to produce a well-documented diagnosis, or perhaps multiple diagnoses, based on behaviors independent of and long pre-dating the crime.

Second, I intended to identify, as clearly as possible, why Mr. Kauffman did the acts constituting the crime, without reference to any potential diagnosis or any criteria for a particular diagnosis. This portion of the project would draw on tools and concepts of the ideographic personology branch of psychology, which addresses a single individual over much or all of his or her lifetime. The goal was to identify causes of the behaviors independently of DSM concepts and jargon.

Finally, the results of those two efforts would be put into a database and analyzed to determine the extent to which any DSM-based diagnosis supported or did not support the identified non-DSM-based causes of the actions constituting the crime.

At this point, nearly a year into the project, I was frustrated. The project was taking longer than I expected and there was no end in sight. It was unclear whether I would be able to develop any kind of meaningful analysis of the information I was gathering.

Also, my relationship with Mr. Kauffman was veering off in directions that made me uncomfortable. I was supposed to be interviewing him. More and more it seemed like he was interviewing me. I had resisted that for a long time, but I seemed to be losing this battle. Was he very good at manipulating me? Or was I more willing to talk about my history than I thought I was? Could talking about myself distort and contaminate my work? Was I really afraid to talk about my history, or had I subconsciously been looking for a chance to do that?

I talked to the professor sponsoring my work, Dr. Jacqueline DeProulx. She said, "Stick with it. Surely you will learn something important at some point."

I puzzled over these things, but what could I do? Really, what choice did I have but to go on?

CHAPTER 3

GETTING RICH AND BEING POOR

June 3, 2012

Katy

About your tattoos. I was shocked when you took your jacket off and I saw them. Lots of young adults have them, but those "sleeves" as you call them, they're something else. I won't lie to you. I don't think they're attractive at all. How old were you when you got them? Why didn't your mom stop you? Maybe that kind of "body art" was normal in your world, but you must have known it wasn't going to help you get jobs and deal with mainstream, middle class people.

You want me to get back to business? Let's talk about recessions. By early 1979 our weekly business strategy meetings started to get gloomy. The mid-1970s had been good for us, a booming economy, stable interest rates, but financial clouds were forming. In 1976 Milton Friedman got the Nobel Prize for economics for his theory that the Federal Reserve should focus on a slow steady increase in the money supply. That became all the rage in Washington and Wall Street. When Paul Volker was appointed chairman of the Federal Reserve Board in mid-1979, he saw his job as wringing inflation out of the economy. The Fed pushed interest rates to ten, twelve, fourteen percent and beyond—the prime rate hit twenty percent in early 1980.

Sharon saw this coming and predicted a severe recession. The financial community (and politicians) seemed oddly oblivious. We talked to some academic economists who agreed with Sharon but didn't seem to know what the government or the private sector should do about it.

We knew what to do: retrench and save up a lot of "dry powder." If real estate crashed, lots of properties could be bought cheap. Extraordinary opportunities were coming for those with cash who could figure out which distressed properties to buy.

We quit starting new projects, sold finished projects, paid down loans. We explained to our investors that we expected unusually good opportunities in a year or so and were building a war chest to take advantage of them when they came. We were in good shape when the crash came in 1980. Many investors lost money on other investments, saw us as smart managers, and would invest more with us when the time was right.

Early in 1982 we started buying distressed properties. Sharon, Eeko, Heinz and I looked at dozens of them, talked about how we could improve them, and bought those where we agreed on a plan to boost their value. Money flowed in from investors as fast as we could spend it. We doubled and tripled the value of our assets. Before then we had gotten money from wealthy individuals, but now we started also getting money from pension funds, charities and other institutions. We became the "go to" place for passive investments in Northwest real estate. From 1982 to 1988 we made far more money than we'd ever dreamed possible, and our investors did very well too.

Early in 1989 we saw the economic situation begin to darken again. We'd expanded very fast. Our limited partnerships owned properties worth over $550 million. Again, we went into a defensive mode, not starting new projects, selling properties, paying down debt. By early 1990 we were in position to buy properties at distressed prices when the recession came.

Where were the best opportunities? The Resolution Trust Corporation, a federal agency formed to sell assets of failed savings and loan associations. Hundreds of S&Ls had failed. The RTC had to sell billions of dollars' worth of properties. Its staff was much too small to sell them one by one or to manage them until it could sell them, so it offered "bulk packages" of properties at distressed prices. Olaf Johansson helped arrange meetings with the RTC staff and gave us good advice on how to deal with them.

We were just a local Seattle firm. We needed to get bigger fast. We merged our four limited partnerships into a single Real Estate Investment Trust. The REIT then did an initial public offering, raising $75 million of new cash. Jim Hawthorne helped us line up a $50 million term loan from United American. Frank Wilson helped us line up a $50 million line of credit with Bank of America, which had taken over Seafirst Bank.

I worked eighty or ninety hours a week. It was exhausting, but we got a very good deal: we bought forty-five properties from the RTC for $120 million. Sharon, Eeko, Heinz and I had worked up plans on what we'd do with each one. Before we made our final offer, I asked them, "Should we do this?" Sharon said, "The numbers look good. We can make this work." Eeko said, "Well, Boss, I wouldn't have the guts to do it myself, but I think you'll make a lot of money." Heinz said, "It'll be a hell of a lot of work, but we'll do it for you."

I said, "One thing I want to make clear: if this goes well, and I think it will, you'll all make money too. But if things get bad, blame me, only me. I don't want any of you blaming yourself or each other. This is my decision. If it doesn't work, it'll be my fault, not yours."

The prior owners had invested over $300 million in the properties, so we got them for about forty cents on the dollar. Values had fallen some but not nearly that much. It was a great deal.

Mark

# # # #

June 10, 2012

Dear Mark,

Mom was high, really zonked, when she let her boyfriend do my tattoos. I didn't care; I just did not want him to touch me anywhere else. I was eleven.

I didn't think I'd ever get a real job or ever deal with mainstream, middle class people. All my life Mom and I had been living on the streets or with dysfunctional men who were hardly middle-class role models.

You are doing a good job of explaining your business career. What came next?

Katy

# # # #

June 17, 2012

Katy

I keep thinking about your mom and you living with guys you hardly knew. That wasn't a good situation for a little kid. Maybe better than being homeless, but it was dangerous. And I can't imagine it was much fun for you or your mom.

Jonathon, then the PI business and real estate editor, wrote a very flattering article on our RTC deal: "Can the Phoenix Rise Again?" It talked about our business from the original "Phoenix house" in 1966 through the recessions of 1970-71 and 1981-82 and into the one that started in 1990. His answer was "Darn right!" (You couldn't use "damn" in the newspaper back then.) His article was picked up in the national business press, so it became widely known that our little regional firm had, three times, done a masterful job of taking advantage of distressed markets. This publicity drove the price of our REIT shares up, so we issued more shares to buy more properties at distressed prices.

Until then, publicity had always been good for us, but we learned it can hurt you bad. It caused the biggest crisis in my life up to that time.

On May 10, 1990, our daughter Julie, then 16, was kidnapped on her way home from school. Two men jumped out of a car, grabbed her and pushed her into the back seat. The car, driven by a woman, sped away. Several of Julie's friends were there but too shaken up to give a good description of the people or the car.

We sat around our house with the police and FBI, waiting for the kidnappers to contact us. About 7:00 that night they called. "We've got her. Check your mailbox." They hung up quickly. In our mailbox was a Polaroid picture of Julie bound and gagged. On the back was a note: WE HAVE HER. YOU HAVE MONEY. LET'S MAKE A DEAL. No amount of money was mentioned. Nor was anything on when and how they would contact us.

Every day we got a picture in the mail, another Polaroid of her holding the front page of the morning newspaper from the day before, postmarked in various cities around the Sound. Every day Julie looked more haggard and disheveled.

I was exhausted but couldn't sleep, frustrated that I couldn't do anything to help. We expected a demand for ransom and I wanted to get ready to pay it. The cops and FBI people were very much against that. "If word gets out that you paid, there'll be more kidnappings. More families will have to go through this."

"Frankly, right now I don't give a shit about other families. This is our daughter we're talking about." Normally I'd never talk to cops or anybody like that, but I was exhausted and stressed.

We asked Grandma Olsen to stay with us, thinking her peaceful calm would help us get through this ordeal. It did. There was something about her. Of course, she was worried and scared too, but she was a calming influence. She prayed a lot, I'm sure, but seldom in front of us. She didn't want to make us uncomfortable. Still, after a couple of days she asked if I had tried praying.

"I did, but it didn't work."

"What do you mean?"

"Well, I tried to make a deal with God. You know, if He'd bring Julie back safe, I'd become a Christian."

"Oh, I see. That's very human, but it doesn't work that way, does it?"

"No, it didn't work. I knew I probably wouldn't change after she got back. It was like I was lying to God. I never lie to people, so it seemed kind of absurd to lie to Him, if He exists."

"Anything else?"

"Well, somehow I felt that I couldn't make God owe me anything. I mean, He can do what He wants, right? I can't make Him do what I want."

"No, we can't overpower Him. We owe Him, a lot. But He cares about us and He'll help us if we let Him."

"Help get Julie back?"

"Maybe, maybe not. But He can help us cope, help us go on no matter what."

I started to cry. I was so tired, so stressed. I'd been trying to hold it together for Cindy and Davie, but I just lost it. Grandma O sat there very quietly. Finally, I quit crying. "So," I said, "I guess I have to just leave it up to Him."

"Yes, that would be best."

"Even if I don't believe in Him?"

"Yes," she said, "I don't think that makes any difference."

I thanked Grandma O for being so patient and went back to thinking about what I could do about the kidnapping.

Of course, we hoped to catch the kidnappers before they could spend any ransom money. But just in case, I wanted the cops or FBI to get us a suitcase full of counterfeit money. "You guys must have a lot of it stashed somewhere; don't you confiscate it all the time?" If we gave the kidnappers mostly counterfeit money with a few thousand dollars of real money on top, we might catch them when they started spending counterfeit bills. I thought it was a good plan. The cops and FBI didn't.

I called my Congressmen friends, Olaf Johansson and Buddy Graves. Both of them, or maybe people on their staffs, called the FBI. The local FBI guy said, "I see you've got friends in Congress." But he still wouldn't agree to get me a suitcase of counterfeit money.

"Why haven't we heard from them?" I asked the FBI guy. "What are they waiting for?"

"They're smart. They know the longer you stew and worry the more you'll be willing to pay."

"I thought you didn't want us to pay anything."

"We don't, but we can't stop you. We think you're going to do it whether we like it or not. If you do, our job will be to watch very carefully and try to make sure that whatever we do doesn't put your daughter at greater risk."

"Oh God." I started crying again. It hurt so much. Anything I did might put Julie at even more risk. I hadn't thought of it that way before.

The ransom dance began. It started with a very short phone call. "Go to the phone booth at the 7-11 in Factoria. 8:00 tonight." I went there a few minutes early. There was a parking lot full of cars and a motel across the street. At least one kidnapper must be watching me, but from where? There were plainclothes police in unmarked cars, but I couldn't see any.

The phone rang as soon as I stepped into the booth. When I picked up the phone, a male voice said, "Go to the phone booth at the Shell station across the street," and hung up. You probably can't imagine this, Katy, because there aren't many phone booths left and most pay phones don't work anymore. This was before cell phones. Phone booths were common; outgoing calls cost a quarter, but you could get a call for nothing.

I walked over to the phone booth at the Shell station. The phone rang again. "One million dollars, small bills, half in 20s, nothing over 100, used, unmarked. How long will it take?"

"Jesus, I'd have to go to twenty or thirty banks, maybe more. And I'd have to get money into the accounts before I could get it back out. Ten days, maybe?"

"Six days. We can be patient, but your daughter needs a bath."

"If you guys hurt her, I will track you down and kill you." I don't know if I really would have, probably not, but that's how I felt. "What do I do with the money?"

"We'll let you know." He hung up.

We had a debrief meeting that night, the cops, FBI guys and me. The caller must have seen me enter both phone booths or been in contact with someone who saw me. The calls couldn't be traced. They probably were made from a nearby motel room, maybe from one of those new mobile phones. You're too young to remember them, Katy. They were as big as a brick and couldn't connect to the internet. The internet was just getting started.

"So, what now?" I asked the lead FBI agent.

"Are you going to do it?" he asked.

"What choice do I have?"

"OK, we don't know how many there are or how good their communication technology is, but we assume they're watching you. We think you should make a show of going from bank to bank to get money, but you'll only need a couple of thousand. We've got counterfeit for the rest. We're busy making it look old and used."

"What do I do with the money? I can't walk around with that much cash, especially with people watching me who know I've got it. I don't want it in my house. That might be risky for my wife and son. Or at my office. That might put my employees in danger."

"We've thought of that. Rent a locker at the airport, put a suitcase in it. Every time you leave a bank go there and put a package in the suitcase."

So, every day I went to about six branches of various banks (some I didn't even have accounts in), asked to see a personal banker, was taken into a private room, and came out carrying a package about the size of a shoebox. Sometimes it was full of tens, twenties, and fifties, all counterfeit. Usually it was empty. All of this was arranged by the FBI. But would it work?

On the third, fourth and fifth days the mail brought another picture of Julie holding the first page of the paper from the day before. The fifth day, a gun was sitting on a table and pointed at her. I didn't let Cindy or Davie see that one.

As expected, I got a call from the kidnapers the evening of the sixth day. “Got the money?”

“Nearly all, over $940,000.” An FBI psychologist had come up with that idea. The number was big enough to satisfy them but the idea that I’d tried hard but couldn’t get it all sounded more credible than saying I had it all. “If you just give me another day, half a day …”

“Go to the phone booth at the Chevron station across from the Renton Cinemas at 9:00 tonight. There’ll be a backpack with instructions inside.” He hung up. We’d hoped to keep him on the line long enough to trace the call. No luck on that.

I got to the Chevron station almost exactly at 9:00. I was afraid if I got there early, they wouldn’t drop off the backpack. The police had it staked out, hoping to at least get a description and maybe a car license number. A guy came on foot, dropped off a backpack, and disappeared into the movie theaters with a pre-paid ticket. They couldn’t figure which of the six theaters he went into. They didn’t get a good description.

There was a beat-up non-descript backpack in the phone booth, a JanSport, like thousands of kids carried. Inside was a note saying to put the money in the backpack, buy a roundtrip ticket to Portland with the return on a particular flight, check the bag for the return flight but not get on it. Did they know the money already was at the airport? Who knew? What difference did it make?

I did what they said. They planned to pick up the backpack at a crowded carousel at a busy time at a busy airport and melt away into the crowd. The police were watching the carousel, hoping whoever picked up the backpack would lead them to where they were holding

Julie. They saw a man disappear into the crowd with the backpack and emerge with one, but they didn't see him swap the one with the money or see the woman sitting on a bench with the backpack between her legs, almost hidden by a long coat.

It was a pretty good plan. It threw the cops and FBI agents off for a few minutes. But then an electronic tracking device in the backpack with the money showed it still was in the terminal near the carousel. Once they figured out that the woman on the bench had the backpack with the money, it wasn't hard to track her to a house near Issaquah where they found Julie and the other kidnappers. When the kidnapper who'd picked up the backpack was on his way out of the parking garage and couldn't communicate with the others, the police picked him up on suspicion of kidnapping. He didn't talk until he saw on the news that the other two kidnappers had been arrested and Julie was safe.

I asked the FBI agent about the tracking device they used to rescue Julie. He wouldn't talk about it. "You're not supposed to know about that technology. Your friends in high places got us to use it but it's secret stuff. Don't tell the press or anybody else about it." Now I think it was just ordinary GPS technology. Everybody has it in their pockets today, but most people had never heard it back then. I've never talked to anybody about the tracking technology for all these years. But GPS technology is common knowledge now, and my loyalty to the federal government has gone down since they locked me up.

Mark

# # # #

June 24, 2012

Dear Mark,

I was so moved by your daughter's kidnapping. It's hard to imagine what your family went through.

As far as my mom and me not "enjoying" life with the guys we lived with, well, the goal was survival, not enjoyment. She told me that sex was "not fun, just something you have to do to get by."

Did the kidnapping cause any changes in your life?

Katy

# # # #

July 1, 2012

Katy

The kidnapping led to a lot of problems for our family. Of course, we were very relieved that Julie was safe, but it caused a twenty percent drop in the price of our REIT shares. Our Board insisted that we get better security.

We moved to a waterfront mansion in a gated community on Lake Washington, not far from Somerset, close enough so the kids wouldn't have to change schools. There was a tennis court, a gym with an indoor lap pool and dressing rooms, a dock and boat house. The main house was three times as big as our Somerset one, not counting a two-bedroom apartment over the garage that our new security service used. It had been built for the founder of a defunct internet sales company. Our REIT had gotten it in the RTC package.

We moved there in June 1990. The kids and their friends and Cindy and I water-skied. We played tennis. I swam laps and worked out in our gym, but I missed seeing my friends at the rec center. None of us felt comfortable there. It was too big, too fancy, too much marble and brass and exotic woods. It felt strange and sterile, not like a real home.

My parents came to visit. "It's lovely," Mom said.

"You throw money around like this, like there's no tomorrow?" Dad asked.

"Dad, it wasn't our idea. We had to get better security. All this stuff just came with it."

"It's got to be expensive, very, very expensive."

"Well, the company owns it. We just rent it, and the Board gave me a raise to cover the rent."

"But you own the company, so isn't that just moving money from one pocket to another?"

"Ah, it's, it's a little more complicated. We own a company that manages the company that owns it. We own about 20% of that company, so our investors pay about 80% of it. And there's tax angles—it's too hard to explain but the taxpayers end up paying for a lot of it."

"I don't understand all that. But I hope you're not borrowing too much. You ought to be saving for a rainy day."

"Dad, it's OK. We've got an independent Board that won't let me go crazy and we're saving a lot, getting richer every day."

"Well, I'm glad to hear that. It brings up another thing."

"What's that?"

"Your sister. You've been paying for her group home, and we appreciate that. But it's time to set up something for after we're gone, in case something happens. Your mom and me, we haven't been able to save enough for that."

"Not a problem, Dad. Cindy and I can do that, right Cindy?"

"Sure. Absolutely. We should have thought of that ourselves."

I said, "We've been paying the group home and sending Lucy a little spending money every month, but maybe we should move it up, give Lucy more."

"No," Mom said, "she wouldn't like that. If you want to send more, give it to the group home so it helps everybody there. She doesn't want special treatment, gets embarrassed about that."

"OK. It's a nonprofit, right? We can send them donations besides paying for Lucy's care and a little spending money."

Mom said, "That would be great."

"But I want something permanent, something that will take care of Lucy even if something happened to your mom and me and even you too," Dad said.

"Like a trust fund?"

"I don't care what you call it. But you know what I want. I want her taken care of no matter what happens, even if we're dead and you're broke."

"OK, OK, I hear you. I'll talk to the lawyers. They'll know how to do it."

"Don't forget," he said. "It'll give me some peace of mind, knowing it's done."

We made one deal after another in the next eighteen months. We bought up three smaller REITs that were in financial trouble. We bought large packages of properties that United American and Bank of America had foreclosed on. Jim Hawthorne and Frank Wilson were the key guys on those deals. The value of the REIT shares shot up, which let us issue more shares to buy another two hundred million worth of properties.

By the end of 1992 our REIT had properties worth over a billion dollars. Over the next few years their value soared to over three billion.

Much as I loved doing deals, I had to spend time hiring more people. There's an art to it. Some people have great resumes and interview well but wouldn't fit in. Personality, character, work ethic, intelligence don't always show up in interviews. If you can find good people who don't interview well, hire them. They'll be more grateful, stay longer and work harder than the golden boys (or girls) that everybody else likes to hire.

Mark

# # # #

July 8, 2012

Dear Mark,

I hear you on being uneasy in a fancy new place. It happened to me, on a much smaller scale of course, when Mom and I finally got off the streets. Sometimes upward mobility is not all it's cracked up to be.

After a while, of course, Mom and I got used to it. Did that happen to you and your family too?

Katy

# # # #

July 15, 2012

Katy

I don't know that we ever got used to living so much differently than ordinary people. Julie was embarrassed about it, and it turned out to cause problems for Cindy too. But I'm glad you and your mom "got off the streets." When and how did that happen?

In late August 1990, an embarrassing thing happened. I went to the boathouse looking for David. When I opened the door, he and his friend Kevin were sprawled in the ski boat seats with their swimsuits around their ankles. I closed the door and left as soon as I saw them, but they'd seen me, and they knew I'd seen them and what they were doing.

I wasn't upset. It seemed like a normal enough thing for thirteen-year-old kids to do. I should have knocked or made some noise to let them know I was coming, but I didn't know they were there, leave alone what was going on.

David and I kind of avoided each other for a couple of days. I needed to do something before Cindy or Julie noticed the tension between us, so one evening I knocked on his door and asked if I could come in. He didn't answer. I waited a few seconds and then went in. "Lookit,

I've been avoiding you and you've been avoiding me, but that's just silly. I know it's embarrassing but we should talk about it. Maybe I can help you feel better." He looked down at his feet and didn't say anything.

"First, I want you to know that what you and Kevin were doing—jacking off, jerking off, beating off, whatever boys call it these days—is perfectly normal. The medical word for it is masturbating. Nearly all guys do it. So, I'm not upset. I don't want you to feel guilty or worried about it." He didn't say anything.

"Second, Kevin hasn't been around since then. He must be as embarrassed as you are. You guys have been friends for a long time. I don't want you to lose a friend over this, and I want him to feel welcome in our home just like always. I would talk to him myself but—"

"Don't, don't, please don't. I don't want to talk about it. I'm sure he doesn't either. Just get out and leave me alone!"

"OK. I won't talk to him. But try to find some way to let him know he's still welcome here."

I thought about telling Cindy about this—I didn't normally keep secrets from her—but if David ever asked if I'd told his mom, I wanted to be able to say "No".

The next Saturday I was on our tennis court hitting balls against the backboard. David and Kevin came out with tennis racquets. It was good to see them together, but I tried not to show it; I didn't want to embarrass them. "You can have the court. I was just leaving, but I could hit you a few for a warm-up if you want."

Kevin said "OK." They stayed on one side and I hit balls from the other. Everybody acted normal, like the boathouse thing never happened. I started hitting the balls harder and they hit them back harder. Soon I was hitting much harder than I'd ever hit to the kids before and they were hitting back just as hard.

David left to go to the bathroom. I began gathering up the jacket and sweatshirt I'd pealed off. Kevin came over and said, "You didn't tell my parents, did you, I mean about the boathouse thing?"

"No, I didn't, and I didn't tell David's mom either. But, you know, they wouldn't have been upset if one of them had walked in on you instead of me."

"Oh, they would have. My dad hates queers, homos, gays, whatever you call them."

"But what you were doing was normal, not gay or anything like that." He looked puzzled. "I mean nearly all boys masturbate, you know, have sex by themselves. It's OK. Your parents know that."

"They're very religious and very old fashioned. You're wrong about them."

"Well, I hope not." Neither of us said anything more for a while. "Look," I said, "don't answer this but do you feel guilty or scared about it? Or wet dreams, or thinking about sex? Don't answer. What I'm trying to tell you is those things are normal. Don't worry about that stuff."

He looked at me as though I was talking, I don't know, Dutch maybe. "Lookit," I said, "if you're worried about this stuff, next time you go to the doctor, ask him about it. Doctors know how to talk about this." He looked down and turned red. He wasn't about to do that. "OK, if that's too embarrassing, how about the library? There's books on this." But he didn't look like he could go that route either. "OK, look, I'll find a book on this and give it to David, and when he's done with it, he can give it to you."

I went to the local Barnes & Noble. A young salesman asked if he could help. "Yes, I've got a thirteen-year old son who's too embarrassed to talk about sex. I meant to talk to him about it several years ago but, somehow, I never got around to it. I don't know what he knows or thinks, but I want him to feel OK about sexual stuff, not guilty or scared or whatever."

"You must be a good dad." He led me to a shelf of books for kids of various ages. The first one I looked at covered the basics but seemed written for younger kids. The next one had parts that seemed to go too far into weird, disgusting stuff. None seemed just right. I bought the first two, thinking at least David will know there isn't anything about sex that I was afraid to talk about.

I knocked on David's door and asked if I could come in. This time he said "OK."

I gave him the books. "Here's two books on sex. The smaller one is pretty basic; you probably know most of it, but the parts about girls may have a few things you don't know. The other covers some stuff that, well, I wish it didn't, but it's more, ah, complete. We can talk about any of this stuff if you want. What I'm trying to say is that if any of this worries you, it's better to talk about it than be afraid to. Understand? When you're done with them, please give them to Kevin."

"OK. And Kevin says you're a really good dad."

I laughed. "The guy in the bookstore thought so too. Lookit, I know this has been embarrassing but I hope our talk the other night helped you feel better."

"I'm sorry I yelled at you. I was upset but, you know, I do feel better. So, thanks."

I was trying to be a good dad for David and help his friend be comfortable at our place again. But this was the first Domino in a chain of events that alienated Kevin's dad, my strongest political supporter, someone who could have done so much to help our industry during the great recession, and maybe helped me stay out of prison.

Mark

# # # #

July 22, 2012

Dear Mark,

It sounds like you were a good dad, and a good father figure for your son's friend. But what would David think if he knew you told me about that incident in the boathouse?

Katy

# # # #

July 29, 2012

Katy

Would David be upset if he knew I told you about the boathouse thing? At the time, he'd have been embarrassed if the story got around at school, but he's over thirty now, married, probably not sensitive about this anymore.

But your question got me thinking. Maybe we should talk about confidentiality, respect for my privacy and for my family and friends. I'm not talking about some big long thing put together by a bunch of lawyers. I just want an understanding between us.

Our original deal, remember, was that I'd tell you about my business career. You're the one who wanted me to talk about personal stuff, but I've come around on that. There's no way you can understand what happened to me unless you understand that I was a terrific husband, father, brother, son, employer, mentor, friend, because it was those qualities that the prosecutors twisted around to make me look like some horrible villain.

I'm not worried about you embarrassing me, but I don't want you doing anything that would embarrass my kids, or my ex-wife, or my friends or colleagues. I guess I'll just have to trust you on that.

Julie couldn't wait to get her driver's license. She wanted a car so she'd have more freedom to get away and be with her friends. I asked, "What sort of car do you want?"

"Nothing fancy. Just an ordinary car that nobody will notice." She picked out an eight-year-old blue Volvo. It didn't cost much. I'd expected to pay a lot more but that's what she wanted. I said, "Nobody'll notice that on the high school parking lot!" She laughed. Lots of eastside parents drove Volvos and passed them on down to their kids as they—the cars and kids—got older. They're supposed to be one of the safest cars. It was nice to know there was a lot of good Swedish steel around my little girl when she was driving.

One day in May 1991, I came home from work and Cindy handed me a condom. "I found this in one of the kid's jeans."

"David's?"

"No, Julie's." Julie had just turned seventeen.

"So, are you going to talk to her about it?"

"No, we are. We're going to do it together."

After dinner, we asked Julie to come to our room. "So, what is this?" Cindy asked her, holding out the condom.

"A condom?"

"I know that. Don't get cute. What was it doing in your pocket?"

"Well, Luke is too embarrassed to buy them and I'm too smart to have sex without them, so I buy them and keep them handy."

There was silence for a while. Cindy and I tried to stay calm. "So," Cindy asked, "you've become sexually active?"

"Uh huh. I'm going on the pill, but this seemed like a good temporary measure. What kind of interrogation is this!"

Julie was losing her cool. All of us were about to lose our cool. I stared at my feet. This should be a mother-daughter conversation. Why am I here?

"Mark," Cindy said, "do you have any input?"

"I, ah, I .... I'm trying to keep calm. I don't want to make things worse. I want to do what's best for Julie, but I, I haven't got a clue what that might be." There was an awkward silence. "Do the security people know about this?"

"Dad, that's part of the problem. That's how we got into this, really, trying to sneak away from them. I hate being watched all the time. It started as a game. Can we make out without them catching us? Can we ditch them? Can we ...."

"Nobody likes it," Cindy said. "Not me, your brother, your dad. But after, you know, the kidnapping, we felt we had to do it."

"I know," Julie said, "but it's ruining my life. I just want to be an ordinary kid. People think it must be cool having a big waterfront house, but it sucks. I'm a freak. I don't have a normal life like my friends. I don't even have many friends anymore."

"I'm sorry," I said. "In a few months you'll go to college. It'll be better there. And we can try to make it easier here. Maybe have the security folks back off a little, Cindy? Give Julie more space to live a more normal life?"

Heads were nodding. Julie had put her finger on something we'd all felt but never talked about. "I suppose it's every father's dream to have a team of security guards follow his daughter around, but maybe that's not all it's cracked up to be." That didn't go over well. "Sorry. That was supposed to be a joke."

We talked a while longer. Nothing else got resolved but we started to feel better. For a little while we forgot about Julie becoming sexually active. We all hugged. That was a pretty good outcome considering where we'd started.

Mark

# # # #

Aug. 5, 2012

Dear Mark,

I understand about Julie's car. It's like if you're living in a homeless camp and everybody else has a blue tarp, you don't want yours to be brown or orange.

There were condoms all over when I was growing up, but I wasn't interested in sex. I just tuned out when kids giggled and smirked about it. It made me feel lonely and different, but the way kids talked seemed so immature and stupid.

Katy

# # # #

Aug. 12, 2012

Katy

Choosing a bland, blue Volvo rather than, say, a red BMW, isn't exactly like your analogy of the tarps, but it seems like maybe we're starting to communicate a little better. But how much did you live in homeless camps? Jeeze, there's a lot I still don't know about you.

I'm surprised you weren't interested in sex as a teenager—most kids are, I think—but after your mom telling you it was "no fun" and your bad experiences, I can see it might seem disgusting.

We started having security guards drive David and his friends around, and Julie's too if they needed a ride. Some kids still came by bike but, especially when the weather was bad, kids and their parents liked having the guards do chauffeur duty and it helped us feel better about having the guards.

Later I realized that this may have been a mistake. Cindy had been a fulltime mom and homemaker. Driving the kids and their friends had been a big part of her life. I didn't mean to take that away from her. And it wasn't good for her to have more time alone, not drive as much, not see the kids and their friends as much. This is when she started drinking during the day and showing signs of depression, warning signs that I missed.

In late August 1991, shortly before Julie left for college, Cindy and I came home one evening and found five or six cars in the driveway. Julie and her friends were out on the dock and in the lake. There were beer bottles all over, piles of clothes here and there, kids skinny dipping. Julie saw me, giggled, handed me a cookie and said, "Have one." Several kids laughed.

"What's in 'em?" asked Cindy.

"They're A-B-T-Rs," one of the kids said, giggling again.

"A-B-T-Rs?" I asked.

"Alice B. Toklas recipe," said Julie.

"Pot," said Cindy.

"Shit," I said. Several kids snuffed out what they were smoking.

"Dad, I'm not a smoker so I can't suck it in far enough or hold it in long enough to do any good, so I use the edibles, most of us do. Try one."

"No, Julie, you know how I feel about that stuff." I handed the cookie back and started to leave. Then I turned around and came back. "Listen, you guys, and that includes you girls too. I wish you hadn't done this, but here we are, and now I'm worried about how you're gonna get home safely. Most of you probably want to get your clothes back on and leave, but please don't drive out of here drunk or high. Stay all night if you want, or at least stay long enough so be safe driving home. Or have the security guards drive you home."

Cindy went in the house and I went to talk to the security guards. "There's some kids out there that look pretty, ah, impaired."

"We know, Boss. We didn't know what we should do about it. What should we have done?"

"I don't know. But try not to let them drive out of here if they seem drunk or high. Give them coffee or something. Drive them home if they'll let you."

I went in the house and got in bed. Cindy said, "She's right you know. If you're not a regular smoker and somebody gives you a joint, it's hard to suck it in far enough and hold it in long enough to get any effect."

"And you know this how?"

"By trying it, of course."

"When you were a kid?"

"No, last month after Buddy's fundraiser." Another warning sign I missed.

"Was he smoking pot?"

"No. He said he promised you not to smoke it in the US until it was legal, and to tell you he'd kept that promise."

"Oh, well, that part's good." I stared at the ceiling. "But this thing with Julie tonight, it's so hard. I try to be a good father, and then this kind of shit comes along. What should I do now?"

"Go to sleep."

"Cindy, this isn't a joke. I really want to do the right thing, but what would that be?"

"I wasn't joking. I know you try hard, but maybe too hard sometimes? Just relax. You're usually so positive, so optimistic. Just be yourself. It'll all be alright." She rolled over and went to sleep. I stared at the ceiling for a long time, with a piece of song looping through my head:

"Try not to worry, try not to hang on to
"Problems that upset you, oh
"Don't you know
"Everything's all right, yes, everything's fine,
"And we want you to sleep well tonight ..."

Is it possible to try too hard to be good?

Mark

# # # #

Aug. 19, 2012

Dear Mark,

I know it is hard when your loved ones start doing drugs, but pot is not so bad. My mom got into stuff a lot harder and worse than that, and there was nothing I could do about it.

Katy

# # # #

Aug. 26, 2012

Katy

Jeeze, Katy, after everything else you've told me, I should have figured your mom got into drugs too. But, you're right, usually there's nothing you can do. Sometimes, though, you can help people with other kinds of problems.

One day in 1992 I walked into Sharon O'Reilly's office and found her crying. I started to back out, but then I closed the door and asked if she wanted to talk. She didn't say anything, just kept crying. I sat on her sofa and said nothing.

After a while I said, "I'll leave if you want." She kept crying. After a few more minutes, I said, "Lookit, you don't have to talk about it, but I care about you and I'd like to help." Gradually her crying slowed down. Finally, she looked up at me, looked back down at her desk, and said "Bob left me." Bob was her husband. They had two teenage kids.

"Oh, I'm so, so sorry." I wanted to say something more comforting, but what could that be? After a while I said, "Well, I could come over and give you a hug if that might help." She didn't react. I thought oh boy, you shouldn't have said that. But after a while she got up and said, "Well, a hug couldn't hurt." So, I got up and hugged her. We sat back down on her sofa. Eventually she said, "He found a younger, prettier woman," and, after another long silence, "I know I've never been pretty but I tried to be a good wife and a good mom."

"You were, you are, and you're a tremendous employee and colleague. Bob's being pretty shallow and short-sighted if he doesn't appreciate you in spite of ...." Oh God, I thought, I'm making this worse. "I'm really sorry. I keep saying the wrong thing."

"It's OK. At least you're trying. You mean well and I appreciate it." She put her arms around me and started crying again. For some stupid reason I started thinking about Zorba the Greek. Remember him? He made love to some lonely old woman just because he felt sorry for her. That led to thinking about having sex with her and that led to an erection. So stupid. Sometimes your body just goes off on its own.

After a while she quit crying, straightened up and said "Well, in your own weird way you are helping me feel better."

"Ah, thanks, I guess. But you know, if we're going to talk about this more, we should have Cindy with us. She's, well, a woman might be more help than me."

"And you'd feel safer with the three of us together, wouldn't you?"

"Yes. Don't get me wrong. I'm not saying we'd ever actually do anything we shouldn't. It's not that, but, you know, when you talk about things that really hurt, things that are hard to talk about, well sometimes feelings kind of morph in ways you don't expect."

I told Cindy about my conversation with Sharon and a few days later we had her over for dinner. Cindy said it had been hard for Bob to watch Sharon's successes. It wasn't just the money, although she was making much more than him, but also the recognition. Sharon was so well known in our industry that they couldn't go to a nice restaurant or through an airport without well dressed, successful men and women stopping her to say hello. It was like he was invisible. Nobody noticed him or knew who he was.

After Sharon went home, I asked Cindy if she ever felt like that, like she was almost a non-person in my shadow. "Not often. I'm not there, but it's like I can see it from here. That's why I feel for Bob—he feels it more." That too was a warning sign, but I didn't see it at the time.

"Oh Cindy, I don't want you to ever feel that way. You know I couldn't do what I do without you."

"You could. You were doing fine before I came along. If anything happened to me, you'd be OK again. You could go on without me if you had too."

"I guess that's a compliment, but let's make sure we never have to find out if it's true."

Sharon got a divorce. Several years later she married a retired widower. He'd been a hard-charging successful executive but, after he married Sharon, he settled into being a house-husband and gardener. He loved her dearly. If he ever noticed that she was not very attractive, it never showed. Sharon came to work every day with a big smile and a lot of energy. She still worked fifty or sixty hours a week, but he went along on her business trips and cooked gourmet dinners when they were home. Everybody could see how much they enjoyed each other.

Early in 1992 we began negotiating a second large bulk purchase from the Resolution Trust Corporation. They didn't have much left in the Northwest that interested us so we looked at their Bay Area properties. Sharon studied that market. I talked with Frank Wilson, then a Senior Vice President at Bank of America, who'd moved to the Bay Area. Olaf Johansson helped behind the scenes.

We agreed on a $140 million package. Again, before I signed the deal, I asked Sharon, Eeko and Heinz, "Do you think we should do this?" Sharon said, "The numbers look good, very good." Eeko said, "There's a lot fewer permit problems than the last one." Heinz said, "Lots of contractors out of work in the Bay Area, so we can get good contractors at good prices."

"Well, I'm pumped about it," I said. "But we'll have to open up a Bay Area office and hire a bunch of new people. I'll need a lot of help from you three on hiring, training and supervising them. And, again, if this doesn't work out, you can blame me but I don't want any of you blaming yourself or each other. OK?"

We closed the deal in March 1992, and started building a Bay Area staff. No trouble finding vacant office space; we'd just bought a million square feet of it.

We began hiring staff for our new Bay Area office. No trouble finding candidates. Lots of developers, contractors, real estate executives, and other skilled professionals were unemployed. We were building an organization as fast as we could, but we didn't want to pass up good opportunities. We bought up two failing REITs and packages of distressed properties from major banks and insurance companies, first Bank of America and United American, later others.

Mark

# # # #

Sept. 3, 2012

Dear Mark,

I appreciate you describing your relationships with your friends and colleagues, and I did ask you to go into that. But now I think we should get to the end of your career. It has been fifteen months and we do not seem to be getting close to your criminal charges and trial yet.

I read the stuff you send me and sometimes I can't help thinking you seem too good to be true. Don't you have any flaws? You seem to be the hero of all your stories. Didn't you make any mistakes?"

Katy

# # # #

Sept. 10, 2012

Katy

About me being "the hero of all my stories," I'm not sure what you meant but it didn't seem like a compliment. Do you think I'm only willing to talk about projects that turned out well? Of course, some didn't work out. We can talk about them if you want.

Other things went wrong too. For example, we had a project manager who thought he was God's gift to women. Heinz talked to him about it, but it didn't get better. Then I told him he was making people uncomfortable and needed to treat people with respect, but it didn't change. Then he started sleeping with an intern, a college student, and flaunting it in front of other employees. Heinz and Eeko said, "We gotta fire him, Boss. You want to do it, or you want us to?"

"Let's do it together, one of you and me."

Heinz and I met with him, told him what we'd heard, and asked if it was true. "Damn right I'm fucking her. She's over twenty-one. We're consenting adults. It's none of your business."

"You're wrong. It is my business. You're making other employees uncomfortable, women and men both. And you're abusing your position as her boss."

"Hey, its construction. We're men, real men. We take any piece of tail we can get."

"No, we're people, real people. We treat everybody with respect."

"Oh, Jesus. A fucking liberal. I should have known. Everybody knows you hang out with queers.

"Don't go there," said Heinz. "Mark and me and other guys don't like the way you treat women. You're out of line. I was going to fire you myself, but Mark came to back me up."

"What are you saying?"

"I'm saying you're fired," said Heinz.

"Oh, come on, she doesn't mean a thing to me. I'll give her up if you want. I'll do better."

I said, "I hope you do, but we warned you and it didn't do any good. And your attitude, well, Jeeze, if she 'doesn't mean a thing' to you, that makes it even worse. Pack up your stuff. A security guard will escort you out of the building."

Here's another example. One day Heinz came into my office, closed the door, and said "Boss, we got a problem."

"What's that?"

"You know our Bay Area construction manager? He's cheating our contractors."

"What do you mean? How?"

"Sometimes he holds back the final payment for no good reason and then negotiates a price reduction. Sometimes he disputes costs for change orders, or claims work is defective, or comes up with some other excuse to argue. He thinks he's doing it 'for the good of the company,' but it's hurting our reputation."

"OK, you and Eeko document it for me, give me examples and details. Then we'll talk to him."

Their report was worse than I expected. Heinz and I met with him. I tried to stay calm and give him a chance to explain himself. He skimmed through the report and then got mad at me. He said, "You bastard. These things made millions for you. I never took a dime for myself. I made you a ton of money. But are you grateful? No, you act like I did something wrong."

"I'm sorry you feel that way, but you did do something wrong. You hurt our reputation. We'll have to go back to those people to apologize and make things right."

"I'm not going back and I'm not going to apologize. All those disputes were settled fair and square. I got releases from all of them. The lawyers OK'd all these settlements."

"It's not OK to gin up fake disputes, force people to settle for less than we owe them."

"Why not? It's business. Business can be rough. If you're not a big boy …."

"Hold it. I'm big enough to admit it when we're wrong. I don't like your attitude. I'm letting you go."

"Let me go? Like fire me? After all I've done for you? After I made you millions?"

"Yes, but it's dirty money. I'm going to give it back and try to fix the damage you caused. You've got to go. You don't fit in here."

On the way back to Seattle, Heinz said, "You know, Mark, I've really like working for you but I'm nearly sixty-five and I want to spend more time with my grandkids. I'm going to retire." He retired before everything blew up. Fortunately, he took his pension and profit sharing in a lump sum, so I didn't take him down along with everybody else.

And I made mistakes with my kids too, embarrassed them when I shouldn't have. For example, when he was about fourteen David came to my home office one evening and said, "Hey, Dad, can you ask Mom to get me some boxers, you know, boxer-type underwear?"

"Sure."

"Thanks." He started to leave.

I should have just left it there, but I thought this was another chance to be a great dad. "Hey, son," I said, "I'm proud of you for having the guts to ask me that."

"Huh? What?"

"Let me tell you a story." I told him about Grandma making my underwear out of chickenfeed sacks, how embarrassed I'd been about that, how much I'd wanted plain white briefs like the other kids in junior high. "So now I guess it's changed, kids are wearing boxers now?"

"Yeah, some of them."

"Well, anyway, the gym teacher told my parents I was embarrassed about my chickenfeed boxers and said maybe they ought to get me briefs like the other kids. My mom asked me about that, and I said, 'Oh no, no, no, it's OK,' because, you know, I was embarrassed about being embarrassed. So, I ended up wearing those awful boxers for another two or three years."

"Whatever," he said. "Can I go now?"

"Sure. I just wanted to explain why I was proud of you about this."

"Whatever."

I told Cindy that David wanted boxers and about my conversation. She said, "I know you meant well, but that must have embarrassed him."

"Yeah, I guess so. But …."

"It's OK. He'll get over it, but I think you were trying too hard." She bought him a couple of packages of boxers and left them on his bed. None of us ever mentioned it again.

Katy, isn't it time to meet again?

Mark

# # # #

Eighth meeting

Mark and I met on September 17, 2012, for the first time nearly four months. We had a lot to talk about but very different agendas. I wanted to talk about his career, his relationships with his family and friends and colleagues, his thinking patterns. He wanted to talk about my mom and my childhood.

KTA: It seems you did a good job of dealing with problem employees. And you must have had a good relationship with your son if it was easier for him to talk to you about the boxers than his mom. I really appreciate your willingness to talk about your career, family, friends and colleagues. I would like to talk a little about some of your thinking patterns, if that is OK.

MK: I keep thinking about you and your mom living with any guy who would "put you up" for a few days or months. It sounds awful. And when you were little, your mom wasn't old enough to be living with guys; they could have been arrested. It wasn't a stable or safe life for a kid, for either of you really.

KTA: No, it was not, but that was long ago and has nothing to do with my research.

MK: Where was Child Protective Services while all this was going on? They should have stepped in and helped you.

KTA: Child Protective Services was the enemy. They would have taken me away from Mom and put me in foster care. Neither of us wanted that. That is why I couldn't go to school. We did not want them to know about me.

MK: But what about friends? Isn't school where most kids make friends?

KTA: I did not have friends. Same reason. Friends would have talked to their parents, parents might have asked questions, and then CPS would have come looking for me.

MK: I guess I'd never thought about it from that point of view. It's too bad you saw CPS as the enemy, but you're right, of course, they probably would have put you in foster care. So, what did you do all day when you were a kid?

KTA: Mom home-schooled me. Not officially, of course, but we read together a lot, practiced arithmetic, played chess.

MK: Chess?

KTA: Mom thought it was good for the brain. We had a set with holes in the board and pegs in the pieces, so you did not need a table. We could play in a car or a tent or anywhere.

MK: Where did she get that?

KTA: Stole it. But, Mark, enough, enough. We need to talk about you.

I had four file drawers of papers: printouts of letters from Mark, notes from our meetings, newspaper articles about his career and trial, all heavily marked up with notes to myself. Whenever I found anything that suggested a diagnostic criterion for a personality disorder or mental illness, I made a notation in a shorthand I had developed for this. For example, N-3.2+3—LM:11-07-28 meant that the item seemed evidence of criteria 3.2 for the Narcissistic personality disorder. The +3 meant that it seemed positive support for that diagnosis, with a strength rating of three out of five. The LM12-09-10 meant it was something from a letter from Mark dated September 10, 2012.

Several thousand of these flags were entered in a database. I had developed algorithms to analyze them. My dissertation would explain my methodology and algorithms, how they demonstrated which personality disorders and mental illness were and were not confirmed, and how the defining characteristics of those diagnoses related to the elements of the crimes.

I had the "mathematical chops" to do this. I thought my methodology and algorithms should be effective. But the computer wasn't producing any meaningful results. Criteria for various personality disorders showed up, but so did contraindications, and none seemed persistent or pervasive.

Mr. Kauffman was a complex person, intelligent, charming, hard-working, persistent, very successful for many years. But did he have an identifiable mental illness or personality disorder? And if he did, why couldn't my methodology identify it?

We had not yet gotten to the elements of the crime. What exactly had Mr. Kauffman done wrong, and why had he done it?

# # # #

Sept. 24, 2012

Katy

One day Jonathon called and said, "There's somebody I want you to meet."

We met in a restaurant. He was with a woman in a long dress with long sleeves, high neckline, no makeup, her hair was kind of, I don't know, severe. He said, "Mark, this is Esther, and Esther, this is Mark, one of my best friends, and definitely the richest." That was awkward.

"Hi. Well, I've done well but Jonathon's articles in the PI made it happen. If I'd given him his fair share ...."

"Money is the root of all evil," he said.

"Love of, love of money," she said. Oh boy, I thought, where this is going?

"I've been saved," he said.

Esther was watching me. I said, "Ah, well, ah, that's OK, I mean that's good, that's good."

"Yes, for God so loved us that He gave his only Son that we might not perish but have everlasting life."

"Well, ah, OK then. I, I'm not sure what to say. Congratulations are in order, I suppose. Ah, this is a bit of a surprise."

"Yes, I've sinned. But everybody has sinned, fallen short, even you, Mark."

"Nobody's perfect, I agree." Luckily a waitress came to take our orders. When she left, I said, "So, Esther, tell me a little about yourself."

"Well, my dad's the pastor of the church where we met, so I'm a P.K., a preacher's kid."

"What kind of church is that, I mean what denomination?"

"Four-square."

"I'm sorry. I don't know what that means."

"I guess you'd say its non-denominational, charismatic, fundamental Christian."

"Oh." (I was thinking "holy rollers" but was pretty sure I shouldn't say that.)

Jonathon said, "You need to find Jesus. You need to be saved."

"Well, ah, but, I mean maybe we should talk about this some other time, some other place." People at the other tables were looking at us, but that didn't slow Jonathon down.

"You could do it right here, right now. Get down on your knees and ask the Lord Jesus to come into your life."

Jesus, I thought, what do I do now? I wished the food would come. "I'm not, I don't know, not ready right now. Let's talk about something else. Esther, tell me about your family. Any brothers and sisters?"

She kind of smiled. "We call everyone in the congregation brothers and sisters, but I know what you mean. My parents have other kids. I've got four brothers and two sisters."

"Wow! Seven of you all together. So, what was it like, being in a big family?"

She talked about her family, about growing up. Finally, she summed it up by saying, "So I guess I've had a sheltered life, not as much experience of 'the world' as you two."

"You haven't missed much," Jonathon said. "It's not all it's cracked up to be."

I didn't know how much he'd told her about his wilder days, but it wasn't my job to clue her in. Sticking with business was safer. "Well, I wasn't kidding about Jonathon's articles in the PI. You couldn't buy the kind of good publicity he's given me."

"So, you've forgiven me for the kidnapping?" he said.

"Oh, Jonathon, I never blamed you. At first I blamed it on that PI article, but I knew you never meant to hurt us. I never thought it was your fault."

"I thought it was my fault. You know, I got a big award for my first series on the Phoenix House. I was trying for another with the Phoenix rising again theme, exploiting our friendship to make money and boost my big ego. But, you're right, I never meant to hurt you or your family."

"And this has been bothering you all this time? Jesus—sorry Esther—we should've talked long ago. We've been friends for a long time. This shouldn't have come between us."

We finished our lunch in a lighter mood, telling Esther about Jonathon's articles and good times we'd had together, leaving out the drinking and drugs and sex stuff.

Mark

# # # #

Oct. 1, 2012

Dear Mark,

Religious fanatics are so naïve, so stupid sometimes. I do not understand how you can be so patient with them. Did this ruin your relationship with Jonathon?

Katy

# # # #

Oct. 8, 2012

Katy

No, my relationship with Jonathon was OK. He called a few days later. "I want to apologize for giving you a rough time in the restaurant, for, ah, trying to convert you. I was out of line. I know you're not religious, but in some ways you're the best Christian I know."

I told Cindy about my lunch with Jonathon and Esther and his phone call. She said, "Let's invite them over." Jonathon said, "We'll come. It'll be a broadening experience for Esther."

A security guard met them at the gate, checked their IDs, confirmed that they were expected. Cindy and I gave them a tour. Then we sat in the living room and watched the sunset. Esther said, "I think I could get used to this."

I realize now she was joking but I took her seriously. "We haven't, really. It's nice but it's, I don't know, maybe too nice, kind of artificial. We were happy in our ordinary house in an ordinary neighborhood with ordinary people around."

"It's the security, isn't it?" Jonathon said.

"Yes. We have to live like this now, but I want to remember where I came from."

"And it's not easy raising kids in a place like this," Cindy said. "They have chores, but it's hard sometimes, trying to be a normal family."

"Chores?" asked Esther. "What do they do?"

"Well, make their beds, scrape and rinse dishes, put them in the dishwasher, put clean dishes and silverware away, clean their bathrooms and vacuum every week." I added mow and edge the lawn, pressure-wash the dock, clean the pool, gym and dressing rooms.

"Um, isn't that more than most kids their age have to do?" asked Esther. "Do they put up a lot of resistance?"

"We started when they were young, and now they pretty much accept it. When Davie was ten or eleven, back in the other house, he said he'd taken a 'survey' and none of his friends had to do as many chores as he did. I asked him, 'Oh, so you think their parents are better than us?'"

"No, but it's not fair."

"Well, some things aren't fair. But, tell me, is it embarrassing that you have to do chores? Are your friends afraid to come over because they think we're big meanies?"

"No, my friends like it here. You guys are nice to them. But still, why do I have to do more than my friends do?"

"I said, 'Look, when I was a kid, we didn't have much money. But lots of families don't have as much as we have now. We don't want you kids getting stuck up or not being nice to kids who don't have as much. We hope the chores help you feel like ordinary kids from an ordinary family, and maybe help keep you from acting like spoiled rich brats'."

Cindy said, "I'm sorry we got off into all this. We shouldn't whine about being rich."

So, Katy, did you have to do chores when you were a kid?

Mark

# # # #

Oct. 15, 2012

Dear Mark,

I had chores, just not like your kids. For example, helped Mom with her street strip routine. We worked with a guy named Jamal. He played guitar and sang. Nobody paid much attention to him until Mom came out, put a couple dollars in his hat, started dancing, and stripped off a piece of clothes every time somebody put money in. I worked the crowd, collecting money. When she got down to a bikini, Jamal chanted, "Itsy, bitsy, tits so tiny, put the bucks in her bikini." I put on quite an act, looking puzzled, afraid, then a little bolder, finally putting money in her top and working the crowd for more. When people started losing interest, he upped the tempo and chanted, "Einy, meany, miny mo, put the money down below." Then I danced around, looking very shy, put money in the mom's bikini bottom, and worked the crowd again, pulling her bikini a little farther down every time, showing more and more pubic hair until the cops made us move on. We made fifty or sixty dollars an hour at this. And, Mom didn't have to have sex to get it, except with Jamal of course.

But we ought to get on with your story.

Katy

# # # #

Oct. 22, 2012

Katy

I guess you wouldn't have conventional chores, being homeless so much. About that "street strip" thing, I saw it once, down at Pike Place Market. Good grief! I don't know what to say about that.

One day after a business meeting, Stephen took me aside and said, "Have you seen Jonathon lately?"

"Yes, a couple of times. We had dinner with him and Esther a couple of weeks ago."

"He's become some kind of religious fanatic. Did he preach at you?"

"Not at dinner, but he laid into me in a restaurant a week or so before that."

"He told you he'd been saved, and you needed to get saved too?"

"Yeah. It's scary, isn't it?"

"Well, it got nasty. It isn't just that he thinks I am going to hell. He attacked my, well, my lifestyle. Said it was an 'abomination' and God was going to strike me and Mario and our friends down. He was so full of anger and hate. You read about people like that, see it on the news. But this was Jonathon. We'd been friends for years. I was best man at his wedding, for Christsake."

"I feel bad about it too. He's gone off the deep end. I hoped he'd get out of drugs and stuff, and if that took getting religious, I'd be OK with it. But, well, he's gone too far."

"Do you think he always was, ah, disgusted about my being gay? And how about you?"

"No, 'disgusted' is too strong. I was uncomfortable at first, and he probably was too, but it was just so new back then. I didn't know any gay people, wasn't even sure there were any. But when you get to know them, you realize they're just people. But now, if we're into questions we've been afraid to ask, I have one for you. Did your sexual relationship with Mario start when you were his student?"

"No, no, not until after we moved into the Phoenix house. By then I'd graduated and was working for that firm. I was also working on my Masters, but I wasn't taking any courses from him and never did after we became lovers."

"OK, that's good.

"So, when did you first realize I was gay?"

"Your dad told me, after the housewarming party. He didn't use that word, but he told me."

"He did? He talked to you about it? He hasn't talked to me about it, not to this day. I mean, we see each other, like for holidays, and we're civil to each other, but we've never talked about Mario and, ah, you know, sexual stuff."

"Yeah, we talked about it. He said he really, really loved you, but you were avoiding him. He asked me to keep on being your friend."

"God, it's been what, '67 to '93, twenty-six years?" We both thought about that.

"I'm sorry. It looks like both of you were waiting for the other to make the first move, but I didn't realize you weren't talking about it. I should have done something...."

"It's not your fault. I should have talked to you. You're probably the easiest guy in the world to talk to. Hell, even my dad could talk to you and he hardly knew you."

"Let's not talk about what we should have done years ago. You need to talk to your dad now. What is he? He must be in his 70s by now."

"Seventy-three or four. You're right. I need to talk to him."

"Don't be too hard on yourself," I said. "None of us spends enough time with our parents. I've hardly talked to my dad for years. I just got so busy with work and kids and stuff."

I told Cindy about my talk with Stephen, and then I said: "Let's take my parents on a vacation, a family vacation. They'd love it. D'you think the kids would be OK with that?"

Cindy laughed. "Well, they're a little unpredictable, aren't they? But we could make it an adventure, go someplace they want to go."

We asked the kids if they had plans for spring vacation. David wanted to go skiing in Colorado or Utah, someplace with good powder. Julie wanted to go to Hawaii or Mexico to lie on a beach. Cindy said we'd been talking about a vacation with grandma and grandpa K. "Before you say no, let's think if we can find something that would be fun for you and them."

"They don't ski, do they?" said David.

"No, and they're over seventy so it wouldn't be a good idea to put them on skis."

"They could do beaches, though," Julie said. "And if we took scuba lessons, they could come on the boat and watch us dive. How about Hawaii?"

David said, "I could go with scuba."

"OK, do we have a plan then?"

"Could we get in a couple of days of skiing first?" David asked.

"Sure," I said. "Now do we have a plan?" Everybody nodded.

Cindy and I talked to my folks about the family vacation. "So where are you talking about?" Dad asked.

"Hawaii, the kids want to go to Hawaii and take scuba lessons. You could come on the boat and watch them dive."

"No, I don't think so."

"You don't think so? It's a chance to spend a week with your grandkids, in a subtropical paradise. Sunny, warm weather. What more could you ask for?"

"No. We wouldn't be comfortable with all those young rich people. And you know I've had cancer spots on my skin. I couldn't take all that sun."

"Well, where would you like to go? England, Europe, Japan, anywhere? Germany? Want to see the old country?"

"No, I don't want to go to some foreign country, especially if they don't speak English."

"Well, there must be places in the U.S. you'd like to see. New York? Los Angeles? New Orleans? Las Vegas?"

He thought for a while. "I've kind of wanted to see Mount Rushmore. And maybe Yellowstone. But not a whole week. Four or five days, max."

The kids weren't enthused. We tried to explain that their grandparents were getting old and not very adventuresome. "We tried to talk them into Hawaii, but they wouldn't have it. This may be our last chance to spend much time with them. Can you do it for them?" They nodded.

We chartered a plane and took off from Boeing Field on a beautiful spring morning. The pilot asked, "Anything you want to see on the way?" The kids wanted to fly over our house. The pilot suggested we check out Mount Rainier and Mount Saint Helens. David said, "Hey, if we're going by Rainier can we check out Crystal Mountain, the ski area?"

"Sure," the pilot said. "We can go wherever you want for five whole days."

"Just so long as Grandma and Grandpa get to see Mount Rushmore and Yellowstone," I said. Everybody laughed.

We saw Mount Rushmore, the Crazy Horse project and Yellowstone. The kids went horseback riding. We took a half day river raft trip. Then we flew to Kalispell for a red bus tour of Glacier National Park. The highlight for my dad was Mount Rushmore. We were there as the sun went down, lighting the rock faces with a golden glow. Dad, who always seemed unemotional, kind of choked up and said, "Gott, I love this country." Even the kids seemed moved a little.

When we got home, I asked my parents about the trip. Mom said it was great seeing the sights and spending time with the grandkids. Dad said, "Well, it must have been expensive. I hope you don't throw money around like that all the time."

I wanted to say something like hey, Dad, I make that much an hour. The year before Cindy and I'd made $60 million and the trip only cost about $20 thousand. Fifty weeks times 60 hours a week. Do the math. Instead, I said, "Dad, it was worth every penny to have you and Mom and the kids together, having fun, doing fun things. They'll never forget those six days with you."

Dad said, "So, have you gotten Lucy taken care of, that trust thing?"

"Oh, sorry Dad. I'm going to get to it. I've been very busy. I'll get it done."

Dad had a stroke a few months later and was in a wheelchair from then on, and Mom's vision was failing, so it was a good thing we did the grandparent trip when we did.

Katy, did you and your mom go on vacations?

Mark

# # # #

Oct. 29, 2012

Dear Mark,

The unemployed do not get vacations. Mom never had a vacation until the last year or so.

Katy

# # # #

Nov. 5. 2012

Katy

The recession of 1991-92, like those before, was short-lived. Real estate prices were rising by the mid-1993. We had properties worth nearly four billion dollars and an excellent credit rating. Shares of many REITs sold for less than their book value but ours traded at a premium. We issued new shares to buy three more struggling REITs and a lot of other distressed properties. By the end of 1995 our REIT owned properties worth more than seven billion dollars. Cindy and I were billionaires.

Grandma Olsen died, and I guess that got Cindy thinking about mortality. We started going to church. I wasn't really into it, but we made friends there and I used it as a time to relax, meditate, quit thinking about business for an hour. And, you know, church is the only place that reminds you to be thankful for what you have. Everything else in our culture just keeps saying "Get more, get more, get more."

Did you and your mom go to church?

Mark

# # # #

Nov. 12, 2012

Dear Mark,

Church? That is a sensitive subject. Mom and I went sometimes, but only to rip them off.

Katy

# # # #

Nov. 19, 2012

Katy

Katy, you shouldn't be embarrassed about your mom "ripping off churches" as you put it. Lots of homeless people do that. I guess some put on quite an act, raising their hands, shouting "hallelujah, praise the Lord" and all that. Your mom may have been one of those, but don't be too hard on her. Maybe if you think of it as a kind of urban survival skill? She had to do something to provide for herself and you. Some church people like to give food and clothes and money, even a place to stay, because they feel good about helping needy people. There's nothing wrong with that. So, there's nothing wrong with accepting their gifts. Right?

Even if what she did was just an act, a fraud, and even if you helped her pull it off, it's not something you should feel embarrassed or guilty about now. You were just a kid, just doing what your mom wanted. She was just trying to stay alive and provide for you, without a lot of resources or other options. Those people felt good about giving to your mom and you. It's not like you were stealing from them. So please, don't be so hard on yourself.

Mark

# # # #

Nov. 26, 2012

Dear Mark,

Mom did steal from churches, and church members, and church pastors. And I helped her. But, Mark, we need to get back to your career.

Katy

# # # #

Dec. 3, 2012

Katy

I'm sorry I wrote that about your mom not stealing from churches. I should have guessed you guys stole stuff too. But I'm really impressed about how far you've come. You're amazing, Katy, a truly strong and talented woman. You should be very proud of yourself. But I'll go on.

Olaf Johansson and Buddy Graves kept advancing in their political careers. Olaf was elected to his fourth term in Congress in 1992. A leader on the revenue and budget committees, he'd become a widely respected expert on federal tax policy and a political dealmaker who could bring together moderates from both parties. (Back then there were moderates in both parties.)

Buddy was elected to Congress in 1992. Two days after he was sworn in the Washington Post ran an article headlined, "Congressmen Caught with Call Girls." A group of newly elected Congressmen met in a hotel. A lot of alcohol was consumed. The paper had photos of Buddy and three other new Congressmen entering or leaving hotel rooms with prostitutes.

Buddy flew back to Tacoma to meet with his wife, advisors, supporters and Democratic Party officials. He didn't want to resign. If he did the Republican governor could appoint a Republican to his seat. Discussions shifted to damage control.

Buddy, his wife, Nikki, and I held a press conference. Buddy spoke first. "Three days ago, I did something very, very stupid. I hurt a lot of people: my wife, the people who supported me, and the people I was elected to serve. Alcohol was involved but that's not an excuse. I did not seek out the woman or initiate our misbehavior, but that's not an excuse either. It was stupid and I am very sorry. I am thankful that some people still support me in spite of my bad behavior. Two of them will speak here today, my wife and my campaign chairman.

Nikki spoke next, saying she was appalled but was trying to forgive him and give him a second chance, and hoped the public would too. I said pretty much the same things. As I was speaking Buddy slipped out and was hidden away until the reporters and photographers were gone.

The press conference got some news media coverage until the next day the Washington Post announced: "Unnamed Persons Provided Prostitutes to Congressmen." Its reporters found the four call-girls were hired to "work" the post-inauguration party and help photographers get incriminating pictures. Who hired the hookers and why? Some people thought it might be the Republican Party, or rich right-wing conservatives, or Islamic priests, or middle eastern sheiks, or Russians or North Koreans, but nobody ever proved who it was. Finally, the news media and the public got tired of it and moved on to other things.

Buddy has been reelected six times since then, but his political career stalled. He never ran for a statewide office. At the time, I think he really meant to behave, but he was a guy who just wouldn't keep his prick in his pants.

In May 1993, with a lot of help from Olaf (but none from Buddy), we did a third deal with the RTC, under its new "equity partnership" program. The government loaned us 65% of the price and kept a share of the profits. We paid $185 million for 62 properties, mostly in the Bay Area, about half what the prior owners had spent on them. The recovery was a year closer. The math probably is beyond you, but our return on investment was even better than the earlier RTC deals.

Mark

# # # #

Dec. 10, 2012

Dear Mark,

I can figure out returns on investments, maybe not in my head but with a calculator. You get pretty good at fractions and decimals when you live with druggies, and I have a college degree in math.

That thing with your friend Buddy, that was high-end prostitution. Quite different from what my mom did.

Even though you seem to think about sex a lot, you are something of a prude, aren't you?

Katy

# # # #

Dec. 17, 2012

Katy

I never made the connection between drugs and arithmetic. And, I didn't know you had a degree in math. I assumed that, ah, well, it never occurred to me you might be good at math.

Your mom was a prostitute? I shouldn't be surprised, I guess.

And you think I'm "something of a prude?" That's not a very positive term. How about "sexually responsible"?

David turned sixteen and got his driver's license. We saw less of him and his friends after they started driving, but they still played tennis on our court, swam laps in our pool, waterskied from our dock, just hung around sometimes. I enjoyed the time I got to spend with them.

Our REIT started a trading division, buying and selling mortgage-backed securities. This let us rapidly expand our assets under management without a lot more employees. A couple of people with Bloomberg terminals can buy and sell hundreds of millions in securities every day.

Inova Development continued to build properties for our REIT and rented office space from it. These arrangements, like many in our industry, were riddled with conflicts of interest. Eeko's job had evolved to cover these issues, but he agreed it was time to bring in someone with more formal ethics training. We hired a law professor to form an ethics department in 1996, five years before the Enron scandal and six years before the Sarbanes-Oxley ethics law. We were proud of it. Could it have prevented what happened to me? Maybe, but nobody reported what I did to our ethics team because nobody thought I was doing anything unethical or illegal.

Mario got lung cancer. As it got close to the end, Stephen didn't want to leave him alone. By then Stephen was the dean. He still taught a few seminars, filled in for professors who had to miss their classes, and had meetings with the faculty and university administration. When he had to do those things, sometimes I sat with Mario.

Mario slept a lot and often didn't have enough energy to talk, but one day he said, "Thanks for being such a good friend to Stephen."

"Well, we've been good friends for a long time, but no thanks are necessary for that."

"Maybe not, but back in the sixties and seventies, even the eighties and nineties, most gay people didn't have many straight friends."

"Yeah, the culture is changing on that, isn't it?"

"Some people are tolerant, like you, but some, like that bastard Jonathon, are not. When he got 'born again' he was cruel and vicious. We'd known him for years. Stephen was best man at his wedding. But he just kept attacking us, the sanctimonious little shithead."

"You saw that?"

"I did. It hurt me and it really, really hurt Stephen. That's what I can't forgive him for. Stephen and I had been so comfortable with each other for many years, and Jonathon wrecked it, on purpose."

"I'm sorry. I didn't know it was that bad."

"It was. For weeks Stephen wouldn't let me touch him. I'm not talking about sex. I'm talking about cuddling, just being comfortable together. We used to cuddle on the couch and watch TV, sit together in bed and read, ordinary stuff all couples do. Jonathon ruined that."

"Stephen didn't say anything to me about that."

"No, he wouldn't have. But after he talked to you and then his dad, we talked about it and things got almost back to normal. I guess that's what I really wanted to thank you for."

"Why he didn't tell me how bad it was?"

"He knew you were still friends with Jonathon and he didn't want to mess that up."

"Well, I am friends with both of them. It's terrible, what happened between them, but both of them needed me at different times, in different ways. I don't like a lot of stuff Jonathon has done, but I felt like he needed me to keep on being his friend."

"Probably true. You're a remarkable friend, a remarkable person. Maybe I should learn to be more like you. But I hate that bastard for what he did to Stephen and me."

"I understand." But still, I felt Mario would be better off if he could forgive. Like, maybe, die a little better death? Maybe it wouldn't have made any difference at that point. But I don't want to die angry like that. Most of the time I feel like I'm doing a pretty good at forgiving the people who hurt me, but sometimes I get mad all over again.

Mario died a few days later. I thought about telling Stephen about this conversation but decided not to. It didn't seem like it would help him at that point.

A few months later Jonathon invited Cindy and me to dinner. His ex-wife had gotten most of his money in the divorce. He lived in a small one-bedroom bachelor pad. Esther talked about things they'd done and places they'd gone. "Jonathon's really broadened my experience," she said, turning a little red.

Did that mean what I thought? I glanced toward the bedroom.

Jonathon said, "Mark, I asked you over because there's something I want to ask you."

"Sure. What's that?"

"Well, Esther and I are getting married, and I'd like you to by my best man."

"I think, yes, that should be OK. But, before I commit, I need to talk to Stephen about it."

"I hope he's OK with it. But you probably should tell him we can't invite him. Esther's dad is going to perform the wedding, and he's, he's kind of, of militant .... Well, back when I first got saved and I was being such an asshole, I got that from him. I'm sorry, Esther, but I was a new Christian and had some pretty rough edges back then."

"It's OK," Esther said. "I'm proud of you for moving away from that. And I'm glad you helped me get away from all that too."

A few days later I told Stephen that Jonathon had asked me to be best man at his second wedding. "But if you're, you know, uncomfortable …."

"No, you should do it. You've been a good friend to him."

"Are you sure it's OK? I know how much he hurt you and Mario."

"Yes. But, frankly, I'm glad Mario isn't here to see it. He couldn't forgive Jonathon for that."

"I know. We talked about it a few days before he died."

"You did? It probably was good for him to talk about it, but I wish he'd been able to forgive."

"I felt the same way, like he was hurting himself, but he just couldn't let go of it."

"I suppose it doesn't make any difference now, but at the time I thought it might help make his death a little easier, for both of us."

"Yes, that's how I felt too. But, well, what's done is done."

"Go ahead and be his best man, but out of respect for Mario I won't come, if I'm invited, which I probably won't be."

"No, you won't. Esther's dad is going to perform the wedding and he's, he's very militant about gay issues, but Jonathon and Esther wanted you to know they've moved away from that."

Mark

# # # #

Dec. 23, 2012

Dear Mark,

I always liked math. It is precise and there are right answers; you can tell when you've got it right. When I was little, Mom and I used to recite multiplication tables to each other. We had them memorized, up to 24 x 24. But everybody uses calculators or their phone now, so that skill is not worth much anymore.

I am sorry about your relationships with Stephen and Mario getting so strained, but I think you handled all that very well, better than I would have.

You remember, way back, I said you must be manipulative, sleazy, unethical. I see now that you took great pride in being ethical.

I still do not understand exactly why you ended up in prison, but I am sure we will get to that soon. I am pleased with how our project has been going. You have been very candid and helpful. I am looking forward to, as Paul Harvey says, "the rest of the story."

Have a very merry Christmas and a happy new year.

Katy

CHAPTER 4

GETTING ANGRY AND DEPRESSED

Jan. 12, 2013

Katy

I'm sorry I didn't write the last few weeks. I'm very angry. Upset. Depressed. I don't know if I can continue helping with your project.

You probably read in the papers or heard on TV, the 9th Circuit turned down my appeal. What you may not know is that Olaf Johansson and Buddy Graves refuse to support my petition for a pardon or clemency. Those ungrateful bastards. It looks like I'm going to sit here for another three years.

I made those people. I was the first to see their political potential. I nurtured their careers, mentored them, hooked them up with influential people, gave them big campaign contributions, chaired their fundraising committees.

I know what you're going to say. You think I did that so I could "use" them. Now who's being cynical? I never tried to compromise their integrity. All I expected was access, a chance to make my "pitch" to them and their staff on things I was interested in. There's nothing wrong with that.

Of course, I can't go see them and I'd never ask them to come here. But they should give my lawyers the same access they gave me all those years. Our relationships weren't just about business and politics. I cared about them and their families. I went to their birthday parties and birthday parties for their wives and kids. I supported their charities. I helped Olaf's kids get into good schools and gave them internships and jobs. We were friends, good friends. Now I'm some kind of political "third rail." They're afraid to touch me. But I'm not asking for public support. All I'm asking is for some quiet support behind the scenes. Is that too much to ask of people who have been good friends for thirty years?

Just because I can't do anything to help them anymore doesn't mean they shouldn't try to help me now, for old time's sake, for friendship's sake. It would be such a comfort to know that my friends still cared about me in spite of everything that's happened. I didn't know they were so shallow.

Damn them. Damn them to hell.

Mark

# # # #

Jan. 16, 2012

Dear Mark,

I am so sorry about your appeal and your political friends refusing to help you. I do not know much about law or politics, but I understand you feel disappointed, betrayed, depressed.

I will not lie to you. I can't help but look at this from a rather selfish perspective. I have a lot invested in this dissertation project and it would be a huge loss it you quit helping on it. I would have start over on some other topic. So, I will try to be patient and hope you will be willing to continue at some point. If there is anything I can do to help, please let me know.

Did writing last week's letter help at all? Wouldn't writing to me help you get over this terrible blow?

Katy

# # # #

Jan. 26, 2013

Katy

No, writing to you a couple of weeks ago didn't help. I'm not sure I can go on. I'm so angry. I've been betrayed by some of my best friends. My wife divorced me. My kids don't come see me much. And my grandson, I don't get to see him at all. I know their lives got trashed too. But I miss them. I'm not really sure I want to see them now, or maybe just I don't want them to see me in here, but I miss them anyway.

Katy, I've had big, big losses. Not just my money, freedom, reputation. I've lost my wife, kids, grandkid, nearly all of my friends, all my reasons to go on living. You probably think I'm depressed? Well, I've got a hell of lot to be depressed about.

Would writing to you help me get over it? No, I'm not up to that.

Mark

Ninth meeting

I almost had a panic attack when I got Mark's letter the morning of January 29. My pulse rate went up; I started breathing hard; my stomach felt queasy.

We were twenty months into my dissertation project. I had developed, tested and refined coding protocols to connect key words, phrases and actions to the DSM-IV criteria for different personality disorders and mental illnesses. Some amount of subjectivity is unavoidable, but I strived to make the protocols as objective as possible so the results would be replicable. I tried to minimize the influence of any personal biases by not speculating about what disorders or illnesses Mr. Kaufmann may have or what might have caused him to commit his crimes.

Mark finally had opened up about his personal life and seemed to have an almost compulsive need to persuade me that he was a "kind, gentle, caring person," and a "terrific husband, father, brother, son, employer, mentor, friend." I could not discern whether this was a lifelong behavioral pattern or just situational, caused by his incarceration and his growing fascination with me, but I had hoped to explore this in our next few meetings.

In short, my dissertation project had been going well but, if he was unwilling to continue, all my work could be wasted. So, I when I got his letter, I threw some clothes and toiletries in a bag and headed for Sheridan. The four-hour drive gave me time to think. How could I get him to go on with our project? Just begging, crying, acting hurt or getting mad probably wouldn't help. I had to persuade him that I cared about him and he cared about me. If he wanted to help me and knew that helping me would also help himself, maybe he could gather the strength to go on.

When I got to the prison Mark looked awful: unshaven, rumpled, lethargic, stooped, grayer, older. I had never seen him like that. I had hoped to cheer him up, but I could see that that would not be easy. Here is a transcript of part of our meeting:

KTA: Hello. How are you doing?

MK: Not good.

KTA: I'm sorry. I hope I can find some way to help you feel better.

MK: No, you hope you can find some way to manipulate me into going on with your project.

KTA: Mark, of course I want to go on with our project. I won't lie to you about that. But I care about you too. I see that you are hurting, and I want to help if I can.

MK: I don't see how you could. You can't imagine how hurt I am.

KTA: I thought it might help to talk about your political friends, but is it still too soon?

MK: I'm just too mad to talk about it now. Maybe sometime. Not now. And it's not just that.

KTA: What else is going on?

MK: Cindy is seeing someone. She's getting remarried.

KTA: How did you find that out?

MK: Julie came and told me. She said "Mom wanted me to tell you. She was afraid you'd find out some other way, because a lot of people know and it might get in the news. But she just couldn't bring herself come here to tell you."

KTA: I'm so sorry.

MK: So, bottom line: I'm gonna be here a lot longer than I expected and I've got a lot less to look forward to when I get out.

KTA: Mark, I understand you feel betrayed and abandoned by people you trusted and depended on. Maybe I haven't been hurt in quite those same ways, but I've had my share of hurts too.

MK: I don't want to talk about it.

KTA: Are you afraid you might just lose it, fall apart, if we talked about it today?

MK: That's a very personal question and I'm not going to answer it.

KTA: Do you want me to leave now? Or can I stay if I respect your space and don't get pushy? [Long pause] Mark, I do want to help you.

MK: I don't want pity, not from you or anybody else.

KTA: But Mark, I'm not talking about pity. I care about you and I'm sure others do too. Why do you make it so difficult for us to express that to you?

MK: Let's talk about your mom.

KTA: Oh, Mark, I don't want to make you any madder, but it's not appropriate to go any further into my life. I'm afraid I've already told you more than I should about that.

MK: Your mom and your childhood are important to me. I understand you were going to be thrown out of your apartment because the guy you'd been living with left and didn't pay the rent. But I thought she seduced the stereo guy just to keep him from calling the cops. Do you really think this was her plan on how to get a new place to live?

KTA: Are you still thinking about that? We talked about that weeks ago. We need to move on.

MK: No we don't. You didn't answer my question. Did she sleep with that stereo guy, and other guys, just to get a place to stay?

KTA: Well, it was better than just quickie sex for money, being an outright whore, wasn't it?

MK: Did she do that too, be an "outright whore"?

KTA: Sure, especially towards the end when her teeth went bad and she didn't look so good.

MK: And where were you when all this was going on?

KTA: Well, sometimes we had two-bedroom apartments, but usually just one. I usually slept with my mom when no guys were there. She sent me to sleep in the living room when guys came.

MK: And you could sleep just a few feet outside their door when this was going on?

KTA: Sometimes they were noisy and it was hard to sleep, but you get used to it, you know?

MK: No, I don't know. It sounds awful. Did your mom enjoy this?

KTA: She told me once she didn't enjoy sex. It was dirty and disgusting, not fun.

MK: Well, yeah. The way she went at it, that must have been true. Sleeping with guys just to get a place to stay, that seems, I don't know, creepy. And not safe, not safe for either of you.

KTA: That was a long time ago. I am safe now and do not want to talk about that. But I have really enjoyed learning about your family which, as you said, was much different from mine. I would like to learn more about your family.

MK: Not now.

KTA: Mark, this may be a bad time to ask, but I would like to start interviewing some of your friends and co-workers and maybe some of your family. Would that be alright with you?

MK: You want to fact-check me, see if I've been making stuff up?

KTA: Well, ah, yes, I guess I would do some of that too. But, really, I would like to see if other people perceived things the same way you did.

MK: Sure, go ahead. Some people may remember different things, or remember some details differently, but nobody's going to tell you I've been lying. But Katy, please, please don't tell any of my family or friends how down and screwed up I am right now. I don't want them to see me like this or know about it.

CHAPTER 5

GETTING ON

Notes of meeting with Jonathon Starke

I met with Jonathon Starke on February 7, 2013, described my meetings and correspondence with Mr. Kauffman, and told him Mr. Kauffman had authorized me to meet with his friends, co-workers and family. Here is a transcript of parts of that meeting:

Jonathon Starke: Mark is the most kind and caring person I ever met. He's, he's, I don't know how to describe it. Maybe the best word is Christian; he's the best Christian I know. He's not religious, doesn't go to church much, pray or read the Bible—which I've tried to get him to do. But there's something about him. You know the love poem from 1st Corinthians, 'love is this and that, love is not X but is Y,' the passage they often read at weddings?"

> KTA: I'm not very familiar with the Bible, but I've been at weddings where they read something like that.

JS: Well, that's Mark. The rest of us aspire to live that way, but he really does it, does it all the time.

KTA: Uh, this seems pretty abstract. Can you give me some examples?

JS: Sure. Way back when we were working on the Phoenix House—did he tell you about that?—I wanted to write an article about him, how he organized the whole thing, raised the money, got everybody to work together. He said, "No, do an article about Stephen and his design." I said the article should focus on him. He said, "No, Stephen is the genius here, the whole thing came from his ideas; he should get credit for it. And, if you focus on his design, you can use a lot of pictures. Nobody wants to see pictures of me begging for money. Besides, Stephen is kind of shy, kind of an introvert. You've got a chance to help him shine, get him some respect, give him self-confidence. Let's do this for him."

KTA: He told me about your article, but he never said anything about this discussion.

JS: No, he wouldn't. But he was like that on other projects too. Like the Maritime Mart. I wanted to do an article focusing on him. He talked me into focusing on Stephen's design work and what he called the "political courage" of public officials who supported the project.

KTA: So, do you think he did it to be a smart businessman, giving public credit (which cost him nothing) where he didn't want to or ethically couldn't give money?

JS: No. He genuinely cared about Stephen and the others. He wanted them to feel good about working with him. It turned out to be good for his business, yes, but caring about the people came first and that's why he did it. I think he was surprised how much it helped his business.

KTA: So, did this continue as he got more successful?

JS: Yes, the same thing with the Green River/United American project. I was going to do an article focusing on him, but he talked me into focusing on Stephen, Frank Wilson, people who supported the project, even environmental groups. None of the environmental groups publicly supported the project, but he wanted me to treat them with respect and recognize their interest in the parks and trails and stuff.

KTA: Mark and I have talked about these projects, but this is new information, a different way of looking at it. But, do you think he took advantage of you to get free publicity to help his business?

JS: No, if anything it was the other way around. I took advantage of our friendship to boost my career and my big ego. His instincts were right; he helped make my articles better. And when I went off on my own and did focus on him, I screwed up his life.

KTA: What do you mean?

JS: The kidnapping. I wrote an article about Mark's first deal with the Resolution Trust Corporation. It was the first time I didn't work closely with him and let him influence my articles about his work. It was supposed to be a surprise.

KTA: Mark mentioned your article, but he didn't seem to blame the kidnapping on it.

JS: No, he wouldn't. He didn't. I blamed myself. I avoided him for a couple of years because I didn't want to face him. When I finally told him how sorry I was, he tried to comfort me.

KTA: Any other examples? Any non-business examples?

JS: Yes. My first wife and I, well, we got a little wild—too much drinking, drugs, playing around. Mark cared about us, worried about us, tried to lead by example, but never, never judged us. And when we divorced, he was there for me, but he never said "I told you so" or put me down.

KTA: He sounds like a good friend.

JS: Yes, he was. And then later, when I first became a Christian, I really hurt him and his friends Stephen and Mario. And yet, even in the worst of all that, he still cared about me, never judged me, never tried to hurt me back.

KTA: How many times have you been down to see him here at Sheridan?

JS: Just two.

KTA: How did the visits go?

JS: OK, I guess, on the surface. He asked about me and our friends, things like that. But he won't talk about himself, you know, life in prison, how he is doing. He is determined to look strong, optimistic,

> in control. I felt like I had to respect that but, you know, you can't really get close to him anymore and, frankly, it made me not want to go back.
>
> KTA: That's very interesting. He would like more visitors, but I don't think he understands that he may be driving them away. Finally, Jonathon, what do you think about his conviction and going to prison?
>
> JS: It is like the story of Job, a good and Godly man who stayed steadfast as everything was taken away from no fault of his own. He's, he's like, I don't know, like a saint.

Notes of meeting with Stephen Hutchinson

I met with Stephen Hutchinson on February 10, 2013 and gave him the same background information that I gave Jonathon Starke. Here is a transcript of parts of that meeting:

> Stephen Hutchinson: Mark is probably the world's best listener. He listens to what you say, understands what you really mean, and never judges anybody. He's a remarkable person.
>
> KTA: Can you give me some examples?
>
> SH: Sure. When we first started talking about the burned out house—he's told you about that, right?—the other guys didn't hear me, like I wasn't even there. Mark listened, asked questions, cared about me and my ideas, like nobody ever had before.

KTA: So, he saw your ideas as a way to get started in real estate, as the first step toward his goal of getting rich?

SH: No, not at first. He was just being a good listener. Later, he realized he might make money at it, but it didn't start that way.

KTA: How about his other early projects? Do you think he used you to get rich on them?

SH: No, that's not how it was at all. I'd talk about ideas, like refurbishing an old art deco apartment house, or redeveloping the urban waterfront, or suspending a building, and he'd listen and understand how these ideas excited me. Then, sometimes, he'd find a way to turn my ideas into reality.

KTA: Do you feel like he stole some of your ideas, tried to take credit for them?

SH: Never. He always bent over backward to give me credit.

KTA: Any other examples? Any non-business examples?

SH: Sure. When I first told my dad I had a sexual relationship Mario—coming out they say now, but we didn't use that term back then— my dad talked to Mark about it. Dad felt comfortable talking to Mark even though he couldn't talk to me.

KTA: Any more examples?

SH: Lots. When Jonathon first became a religious fanatic, he lashed into me and Mario about being gay. Mario and I hated him for that. Mark never did. He listened to us and understood how hurt we were, but he listened to Jonathon too, and stayed friends with all three of us. And when he was dying, Mario talked to Mark about how much Jonathon had hurt us. That's amazing because Mario couldn't talk to me about it, even though we lived together and loved each other very much. Mark is somebody that anyone can talk to about anything. Haven't you noticed that?

KTA: [laughing] Well, he has gotten me to talk about things I never wanted to talk about.

SH: And later, when my reputation and career were almost destroyed, he was there for me.

KTA: Can you explain what that was about?

SH: Ask Mark. I'd rather not talk about that.

KTA: He must have been a very special friend, to you and Jonathon both.

SH: He was. But at the end, when his life was falling apart, we both deserted him. Even then, though, he never quit caring about us, never judged us, never held that against us.

KTA: So, what do you think about his conviction and going to prison?

SH: A terrible miscarriage of justice. I don't understand securities law, but he didn't do anything morally wrong. They made him a scapegoat for the recession. He's an amazing and wonderful guy. It's a tragedy.

# # # #

February 14, 2013

Dear Mark,

I met with your friends Jonathon and Stephen. They have nothing but good things to say about you, very deep respect and admiration for you. It is taking me a while to process this.

You tried to tell me that you are kind and caring, but I found that hard to believe. I am so sorry. I am rethinking a lot of what we have talked about all these months.

One question: Stephen talked about you "being there for him" when his reputation and career were almost destroyed. What that was about?

Love, Katy

# # # #

Feb. 21, 2013

Dear Katy

"Love, Katy"? It may not mean anything, but I like it.

You were surprised that Jonathon and Stephen had good things to say about me? You've always seemed suspicious, skeptical, never quite trusted me. So, I'm glad you talked to them.

I'm still pretty bummed out, but I know your dissertation means a lot to you. And, you know, helping you did help pull me out of my last funk. Maybe it'll work for me again.

What Stephen was talking about happened much later, in 2006. Jonathon wrote a front-page article in the Sunday PI called "Phoenix House—Forty Years Later." It summarized his original articles, Stephen's career and mine, and changes in the housing industry since then. He mentioned that Stephen had lived with Professor Piccolo for over thirty years and then with a younger man after Mario died and left the house to him, implying that Stephen's relationships with them were sexual. When another reporter questioned him about that, Stephen didn't deny it. This triggered lots of letters to the editors, many supportive but some hostile, including one from a "Concerned Christian" saying the University should fire Stephen. Then a male student claimed Stephen had tried to seduce him, and then a second one did. Stephen denied having any sexual contact with them, or any students or minors, but the university suspended him, banned him from the campus, and scheduled a public hearing on whether to terminate his tenure and fire him.

I hired a lawyer for him and an expert, your Professor Jacqueline DeProulx. She coached us on questions to ask the accusers and testified about the scientific literature on false memories.

I had tried to avoid publicity ever since Julie's kidnapping, but I testified for him. Also, before the hearing I told the university President that I'd been a major donor to the Department of Architecture and Urban Planning for many years and had been planning to endow a chair in Stephen's honor. I didn't threaten to withhold that donation, of course, but I think he got the message.

The accusing students were not credible and Jackie, Professor DeProulx, was very helpful. The Hearing Officer found insufficient evidence to discipline Stephen and the university reinstated him. A couple of months later, I contributed five million dollars to endow a chair in his honor. That June the university awarded me an honorary doctorate. My parents were proud of that, but I never told them the whole story.

But, Katy, it feels like you're trying to distract me from learning more about your life. I was right that you aren't what you appear to be, but something's still missing. How did you get from that awful childhood to become such an awesome professional woman?

Love, Mark

# # # #

Feb. 28, 2013

Dear Mark,

I do not think it is possible to distract you. But you are right: I do not want us to focus on my mom and me. What happened next in your life?

Love, Katy

# # # #

Mar. 7, 2013

Dear Katy

Our business kept growing and so did the kids. I enjoyed the kids and their friends, but you can't expect to get through the teen years without a few awkward incidents.

One evening in June 1994, David's friend Kevin came to my home office, looking pretty upset. "I dinged your car," he said. "I'm very, very sorry."

"What happened?"

"Well, I backed into it with my dad's car. I just got careless. Stupid. Stupid. It's a pretty big dent."

"It's OK," I said. "We've got insurance."

"I'll pay you the de…, the de…, the de…."

"The deductible?"

"Yeah, yeah, the deduct."

"Oh, that won't be necessary. These things happen. How about your dad's car? Any damage to it?"

"Not really. Some black paint from your Expedition got on the corner of his bumper, but I think I can get it off, at least good enough so he won't notice."

"So, you don't plan to tell him?"

"No. And I hope you won't either. Will you?"

"No, not unless you ask me to. But didn't telling me help you feel better? Or maybe not yet, but after a while won't you be glad you told me?" He nodded. "So, shouldn't it be the same with him? Don't you think you'd feel better if you told him?"

"No."

"Well, it's your call. But I've known your dad since before you were born. I think he'd handle it OK. Or if he got upset, you could have him call me and I'd tell him it's no big deal."

"No, I'd rather not take a chance on that."

"I'm sorry," I said. "I think you're wrong about your dad but, like I said, it's your decision."

Then, about 10:00 one Saturday morning in early June, 1995, David and Kevin come downstairs for breakfast. I gave them a few minutes to wake up before confronting them. "When I went out to get the paper this morning there was vomit on the lawn. There's no flu epidemic going on, so I assume you guys must be hung over."

David said, "Ah, ah Dad, we stole a bottle of wine out of the garage last night."

"Two, actually," said Kevin.

"Yeah but there were four of us. We tried to wash it away with the hose, thought we had it cleaned up, but it was dark so …."

"Those were the big bottles, right? A liter and a half each? That works out to a regular bottle a person."

"I guess so."

"So where are the other two? Are they still asleep?"

"They went home."

"They drove home?" I asked.

"Yeah, I guess."

"Oh, guys, guys. I'm not really mad about you stealing the wine or getting drunk. That's pretty normal stuff for kids your age. But I'm very, very pissed about you letting the other guys drive home. Don't you know how dangerous that is? What a big chance they were taking? And what a big chance you were taking by letting them do it? This is just, just …."

"Wait, Dad, Dad. They weren't guys. They were girls. Their parents would have gone ape-shit if they hadn't gotten home."

"Oh, shit." I tried to figure out what to say next. "That does make it more complicated. But, you know, I still wish you hadn't let them drive home. There were other options. You could have gotten me or Mom to drive them home. Or you could have had the security guards drive them home. Or you could have had some sober friend come get them. Or you could have called a cab." (This was long before Uber.)

I wanted to make an impression, scare them, do something they'd remember, so I went on. "You kids think nothing bad will ever happen, but it does. Every year, especially about this time, just before school gets out, kids your age get killed or hurt in drunk driving accidents. How would you feel if one of those girls got killed last night? Or ended up in a wheelchair for the rest of her life? How would her parents feel? Her brothers and sisters and friends? I know you weren't thinking about those things last night. But that's my point. Next time, every time, I want you to think about those things."

After a while I said: "Sure, lots of times, most times, nothing that bad happens. But sometimes it does. The risks are too great. It's not worth it. Please, please, don't ever drive drunk. Don't ride with anybody who's driving drunk. And if you possibly can, don't let your friends drive drunk. I'm really, really serious about this."

They just stared into their cereal bowls. After a while I continued. "There won't be any more punishment this time but please, please think about what I said. Get some breakfast. Then you've got some cleanup work to do. Try running the lawnmower over the puke, or try the shop vac."

Kevin asked, "Are you going to tell my dad about this?"

"Well, I wouldn't bring it up but, if he asks, I wouldn't want to lie. Why don't you eat some Tums or drink some Pepto-Bismol or something, maybe take a nap, get cleaned up, so you don't look so hung over. Then he'll probably never think to ask."

"He's in D.C., gone all week. But you're right; I'd better clean up so Mom won't be suspicious."

Cindy and I were fond of Kevin, and he was fond of us. I knew Kevin trusted me more than he trusted his father, but I didn't foresee the problem that would cause a few years later.

Julie went to Stanford. We offered to buy her a condo near there, but she wanted to live in the dorms "like an ordinary kid." Where did you live when you went to college, Katy?

She majored in art. The third summer she interned at a fashion designer, not high fashion but mass-market fashions for kids, teens and young adults. She'd had computer-based art courses. The fashion industry was just beginning to convert from hand-drawn to computer-drawn designs. Julie was on the leading edge of that. When she graduated in June 1995, she had job offers from several national clothing brands and took a job in New York City.

She said there were fantastic opportunities for young people in the fashion industry because so many people had died of AIDS. Julie's boss had lost more than twenty friends. I'd been aware of the epidemic, of course, but AIDS wasn't very visible in the real estate industry.

Julie moved in with a young man, Nathan. They lived in a small fourth-floor walkup. She got pregnant. Cindy and I offered to buy her a condo or co-op. Nathan was against it. "We're doing OK. We've got degrees, good jobs. We want to make it on our own without help from you."

Cindy said lots of parents give their kids a down payment and their friends wouldn't "look down on them" if we helped them get a modest place. After a few weeks, the kids relented. We helped Julie buy a brownstone in Brooklyn. Rents from the top three floors paid the mortgage. So, we'd solved their housing problem and were excited about becoming grandparents. We thought it would be nice if they got married, but young people don't seem to think that's important anymore.

Cindy and I thought David might follow his sister to Stanford, but he chose to go to Harvey Mudd in Claremont, California. He loved it there. He came home for Christmas so excited. "Dad, it's like heaven for nerds!"

"Oh, I never thought of you as a nerd. You had friends and sports: swimming, tennis, cross-country."

"Yeah, the nerd sports. But I meant the classes. Everybody is smart and interested in school. You don't have to pretend you're dumb or be afraid to ask questions."

He was interested in all his classes: math, chemistry, physics, biology, history, literature, everything. He was getting a lot of support for being smart. We hadn't realized how much he'd wanted that. We should have been more supportive when he was in high school, but we didn't know being smart made him feel "different".

So, we were empty nesters. Our children were doing well. I thought we had it made, but another big crisis was just around the corner.

Love, Mark

# # # #

Mar. 14, 2013

Dear Mark,

I could have gone to Stanford, but I went to the UW instead. I lived with my Mom. She started college a couple of years before me, but she would have felt old or out of place in the dorms and neither one of us wanted to live alone, so we kept on living together. Still do.

But back to your life. What was the crisis about?

Love, Katy

# # # #

Mar. 21, 2013

Dear Katy

One evening in October 1997, I got a call from an hysterical woman. “Mark Kauffman?”

“Yes, who is this?”

“Nikki. Your wife has been sleeping with my husband, and if it doesn’t stop—”

“Wait, wait. Nikki who?”

"Nikki Graves, Buddy's wife, you asshole. You know damn well who I am."

"I'm sorry. I, I didn't recognize your voice." I hardly knew the woman, hadn't seen her since the press conference over Buddy's call-girl scandal.

"Well, you tell her—like I already told Buddy—if this happens again, they're both going to be all over the 6:00 news and the front page of every newspaper. I'm not kidding. I will destroy him, both of them."

"Well, I, ah, really, ah, don't know what to say. Of course, I'll talk to her. But let's try to stay calm, not do something everybody will regret."

"I'm not calm but I am very, very serious. They won't get a second chance. Good night, Mark."

I waited for Cindy. Fortunately, both kids were away at college. I don't think I could have coped with this if they were around. Cindy came home about 10:30 or 11:00. I'd seldom seen her so drunk. That wasn't going to make things any easier, at least for me. My whole adult life I've taken great pride in staying calm in crises, but this was a new kind. I was about to lose it. I just looked at her for a while, trying to keep control and figure out what to do. "So, can you tell me what happened?"

"You know what happened."

"No, I mean, how it got started, the, ah, the sexual relationship?"

"So, it's true confession time, is it?"

"Well, maybe this isn't a good time. Some time, though, we should talk about it. But it's late. Maybe we should get some sleep."

"So where are you going to sleep?"

"In our bed of course."

"Fine. Then I'll sleep in Julie's room."

I didn't think that was necessary but was afraid to say so. This was the first night we hadn't slept together in twenty-five years, except when I was away on business.

The next morning, I cancelled all my appointments. I hadn't slept much. I made myself coffee and breakfast and waited. Cindy came down about 10:00, in a robe borrowed from Julie's closet, no makeup, hair uncombed, bags under her eyes. I loved her so much.

She poured herself a cup of coffee. After a while she said "You're right, of course. At some point we should talk about it."

"Yes, but first I want you to know that I really, really love you. I see you're hurting. I want to help."

She started to cry. "That wasn't helpful. I know you meant well but .... I tell you what: I'll go have a shower and get cleaned up, and then maybe we'll talk about it."

She came back in half an hour or so, got another cup of coffee and fixed herself some breakfast. "If it's any comfort, Buddy isn't very good at it, sex I mean."

"I don't care about that. What I want to know is why? Why did you do it?"

"I don't know. Boredom, loneliness, frustration. Who knows?"

"I thought our life was going along pretty well. The kids are doing fine. I'm working hard but I still enjoy it."

"Yes, your life has been going fine. But it's been going along without me. I haven't had much to do since David went to college. Since he got his driver license really."

"I'm sorry. I didn't know the empty nester thing was so hard for you."

"It's not so much the kids being gone. It's you being gone."

"You mean you get horny when I'm gone?"

"Mark, come on. You know we do it just once or twice a week when you're here, and you're gone for only two or three days at the most. So, it's not that, mainly. But the house is just so empty, watching TV or reading or just sitting around by myself at night."

We talked for a while, but nothing seemed to get resolved. She said, "Don't you have meetings or something?"

"I cancelled them."

"I'd rather you go to work. Go somewhere. I'm talked out for now."

I got out my bike. In the garage I found an extra garbage can nearly full of empty wine bottles, cheap Chardonnay, Yellow Tail from Australia. I wanted to go back to confront her, but then thought I'd better not. I got on my bike, rode out the driveway, and waved at the guards. "No need to follow me; just going for a short ride." If any kidnappers were around, they wouldn't expect me to go for a bike ride in the middle of a workday.

I rode across the Mercer Island bridge and the floating bridge, south to Renton and back up the east side of the lake, about 40 miles. I was out of shape; my legs and back got sore. But I wasn't ready to face Cindy until I got really tired.

I took a shower, got a sparkling water to drink, and looked for her. She was out on the deck, a book face down in her lap, a glass of wine in her hand. "How much of that have you been drinking?"

She almost yelled at me. “What, so now you think I’m an alcoholic?” I’d left like she told me to. What was I supposed to do now?

“I don’t think you’re an alcoholic—not yet at least. But I found a whole garbage can of wine bottles in the garage.”

“I recycle, you asshole. Anything wrong with that?”

This wasn’t the Cindy I knew, that I’d lived with for twenty-five years. I’d never seen her like this. I didn’t know what to do. I drove to my office, got some papers, came back, went to my home office, tried to work. I heard the refrigerator door open and close. Refilling her wine glass? Probably.

I went out on the deck to watch the sunset with her. It was getting cool. I brought an afghan, put it over her, and sat in a lounge chair, maybe ten feet away from her. Neither of us said anything. After the sun went down, I went to bed. I don’t know when she did, but she slept in Julie’s room again. She’d moved a lot of her clothes and makeup over there.

This went on for nearly a month, seeing each other in the kitchen or around the house, usually saying nothing. I didn’t know what to do.

One day I called Buddy and asked if he’d meet with me. He said, “You’re not talking about a duel or anything like that?”

“No, I just want to understand what happened. I was mad, but I’m pretty much over that now. I’m just trying to figure out what to do, how to get her back.” He wouldn’t meet in a restaurant, too much risk of being interrupted by people wanting to talk to him. We met for a walk at the McMillan trailhead on the Foothills

Trail. It was awkward. Finally, I said, "Can you just tell me how it happened, you know, the first time?"

"Yes, of course. Cindy had organized a joint fundraiser for the Sierra Club and my campaign at the Sheraton in Tacoma. She'd written out this cute dialogue where we finished each other's statements. It went something like this:

> [her] We've asked you all to come today because each of you has contributed ...
>
> [me] either to the Sierra Club or my campaigns ...
>
> [her] or both. We thought it might be fun for you all to get together ...
>
> [me] to see old friends ...
>
> [her] and make new ones. We're going to have some introductions and a few drinks...
>
> [me] and get to know each other a little.
>
> [her] And then we're going to ask each of you to make a contribution ...
>
> [me] to the Sierra Club if you've previously contributed to my campaigns or ...
>
> [her] or to Buddy's campaign if you have previously contributed to the Sierra Club.
>
> [me] And if you previously contributed to both ...
>
> [together] please contribute to both."

"People laughed. It was fun. We raised over six hundred thousand dollars, and each of us got a list of new donors. Everybody got in the spirit of it. Cindy is a fundraising genius."

"When it was over Cindy was feeling good and a bit drunk. I didn't want her to drive home. I said, 'Why don't you rest up at my condo while I go to my district office?' That's what I meant to do. But when I let her into my condo, she kissed me and started leading me around until she found the bedroom. I should have resisted. I'm so sorry."

"And after that?"

"The next time I was in Tacoma we agreed to meet at my condo again. Nikki was going to visit friends on Vashon Island. We thought she'd be gone all day, but the ferry broke down. She came back and caught us, not in the act but in bed with our clothes off."

"So that was the second and last time?"

"Yes."

Cindy and I have not contributed to Buddy's campaigns since then, but his political career was well established. He's had so many terms in Congress, he's a fixture now, in this state and nationally. After the 2000 census, his district was modified to include Auburn, Black Diamond, Renton and the east side up to I-90, so he's been "our" Congressman since then.

After another week or so, I went to Brett Jamison, our General Counsel. "Got a few minutes? I want to talk about a personal problem."

"I can spend as much time as you want but, if there are legal problems, you know I represent the company and can't represent you."

"OK, I understand that. It's not a legal problem yet, but Cindy and I are kind of estranged. I'm trying to find some way to get back together, but everything I do seems to make it worse."

"Well, I'm not a divorce lawyer, but I know something about these things. Are you ready to start thinking about what would happen if you decide to get a divorce?

"Like what do you mean?"

"Well, let's start with one of the tough ones. Who gets the kids? Or who gets which kid?"

"What are you talking about? Both kids are away at college. When they come home on vacations and stuff, we'd share them."

"It usually doesn't work that way. At least one attaches to the weaker, more fragile parent. In your case that would be Cindy, I assume?"

"So, you're saying I'd probably lose my relationship with at least one of the kids?"

"Probably. You might be able to have some kind of relationship with one, maybe both, but it would be a lot different, especially the one who attaches most to Cindy. He or she may be hostile for a few years, maybe forever."

"Oh, God, I hope you're wrong."

"Of course. I do too. But 'friendly divorces' are rare. Both of you may want that, but things usually get far worse than you expect, especially if kids are involved, even adult kids."

"I ... I ... I just can't imagine that happening to my family." There was quite a long silence. "And the second thing?"

"Money and assets. You were more or less poor when you got married, right? Neither of you got a big inheritance and you've always lived in Washington, so everything is community property. She gets half, you get half, plus or minus a little. You wouldn't want her owning half of the development company, so you'd probably end up owning Inova Development and she'd end up with most of your REIT shares and other investments."

"I suppose then she sells a lot of it?"

"Probably. That's part of why, if this gets close to happening, we need to issue a press release explaining the divorce and the settlement if there is one. On that I'd represent the company. Your lawyer might have some input, but the company would have to make public disclosures."

"We couldn't keep all this private?"

"No. Your REIT was built around your reputation as a real estate genius. If investors thought you were distracted or upset over a divorce, the price of shares in your REIT probably would drop. If Cindy will get a lot of REIT shares, investors would assume she'll sell most of them, and that could depress their price even more. We can't withhold information that investors probably would consider in deciding whether to buy or sell or hold shares in the REIT."

"Any other big problems?"

"Yes. The divorce would be big news. You and Cindy would live in a fishbowl. There would be headlines like: 'Stay-at-home Mom Gets $800 million divorce settlement.' And after that they'd want follow-up stories and you'd both be fair game for tabloid rumors and late-night comedians. The media might leave your kids alone, but don't count on it."

"Jeeze. I still love Cindy and want us to find some way through this. You've given me lots of motivation to try harder."

"As your friend, I hope you can work it out. If you can't, I could help you choose a lawyer, but my job would be to protect the company, even if that means I have to do things that hurt you."

"You've been a good friend for a long time. We can still be friends, no matter what happens."

At home I found Cindy in the living room looking out across the channel. "You look glum," she said. "What did you do today?"

"I talked to Brett Jamison about a divorce. I mean, what it would be like, what would happen if we decide to go that way."

She gave me a funny smile. "I talked to a divorce lawyer. It didn't go well. The kids, the money, the publicity, it would be awful."

"Lawyers must all think alike," I said, a weak joke. "We talked about the same things. I really, really don't want to go down that road."

"I don't either. I know that now. Let's have something to eat."

She made a salad and cooked some vegetables. I grilled a couple of chicken breasts. She didn't drink any wine. After dinner she led me up to our room. We made love for the first time in months, and she slept in our bed that night. I thought we'd turned a corner. Turns out I was a bit premature on that.

The next morning, we slept in, got up, showered and had breakfast. Cindy talked about her depression, not using that word, but saying that being empty nesters was hard for her and so was our business expanding into the Bay Area, which took me away a lot of nights. Her volunteer work with environmental groups had become frustrating; people were more polarized and many activists, especially younger ones, seemed to view her as a "rich bitch" (her term) who dabbled in environmental causes but drove a big Mercedes to their meetings.

I said, "We can come up with a plan to deal with all this."

"Shut up! I don't want you to come up with a God-damn plan. You can't just bring in experts to fix me. I'm a person, not a project. Don't try to come up with a plan to fix me."

I was stunned. What had I done wrong? I hadn't said I would come up with a plan. I'd said "we". All the progress we'd made in the last sixteen hours seemed gone. Now I understand she meant I should just listen, but I'd gone into my business problem-solving mode. Wrong time for that.

"I'm sorry, Mark. I shouldn't have yelled at you. I know you were trying to be helpful, but I was just trying to explain how I feel. There'll be a time for action plans later, but I'm not ready for that. I'm still trying to figure out where I am."

We talked, or she talked, for several hours. I tried to listen and say very little. Sometimes I tried to assure her that I did understand. Finally, she said, "Maybe I was too hasty when I yelled at you about bringing in experts. Maybe a good counselor could help me, help us, think our way through this."

"Maybe, but how do you find a good one? I hear a lot of 'em are quacks."

"A couple of friends recommended this woman. I don't know if she's available, but maybe we should try her?"

"It's worth a try. Let's do it."

She met with the counselor, Bonnie, several times without me before they decided it was time for me to join them. Bonnie had a warm smile and was soft spoken, but she could be tough. At our first meeting I was tired, apprehensive, fidgety. She said, "You look stressed. Is there anything I can do to make this easier for you?"

"I want this to work, it's just, I don't know, just a new thing for me."

"I understand. You're used to being in control and you must wonder how somebody like me could possibly understand the problems of a wealthy and powerful person like you."

"Yeah, kind of, a little."

"Here's the deal," she said. "I don't know a lot about problems that are unique to rich and powerful people, but they're still people. I'm going to concentrate on things you have in common with ordinary people, where I do have some expertise. Anything unique to being rich and powerful, you'll be on your own on that. Fair enough?"

"OK, fair enough."

We met twice a week. There were a lot of tears, mostly Cindy's but I choked up and got teary-eyed a few times too. Cindy came out with a long list of grudges—no, that's too strong—incidents where I'd slighted her or disappointed her: missed kid events, birthdays, anniversaries. These came out one or two at a time over several weeks. It bothered me to think she might have been brooding over them for so long. It wasn't like her. Cindy had always been resilient, not carried grudges.

Eventually we started to talk about what a happier future might look like. I wanted to jump ahead, but I'd learned something. We had to go at Cindy's pace. There's an old joke, I forget how it goes, but the punchline is "Patience, Jackass." Many, many times I said to myself, "Patience, Jackass. Patience, Jackass."

Finally, one day Bonnie said to me, "Are we ready to talk about your job?"

"Yes. I've been thinking about that. I want to cut back on my hours and work more from home, but I'm not ready to quit completely. I still enjoy it and I'm still young. Barely fifty."

"Would you quit if I asked you to?" Cindy asked.

I hesitated for a minute but then I said, "Yes. It probably would be a mistake, but I would."

"Why a mistake?" Bonnie asked.

"Well, for one thing I might regret it, feel I got pushed into it when I didn't want to, or feel like I've become a burden on her. And I don't want Cindy to feel like she has to take care of me."

"Don't worry," Cindy said. "I'm not going to do that. I'm not worried about the things you said, but it probably would be the other way around. You might feel like you had to spend a lot of time taking care of me. I'm not that fragile. I'm going to find a way to live that doesn't depend on you propping me up all the time."

In another session we talked about Cindy's role in our business. "I thought about offering you a full-time job with the company, but most of our people work at least 60 hours a week and we shouldn't both be workaholics. Maybe something part time though."

"No," Cindy said, "Everybody would see me as the boss's wife. I'd never know whether people listened to me because they thought I might be right or just because I'm your wife."

"Well, I like having you on the Board." Cindy had always been on our Board of Directors. We sent large envelopes of materials to Board members before every meeting. Cindy and I always went through them together, trying to figure out what each member might say and how we should respond. "It's been very helpful having you review the Board packets with me."

"Is that right? I didn't know you saw any value in that."

"Yikes, yet another thing we haven't been communicating about!" That was partly a joke, but how could she not know how much I valued her advice?

Bonnie opened another session with this question: "Are we ready to talk about Cindy's drinking?" Nobody said anything. Finally, I said, "It scares me, really scares me." I choked up. This was harder than talking about my job or anything else we'd covered. "I feel so helpless. I want to help. I'd do anything I could to help. But I'm afraid that anything I do or say might make it worse."

"You're learning," Bonnie said. "You're a pretty quick learner."

Cindy still didn't say anything. After a while Bonnie said, "Some people keep drinking until they hit bottom, but it doesn't have to be that way. Some people learn enough about the disease early enough to head it off before it gets too bad. I can recommend some books or things to help you understand it better. And you could try AA."

Cindy said, "No, I've read some of those books. I think I'll be OK after I figure out what I want to do with the rest of my life."

Finally, we got to the big, big issue: what could Cindy do to regain a sense of purpose? We'd talked all around it, how important it is to care about other people and about issues or causes outside yourself. For Cindy, volunteering for environmental groups had helped meet those needs for many years but didn't seem to meet them anymore.

We decided to fund a foundation focused on social issues. At first Cindy wanted it to operate only in the Puget Sound area. I pointed out that half our business now was in the Bay Area, I'd be spending a lot of time there, and I'd like Cindy to come with me more often. Also, it's sunny there a lot in winter. If Cindy suffered from Seasonal Affective Disorder, spending more time in the Bay Area might help. Cindy decided that the Foundation would operate in both the Northwest and the Bay Area.

I kept working but only about fifty hours a week, much of that from home or our condo in Redwood City. Cindy stayed on our company's Board but worked mainly as CEO of our charity, the Cascade-Sierra Foundation. She was energized. Her depression melted away. She quit drinking, even though she hosted many fundraisers where alcohol was served.

Cindy talked to founders and managers of other foundations, asking questions, looking for ideas. She recruited people to serve on the Foundation's board, and people with social service experience to serve on advisory boards for the Puget Sound and Bay Area divisions. She hired a small staff and picked out office space in Bellevue and Redwood City.

To get the Foundation started, we transferred from our personal brokerage account $100 million worth of shares in our REIT. At first, we didn't plan to seek other donations. Most wealthy people we knew had business relationships with Inova or the REIT, and we didn't want them to feel pressured to contribute. But, as Buddy had pointed out, Cindy was a master fundraiser. Many people asked us to donate to various causes. Cindy would say yes, but she hoped they'd make a donation to our

Foundation too. She never talked about how much people were expected to contribute, but this generated a rapidly growing stream of donations. Many people donated stock, which helped diversify the Foundation's assets. By late 2007 the Foundation had an endowment of about five hundred million dollars.

Love, Mark

# # # #

Mar. 28, 2013

Dear Mark,

I am so sorry about your marriage difficulties. It is hard for me to relate to them because Mom never married or had any stable, long-term relationships, and I have not had any either. But a stable, long-term, loving relationship? That would be a dream. Having one threatened by infidelity would be a nightmare.

What happened next with your business?

Love, Katy

# # # #

Apr. 5, 2013

Dear Katy

While Cindy was building the Foundation, I was building Inova Development into a more durable organization. We'd done a lot with remarkably few people, but we'd grown very fast and everybody worked long hours.

I talked with our key employees about the risk of burnout. What else could we delegate? What kinds of people should we promote or hire to delegate things to? What could we quit doing? At first they said they were too busy to figure out how to be less busy, but they came to see the value of this.

I wanted to build an institution that would continually improve and regenerate itself, even after I was gone. I thought I was doing a good job at this, but that turned out to be delusional. When I went down, I took the whole organization with me. That really hurt.

We saw my parents every month or so. One evening after we talked about Cindy's Foundation work, Dad said, "Giving all that money to strangers is OK, but have you taken care of your sister yet? You know, the trust thing?"

"Oh Dad, I'm sorry. I know that worries you. But things have been really hectic. I'll do it. I'll get right on it."

By the middle of David's junior year, he began to focus on biochemistry and bioengineering. "Dad, this is the future. Amazing things are going on. Technology can help solve most of the world's problems. We can feed billions more people, with better nutrition, using less land, fewer chemicals. We can grow trees faster, produce more forest products on less land and put a lot of our forests into parks and wilderness. We can prevent and cure diseases, we can …." Well, you get the point, Katy. He was so enthusiastic. You watch the news and you might think today's young people are all lazy, selfish, self-absorbed. But spend time with a kid like David, you'll be more optimistic about the future.

Not all kids are over-achievers like him, of course. One evening I said to Cindy, "I'd like to know more about the programs you support. Maybe I could be more supportive if I knew more about what you do. Make sense?"

"Yes, it does. And with the kids and their friends gone most of the time, maybe you'd enjoy spending some time around teenagers again. You could visit our 'Out of the Storm' shelter."

"What's that?"

"It takes in street kids, mostly druggies, run-aways, kids with no safe place to go."

I went to Out of the Storm. The house mother, Ms. Hampton-Gruenwold, explained the purposes and goals of their program and how it operated. Then she took me to meet the kids, twelve girls and eight boys, and asked them to explain what the program meant to them. They were quite articulate; their little speeches probably had been well-rehearsed. But then a girl in the back, dressed in black with lots of tattoos, said, "Mister, I don't think you give a shit about us."

"Well," I said, "I don't really know any of you. But I'll tell you this: I love my wife and she cares about the program here and cares about you too."

"The rich lady with the fancy clothes?"

"Yeah, that's probably her."

"Well, she's a looker, but she don't know nothing about real life, where we come from, how we got here, all that shit."

"Maybe you're right. She's very busy. She doesn't have time to get to know you."

"I know something about guys like you, though. Lots of rich guys like blow jobs."

"Well, that's not what I'm here for."

"How about me?" said the boy next to her. "You like it from boys? I'll do it for two hundred bucks."

"Hey, enough of this," Ms. Hampton-Gruenwold said. "You're going to embarrass Mr. Kauffman."

"So," I said to the girl, "what's your name, Goth girl?"

"Moonbeam."

"So, does that make you Mr. Sunshine?" I said to the boy.

"Yeah, call me Sonny."

"OK. I don't know any of you. Still, I'm sorry my wife is too busy to get to know you. Maybe I'll come back and try to get to know some of you a little better."

I visited Out of the Storm every other week or so. Kids came and went but Moonbeam and Sonny were there for several years. Most of the kids would rather watch TV or play video games, but some would hang out with me. After a couple of months, Moonbeam said, "Hey, Mark, why don't you take us out some place, get us away from here for a few hours? There's lots of fun places we could go."

"I've thought about that, but The Warden says it would be too dangerous." The Warden, that's what we called Ms. Hampton-Gruenwold when she wasn't around.

"What d'you mean? Aren't you a good driver?" said Sonny.

"Not that. I guess she's afraid one of you might accuse me of something, you know, something sexual."

"Maybe she's smarter than I thought," said Sonny. "I've thought about that. I bet you'd pay big bucks to avoid a scandal."

"Come on, Sonny, you don't really think I'd try anything like that, do you?"

"Nah, but you'd pay big bucks to keep me quiet if I was gonna to say you did."

"Don't count on it. But thanks for the warning."

Some years later I took Moonbeam out to restaurants and other places. By then she'd changed her name to Melody and started college. I never was alone with Sonny. He left Out of the Storm when he turned eighteen but died a month or so later, probably an overdose. I helped Melody through college. A scholarship covered her tuition. I paid for her books and living expenses. I would have given her a job when she graduated but she wanted to teach in an inner-city school. She's doing that now. I haven't had many visitors, but she's come here several times.

The Director said she was amazed at how well I related to the street kids. I told her I could relate to anybody, rich or poor, old or young, black or white, straight or gay, educated or not. I was proud of that, but it turned out that's another thing that helped put me in here.

Cindy and I talked about the kids at Out of the Storm and how to get help earlier for kids like them. We knew that school counselors, social workers and people in the juvenile courts could identify kids at risk, but what kind of help should we try to provide? Experts told us the most successful programs, like Big Brothers/Big Sisters, focused on mentoring relationships with volunteers who spent significant amounts of time with kids. We wanted volunteers to work closely with both kids and their parents. Cindy set up a new non-profit to do this, called Families At Risk Resources and Support, or FARRS.

Love, Mark

CHAPTER 6

GETTING OFF THE STREETS

Apr. 12, 2013

Dear Mark,

I know about FARRS—it got my mom and me off the streets, put me through junior high, high school and college. I knew it was funded by some big charity but I had never heard of the Cascade-Sierra Foundation. Does Dr. DeProulx know you funded FARRS?

I knew some street kids, including a few who spent time at Out of the Storm, but the names Moonbeam and Sonny don't ring a bell. Do you know what names or nick-names they used on the streets?

Love, Katy

# # # #

Apr. 19, 2013

Dear Katy

Your mom and you were a FARRS family? You were just the kind of family we were trying to help. I'd like to know more about how you got into the program and how it worked for you and your mom. Of course, I'm not involved with it anymore. It may not still exist. There's not much left of our Foundation and a lot of programs it supported. Still, I'd like to learn more about your experiences.

Jackie knows that Cindy and I funded the Cascade-Sierra Foundation. I don't know if she knows it funded FARRS. Does she know you were a FARRS kid? I don't know what other names Moonbeam and Sonny used except Moonbeam went by Melody after she got out of FARRS.

Cindy worked hard to support the boards and staffs of non-profits the Foundation was funding and, of course, to raise money. She got to know the wives of most of the billionaires in the Puget Sound and Bay areas, and many of their husbands. Bill and Melinda Gates lived just up the lake from us; they contributed to our Foundation and we contributed to theirs. Craig and Wendy McCaw had given mainly to environmental causes and Cindy knew them through that. After the McCaw brothers sold their cell phone company to AT&T, all of them supported our Foundation. In the Bay Area Larry Ellison was a supporter, although he was between wives during most of this time. Steve Jobs and his wife, Laurene, were supporters. He was working at NeXT Computers and Pixar for much of this time, but they became more important donors after he returned to Apple and revived its fortunes (along with his own). There were many others.

Inova Development built new buildings for their companies, so I'd met some of these billionaires but didn't really know them. Cindy got to know them better than I did. They'd come to our house for charity fundraisers and not recognize me. That was OK. I never wanted to hang out with billionaires—I just wanted to be one.

David's friend Kevin got married in June 1999. David was his best man. Kevin invited Cindy and me to the rehearsal dinner. Everything went smoothly through the dinner and introductions of the groomsmen and bridesmaids. David roasted Kevin and handed the microphone to him. Kevin thanked everyone for coming, took a jab or two at David to get even for the roasting, and then got more serious. "Some of you may be unhappy about the bar closing early, no wine with dinner, sparkling cider instead of champagne for the toasts. We're donating what the wine and champagne would have cost to MADD, Mothers Against Drunk Driving. I don't want anybody driving home impaired. Cabs will be available if you need them. Many of my friends think I've been fanatic about this, but please don't ever drive drunk, don't ever ride with anybody who is driving drunk, and try to stop your friends from driving drunk if you can."

There was a stunned silence for a minute or so. Then he went on. "David is my best man tomorrow because we've been best friends all of our lives. But I want all of you to know that the very best man here tonight isn't

David but his father, Mark Kauffman. Mark has been like a second father to me all those years, and his wife, Cindy, has been like a second mother. They've both been such great, positive, loving influences on my life. I want to take this opportunity to thank them and say how much I love them both."

Three groomsmen, who I knew from countless times they had been at our house, stood up. One of them yelled, "Speech! Speech!" I looked at Olaf and saw he was upset. People started passing the microphone to me. By the time it got to me most of the wedding party was chanting "Speech! Speech!"

I had to say something. "Well, we—my wife, Cindy, and I—have been friends with Kevin's parents since before Kevin and David were born. We've camped together, eaten lots of meals together, played together, waterskiing, tennis, swimming, card games, board games, you name it. Kevin has stayed at our house many times and David has stayed at theirs. Cindy and I have warm feelings for everyone in Kevin's family. We are so honored that he seems to have warm feelings for us. To the bride, I say you are lucky to be marrying into such a fine and fun-loving family. To Kevin's parents, I say thank you for sharing this fine young man with us for all those years."

I looked at Olaf. My talk hadn't done much good. He was leaving, dragging Carol behind him. The next day Olaf shook my hand in the receiving line, but he didn't smile and didn't want to talk. Clearly, he was still hurt. I didn't know if Kevin had hurt his dad on purpose or just hadn't understood how his dad would react to what he said. I think he meant well, but this put a big strain on my relationship with Olaf.

I talked to Olaf a couple of weeks later in D.C., told him I'd had no idea what Kevin was going to say at the rehearsal dinner, and was very sorry if it had embarrassed him. I didn't know what else I could do to restore our friendship. He seemed to accept my apology, but our relationship has been very cool ever since. Like I said, he could have helped me when the prosecutors came after me, but he didn't. Then I thought he would help me get a pardon or get my sentence commuted or something if I lost my appeal, but he wouldn't help with that either.

Love, Mark

# # # #

Apr. 26, 2013

Dear Mark,

How did Mom and I get into the FARRS program? Her boyfriend molested me, and she was too high to notice. For once, I was in school at the time. I told the school counselor. She took me to the police and then a social worker. The cops and prosecutors agreed to defer the charges against Mom if we got in the FARRS program and drop them if we stayed in and she stayed clean for two years. I was twelve.

Mom and I had an intake session with the FARRS Director. She outlined the kinds of resources they could provide, and the responsibilities Mom and I would have if we agreed to participate in the program. Like we had any choice! It was that or jail for her and a foster home for me.

The Director, Mom and I worked out a short-term plan and longer-term goals. The Director printed up copies and all three of us signed them. We were in.

FARRS has closed down now but it got Mom and me through college before it went under.

Dr. DeProulx says she did not know your foundation funded FARRS, and she did not know that Mom and I were in the FARRS program, so she never made the connection.

Love, Katy

# # # #

May 3, 2013

Dear Katy

What an ordeal for you. What would have happened if your mom had not gone along with the program? You would have ended up in the regular foster care program, that's what. Maybe that's what it took to get her clean and sober. But having to turn your mom in just to get rid of a pervert. That's awful.

So sad to hear FARRS closed down. Another casualty from the collapse of my fortune, I guess. But I'm glad it survived long enough to get you through college.

Did getting into the FARRS program feel good? We thought something like a contract would help assure families that we'd provide resources and support if they'd make good use of them, and this would help get relationships off on the right foot. Any feedback on that? I'd like to talk more about how the program worked, but I know you want to keep moving on our project.

One Sunday, I flew down to the Bay Area. When I got to our condo, I was surprised to see David come out of the bedroom, pulling up his pants and blocking my way. "Hey, Dad, don't come in. There's, ah, a, a girl in there."

"Oh, I didn't know you were here. Yes, well, tell you what: I'll go to the IHOP down the street and have some coffee or something. Come join me, both of you."

I went to the IHOP, ordered coffee, wondering if they'd come. I wasn't shocked. He was 22. Like most kids he never said anything about his sex life. Like most parents, we never asked. Still, the fact that I'd "caught" them could make things awkward.

After about forty-five minutes they both came to the restaurant. David said, "Hi"

"Hi. Glad you came."

"This is Kaitlyn."

"Nice to meet you." She nodded and they sat down.

"Want something to eat?" I asked. A waitress brought menus.

"OK," David said. "You buying?" He grinned.

"Sure, oldest one buys." This was an old family ritual. We ordered breakfast.

David said, "Well, if I'd called you or Mom, I'd have found out you were coming."

"Yeah, but it's OK. Hey, I'm glad I got a chance to see you." Then I asked Kaitlyn if she called her parents every Sunday morning.

"Yes, but odd you should ask."

"Well, David seldom called us until a couple of months ago and then he started calling on Sunday mornings. I should have put two and two together." Both of them turned a little red.

"Yeah, it's been a couple of months," David said. "I meant to tell you about Kaitlyn, I mean not, well, you know, but that I was dating someone ...."

"It's OK. Kaitlyn, tell me a little about yourself. Are you from the LA area?"

"Yes, Santa Monica."

"So, are you a surfer?"

"Well, I've surfed some, pretty much everybody did, but I was more the nerdy-type, not a major surfer-dudette."

"What's your major?"

"Architecture and urban planning."

"That's right up my alley, but I never got a degree in it. Actually, I never got any degree, but I've worked with a lot of architects and urban planners."

"I bet. David told me some about your business. My father's an oncologist and part time adjunct professor at UCLA medical school, so I never got much exposure to the business world."

"It's very interesting. I've always enjoyed it."

We chatted for another forty-five minutes or so. The tension over me barging in on them seemed to be fading away. Kaitlyn excused herself to go to the restroom.

David said, "So I guess you'll probably tell Mom about finding Kaitlyn and me in the condo?"

"We don't normally keep secrets from each other, so, yes, we'll talk about it, but not 'til I get back on Wednesday. D'you want to call her and tell her about it before then?"

"That's just what I was wondering."

"She'll be OK with it, either way, I mean whether you tell her or I do. We may seem a little old-fashioned, but she won't be too shocked. And, of course, we got some practice at this with your sister. So, don't worry about upsetting her."

"Yeah, I think you're right. I think I'll call her, but I want to talk to Kaitlyn about it first."

Just then Kaitlyn came back. "You guys look serious. What are you talking about?"

I tried to think of something light and funny to say, but I didn't want to joke about "guy talk" under the circumstances. Before I could think of anything David said, "We were talking about whether it would be better for me to call my mom and tell her he found us in the condo or if he should tell her when he gets home."

I said, "Please don't worry about David's mom. She'll be OK. I'm sure she'll look forward to meeting you. It's just that, well, I don't like to keep secrets from her, so one of us ought to tell her."

Kaitlyn looked at me and at David, back and forth, back and forth. "That is so, so cool, that you can talk about it and . . . and, well, um, be calm and sensible. I won't be telling my parents anything even though we talk every week."

"Well," I said, "different families handle these things differently. Don't be too hard on your parents. Some people in our generation never got comfortable talking about this kind of stuff."

"My family doesn't really communicate about anything." She started to cry. David tried to comfort her. I couldn't think of anything helpful to say. "I'm sorry," she said. "It's just so cool listening to you two talk and seeing how much you enjoy each other. David is a lucky guy. And you are a great father."

"Thanks. I'm sorry your family is more …, I don't know, formal maybe, but you seem like a warm and loving person. David's lucky to have you. I think his mom will like you too. I'm sure she will."

And she did. We both became very fond of Kaitlyn.

Love, Mark

# # # #

May 10, 2013

Dear Mark,

The FARRS intake process felt manipulative and degrading. For poor families, nothing good ever comes from signing papers. The thing we signed was not comforting; it felt threatening. If you get a bunch of goodies dangled in front of you, you will sign almost anything. But then you owe people; they can hold it over you; they can take it all away.

Mom went into rehab and I was allowed to visit her after the first couple of weeks. I went to live with a nice couple, the Andersons. They promised that Mom and I could have our own apartment after she got out of rehab.

I got new clothes and a new hairdo, got my fingernails and toenails done, learned to ride a bike, how to make a bed, how to use a knife and fork, how to set a table, lots of stuff like that. I had a room of my own, and my own bathroom down the hall.

But there was a culture shock. Hand washing, for example. I was astounded at how often I was supposed to wash my hands. Every time you pee, or shit, or use a pad or tampon, and not just stuff down there, but before you eat or cook or use a computer. Mrs. Anderson seemed fanatic about this. Over and over, "Did you wash your hands?" and "You need to wash your hands first."

Finally, I asked her, "How come? Why all this hand washing?" She said it was to keep you from getting sick but, when I questioned that, she admitted that people just expected it. "Make it a habit," she said, "and then you won't embarrass yourself by forgetting." I still did not understand. Finally, she said, "Look, if somebody sees you come out of a stall and not wash your hands, they may think you weren't raised right." I was glad Mom did not hear that. It would have hurt her to hear that I "weren't raised right." Mom and I did not wash our hands much. If you pee between parked cars or in bushes or alleys or phone booths, it never becomes a habit.

And brushing teeth and wearing pajamas and taking a bath or shower every day. Upscale people have a lot of rituals like that, which are OK if you are used to them but do not make much sense if you are not. These personal hygiene things may have some small health benefits, but mostly they are just social conventions, things people expect everybody to do. Still, I have been so well trained that I am a little obsessive-compulsive about them now.

When Mom got out of rehab she stayed at Andersons' for a few weeks while we looked for an apartment. It was kind of weird watching her go through what I'd been through already, getting new clothes, new hairdo, her nails and toenails done, getting used to washing her hands and brushing her teeth and wearing pajamas to bed, getting used to having a safe place to stay and three meals a day.

But it seemed like she was being transformed into somebody I didn't know, and she said I seemed like a different person already. On the surface the changes all were good, but underneath there was fear that we might not know each other anymore, that all the good new things might be taken away, and maybe some regret that we hadn't had the good stuff all along.

One of the best things that first year in the program was getting Mom's teeth fixed. Meth had rotted her teeth. She had taken less and less care of herself and looked worse and worse because her teeth were ugly. That lead to a string of worse and worse guys, guys who beat her and sometimes molested me. FARRS worked with the UW Dentistry School to get her implants, which were still experimental back then. Her new teeth, as much as anything else, is what started to turn her life around.

We were really happy to move into our own place. It seemed odd at first, but we kept working on things Mrs. Anderson had been trying to teach us, asking each other, "Did you wash your hands?" and "Did you brush your teeth?" and saying things like "Forks on the left, spoons and knives on the right." At first it was kind of a joke, making fun of Mrs. Anderson. But she and other FARRS people came by every week and seemed to be checking up on things like that, so it was not just a joke. It is what we were expected to do. We were afraid that if we didn't, they might take away the apartment and food and clothes and all the other things they were giving us.

We got back to playing chess. We had started playing when I was eight or nine. When she got addicted, she could not concentrate; I beat her all the time and we quit playing. After we got the apartment, we started playing again. It felt good so see her mind clearing up. We had some really good chess games. When I was in eighth grade, Mom and the Andersons talked me into playing on the school chess team. I was the best player, but I still did not make any friends.

But, Mark, we need to get on with your story.

Love, Katy

# # # #

May 17, 2013

Dear Katy

Well, I asked for your feelings and at least you were honest. I've got to admit, though, I was surprised by what you wrote. We never intended to make people feel threatened. We thought written plans and goals would help make families feel more secure and comfortable. We should have asked for feedback on this long ago.

Still, it sounds like the short-term plan did work. You probably didn't know this, but to be able to take you in the Andersons had to become licensed foster care providers. FARRS never used the term "foster care." We knew that program had a bad reputation with the families we wanted to serve.

The "dot.com" bubble burst and the stock market collapsed in 2000. This hit the Puget Sound and Bay Areas hard. There were lots of empty and half-completed buildings. Lots of developers went bankrupt. Many other REITs had to reduce or suspend distributions to their shareholders. People who'd become afraid of the stock market looked for investments supported by real assets and companies with track records of thriving in hard times. That's the reputation we had. Again, we'd seen the downturn coming and prepared for it. Again, we bought a lot of properties at distressed prices.

The stocks of many companies, especially high-tech companies, fell a lot, but demand for office space took only a small, short dip. Microsoft, Hewlett-Packard, Intel, Apple, Adobe, Oracle and many older tech companies kept expanding, and new ones like Google, Amazon and Facebook came along. We built buildings, sometimes whole campuses, for most of them.

Our economics team helped identify the tech firms most likely to succeed and expand. Cindy and I started buying stock in them. I was never a stock market guy, but we got in near the bottom and rode the tech boom from late 2001 through mid-2008. We invested about $50 million in tech stocks. By mid-2008 they were worth about $240 million.

David went to graduate school at Caltech and continued to thrive. He got a masters in biochemistry and began work on his PhD. He came home for a few days in June 2003. He and Kaitlyn lived together. "Where's Kaitlyn?" I asked.

"She's got a project to finish up. She'll be up in a couple of days."

He seemed kind of pensive. "What are you thinking about?" I asked.

"Oh, career stuff. One of my professors asked about my career plans. I told him I'd been focused on getting my PhD and hadn't thought much about what I'd do after that. Go into research with a company or teach, I suppose." I nodded. "Then he said I could be successful in either research or teaching or both, but asked 'Have you thought about business? You've got the people skills to lead an organization, and you might find that more satisfying than just being a researcher or professor'." He was embarrassed.

"Go on. Did he say what he meant by that?"

"Yeah, a little. He said, 'I've watched you working on group projects and people look to you for leadership, not because you're bossy or try to take over but because you're good at helping people work together'." Now he was even more embarrassed.

"Lookit, this isn't easy for you to talk about, but you're not bragging, not coming across that way at all. You seem to be really wrestling with this, which is good."

"So, what do you think?"

"Oh, what I think isn't important. You'll have to decide. I've found my work satisfying and rewarding, and I'm not just talking about the money. Your mom finds her work, which is a lot like running a company, very satisfying too. So maybe it's in your blood. But good social skills are a blessing no matter what you do. University faculties are riddled with politics and personality conflicts, so the things that would make you good at business could make you a good dean someday too."

"Thanks."

"Hey, I've said many times, better to have to choose between good things than not have choices. There's no wrong answer. You just have to figure out what you want to do. Your mom and I will be supportive, whatever you decide."

"Well, I don't have to decide now but I think I'll take a couple of business courses and see how that feels."

Katy, what happened next with you and your mom in the FARRS program?

Love, Mark

# # # #

May 24, 2013

Dear Mark,

Mom was uncomfortable about what the Andersons were doing for us. She was embarrassed about the bike and them teaching me how to ride it. Maybe she felt she should have done that, but she never could have. If she had gotten me a bike, it just would have been stolen. There is no place to keep stuff when you are homeless.

And learning to use knives and forks and table napkins, make your bed, stuff like that. It wouldn't have made any sense to have fancy place settings when we were eating McDonalds food or popcorn and government cheese under a bridge. You don't need to make your bed if you're sleeping in a car or tent. They meant well, but Mom felt like they were putting her down for not being a better mother and teaching me all those things when I was younger.

The Andersons gave me a crash course in American culture, exposing me to all kinds of music, books, old TV shows, old movies. They were trying to fill in a lot of gaps, to help me fit in socially when these subjects came up. It was not much fun for me at the time, but they tried hard and meant well, and it kind of worked. I got to be less of a freak to my peers.

They taught Mom and me about credit cards, bank accounts, computers, stuff like that. We'd been on a cash only economy, except for a few credit card frauds.

Since Mom dropped out of seventh grade, or got kicked out because she was pregnant, we were at about the same level as far as school went. We studied together. Helping her helped me learn faster. My grades were good.

I see now why the Andersons put so much effort into things like clothes, table manners, piano lessons, art lessons, making friends with kids my age. They were trying to help me "catch up" socially and academically, trying to give me the kinds of experiences the other kids had. But it was like force-feeding: too much coming in too fast.

One day I overheard them refer to me as their "little Pygmalion project." I thought they said "little piggy." I cried and cried and, finally, I told them what I had heard and said I wasn't a little piggy, I hadn't asked for all the stuff they had given me. They said they were very sorry, took me to see "My Fair Lady," tried to assure me that they didn't see me as an Eliza Doolittle or see themselves as Henry Higgins types. But, really, it was just like that. I was a project for them: they were doing a makeover on me, whether I wanted it or not.

Seventh grade was tough. I didn't have any friends. I was being trained to act like the other kids, being turned into an upscale suburban kid practically overnight, but my life experiences had been so different. Kids would giggle about sex like it was a fun, cool thing, but I couldn't tell them about my Mom's experiences or me being molested. I did not fit in.

Then Mom went to her first PTA meeting and made everything worse. She didn't mean to, of course. Looking back now, it is even kind of funny. She was 25, must have been at least ten years younger than any of the other parents. She had new clothes, new hairdo, and had gotten some pounds back on and her shape back during ten weeks in rehab. She looked good. It's too bad the subject of sex education for seventh graders came up. She had strong feelings about that, of course, and the Andersons hadn't had time to get her language toned down. Still, she probably should not have referred to my classmates as "little fuckers."

The Andersons tried to reassure the other parents that their home was a safe place for kids. They went to all my soccer games and school events to try to get to know the other parents, encouraged me to invite friends over, asked other parents to let their kids come. But sometimes they called it a "play date" and that embarrassed me. Sometimes kids came over to play with me, but only because their parents wanted them to "help me adjust." Playing with me was a good deed, like serving soup to homeless people.

And then there were the "inspections." When the Andersons or FARRS people came to visit, they always seemed to be checking things out, seeing if our place was clean and orderly. We always had to keep the beds made, dishes done, dirty clothes put away, vacuuming done, all that, because you never knew when they were coming.

A lot of good came out of it, of course. I had plenty to eat and a safe place to sleep. I grew six inches taller, changed shape and all that. But the transition from street kid to middle class was hard.

FARRS provided a counselor but, somehow, she managed to be condescending and overbearing at the same time. She pushed me to talk about bad stuff too soon. I quit going after a couple of sessions.

Love, Katy

# # # #

May 31, 2013

Dear Katy

Sorry your counselor was such a bad fit. But how could you sort all this out by yourself when you were only twelve or thirteen? It's not good to bottle stuff up. Maybe you should find a better counselor and try again. Just saying.

I'm sure the Andersons didn't mean to put your mom down. When we were planning the program, these kinds of problems never occurred to us. Still, it sounds like things worked out pretty well, eventually. The PTA thing must have been painful at the time, but it seems like you can see the funny side of it now. That's good.

Social workers assess peoples' mental health by checking their self-care and living conditions. Those inspections weren't just to be "nosey". They were looking to see if you needed more help. Sounds like you passed with flying colors, but I'm sorry this was so stressful.

A question: did you and your mom, or you and the Andersons, ever talk about the risk of your mom backsliding, getting back into drugs? Experts told us the first few weeks out of rehab were the highest risk time for recovering addicts.

Was high school any easier for you?

I'll go on with my story. In June 2007, David came home for a few days. He'd nearly finished the classroom work for his PhD, chosen a topic for his dissertation, and talked to potential faculty sponsors about it. He'd also finished most of the classes for an MBA.

"So," I said, "still on the fence between a research track and a business track?"

"No, I'm leaning toward the business track, but still in the biotech or biomedical field."

"Um, that sounds good. There must be lots of interesting opportunities."

"Yeah, I was just about to start sending out some resumes but ...." He didn't finish the sentence.

"But what?"

"Oh, I'm not ready to talk about it. I thought I was. But now I'm not sure."

"We've usually been able to talk about things, haven't we? Even things that are awkward or embarrassing. What makes this so difficult to talk about?"

"Well, this one is hard. It's not embarrassing or anything like that. It's a business opportunity. But still ...."

"So, you'd have to drop out of school? Is that the problem?"

"No, I mean, yes, I'd drop out of school. But that's not the problem."

"So, what is the problem?"

"Look, you've been a great father, a terrific father, and you've given me so much, so much support."

"Thanks, but you haven't gotten to the problem yet. What's bothering you?"

"I don't want to beg or have you feel like I am begging. That's what's so hard. I have this opportunity but going after it would take a lot of money, money I'd have to get from you."

"Well, we can talk about that."

"You don't have to give it to me. I'll be just fine if you don't. You don't owe me anything."

"Tell me about this opportunity."

"It's a biomedical start-up. They're working on gene-related aspects of autoimmune diseases. One of my professors and a couple of his post-doc students started it. Some angel investors helped get it going but they're burning through their cash. There's personality problems among the investors that'll make it hard to get another round of funding. The science looks good but they're going under."

"So, what would you like to do?"

"If I had the money, I'd buy out the original investors, manage the company and fund it for a few years. If we could get through the proof of concept stage and some Phase I trials underway, we should be able to get venture company funding and, if things go well, maybe partner with a big drug company."

"And if it fails?"

"Good question. I'd have experience as the CEO of a failed start-up, so somebody might hire me for that. I'd have a lot of contacts in the industry and still have contacts in the academic world, so something might come up through those. If not, I'd go back and finish my MBA and maybe my PhD and figure out what my options were. Don't worry. I wouldn't fall apart or anything like that. I wouldn't be the first guy to dream big and fail the first time. I'd bounce back. I think I'm pretty resilient."

"I like that attitude. You're the kind of person I like to hire."

"I'm not much interested in real estate. Nothing personal. It's just that I'm really into in science and technology. There's so much cool stuff going on. There'll be opportunities of some kind."

"Yes, I think you're right. So, how much money are we talking about for, ah, say, the first two or three years?"

"Hard to say. My friends say the cash burn is about $300,000 a month. And the odd thing about this kind of business, the better things go the faster you want to spend money. If it goes as well as we hope, the cash needs would go up pretty fast. I'd guess ten or twelve million for the first couple of years, maybe more if things go really well, and another seven or eight million for the third year."

"And how would this work? Would it be a gift or a loan or would we buy stock in your company?"

"Some combination of those, I guess. I haven't thought that through."

"I understand. But you know, it's not like losing that kind of money would risk our lifestyle or retirement. And, some day you and your sister will inherit a lot. That's probably a long way off—I'm only 63. Giving you some money now could be a lot better than having you inherit it in twenty or thirty years. So, it's not out of the question, but I need to talk to your mom before we go any further."

Cindy and I talked it over. We didn't want to leave David in suspense too long, but we wanted to figure out what would be best for our family. By the next afternoon we were ready to talk to him. I asked Cindy, "Do you want to do the talking or should I?"

"You start off, but I'll chip in at some point."

We met with David. Cindy and I were nervous. We'd never talked about money with the kids. They knew we had a lot, but we'd never given them much and never talked to them about how much we had.

"So," I said, "your mom and I have talked about the biotech thing. Here's what we want to offer: we will give you shares in our REIT worth ten million dollars and, after you buy control of the company, we will match whatever new money you put into it. For example, if you put in three million dollars, then we'd do the same; the company would get six million and we'd get the same number of new shares as you. Since you'd buy up the existing shares first with your own money, you'd always have more shares than us and have control. If the company does well, we'll do well too, like a junior partner.

"That is very, very generous. I was thinking of just a loan."

"We talked about that but, you know, it doesn't make sense for you to owe us money. It makes more sense to give you some now."

Cindy chimed in. "Yes, look at it as an advance on your inheritance. We'll do something for your sister too. We're not sure what, but we'll do something to be fair to her."

"Thanks," David said. "I'd thought about that too. Right now, Julie and Nathan don't want any more help from you; they want to make it on their own."

"And one more thing," Cindy said. "I want to make sure this isn't going to hurt our relationship with you. We hope your business is a great success. But if it isn't, we will not regret helping you and we will not put you down or make you feel bad about losing the money. It may seem like a lot of money to you, and for most families it would be, but it's not much for us. Our only concern is that if you lose the money, we don't want you to be ashamed or worry that we might think less of you. We know this has a lot of risk. If it fails, please, please remember this conversation and know that we still love you as much as ever."

"I love you too, both of you. And not just because of this."

In June 2007, David bought out the original AutoimuneX investors. They'd owned 80% of the company, and three key scientists owned the other 20%. The company was running out of money. The investors weren't willing to put more in, and neither they nor the scientists could find any other source of funds. After David got control, he invested two million dollars in new shares. Cindy and I matched that, so the company got four million dollars to continue its scientific work. The frictions among the investors and scientists were solved. The next phase of research was funded.

We offered to give Julie ten million dollars or put that much in a trust for her. "Oh Dad," she said, "you've already been so generous on our house. We couldn't have afforded such a nice place on our own. Just because you gave us what, half a million dollars, for that didn't mean you had to rush out and give David half a million too. You helped us first. Now it's David's turn. At some point we may need your help, but right now we're doing fine." So, we didn't do anything more for Julie.

We told my parents about David's business adventure and how proud we were of him. They probably were proud too, but Dad said, "Son, it's fine to help your kid but what about your sister? Have you set up that trust fund?"

"Oh, Dad, I'm sorry. I haven't yet but I will, soon, right away."

"You've been saying that for years. I'm 91 now. I'm not in good health, you know. It needs to get done. Please, please do it now."

"OK, OK," I said.

Love, Mark

# # # #

June 7, 2013

Dear Mark,

Giving one kid half a million dollars to buy a house, and then giving the other ten million dollars to buy a company, and then offering the first one another ten million dollars, that's crazy. I remember when Mom couldn't come up with enough to buy food.

Yes, I worried about Mom backsliding into drugs again, but nobody ever talked to me about it. It was like the subject was taboo.

High school went better. I was in Advanced Placement classes and they were great, like your Honors classes. I got into track and cross country. Dating? No, guys were mainly looking for girls who would "put out" and, like I said, I was brought up to believe sex was dirty, disgusting, no fun at all. Watching girls get "all gaga" over boys was hard, even when they weren't really doing anything yet. When they talked about making out and going farther, well, it made me want to puke.

And it was hard remembering to be "prim and proper" all the time, acting like an upper middle-class kid. It is tiring to be "on stage" all the time.

I know you love your son, and all this about him buying a business is interesting, but does it have anything to do with what you are in prison for?

Love, Katy

# # # #

June 14, 2013

Dear Katy

Yes, David's purchase of AutoimuneX did have a lot to do with me being here, but it's not his fault.

I understand about the Advanced Placement classes. I've never forgotten how challenging and fun it was to have classes full of smart kids who wanted to learn, with great teachers who knew how to teach. It's very cool to be in a place where being smart and working hard are OK.

I know you feel it's hard sometimes, acting "prim and proper," smooth and sophisticated, middle class. You do it very well; I've only seen you "slip" a couple of times. But why is it so important not to slip? There's no reason to be ashamed of your childhood. Quite the opposite. You should be proud of how far you've come.

One thing has been bothering me, though. I hope you don't mind me asking this, but did your mom have brain damage or learning disabilities from all the drugs she took?

The AutoimuneX research was going well. David sold more of the REIT stock we'd given him and invested another two million dollars in it. Cindy and I matched that.

In November 2007, David and Kaitlyn came up for Thanksgiving. Kevin and his wife came by to see them. Kevin had big news. They were moving back to Bellevue and he was going to work for the U.S. Attorney in Seattle. He'd been a top graduate from the Law School at UC Berkeley and gone to work for a big Wall Street law firm. Those are the highest paid, most sought-after jobs for new law graduates, but that kind of work isn't for everybody.

"Hey, we're really glad to have you back. But why the change? What brings you back?"

"Oh, the usual. The work was dull, little contact with clients, long hours, long commutes, no social life, no way to raise kids. New York was exciting for a year or so, but it's no place to live and raise a family."

"And why the U.S. Attorney's office?"

"Well, I'm burned out on Wall Street kinds of stuff. I thought about what I want to do and kept coming back to public interest, public policy stuff. But I didn't want to start as a Congressional staffer. My dad could have fixed that up of course, but I wanted to do something on my own."

"So, you applied to the U.S. Attorney?" David asked.

"Yeah. He'd known me since I was a kid, and of course my dad helped get him the job. It's not like I got away from Dad completely."

"You're well qualified," I said.

"Oh, my resume is good, so I could have gotten on with a US Attorney somewhere, but I wanted to get back to the Northwest."

David said, "It's neat to have you back. Kaitlyn and I get up here every few months and it'll be fun to get together."

"Mark and I are glad to have you back, too," said Cindy. "We hope you'll come visit us too sometimes."

Kevin laughed. "Hey, we gotta see my parents once in a while, so that would make coming across the lake much more, ah, appealing."

I winced. "Come on, your dad's not so bad."

"That was kind of a joke. He's OK. But you guys, you're still my favorite people."

Katy, how was college? Any better?

Love, Mark

# # # #

June 21, 2013

Dear Mark,

The Andersons wanted me to go to Stanford. Mr. Anderson said my SATs and grades were good enough and he had connections with the admissions people. But Mom went to the UW. It seemed too risky to go away and leave her alone. The college scene is full of drugs and I didn't want to risk her getting back into that. She was more fragile than people realized, and I had kind of taken care of her ever since she got addicted. It was safer for us to stay together.

College went well. I fitted in better than in high school. I got good grades without working very hard, so the academic side wasn't stressful. The party scene didn't appeal to me. I still didn't date much, no serious boyfriends.

The Andersons came over to see Mom and me every week. One day they were surprised to see us playing chess. They asked about it and Mom said, "I always thought it was good for the brain. We've played since Katy was eight."

"Oh," said Mrs. Anderson. "We play bridge. Would you like to learn?" They taught us bridge and we played whenever they came over. It gave us a chance to be together without feeling like we were being inspected again and grilled for information.

Mom does not have any brain damage. She did very well in her GED classes and her undergraduate and graduate work.

While she was an undergrad, she worked nights doing medical records transcription, thinking she could just sit in a back room with earphones on, quietly keyboard away, and not have to deal with the public or co-workers. She was shy and insecure after we got off the streets. But she is strong and determined, and the FARRS social training helped. She made friends, got into a running club, volunteered as a Big Sister, had some of her tattoos removed. That hurts and leaves scars, but it was easier having people ask if she'd been burned than asking about the "tats".

She stayed in school and got a masters' degree in computer science. Now she manages the IT system for a major hospital. She is very smart. She gave me good genes.

I'm not ashamed of my childhood but I don't like to talk about it. I am just kind of a private person, I guess. And lots of people pity me if they hear about it. Others smirk, like they are titillated about sex and drugs. I do not like being pitied or being smirked at. Would you?

I am proud of my mom and everything she has accomplished. And I am proud of myself too, even though you seem to think I am not.

I hope you are not too disappointed that I was so angry during those first few years in the FARRS program. But people were working so hard to change me, I couldn't help but feel they must think something was wrong with the way I was. Why else would it be so important to change me?

But I should not complain so much about that time. Of course, there was a lot of good stuff too. Being clean and safe and warm was very cool. I never wanted to go back to the streets. But the risk that Mom or I might screw up and get us sent back, well, that was hanging over our heads all the time.

So, I felt a lot of stress but also a lot of gratitude at the same time. Is it inconsistent to be grateful and angry about the same things at the same time?

Love, Katy

# # # #

June 28, 2013

Dear Katy

You didn't miss much by not getting into the party scene and living with your mom is nothing to be ashamed about. It was a very kind and caring thing to do. It sounds like sometimes it was hard to tell which of you was the parent, but if the roles got switched back when she was addicted, well, I can see how they might kind of stay that way.

It's good that you can express how angry the FARRS program made you. And, no, it isn't inconsistent to be grateful and angry about the same things at the same time. Lots of times that happens. Like, for instance, when your kids are out late and you've been up worrying and hoping they're OK. When they walk in the door you don't know whether you'll hug them or yell at them. You're mad but love them more than ever.

I'm glad your mom didn't have any brain damage. Maybe she got clean in time or just got lucky. She may have been kind of shy, but it must have taken a lot of guts to keep going to school. She would have been older than most of her classmates, so college probably didn't give her much of a social life. You're too modest to say it, but it looks to me like your support made her successes possible.

Like I said before, you shouldn't be ashamed about your childhood or your mom. You should be very, very proud about how much you've accomplished and how you helped your mom recover and thrive as a sober, clean, productive adult.

We talked to a lot of experts when we were designing the FARRS program, but you've brought up things we never thought about. It's too bad I can't use your input to make the program better. We always focused on the positive, the benefits we could provide parents and kids. We thought parents would feel good that their good behavior was helping get benefits for their kids, and kids would feel good that their good behavior was helping get benefits for their parents. We never realized there was a dark side to it, how much pressure the program put on them. We didn't understand how hard it is for people like your mom and you to accept help and trust people who are trying to help.

Katy, I think we should meet in person again. It's been a long time.

Love, Mark

Tenth meeting

I met with Mark on July 5, 2013. We had not met since January 9. A lot of changes had been happening in my life.

Mom had settled into her IT management job. She was the healthiest I had ever seen her. At 42, with her unique combination of "hard knock" life experiences, cultural makeover under FARRS, and advanced degree in IT, she had quickly become a valued and respected employee at the hospital. She was excited about her new responsibilities and challenges, making new friends, enjoying her professional successes and financial independence. She was saving to buy a house or condo. I still lived with her, but she no longer needed me. We had not talked about it yet but, at some point, we would need to decide if I would continue living with her or we would each live on our own for the first time.

Also, I had started dating an assistant professor in the business school, Dr. Brandon Moore. Some of our friends had a bridge group and sometimes they needed a "fourth". They were into competitive duplicate bridge. I felt like a fool the first few times I played with them, so I studied bridge books and websites and became a much better player. Brandon also subbed sometimes. After the group got to know us as individual players, sometimes they would call both of us when they needed another couple to fill out a table. Then one of the regular couples moved away and we became regulars. Our friends started to think of us as a couple. We laughed about that at first, but we started seeing each other outside of the bridge group. It was a surprise, to me at least, when we started kissing and then making out. He knew I had no sexual experience and was very gentle and patient with me. I kept thinking about Mark's advice: go slow and be old fashioned as long as you can. We had not become intimate yet, but things seemed to be heading in that direction.

Finally, I had not looked forward to meeting with Mark because it seemed that most of our meetings went badly. This meeting went better for a while, but then it took an odd twist:

> MK: It's been a long time. Have you been avoiding me?
>
> KTA: Well, kind of. You always seem to want to talk about my childhood and my mom, and I want to about you, so we are never on the same page.

MK: OK, I won't do that this time. I won't ask for more information about your past. It's time to talk about the present and future.

KTA: Thanks, but what do you mean by that?

MK: Early on, I said you seemed to have an angry streak in you. I couldn't figure that out for a long time, but I think I understand it now.

KTA: Let's not get into that. You're doing the same thing again, making this about me.

MK: Not really. I've been struggling to suppress anger too, you know.

KTA: What are you are talking about?

MK: I'm talking about how both of us deal with anger, try to suppress it. That doesn't work. You can't just will it to go away.

KTA: Jesus, Mark, this is way off topic. Can't we get back to your career and legal problems and all that?

MK: Look, you don't want to think about how angry you are about your forced makeover, or how hard it is to keep being somebody so radically different from who you started out to be. I don't like to think about how mad I am about getting screwed by the legal system. But we ought to deal with these things.

KTA: You're not my counselor.

MK: No, and I shouldn't be. But maybe you ought to find a good one.

KTA: But you don't need one, right? You've got life all figured out.

MK: Maybe not everything, but as far as anger management goes, I'm probably doing a little better than you are.

KTA: I can't believe this. Where are you coming from? This is like FARRS all over. You think there is something wrong with me, that I need another makeover?

MK: Katy, I'm trying to help you. I care about you, care about you a lot. You work so hard trying to be prissy, prim, poised and perfect, always in control. You must be exhausted. You don't have to be so perfect all the time. You're a wonderful person. Can't you just relax and feel good about yourself?

KTA: Look, you're no different. You pretend to be just fine, strong, in control, looking at everything with a wry, bemused detachment, but, really, sometimes you are barely holding yourself together.

MK: Touché. But what I'm doing is healthy. What you're doing is hurting you.

KTA: This is so inappropriate. I should never have told you so much about my personal life. We need to get on to your criminal case and trial. You have been turning this into something like Scheherazade: is this going to go on for 1001 nights? It's been over two years. I need to get my dissertation finished.

CHAPTER 7

GETTING BACK TO BUSINESS AND INTO TROUBLE

July 12, 2013

Dear Katy

Early in 2008 our economic teams felt a dangerous bubble was building in single family housing markets. Countrywide Financial, the biggest US housing lender, was taken over for a small fraction of what it had been worth just months before. It was known for high risk loans and most people thought "conventional" and FHA-insured loans were still very safe, but Sharon thought the risks were higher than people realized.

Our REIT was mainly in commercial real estate: office buildings, shopping centers, malls, warehouses. But Sharon said if a bubble in single family homes did burst, commercial properties would be hurt too, partly because people who lost jobs would cut other spending to keep up with their house payments. We thought a commercial property recession would be shallow and short, like the ones we'd been through before. Boy, were we wrong about that!

In March 2008, Bear Stearns, an investment bank, got in trouble; Chase took it over, with help (or pressure) from the Federal Reserve. I told Olaf Johansson, by then a leading member of the Senate Finance Committee, that we were worried. He said, "Paulson and his people brought some ideas to our committee. It's pretty much under the radar, but they're concerned." He was referring to Henry Paulson, Secretary of the Treasury. So, people at the highest level of government were worried too. The news media and business community seemed blissfully unaware of the risks, but Olaf's comments reinforced our decision to get ready for another downturn.

As we'd done before, we cut back on new investments, paid down debt, got more liquid. If we'd we done only that, we'd have made a lot money from the Great Recession, but we also started working on a large borrowing.

Dad died in June. He'd worked hard to provide for us kids and was a good dad in lots of ways. I loved him, but I never told him that. For years I'd wanted to be closer to him, but he wasn't a guy you could get close too. So, I grieved over his death and felt guilty about not setting up a trust fund for my sister. I got our lawyer working on that.

David and Kaitlyn came home for the 4th of July weekend. The weather was beautiful. We all enjoyed ourselves, but something was on David's mind. I asked him, "Why so serious? Everything going OK with the company?"

"Oh, the company is doing fine, very fine. It looks like we may want to up our spending sooner than we thought."

"That's good. Early on you said the better things went the faster you'd want to spend."

"Yeah, that's true. I'll run out of REIT shares in a year or two, so we need to start looking for new investors. I don't want to risk running out of cash."

"That's wise. But you don't need to look for new investors yet. Your mom and I could give you another five or ten million and then keep matching whatever you put in the company, so you can concentrate on running it. Can't we, Cindy?

"Sure. I think you should have enough cash for a couple of years, maybe more."

"I think so too," he said. "I'm kind of worried about the stock market. The REIT shares quit going up and it looks like they're starting to drift down. Of course, you know a lot more about that than I do."

I said, "Well, I won't make any recommendations on when to sell or how much to sell. But we do see some turmoil coming in the next couple of quarters, and we're gearing up to take advantage of opportunities that will come along after that."

"What do you mean? Are you talking a recession or anything like that?"

"Well, we think there's kind of a bubble in single family housing which could spread to commercial properties for a while. We've always made our best deals during slumps. We're getting ready to make a lot of money from the next one."

"But are you saying that it's likely to go down before the, ah, opportunities get here?"

"Yeah, of course, that's the way it always works. But most of the downs are rather short, a year or two, maybe a little more."

"That's a pretty long time for us. We're burning through cash. A year or two slump could be very painful for us."

Cindy chimed in, "Yes, we've thought about that at the Foundation too. If the economy gets bad, the needs for non-profit services go up. We probably should be getting more liquid too."

I said, "OK, OK, enough talk about business. Let's get some steaks on the grill. Anybody need another beer?"

Cindy said, "Yes, let's relax and enjoy the holiday. It's back to work tomorrow."

So, Katy, does that sound like a big-time financial crime to you? Should I be locked up in here because of a simple family conversation like that? You're not going to figure that out by studying me. You want answers? Go study law, political science, that kind of stuff.

It still makes me so mad. I think I'm over it, think I've been able to move on, and then I think about how this mess started and get mad all over again. But I'll try to calm down. I'll try to explain it, Katy. But if it doesn't make sense to you, well, it doesn't make sense to me either.

The next Monday Cindy and I transferred another 600,000 REIT shares to David's brokerage account. We could have given him cash. Our net worth was nearly two billion dollars. But we'd given David REIT shares before, so we did it again without thinking about the problems that might cause.

A week or so later David called and said he was putting another five million dollars into his company. "Can you match it?"

"Sure," I said, and wired his company five million dollars.

The lawyer finally got Lucy's trust put together. We transferred REIT shares worth ten million dollars to it. Part of the trust income would pay for her care and a small allowance for her to spend. The rest would be donated to the nonprofit organization that provided her care. The lawyer said, "I advise you to diversity the trust investments. As trustee, you have an obligation to do that and if you don't, the beneficiary could sue you."

"Well, my sister isn't going to do that."

"No, but her guardian might."

"My mom's her guardian now, and after that it's me."

"Yes, but if something went wrong an independent guardian might be appointed. I'm advising you to diversify."

So, I had the trust sell six million dollars of REIT shares and put the money in conservative stuff.

We donated another forty million worth of our REIT shares to the Foundation. The non-profits it supported had already started to see increased needs for their services.

On August 1, 2008, our REIT borrowed $850 million. We wouldn't be investing in more properties anytime soon, but we had to put that (and other cash) to work where it would get a decent return until it was time to buy distressed properties again. We put nearly a billion dollars into mortgage-backed securities. They were very liquid; hundreds of millions of dollars of them changed hands every day. We had a team of experts buying and selling them, and we were one of the most elite firms in this business. The risks seemed low and manageable.

We disclosed our borrowing to the Securities and Exchange Commission and issued a press release. Security analysts asked for more information. You can't give some investors more information than others, so we held a press conference. We explained the steps we'd taken to get more liquid, ready for opportunities we expected to come in the next few quarters. People asked if we thought there would be a recession, how deep it might be, how long it might last, and how it might affect distributions to our REIT shareholders. We said we expected a brief "dip" and our funds from operations would be a little lower until we made major new investments, but we intended to maintain our REIT distributions and could easily do that.

Our REIT shares had been selling for over fourteen dollars. They started falling when we announced the borrowing. We hoped the press conference would reassure investors, but it didn't. I was frustrated that investors were so short-sighted. I said to Cindy, "Why won't they just ride out the downturns? The market always recovers pretty quickly."

She was more philosophical. "Sometimes the short term is more important for some people. Look at David. Last month he sold seven million dollars of REIT shares to make sure he had enough liquidity for the next couple of years."

"I thought it was five million."

"No, he put five million into AutoimuneX, but he sold five hundred thousand REIT shares at a little over fourteen dollars, so he raised over seven million. He put the rest in treasury bills, safe and liquid, so he wouldn't have to worry about the market for the next year or so. Right now, I bet he's glad he did."

"I didn't know that. But you're right; right now he's probably glad he did it."

"And the Foundation did the same thing. Last month we sold thirty million dollars of REIT shares."

"Oh, I didn't know that. When?"

"A few days after David did. I meant to tell you about it, but we were so busy."

"Yeah, things have been hectic."

"But we talked about it with David on the 4th of July. Remember? Not the number of shares or dollars, of course, but his need to keep AutoimuneX liquid and the Foundation's need to be ready for a downturn."

"Well, I didn't know either of you was seriously thinking about selling so many REIT shares. Still, like you say, right now it looks like you were pretty smart. If a slump comes, though, we'll make a lot of money, just like we've done before."

Love, Mark

# # # #

July 19, 2013

Dear Mark,

Would you have borrowed the $850 million if your dad hadn't died or had tried to talk you out of it? Would Heinz and Eeko have tried to talk you out of it if they hadn't retired?

Love, Katy

# # # #

July 26, 2013

Dear Katy

Dad never approved of any borrowings, so I quit telling him about them. Part of me is glad, though, he didn't live to see everything blow up the way it did, the way he worried it would.

Would Heinz and Eeko have tried to talk me out of the big borrowing? I don't think so. They supported all our earlier borrowings. Anyway, it was my decision and I won't blame it on them or anybody else.

In hindsight, borrowing that money looks like a huge mistake. Still, the basic idea was good. We just did it a few months too early and we parked the money in the wrong place. But nobody could see what was coming.

On September 15, 2008, Lehman Brothers went bankrupt. This rocked the world. The worldwide financial system was collapsing. Nobody knew what was happening. It was impossible to sell many investments, especially mortgage-backed securities. Washington Mutual, the country's largest home lender went under; Chase took it over for pennies on the dollar. The government took over Fannie Mae and Freddy Mac, semi-government firms that issued mortgage-backed securities. A subsidiary of American International Group, a big insurance company, had guaranteed a lot of them, and the government had to take over AIG too.

This Great Recession hit our REIT hard. Our expenses were up but less money was coming in. We signed contracts to sell undeveloped land, but the buyers couldn't get financing or sell other properties so most of those fell through. Newer buildings could be sold only at huge losses. Some older buildings could be sold for a "paper profit," but they were our biggest sources of cash and earnings.

The REIT paid Inova management fees based on the value of its assets. We wrote down its asset values, which reduced the REIT's costs but hurt Inova.

We notified the SEC that we couldn't file the REIT's quarterly report on time because it was impossible to determine the fair value of its assets. The REIT shares dropped below seven dollars, down more than half in three months.

Our key managers and I worked seventy and eighty hours a week, scrambling to find money and send it where it was needed the most. The hardest part was knowing we'd been almost right: we'd seen that a recession was likely and taken steps to prepare for it, but we'd wildly underestimated how deep it would be and how our "dry powder" would suddenly become illiquid.

Katy, as I told you, business was my life. Normally I loved it. But this time I was desperately trying to save the business I'd built up over more than forty years. And I missed Heinz and Eeko.

Love, Mark

# # # #

Aug. 2, 2013

Dear Katy

One day in mid-October, Cindy and I were in the Bay Area, me for business and her for Foundation meetings. David and Kaitlyn came see us. Cindy and I both gave Kaitlyn a big hug. Cindy hugged David too. David and I kind of nodded at each other. We hadn't hugged since he was about ten and shaking hands seemed awkward. It's a guy thing.

Cindy noticed a ring on Kaitlyn's hand. I didn't notice it. Another guy thing, I guess. "So, you've got something exciting to tell us," Cindy said, grinning.

Kaitlyn looked at her hand and then back at Cindy and me. "Oops! I guess we gave the surprise away."

Cindy said, "Congratulations anyway. We're happy for you, both of you. When's the date?"

"No date yet. Probably after school's out in June." Then Kaitlyn said, "Mark, you look tired."

"Things have been hectic."

"I bet," David said. "I've been reading the papers. Are you worried?"

"Not worried, just frustrated. There are so many great opportunities out there right now, and we can't take advantage of them. We were so right; we did so many things right, but we borrowed too early and parked the money in the wrong place.

Still, Congress and the Administration are trying to unfreeze the mortgage bond market. We'll have to take some losses, but if we can get some cash there are spectacular deals out there. When it's over we'll make a lot of money from all this. How's things at AutoimuneX?"

"Good, good. I'm working hard too, but it's OK, I'm not complaining. And when I talk to other startup CEOs, they all tell me how lucky I am to have you and Mom backing us. They spend most of their time raising money and trying to keep their investors happy. I've been very, very lucky having you and Mom back us."

"We're very proud of you and it's exciting for us to watch and try to help."

"You've been tremendous. But, you know, maybe I've been a little spoiled, the money coming so easy. I need to develop skills of making pitches to investors and reassuring them. Maybe we should have more formal board meetings, where I treat you and mom more like strangers, you know, like ordinary investors who don't know me. Make sense?"

"Yes, it does. At some point you may want to bring in outside investors, and you'll need to 'sell' your products and your intellectual property and, of course, sell yourself. It takes practice."

"Yeah, I better brush up on PowerPoint."

In late November 2008, Sharon came to my office, closed the door, and burst into tears. "I'm so sorry. I should have known the mortgage bond market might freeze up. I should have warned you not to buy those mortgage-backed securities."

"No, no, Sharon. Nobody blames you. Not me or the Board or anybody. Nobody saw this coming. Don't blame yourself."

"I can't help it. I keep waking up in the middle of the night thinking I should have seen it coming, should have warned you. I, I just don't know if I can keep on going. Maybe I should retire."

"Please don't do that. How about a vacation. Why don't you guys get away for a couple of weeks. Go someplace with beaches and no cell phones, no internet, no news."

"How about you? Are you going to do that?"

"No, I've got too much work to do, a lot of people to cheer up. But we shouldn't make any big decisions for the next few weeks, so why don't you go rest up? When you come back, we'll know more, and we can make decisions then."

She and her husband went to a small island in the eastern Caribbean, without cell phone or internet coverage. It's harder to find places like that now, people are so attached to their devices. Today you'd have to go to a monastery in Tibet or something to get away like that.

I tried and tried to cheer up our employees. Many asked me what was going to happen. The only thing I could say was, "I don't know, but we will get through this, we'll be OK." I believed that.

I kept trying to think up jokes that might make people at work laugh. It's not easy to make jokes about financial disasters and you know I'm not much of a comedian. Well, even the best comedians probably couldn't have done much to cheer up our employees at that point. But we were only scared about losing money, not about going to jail.

Love, Mark

# # # #

Aug. 9, 2013

Dear Mark,

I have been thinking about what you said. I have been angry. I have become a perfectionist. I do feel like I am "on stage" all the time and can never let my guard down, never be out of character. But this is not the time to deal with that. I need to get my dissertation done.

Thank you for your last two letters. I appreciate you trying to get this project wrapped up for me.

Love, Katy

# # # #

Aug. 16, 2013

Dear Katy

For once the Federal government moved pretty quickly. On October 3 Congress passed and President Bush signed the "Emergency Economic Stabilization Act." It created a "Troubled Asset Relief Program," called the TARP. Olaf Johansson was heavily involved in shaping it.

The TARP provided seven hundred billion dollars to buy "toxic assets," so companies could sell mortgage-backed securities and the cash could be recycled into other investments. That's what we desperately needed. That's what Congress said the money would be used for. If the agencies had done that, I wouldn't be here today.

But less than two weeks later President Bush and Treasury Secretary Paulson diverted most of the TARP money to bail out big banks. I called Olaf Johansson's office several times, but he never called back. Finally, I got him at home on his personal cell phone, told him how concerned I was about the direction the TARP was going, and asked him to help get it back on track. He was evasive, wouldn't promise anything. We'd been friends for many years. I thought maybe he was avoiding me because of what Kevin said at the rehearsal dinner. Now I realize he was involved in very confidential talks at very high levels, with the Secretary of the Treasury, Chair of the Federal Reserve Board, even the President. This mess was bigger than our friendship, too big for him to do me any favors or risk anybody thinking he had.

Instead of buying mortgage-backed securities, the government spent hundreds of billions to buy preferred stock in big banks and AIG, which was good for them but didn't do squat for our REIT or other companies like ours. Later, a little TARP money was diverted to help homebuyers who owed more on their mortgages than the houses were worth. That didn't help us. Finally, the Obama administration used the rest of the TARP money to bail out General Motors and Chrysler. That didn't help us either.

Katy, I'm not saying these decisions were bad for the country. The financial system stabilized. The government got nearly all the TARP money back. Auto industry jobs were saved. The recession was sharp and deep, but stock prices bottomed in March and began to recover in April 2009, only eight months after Lehman Brothers collapsed. For most of the economy the recovery has continued for years now.

But the real estate industry was hung out to dry. Maybe the big banks and car companies had better political connections and lobbyists. Maybe our industry became scapegoats because people thought we caused the crisis. Maybe it was easier to bail out a few big banks and two huge car companies than help the thousands of small companies in our industry. Home prices and commercial real estate kept falling until 2012.

Big decisions had to be made quickly. I understand that. I try not to be bitter. But, you know, deep down I can't help feeling it wasn't fair. It wasn't fair to me, or our investors, or a lot of other people.

It wasn't just a few rich people who got hurt. Most of our REIT shares were owned by pension funds, insurance companies, non-profits like colleges and charities and hospitals. The collapse of our REIT hurt millions of people, most of whom had never heard of us.

Did I make mistakes? Of course. I'm not trying to make excuses. I'm just saying the government started out with a program that would have helped us. If they'd stuck with it, we could have survived and thrived. But somehow it morphed into a bailout for a few big banks, one big insurance company, and two big car companies. Nobody paid much attention to how much we little folks were suffering.

Love, Mark

# # # #

Aug. 23, 2013

Dear Mark,

It seems odd for a billionaire to think of himself as a "little folk." Still, I do not mean to make fun of you.

I understand you feel the government turned its back on the real estate industry. I guess it is hard to really own a politician. Rumor is you can rent them, though.

Love, Katy

# # # #

Aug. 30, 2013

Dear Katy

Good one on politicians. I like to see you lighten up, even on stuff that is painful for me.

I told Jim Hawthorne, who had retired from United American but still was active as a consultant on its political affairs, "I struck out on getting Olaf to help on the financial crisis."

"Us too. He won't talk to me and his staff won't talk to our lobbyists."

"I'm thinking we may have to go to Buddy Graves. He's not much into financial stuff, but he's our Congressmen. Your company and mine are the biggest financial institutions in his district."

"Yeah, we're thinking that too. The government's bailing out AIG because it's 'systemically important', but they're not lifting a finger for regional insurers like us."

"Exactly. And the TARP was supposed to create demand for mortgage-backed securities, which would help my REIT and your company."

"We've got tens of billions in MBSs, far more than you."

"And that's supposed to comfort me?" We were both too stressed for jokes like that. But he was right. United American had more invested in mortgage-backed securities than our REIT did.

"Our folks are working on a PowerPoint presentation for Buddy and his staff. He's got a tough election next month, especially with his divorce." Buddy had been caught with his pants off again, and this time Nikki had filed for divorce and called the news media.

"Good, good. I'll have Sharon put one together too. Can you call Buddy to set up a meeting?"

But before Jim had a chance to do that, Buddy called and asked me to meet him at his district office. "I'll explain why when you get there."

My next call was from Jim Hawthorne. "Buddy wants to meet next Wednesday at 2:00."

"I got the same call, same meeting, same time. What do you think this is about?"

"Well, there is nothing more important for either of us, or the country, than the financial crisis. It must be that."

But it wasn't. Buddy started the meeting by saying, "Thanks for coming. I need your help. I've got a tough election next month and the environmental groups are putting a lot of pressure on me to support demolition of the United American headquarters building."

Jim and I were stunned. "What?"

"They say it's a blight on the Gorge. Why should one of the most popular state parks have a big office building hanging over it?"

Jim said, "Well, they've got it backwards, Buddy. United American and Mark created the park. It wouldn't be there if it weren't for us."

"Ancient history. Most of my constituents are too young to remember that."

"Well, we can work together to educate them."

"No, I haven't got time. I promised them I'd try to get your support. They'll help us get federal money for the demolition if we'll support their cause."

"But there's thousands of tons of steel and concrete and glass suspended over the gorge. You're talking tens of millions of dollars just for the demolition, and over a hundred million to build us a replacement building."

"Chump change for the feds. We'll bury it in an Appropriations committee report. The only people who will know about it are the ones who support it. You know how these things work."

Jim and I refused to help get the United American headquarters building demolished, Buddy got re-elected anyway, but my relationship with him got even more strained. Still, is that a good enough reason for him not to help get me out of here?

Love, Mark

# # # #

Sept. 6, 2013

Dear Katy

In December I got a call from a man at the Securities and Exchange Commission. He said the SEC was looking into the real estate crisis, trying to figure out what had happened and what might be done to help our industry. He asked if I could spend a couple of hours with him to discuss the state of the industry. I said sure.

I didn't tell Brett Jamison or any of our other lawyers about the meeting. I didn't have anything to hide. I didn't think he was investigating me or thinking I might be a suspect or anything like that. Now I know this was naïve, but I was tired and worried and looking for somebody to listen and help me understand what was going on. The world had become so topsy-turvy. I wasn't thinking clearly.

The SEC guy was a well-dressed, articulate young man, about the same age as David, late twenties probably, soft spoken, somewhat shy, polite and deferential. He seemed a little in awe of me. He probably was—he'd probably never talked to a billionaire before. I'd always gotten along well with my kids and their friends and other young people. I was really good at establishing a rapport with smart young people like him.

We talked for an hour and a half or so about the real estate business, how the Lehman Brothers bankruptcy triggered a liquidity crisis, how nobody seemed to know what to do about it, how we'd hoped the TARP would be a big help until it morphed into something that didn't help to us or our industry. The same stuff I've told you.

He asked me when I first began to think that a recession might be coming. I explained how early in 2008 we'd become concerned about sub-prime home loans, how our concerns grew after Countrywide collapsed, how we thought a single-family housing bubble might burst and spread to commercial properties. He kept nodding and encouraging me to go on. I didn't see a trap coming.

Then he asked me what we'd done to "adjust" or prepare for a recession. Again, I told him the same things I've told you, how we quit taking on speculative new projects, quit buying land, conserved cash, began working toward the large borrowing we did in August.

He asked who I'd talked to over the summer about that borrowing. I said, "Well, our Board of course, our senior managers, investment bankers, lawyers. You can't borrow $850 million without talking to a lot of people."

"Of course, of course. I meant securities analysts, major investors, people like that."

"No, these things are very confidential. I suppose the Bank of America folks must have talked to firms that might take pieces of the loan—this was a syndication deal with a bunch of banks—but I wasn't involved in any of that."

"How about friends and family? You must have a pretty active social life, see a lot of people, friends, business acquaintances, people like that."

"Well, I try not to mix business and social stuff. Our lawyers have me trained not to blab about stuff that hasn't been made public yet. So, no, I don't think I talked to anybody about it before the public announcement."

"How about your wife? I understand she's on your Board and also the boards your Foundation and knows a lot of rich folks. Do you think she might have talked to people about it?"

"No. She's very focused on her charity stuff. She doesn't pay much attention to the business except the last day or so before our Board meetings. Then she'll study hard, ask questions at the meeting, participate in discussions, vote, and forget about it until a day or two before the next meeting. The only time I remember her talking about business between Board meetings is last 4th of July when we talked about this stuff a little with our son, David."

The meeting wound down and he left. It was a very friendly meeting. He seemed genuinely interested in me and our industry and the struggles we were going through. I thought it went well. I liked the guy.

A few days later I told Brett Jamison about the meeting. He was upset. "You met with an SEC investigator? Alone, without a lawyer?"

"Yeah, but he wasn't investigating me. We talked about conditions in the industry, a little bit about how we prepared for the recession, the crash. I'm not a suspect or anything like that."

"Maybe not, or at least not yet. But I can picture you trying to charm the socks off the guy. It's dangerous, Mark. For such a successful person, sometimes you can be so damn naïve. Don't you ever watch cop shows on TV? Whatever you say can be used against you, and all that?"

"Brett, Brett, take off your lawyer hat a minute. I've been working hard. Really stressed. I needed to talk to somebody. He was a good listener. I liked the kid. I haven't done anything wrong. I haven't got anything to hide. It'll be alright. Nothing bad will come from this."

"I hope you're right, I really do."

So, Katy, I guess I did try to charm the SEC guy. But it wasn't part of some evil scheme. I just wanted a little sympathy. I just wanted somebody to try to understand me.

The whole family was together for Christmas. David and Kaitlyn came up from Los Angeles. Julie and our grandson, Major, flew in from New York. Nathan didn't come. Julie said he was busy at work and would join us before New Year's.

I was exhausted. Our REIT shares kept drifting down, with a little bump up when the TARP was announced but another slide after the TARP money got diverted away from the kinds of assets we needed to sell. For a while Cindy and I tried to support the REIT share price by buying more shares ourselves. Then, when the REIT almost ran out of cash, we bought new shares directly from it, by borrowing from our brokerage account. Our personal margin debt soared to nearly a hundred million dollars. Still, we expected to make a lot of money from this in a few years. We were buying REIT shares for a third of what they'd cost a few months before.

Of course, we filed the required notices with the SEC showing how many shares we bought and what we paid for them. Normally, such "insider purchases" boost share prices, but the price of our REIT shares kept going down, down, down.

Cindy was tired too. Contributions to the Foundation, and the non-profits it supported, had fallen a lot.

Still, we had a lot to be thankful for. David's business was going well. Kaitlyn had a good job lined up at an architecture and urban planning firm. Julie was taking a new job at Nordstrom. She and Major, who was seven, would be moving back to Seattle in January. Nathan was not coming, though. His company downsized and let him go just before Christmas, and he decided to stay in New York.

We were optimistic about the incoming Obama administration. It seemed good to have a young, optimistic, smart president, and real estate usually does better under Democrats.

This turned out to be our last Christmas as a family. On January 5 the government filed criminal insider trading charges against David and me and said it was considering charges against the Foundation and Cindy.

I called Brett Jamison. "What do we do?"

"Well, first you all need lawyers."

"What do you mean 'all'? We're in this together."

"No, there may be ethical problems with the same lawyers representing all of you. What's best for one may not be best for the others."

"We're family. You don't think we are going to turn on each other, do you?"

"Not right away, and I hope it doesn't get to that. But when it comes time to talk about deals, your interests may not be the same."

"I don't like it. Lawyers might make it worse, get too aggressive, drive wedges."

"That's why you need them, why each of you needs a different one. You don't have to take their advice, but having different teams looking at it for different clients could open up opportunities you'd never have if one team tried to represent all of you."

"That's probably good advice, but I still don't like it."

"I'm not asking you to like it. You asked for my advice and you got it."

"OK, OK. Can you recommend some people for us?"

"Yes. I'll ask around to see who's most qualified and available. It won't be cheap, you know."

"So, how much are we talking about?"

"Probably about two hundred fifty thousand to get started on the criminal side. Maybe a half million if you can get a good deal quickly, millions if you go to trial. The big bucks will be for the shareholder class action suits. They'll start coming in the next few days."

"But what have they got to go on?"

"Oh, the Feds are giving them enough to get started. Then there'll be massive discovery looking at your records, calendars, emails, hard drives, phone logs, everything."

The first seven class action suits were filed the next day.

We hired white collar criminal defense lawyers for David, Cindy and me, and securities lawyers to defend the class actions: $650 an hour for senior lawyers and up to $300 for associates. We had over a dozen lawyers involved and nothing had really happened yet.

David flew back from Los Angeles. He'd been excited about getting back to AutoimuneX after the holidays. Now suddenly he had to shift from being a CEO to being a defendant in a major federal criminal case. At some level both of us must have known we could end up in prison, but that hadn't really sunk in yet.

On Thursday we met with our defense lawyers. My lawyer summarized the criminal cases: "They say that in July you and Cindy transferred eight point five million dollars of REIT shares from your personal account to David's, knowing the REIT might be headed for financial trouble and was about to borrow $850 million, which had not been publicly disclosed. Then David immediately sold seven million dollars of those REIT shares before there had been any public disclosure of the upcoming borrowing or the REIT's financial problems. About this time, you and Cindy donated forty million dollars of REIT shares to your Foundation, and then it sold thirty million of them almost immediately, again before any such public disclosures. Finally, about this time you set up a trust for your sister, transferred ten million dollars of REIT shares to it, and immediately had it sell six million of those. At all these times Cindy was on the board of Inova Development, which manages your REIT, and of your Foundation, and of AutoimuneX, an untraded private company that David owns, and you were the sole trustee of the trust for your sister. Is all that true?"

"Well, mainly true, but we didn't know the REIT was 'headed for financial trouble' and none of those transfers had anything to do with the borrowing or any concerns about the market. And my sister's trust, I'd promised my dad I'd do that years ago, but didn't get around to it until he died."

David and I turned ourselves in to be booked and fingerprinted the next afternoon. Somebody at the SEC or the U.S. Attorney's office tipped off the press so we were videotaped walking into the courthouse. They call it a "Perp Walk." The tape was played on network news all over the country and viewed over 400,000 times on YouTube. We were being made scapegoats for the whole worldwide financial mess. Utter nonsense. We were victims, not perpetrators.

The only person who seemed to recognize that was a guy who took our fingerprints in the courthouse basement. "Oh boy," he said, "they're going to ream big new ones in you guys."

We were released on our own recognizance. We weren't the sort of people likely to run away. Still, it was awful. Some people, even friends and people we worked with every day, didn't want to look at us. Others went out of their way to get a peep at us. Cindy and I quit going out in public because of people staring, whispering, pointing.

The next week we pled "Not Guilty." It's the first step in the process. Most cases end with a plea bargain, pleading guilty to a lesser crime, often with the prosecutors agreeing to recommend lenient punishment. I was naïve. David and I hoped the prosecutors would drop the charges or, if we had to go to trial, we'd win.

Love, Mark

# # # #

Sept. 13, 2013

Dear Katy

A couple of nights after we pled not guilty, our doorbell rang. Cindy answered it. "Kevin, what a surprise, so good to see you."

David, Kaitlyn, Julie and I all went to greet him. Cindy tried to give him a hug. He put his hands up and said, "Sorry, no hugs tonight." He looked haggard, big black bags under his eyes. "Can't stay long. Can't say much either. But I had to come."

We all sat in the living room, Kevin on a footstool, the rest of us in a semicircle around him. I wanted to lighten things up, so I said: "Kevin, I'd offer you a drink, but I assume you're driving." Nobody laughed. "Sorry, that wasn't much of a joke."

Kevin sat with his elbows on his knees, his head in his hands. Finally, he said to David, "When we first started investigating you and your dad, I told my boss you were my best friend and best man at my wedding."

There was another long silence. David said, "It's OK. Go on."

"And I told him what I'd said about you, Mark, at the rehearsal dinner." After a while he went on. "So, he took me off the case and tried to isolate me from it. He had to do that. And, well, you know, it was best for me ...." He was having a hard time holding it together.

I said, "It's OK, Kevin, we appreciate you coming."

"I can't talk about your case. You know that. I'm not supposed to talk to any of you at all, but I just couldn't, you know, keep avoiding you without any explanation."

David said, "We understand. Like Dad said, we appreciate you coming."

"I know you must be going through hell. Well, I can't imagine, really. But it's been hard for me too. When I walk around the office everybody shuts up. Maybe they want to protect me from having to hear about your case, or maybe they worry that I might tip you off on their strategy. Either way, it's hard. So, I'm getting a transfer. Some other office, some place where I won't run into anybody working on your case."

"Oh, I'm sorry," said Cindy. "We know how much you love the Northwest, how happy you were to get back."

"Yeah, but that's the way it has to be, at least until it's over, your case I mean."

We all sat there for a while, letting it sink in. Everyone's relationship with Kevin and his wife would be suspended and probably never be the same again. Finally, Kevin said, "I can't say any more. I'd better go now."

We all stood up. David hugged Kevin. Then, one by one the rest of us did too. Cindy walked him to the door. Nobody said goodbye.

Except for that, there was kind of a lull after our not guilty pleas. Stuff was going on behind the scenes, of course, but there wasn't a lot for me or David to do. We tried to go back to work, to live normal lives as much as we could, but it was hanging over our heads all the time. I'd wake up thinking it all was a bad dream, and then I'd realize oh, no, it's not.

I was afraid Cindy might start drinking again. I said, "Lookit, we've got really big problems and we've got to stay focused on dealing with them. We can't risk having alcohol screw us up. I'm not going to have another drink until all this is over."

"Me too," David said. "I've been drinking too much. It hurts my stomach and messes up my sleep."

Cindy looked at us both and hesitated. "OK, I know you're doing this because you're worried about me. I admit I wanted to get drunk a few times since this started, but I'm with you guys—drinking would make all this worse. Let's make sure we don't go down that road."

"OK, let's be an alcohol-free house then," said Julie. She was staying with us. She didn't pledge not to drink, and we didn't ask her to. Sometimes she drank with friends after work or when she went out with other people, but she didn't drink at home or in front of us.

I was exhausted. We all were. Cindy and I went to bed earlier than usual, but we hardly ever made love. I thought about getting separate beds, but neither of us wanted to talk about that. When we did make love, it was kind of like taking a prescription, something that was supposed to be good for us but wasn't particularly fun.

I tried to make friends with Major. Cindy and I had seen him a few times a year, sometimes in New York and sometimes at our house, but he didn't really know us. Maybe he was upset about being separated from his dad. Maybe he missed his friends in New York. Maybe he was a little overwhelmed by moving from an 800 square foot Brooklyn apartment to a 7,800 square foot mansion on Lake Washington. Maybe he was just a difficult kid to get to know. Usually I was really good with kids, but he was kind of a mystery.

I tried reading to him, but he said he he'd rather read to himself. I cranked the heat up in our swimming pool for him, but he didn't like swimming. He was willing to play video games but I'd never liked them and I couldn't concentrate on them (or anything else). It hurt that he didn't warm up to me.

The shares of our REIT kept drifting down. By the end of January, they were down over 80%. Those in our personal brokerage account had fallen from over $1.6 billion to about $250 million in just seven months. Many other industries were hit hard too, even tech companies.

Our tech stocks fell by over half. Cindy and I weren't billionaires anymore, not even close.

Our personal legal fees were running over two hundred thousand dollars a month. I hadn't taken my salary since October. Inova Development and the REIT were both losing money and paying over two million dollars a month in legal fees, mostly for discovery in the class action suits. We'd borrowed close to $120 million from our brokerage account, and this margin debt was getting bigger because we couldn't pay the interest.

The Inova Development Board gave me a four-million-dollar bonus for 2008. Since it wasn't a public company, we didn't have to make a public announcement about that, thank goodness. Can you imagine what the press would have said about me getting a bonus at that point?

Security analysts, investors and employees were asking if our REIT could survive and who might take it over if I went to jail. I tried to focus on making good business decisions, and get everybody else to do that, but it was impossible.

Love, Mark

CHAPTER 8

GETTING IN DEEPER

Sept. 20, 2013

Dear Katy

We tried to figure out some way to settle the cases against David and his company. If he lost the civil suits, the plaintiffs could seize all his assets including his company. With criminal charges hanging over his head, his company couldn't borrow or attract investors. Cindy and I agreed: our first priority was getting David and his company out of this mess as soon as we could.

Our lawyers didn't like that. If we settled the civil cases against David and his company, the plaintiffs' lawyers would use the settlement money to fund more aggressive actions against me, our companies, Cindy and our Foundation. I said, "I don't care. We've got to get David and his company out of this as fast as possible." Cindy agreed.

I tried to get Olaf Johansson to help behind the scenes with the Justice Department and the SEC. I wasn't asking for help with my case, only for David. David had been his son's best friend all their lives. I remembered how hurt he'd been about the rehearsal dinner, but I thought all that was behind us. Olaf was evasive, saying the prosecutors and SEC people didn't like elected officials trying to influence their decisions. Anyway, the Democrats were now in charge, so the influence he had with the Bush folks was gone. Probably true but, also, he was up for reelection in eighteen months. He seemed to want to keep a lot of distance between us.

Like any good negotiator, I set out to find as much as I could about the opposition. Some lawyers thought the charges had been filed early in January because the U.S. Attorney probably would be replaced when the Obama administration came in. Filing charges against me might burnish his reputation and help him get a good job at a law firm. Some thought maybe it was a ploy to try to stay in office; the Obama people might keep him if he was prosecuting "one of those financial villains." Others thought the Republicans wanted to be seen as tough on white collar crime and were afraid Democrats might harp on how few cases the Bush people brought against officers of financial institutions. Some lawyers pooh-poohed the political angles and said maybe the prosecutors were just trying to do their jobs. Some asked what difference does it make?

Still, I looked for ways to make it easier for the prosecutors to drop the charges against David and harder for the news media to attack them if they did. Jonathon wrote a long and sympathetic article for the Huffington Post about David's company and how tragic it was that the criminal charges and class action suits might destroy its important research. The plaintiffs' lawyers probably didn't give a damn, but the real audience was the prosecutors and, of course, the news media. Did it help? Nobody knows, but we figured it couldn't hurt.

By June a framework for a possible settlement began to emerge. The criminal charges against David would be dropped. The civil suits against him and his company would be consolidated and settled. But the prosecutors were not willing to drop the criminal charges against David without getting some kind of victory against me.

David said, "You shouldn't take a fall for me." Cindy was torn.

I said, "Lookit, let's find out what's doable. We can decide whether to take a deal after we know what it is."

We hoped the prosecutors would settle for a "no contest" plea. They balked. The best we could get was an "Alford plea": I'd plead guilty, not admitting I was but agreeing the prosecutors had enough evidence so a jury probably would convict me. It was a bitter pill. But the prosecutors would agree not to file criminal charges against Cindy or the Foundation.

David said, "Dad, I told you, I don't want you to take a fall for me."

"Son, listen. I've had a long and great run. I'm only 65, but my life as I've known it is over anyway. I probably won't have to serve much time, maybe none. But if I don't do this, we might lose our business and you might lose yours. And it gets your mom and the Foundation out of trouble. I want to do this partly for you and your mom, but for myself too."

We all looked at each other and nodded. Wouldn't any good husband and father do this? I loved my wife and son very much. Cindy would have been devastated if David had gone to jail. It wasn't crazy to do the Alford plea, but it didn't work out like we thought it would.

To settle the civil cases against David and his company, Cindy and I agreed to pay twenty percent of what David got from selling REIT shares. The money went into a settlement fund, with a distribution formula to be determined later. The judge approved this. The plaintiffs' lawyers racked up so many billable hours fighting over the distribution formula that nearly all the money went to them; their clients got almost nothing. Of course, the whole thing was about lawyer fees all along. If anyone had asked the class members if they thought David and I had done them wrong, most would have said no—they'd never heard of him and had no reason to blame their losses on me.

I entered my Alford plea on August 30. The prosecutors dismissed the criminal charges against David and recommended a one-year sentence for me. I agreed that the court could sentence me to more time. The court ordered a pre-sentencing report. We expected it to be very favorable and maybe lead to only a suspended sentence. A sentencing hearing was scheduled for October 30.

Next, we focused on settling the class action suits against Cindy and the Foundation. The government had dropped its investigation with no charges filed. We told the plaintiffs' lawyers that they'd get a lot of bad publicity if they kept attacking the Foundation. We demanded the names and addresses of all known class members so we could urge them to "opt out" of the suits. The plaintiffs' lawyers realized they probably couldn't recover all their fees and expenses. We settled the Foundation cases for two percent of what the Foundation had gotten from selling REIT shares.

We'd made a lot of progress. Except for the sentencing hanging over my head and the class action suits against me and our companies, things were looking better. I thought our companies could survive, at least in shrunken forms.

Then it really hit the fan. New federal criminal charges against me for violating securities laws, namely Rule 10b-5. This was total nonsense. Total crap. The government double-crossed me. It was an unfair bait and switch. They tricked me into the Alford plea on insider trading, leading me to think that would end my troubles with them, and then came out with this shit. I was very, very angry. Still am. I thought was over it. But writing this down just makes me boil over again.

Rule 10b-5 is called the "fraud rule." Fraud is a very nasty word. It's also misleading. That rule has been interpreted to cover lots of things that ordinary people wouldn't consider fraud at all. Still, we had good legal arguments that it couldn't be stretched far enough to cover what I'd done.

They claimed I led a conspiracy to keep the investing public from understanding how risky our REIT was. What bullshit. Our lawyers had made sure every presentation and press release had the usual disclaimers about forward-looking statements. This is standard stuff for any public company. We did it the same way everybody else did. That should have protected us from this kind of hindsight-based crap.

I was tired, very tired. Things had just piled up so bad for so long. But I tried to focus, tried to get ready for trial.

One of the best things we did was to hire Jackie, yes, your Dr. DeProulx, as a possible expert witness. Jackie and I spent a lot of time together. I took personality tests. Has she given those to you? Maybe she can't without my consent. If you want my consent, I'll give it. I don't know if they'll help you, but you can have them if you want.

But mainly we talked. She was such a good listener. It felt so good to have somebody willing to listen to me. The lawyers weren't. They wanted me to answer picky little questions and help find documents, but they didn't want to hear about how I felt or what was important to me. Once they're in their professional work mode, they're just highly trained technicians playing technical games. I know that's their job; that's what you pay them for. But you can't look to them for any comfort in times of trouble.

Jackie was genuinely interested in me and really cared about me. In the end, she didn't testify at my trial or my sentencing hearing. What could she have said that would make a difference? Of course, she could have testified that I was a nice guy, a good guy, a kind and loving husband and father, a kind and caring boss, but we had lots of character witnesses for that.

But I'm really glad we hired her. She helped me get through very rough times. We spent a lot of time together. As I said, she really cared about me and gave me a lot of support and comfort when I needed it.

And she brought you into my life, didn't she?

Love, Mark

# # # #

Sept. 27, 2013

Dear Katy,

We asked the court to let me withdraw my Alford plea, arguing that the government tricked me into doing it, not telling us about their plan to hit me with new charges. For months they'd been sitting on all the information the 10b-5 charges were based on.

We lost on that. We appealed and tried to expedite the appeal, arguing it would be unfair to have to go to trial on the new charges without knowing whether we could withdraw the Alford plea on the old one. The 9th Circuit refused to expedite our appeal.

I refused to consider any plea bargain on the new charges. I was too mad. And fighting them gave me a chance—maybe not a great one but still some chance—of being vindicated. So, we dug in to get ready for trial.

New class actions were filed against me and our REIT, each with its own law firm, each having a lead lawyer with a huge ego who wanted to be the lead lawyer for a consolidated class. We spent hundreds of thousands in extra legal fees because of their bickering over how to organize their attacks on us. How's that for a screwed up "justice" system?

Cindy came home one night in tears. "My lawyers say I have to divorce you."

"What? Cindy, I love you very much. I thought you still loved me."

"Yes, I do, but my lawyers say the only way to salvage anything for the kids and me is to distance myself from you. A divorce is the first step."

"Oh God." That's one of the very few times I ever swore in front of Cindy. We talked about it for a long time. I began to realize that her lawyers and a lot of other people thought I was headed for prison and our businesses were headed for bankruptcy. I asked, "What about the kids? Can you help them understand that you don't hate me?"

"They understand. I've already talked to them. And they don't hate you either."

"Well, that's something, I guess."

About Jackie, your Dr. DeProulx. does she ever talk about me? I think I've figured it out. Jackie sent you, didn't she? Well, maybe "sent" is too strong, but this whole dissertation thing was her idea, wasn't it? She must have missed our meetings almost as much as I did. She couldn't come see me herself, so she had you come for her. That's what's been going on for over two years, isn't it?

It makes sense. You know, underneath my cool, analytical, businesslike exterior, I'm really a loveable guy. You know the old song, "To know, know, know him is to love, love, love him …." Maybe you don't remember that song; it was popular before you were born. Still, the point is that she knew me so well she couldn't help loving me. Maybe not in a sexual way, but maybe that too. I'm not that bad looking, for a guy my age.

OK, Katy. I might as well tell you, as Paul Harvey used to say, the rest of the story. As I said, Jackie and I got to be very close. There was nothing sexual about it but one time when we were talking about my family, I started crying. She hugged me and tried to comfort me. It was nothing sexual on her side. I didn't mean for it to turn into anything like that on mine. But, you know, well, we've talked about this before, how other forms of intimacy sometimes morph into sexual feelings when you don't want them to? I started to get turned on. I tried to kiss her. She pushed me away, but she was very kind and gentle about it. Maybe in other circumstances we could have become lovers, but this wouldn't have been a good time for either of us. She did the right thing.

I'm not proud of that one-time mistake. I'd been faithful to Cindy all those years. Still have. But even Jimmy Carter says he'd felt lust in his heart. Nothing happened. But I suppose you ought to know that one time, just that one time, I might have been unfaithful if Jackie had let me.

Oh, well, what does it matter?

Love, Mark

# # # #

Oct. 4, 2013

Dear Katy

I asked Sharon to come out of retirement and take over as CEO of Inova Development and our REIT so I could spend full time on my legal problems. She said, "I'm flattered, Mark, I really am, but my husband isn't well. I need to take care of him, and I just don't have the energy."

In March 2010, there were hostile takeover bids for our REIT. The share prices of most other REITs had started to recover, but not ours. Because of the criminal charges and class action suits, our REIT couldn't refinance loans coming due. Interest rates were at all-time lows; our competitors could borrow very cheaply but we couldn't borrow at any cost. The REIT filed for bankruptcy.

We hoped there would be a bidding war for the REIT assets, but our competitors organized coalitions to bid together, get our assets cheap and divide them up among themselves. Isn't this an antitrust violation? Where is the Justice Department when you need them?

The REIT sold all its assets in a bulk sale for less than fifty cents on the dollar. Of course, this was exactly what we'd hoped to do to others when we saw the recession coming. All the money went to the REIT creditors; we and the other shareholders got nothing. The firms that bought our assets hired a few of our key employees. We closed down the subsidiary that had managed our REIT and laid off the rest. That wasn't enough to save Inova Development. It filed for bankruptcy too.

I was unemployed. My legal expenses were nearly three hundred thousand dollars a month. We owed the IRS for gift taxes on the money we gave David in 2008. The IRS audited our tax returns for 2003 through 2008 and claimed we owed another fifteen million dollars. We'd already sold our tech stocks and other investments to pay our margin debt and attorney fees. Cindy and I were nearly broke.

Our divorce was final in April. We had gotten the house and a few other assets into Cindy's name, and tried to protect her from our creditors. I agreed take responsibility for defending the class action suits and paying all federal taxes and other marital obligations. It wasn't clear if this would work, but there was so little left we hoped people wouldn't bother to go after Cindy.

Cindy and I had bought the Lake Washington home from our REIT back in 2004. She got it in the divorce and sold it soon after. I heard she only got eight million dollars and she owed that much on it, so she didn't get a penny from that. Back in mid-2008 it had been worth more than fifteen million. I heard a pro football player owns it now. He probably can afford it.

I got some of the federal tax claims paid off and kept paying my lawyers as long as I could, but by August 2010 I was totally out of money. I filed for personal bankruptcy.

My legal defense team was down to a couple of people, being paid by a legal defense fund. Many of my friends contributed: Stephen Hutchinson, Jonathon Starke, Jim Hawthorne, Frank Wilson, Branson Stackhouse, Brett Jamison, Gretchen Jaeger, Eeko Watanabe, Sharon O'Reilly, Heinz Vandenhof, Kevin Johansson, and others. I mention these people, Katy, because I want you to understand how loyal my friends have been. These people still care about me. It's just sad that the only way they have to show it is by contributing to my legal defense fund.

Love, Mark

# # # #

Sept. 27, 2013

Dear Katy

My trial was in September 2010. It was a farce. The prosecutor used every trick in the book.

I had to take the stand because the whole case turned on my intent. Only I could explain that and, if I didn't take the stand, the prosecutors would twist perfectly innocent stuff around to make me look bad. But the cross examination was brutal. At first, the prosecutor kept putting words into my mouth, not letting me explain anything. You've seen the transcript, haven't you?

[Note: Here is the portion of the trial transcript that Mark is referring to. K.T.]

> Prosecutor: Isn't it true, Mr. Kauffman, that during the July 4 weekend, in 2008, you and your wife and son talked about how you expected the housing market to crash and the shares in your REIT to go down?
>
> MK: It wasn't like that, exactly, but—
>
> Prosecutor: Just answer the questions, Mr. Kaufman, just "yes" or "no".
>
> MK: But—
>
> Prosecutor: Just answer the questions, Mr. Kaufman, just yes or no. Your Honor, could you please advise Mr. Kauffman ....
>
> MK: OK, OK.

Prosecutor: Isn't it true, Mr. Kauffman, that during the July 4 weekend, in 2008, you and your wife and son talked about how you expected the housing market to crash and the shares in your REIT to go down?

MK: Yes. No.

Prosecutor: And isn't it also true, Mr. Kauffman, that on or about July 14 you transferred about eight point five million dollars worth of shares in your REIT from your personal brokerage account to your son, David Kauffman?

MK: "Yes, but—"

Prosecutor: Just answer the questions, Mr. Kaufman, just yes or no.

MK: OK, OK. Yes.

Prosecutor: That was "yes", on or about July 14 you transferred about eight point five million dollars worth of shares in your REIT to your son, David Kauffman?

MK: Yes.

Prosecutor: And, Mr. Kauffman, do you know that three days later your son, David Kauffman, sold most of those shares in your REIT for approximately seven million dollars?

MK: Well, I don't know if it was the same shares. He already had a bunch of REIT shares, but some of them may have been the same shares.

Prosecutor: Alright, Mr. Kauffman, do you know that three days later your son, David Kauffman, sold those or other shares in your REIT for approximately seven million dollars?

MK: Yes.

Prosecutor: And isn't it also true, Mr. Kauffman, that on or about July 15 you transferred about ten million dollars worth of shares in your REIT to a trust for your sister, Lucy Kauffman?

MK: Yes, but—

Prosecutor: Your Honor, will you please advise the witness ....

MK: OK, OK.

Prosecutor: So, for the record, isn't it also true, Mr. Kauffman, that on or about July 15, 2008, you transferred about ten million dollars of shares in your REIT to a trust for your sister, Lucy Kauffman?

MK: Yes.

Prosecutor: And who was the trustee for that trust?

MK: I was, still am.

Prosecutor: So, you must be aware, then, that on or about July 18, 2008, the trust sold about six million dollars of those REIT shares?

MK: Yes.

Prosecutor: So, did you, as trustee, order the sale of those shares?

Me: Yes, my lawyer ....

Prosecutor: Just answer the questions, Mr. Kaufman, just 'yes' or 'no'. Do I have to ask the Court to remind you?

MK: No.

Prosecutor: And now, Mr. Kauffman, isn't it also true that on or about July 16, 2008, you transferred another forty million dollars worth of your REIT shares to the Cascade-Sierra Foundation, a non-profit organization of which your wife, Cindy, was the Chief Executive Officer?

MK: Yes, but—

Prosecutor: No buts, Mr. Kauffman. So, the answer was 'Yes'?

MK: Yes.

Prosecutor: And, Mr. Kauffman, did that foundation on or about July 21, 2008, sell about thirty million dollars of shares in your REIT, at the direction of your wife, its CEO, who also was on the Board of Directors of your company, Inova Development?

MK: Yes, I think that is correct.

Prosecutor: So, Mr. Kauffman, to summarize: (1) on or about July 14, 2008, you transferred approximately eight point five million dollars of shares in your REIT to your son, David Kauffman, and three days later on July 17 he sold approximately seven million dollars of shares in your REIT; (2) on or about July 15, 2008, you transferred ten million dollars of shares in your REIT to a trust for your sister, Lucy Kauffman, and three days later, on July 18, the trust, at your direction as trustee, sold a majority of those shares for about six million dollars; (3) on or about July 16, 2008, you transferred another forty million dollars of your REIT shares to the Cascade-Sierra Foundation which, five days later, sold thirty million dollars of such shares, at the direction of your wife, a member of your Board of Directors?"

MK: Yes.

Prosecutor: And during that time, Mr. Kauffman, say from July 4, 2008, through July 21, 2008, isn't it true that you believed that a real estate recession would come soon and you expected the value of your REIT shares to fall when that happened?

MK: No. I expected a recession but I had no—

Prosecutor: Isn't it true, Mr. Kauffman, that on August 1, 2008, your REIT borrowed eight hundred fifty million dollars?

MK: Yes.

Prosecutor: And you expected a recession at the time you borrowed that money, did you not?

MK: No.

Prosecutor: But just a minute ago you testified that you expected a recession during the time of July 4 through July 21. Did anything happen between July 21, 2008, and August 1, 2008, that changed your expectations about a recession?

MK: No.

Prosecutor: So, Mr. Kauffman, are you changing your testimony regarding whether you expected a recession?

MK: No. I can explain—

Prosecutor: Your counsel can give you a chance to explain yourself on redirect. Now, Mr. Kauffman, I would like to go on to a related subject. Mr. Kauffman, approximately how long did it take to arrange that borrowing?

MK: About eight weeks.

Prosecutor: So, it was about eight weeks from the time you first began talking to investment bankers about this borrowing until August 1, 2008, when the borrowing occurred.

MK: Yes.

Prosecutor: And when was that eight hundred fifty million dollar borrowing first announced to the public?

MK: On August 1, the day it happened.

Prosecutor: So, Mr. Kauffman, you were secretly transferring REIT shares to your son, your sister's trust and your wife's foundation, before the public had any way of knowing that you were planning to borrow all that money?

MK: Well, that's just not a fair way—

Prosecutor: Just yes or no Mr. Kauffman. If you want to say more your attorneys can give you a chance when they cross-examine you, if they are foolish enough to ...."

MK attorney: Objection!

Judge: Sustained. Gentlemen, I've given the prosecution a lot of rope because this is a hostile witness, but—

MK: I'm not hostile, or I wasn't until—

MK lawyer: Shut up Mark, shut up! It's just a technical term. Don't take it personally.

Prosecutor: I withdraw my question.

[Returning to Mark's letter of September 27, 2013]

The judge called a recess and met with the lawyers in his chambers. When everybody got back, the questioning took a different turn. The prosecutor said, "Now, Mr. Kauffman, please explain in your own words why your REIT borrowed eight hundred fifty million dollars on or about August 1, 2008?"

By then I was very angry and wanted to say, "Who else's words could I use, you asshole." But I suspected that he'd made me angry on purpose and I didn't want to look hostile. I took a deep breath, a long drink of water, and explained why we'd borrowed the money.

The rest of the day, most of the prosecutor's questions started with, "You said in your own words that ...". If I said yes, he would strut around like I'd just admitted something terrible. If I tried to clarify or correct what I'd said, he would say, "So you're changing your testimony?"

At the end of the day my lead lawyer sighed but was pretty poker-faced. Brett Jamison, who'd watched my testimony from the back of the courtroom, was more candid. "You were a lousy witness. You tried to be too honest. He played you like a fiddle."

So, I was convicted—but you knew that all along.

I'm trying to calm down. Being angry isn't good for me; it's bad for my health. I've tried to get over it. I don't sit around making circles with my thumbs and fingers and chanting "omm, omm, omm" or anything like that, but in my own way I meditate a lot. I knew there was a lot of anger still simmering in me, but I'm surprised how much rage got churned when I wrote this.

I was a victim of the times. The horrible financial and emotional pain of the great recession, people losing their jobs, houses, retirement funds, was still fresh. People thought Wall Street financial wheelers and dealers should be punished, and maybe some should have been. But way out west, I seemed to be the only wheeler/dealer people could get their hands on.

Love, Mark

# # # #

Oct. 18, 2013

Dear Katy,

The legal fireworks weren't over yet. My lawyers and I assumed it would take at least several months for the Justice Department to finish a presentencing report, but the prosecutors moved for a sentencing hearing only a week after the verdict, based on the presentencing report prepared after my Alford plea.

I was sentenced to six years in federal prison. We asked that I be given a reasonable time to "wind up my affairs," but the prosecutors argued that I was in bankruptcy so my "affairs" were being taken care of that way. We lost on that too. I had to report to the prison ten days after the trial ended.

The day before I had to start serving my sentence, I sat in my apartment in Factoria, watching cars creeping along on I-90 and I-405, thinking about all those people feeling sorry for themselves over being stuck in traffic. How lucky they were. They could get in their cars and go wherever they wanted, any time they wanted. I was going to lose that freedom.

My doorbell rang. I looked out the peephole but didn't see anybody. "Who is it?"

"Jonathon," said a voice, "and Stephen."

"Come in, come in. It's good to see you." They came in and looked around my small apartment for a place to sit. The living room was empty except for one old recliner from St. Vincent de Paul. "Sorry about the furniture situation. I've got a couple chairs. I'll get them."

I got my two folding chairs from the kitchen. They sat down. Nobody said anything for a minute or so. "It's good to see you," I said again. "And, I mean, well, together after, what, how many years? Tell me, how did it happen, you two getting back together?"

"We were at your sentencing," Jonathon said.

"Yes, I saw you there. But you were on opposite sides of the room."

Jonathon said, "Well, we kind of bumped into each other on the way out, and I suggested we get a cup of coffee. While we were drinking it, I asked, 'How long since you've seen him'? (meaning you)."

"And I said, 'Oh, I don't know, nearly two years I guess'."

Jonathon said, "So, I asked, 'Have you been mad at him too?' and he said, 'Well, yes, mad, but mainly hurt, I think'."

Stephen said, "It's hard to explain, Mark, but I was hurt. All these years I looked up to you and was so proud to be your friend. And you've been such a good friend to me. But then when you needed friends the most, I, ah, I, I just didn't want to see you."

Jonathon said, "Me too. You were always there for me when I needed you but, when you needed friends, I crapped out on you. I'm so sorry."

"Well, it must have been hard. Isn't it a lot like having terminal cancer: people just don't know what to say so they avoid you? Still, I missed you guys and I'm glad you came."

"You're right about the cancer thing," Jonathon said, "but it wasn't just that. This is, well, embarrassing, but I was mad about losing so much money. I'd invested most of what I inherited from my parents, about four million dollars, in your REIT. I should have been more diversified, but I'd always done well investing in you, in your firm, and it never occurred to me that anything might go wrong. I'm a Christian, you know, so I shouldn't care about money, but it really hurt, losing so much money like that."

"Yes, me too," Stephen said. "Most of my life I didn't care about money. I mainly cared about getting things designed and built; money just came along. But remember when I was suspended, when it looked like my career might be over? At first, I felt sorry for myself but then I realized I had nearly six million dollars. I didn't need to work. I could travel the world photographing architectural masterpieces. I might even write a book on the history of architecture. The point is, having all that money gave me lots of options, a kind of security. I was so thankful for that at the time, and I've been very thankful for it ever since."

"But you must have lost a lot in the crash too, didn't you?" I asked.

"Yeah, I had about half of it in your REIT, but I got some out before it fell too far. I lost on other stuff too, but most of it bounced back. And I've got my pension and Social Security. I'll be OK. It was scary, losing so much and not knowing how much more I might lose. I've pretty much gotten over it, but I was angry when things were really bad."

"I'm so sorry, so very sorry. I didn't mean for you guys, or anybody, to get hurt. It just, well, it just .... I don't know what to say."

"Well, we're sorry too. But we care about you, we really do," said Jonathon.

"Yes, that's right, and we should have stayed with you through all of this, should have been the kind of friends you always were for us."

"Thanks. It means a lot to me. I understand why you didn't come sooner, but I'm glad you came tonight."

Until then, Katy, I hadn't really thought much about the people who lost money in our REIT. Most of its shares were owned by insurance companies, mutual funds, pension funds, other institutions. Of course, real people lost money from investing through them, and a lot of people like Jonathon and Stephen invested their hard-earned money directly in our REIT. At some level I knew that, of course, but it hadn't been real to me. Maybe I was just too self-centered, feeling sorry for myself, not feeling anything about all the other people who suffered losses.

Do you think that's what the prosecutor and the judge were talking about when they said I showed no "remorse," no "guilt," no "responsibility" for the damage I'd done? Maybe so. Maybe that's the message they were trying to send. Well, if that was their message, it did get through.

It hurts that so few people have come to visit me here. Kaitlyn has come a couple of times and David once. Kevin several times. Moonbeam, now called Melody, three or four times. Early on Cindy wrote a couple of letters, but she says it would be just too painful to come. She's remarried now. I hope she's happy. Julie comes every month but won't bring Major; she says it would be too upsetting for him.

I thought Jonathon and Stephen would come regularly, but they've only come once.

I thought Jackie DeProulx might come to see me once in a while, but she hasn't. Does she ever ask about me?

Love, Mark

Eleventh meeting

I thought our correspondence would end when we had covered his trial and conviction, so I did not expect that last letter. I decided we should meet one more time so I could thank him in person and tie off our relationship. We met on October 23, 2013.

I was nearly two and a half years into my dissertation project and very frustrated. No matter how I manipulated my data and algorithms, I could not document a clear diagnosis of any mental illness or personality disorder as defined in the DSM-IV. At various times, Mark exhibited some criteria for various disorders, but no clear pattern was pervasive or well established before the crimes were committed. But it was not his fault that my project appeared to be an utter failure. He had been cooperative, open and honest, just like he had promised.

Finally, I had detailed information on the acts constituting his crimes and the reasons he had done them. But even if I had been able to document a clear diagnosis, would any mental illness or personality disorder explain the root causes of those acts? Supporting his son's business and his wife's charity work, caring for his sister and honoring promises to his father—could they be explained by any disorder in the DSM-IV?

Was there any way forward? Dr. DeProulx was kind and understanding. She listened to me for a long time. I had discussed my methodologies with her periodically, but this was the first time we had discussed the results, or lack of them. Finally, she said, "Katy, it is more satisfying when our research produces positive results, confirms that a hypothesis is true. But frequently science makes progress from failing to prove hypotheses. Maybe if you look at it that way, you can produce a meaningful and useful dissertation."

Oddly, the apparent failure of my research was not as devastating as it could have been. My relationship with Brandon had progressed. Without his loving support, unfailing belief in me, and patient encouragement, I would not have been able to complete my dissertation.

I expected this to be my last meeting with Mark. I wanted it to go well and our relationship to end on an upbeat note, with warm feelings and a sense that, as we had hoped, our project had been a positive experience for both of us.

KTA: Mark, I really want to thank you for your hard work on our project. You have been wonderfully forthcoming and candid. I cannot tell you how much I appreciate it.

MK: Well, thank you. It turned out to be good for me, so I guess I should thank you too.

KTA: I am glad you feel that way, glad you feel you got some benefits from it too. And, Mark, I owe you an apology. Until recently, I assumed you were guilty, I mean not just legally guilty, but that you must have done things that were morally wrong. You tried to tell me at the beginning that you had not, but I did not believe you. Now I understand that you were an honest businessperson acting out of genuine love for your wife, son, sister and father.

MK: Well, I was wrong about you too. I thought you were just a spoiled debutante who'd never done anything except, maybe, be an officer in a sorority or something. I had no idea you were a survivor of, ah, um, of so much.

KTA: Well, it has been quite a ride.

MK: You sound like this is the end, like we won't be seeing each other anymore.

KTA: Probably not, but—

MK: Is that why you look so happy? Because you won't have to see me anymore?

KTA: No, Mark, it is not like that. Not at all. Naturally I am happy to be coming to the end of a long project, but I will miss you.

MK: Katy, you are just glowing today, you look so good, so happy, it seems like it must be more than that. Like a cat who just ate a canary. Like you just lost your virginity or something.

KTA: Mark, come on—

MK: Sorry, sorry. That was out of line.

KTA: I'll forget you said that. I want us to part on a friendly, comfortable basis. Can't we do that?

MK: I don't want us to part at all. By the way, what did you conclude about me after all this time?

KTA: Ah, that will get us back to something more upbeat. I concluded that you do not suffer any of the generally recognized mental illnesses or any of the common personality disorders.

MK: But maybe a mental illness that is not generally recognized? Or a personality disorder that is not common?

KTA: No, no. I just lapsed into academic talk for a minute. You're not crazy and your personality is fine, pretty healthy.

MK: And that was a surprise?

KTA: Well, for a long time I assumed there probably was something wrong with you. Why else would you be in prison? You told me you were kind and gentle, warm and loveable, open and honest. I didn't believe it at first, but I was wrong about that. You've taught me a lot.

MK: Yes, I tried to teach you about real estate, business, finance, politics, how much our culture has changed over the years, how the world really works.

KTA: All that too. But I was thinking more about giving and accepting love, caring and sharing, anger and forgiveness, shame and pride, even sex.

MK: Oh, Katy. That is so, so, ah, flattering, I guess is the word. Do you really mean that?

KTA: Yes, but let's not get too mushy here. I don't want to cry.

MK: I've never seen you cry. I've seldom seen you laugh either, but I love to see you laugh. I'm trying to think up a joke or something, anything to make you laugh.

I didn't laugh but I smiled at that.

MK: I don't want our relationship to end.

KTA: Well, if you think of anything you left out, you can still write to me.

MK: That's not what I meant.

KTA: I am going to be very busy the next couple of months, writing up the final version of my dissertation and preparing to defend it. I am not going to

> forget you, of course, but I do not think I will have time to continue writing to you and, you know, it seems it would be best if I did not do that.

I got up, walked around the table and gave him a hug. I was a little teary but, like I told him, I didn't want to cry.

When I got home, I called the assistant warden and asked him to send me the computer I had loaned to Mark.

CHAPTER 9

GETTING TOGETHER

I submitted my dissertation on February 16, 2014. It did not turn out the way I originally expected. I explained my goal of attempting to document, based primarily on events occurring long before the crimes were committed, that one or more mental illnesses or personality disorders as defined in the DSM-IV caused or at least explained the behaviors constituting the crime. Then I explained the methodologies used to document events that seemed to indicate or counter-indicate one or more diagnostic criteria for various mental illnesses and personality disorders, my database to collate them, my algorithms to analyze them, and my computer program to crunch those data. But, for me, at least, the conclusion was quite unexpected: these methodologies, and most likely any similar methodologies, were of no practical use in determining why Mr. Kauffman did what he did and, by extension, might be of no practical use in determining why other white-collar criminals do what they do.

That might not come as a surprise to the average layperson, but for me, after years of academic training in psychology, it was like saying the emperor has no clothes. The DSM has become so important in our field, and used for so many purposes, that I (and probably many others) had lost sight of its limitations.

To my surprise, just before I finished the final rewrite of my dissertation, I got a handwritten letter from Mark:

Feb. 10, 2014

Dear Katy

They took away my computer. Or, I guess it was your computer. If I have to write by hand, maybe I'll be a little more succinct. That could be a relief for you (just kidding).

I miss our meetings and getting your letters. You were right at the beginning. It was therapeutic. It was so nice to have a sympathetic listener. I tried to be honest, to not leave out mistakes I made or the dark moments in my life. I don't claim to be a saint. I've got flaws, like anybody else, but I'm not a bad person. And I feel good about your comment that I taught you a lot.

I wish you success with your dissertation, your career, everything.

You're such a kind and caring person. I've grown very fond of you. I hope you'll stay in touch, let me know how you are doing, what's going on in your life. I know you'll be busy and have your own life to live. But it would be great if you could find time to visit me now and then.

I'll never forget you and I'll always be thankful for all you've done for me.

Love, Mark

I did not respond to this or any of his subsequent letters. I was busy finishing my dissertation, and then settling into my career as an associate professor, and later a wife and mother. I wanted to focus on the new phases of my life. I did not want to hurt him, but I did not want him to become dependent on me, to rely on our relationship as a way to cope with his losses, loneliness and isolation. After all, I had never been his therapist.

I defended my dissertation on April 25, 2014. I was worried that Dr. DeProulx and the other two reviewing professors might find my whole approach unprofessional and my conclusions undefendable. However, she was very supportive. The others were somewhat less so, but they seemed impressed with my methodologies and intrigued by the results of the numerous computer runs analyzing my data.

While I was stressing over whether my dissertation would be accepted, I got another letter from Mark:

Mar. 20, 2014

Dear Katy

I am turning 69. Maybe it's the birthday that got me thinking about what my life will be like after I get out. That's nearly two years away, but I don't have a lot of other things to think about.

I'm going to be OK. It will be a lot different, Mark Kauffman 4.0. Or 5.0 or 6.0? Really, I think there have only been three main phases in my adult life so far: insecure adolescent, rising businessman, convict.

I won't be rich anymore. I'll have Social Security. I've got my IRA. It's not nearly as big as it was, of course, but I'll get some money out of it. I'll have part of my pension. Our pension plan had been fully funded, but it went under along with everything else. The Pension Benefit Guarantee Corporation gives our retirees something, but higher paid people, especially me, get a lot less than we expected. But I'm not asking for pity. I won't need a lot of money.

Many people assumed I'd squirreled away at least a few million. We went 'round and 'round on that in the class action suits and bankruptcies. No, I don't have any money in Swiss bank accounts, or any other tax haven, or any gold buried someplace or any other hidden assets.

Maybe I could work. Not in securities; I've been banned from that. Maybe a Walmart greeter? Do they do a background check for that? I don't know. Maybe they don't hire convicted felons.

Well, I won't really have to work. I can get by. But who will I live with? I can live with one of my kids, for a while at least. Maybe I'll meet a new woman. But even if I do, I'd still like to have some kind of relationship with you. It wouldn't have to be the biggest thing in your life, but it would be nice if I could see you sometimes.

My life is boring now. And I can't help but think you must miss me too, at least a little. Didn't we have something special going? Most people are close to only a very few others their whole lives.

When you get close to somebody you ought to hang on to that. It's something very special. Let's not waste a chance to keep a good thing going.

Love, Mark

I was awarded my PhD on June 10, 2014, and then was offered an assistant professor position at the UW. I began to settle into what some of my graduate student friends called life AD, After Dissertation. I would co-teach one class Summer Quarter, with an experienced professor who had taught it many times before and had the materials already prepared. Not a tough job.

Although we were not yet married, Brandon and I went into what we thought of as our honeymoon phase. Brandon taught only one course that quarter too, so we had lots of time to play. We spent weekends in La Conner, Port Ludlow, Semiahmoo, Leavenworth, Cannon Beach, Vancouver, Whistler. We hiked, rode mountain bikes, paddled kayaks and stand-up boards, all the things young adults do in in the Northwest. We bought a Prius to get around without putting so much CO2 into the atmosphere.

After many years of being a student and then a teaching assistant, for the first time I had a real job, a real income, and the social status of being an assistant professor. Brandon was a couple years ahead of me on that, but he too was still enjoying that transition. We were not rich, of course, but we had no mortgage, no children, no big financial commitments except our student loans. We could spend most of our income just having fun.

Brandon and I were so happy. It was a beautiful, almost magical summer.

I was spending less and less time with my mom. She continued to blossom and advance in her late-starting career and was looking for a condo to buy. Brandon and I moved into an apartment in July 2014, with office space for each of us. This was the first time I had not lived with Mom, except the few weeks she was in rehab. I was quite aware that this sent Mom two messages: (1) she did not need to buy a place big enough to share with me, and (2) I felt confident she could live on her own without a risk of backsliding into addiction. It was a major milestone in our relationship. It felt like a great weight had been lifted off of me. At last I was free to focus on my own life.

Then I got another letter from Mark.

July 28, 2014

Dear Katy

I'm still overwhelmed by what you said about what you learned from me. And I can't believe how much I miss you.

Time drags slowly now. I should try to find something else to do, not just stare at the walls and feel depressed. Don't take that literally. I'm not what you'd call "clinically depressed." I'm just down a little, bored, not sleeping well. It's not your fault. I'm not trying to lay a guilt trip on you or anything like that.

I'd really like it if you could come for a visit, just an hour or so, for old times' sake.

I'm disappointed that you have not replied to my last two letters. I suppose you want to put some distance between us before we resume our relationship or begin to develop a new one that is not based on your dissertation project. I can give you space to do that. I will not write again for six months unless I hear from you sooner. But every day I hope to get a letter from you, so I hope I don't have to wait so long.

You remember, Katy, I said there are two things you've got to do to be happy: care about other people and have some kind of work you care about doing. You provided both for me. I was a little hostile at first, but I came to care about you, care about you a lot. And writing to you became a big part of my life. I didn't like it at first, but as I got more into it, it became a big project for me. It gave me a purpose, trying to help you understand who I am and how I got this way.

You're a very good listener, a very kind and caring person. And I shared a lot of very personal, intimate stuff with you, some things I hadn't talked about for years and some I'd never ever talked about ever. Didn't we have a closeness, a kind of intimacy that you don't have very often? It's a very special thing, that kind of closeness. You're lucky to get it just a few times in your life. We shouldn't let it slip away.

Love, Mark

Brandon read the letter. "Pathetic," he said. "Don't encourage him."

"I'm not. At our last meeting I told him I would not write to him again. I have ignored his letters since then and will keep ignoring him. With no positive reinforcement, his behavior should extinguish itself over time, don't you think?"

"It's supposed to work that way, at least with rats."

My dissertation was published, with a few minor edits, in the Journal of the American Association of Forensic Psychologists. 37 AAFP Journal, Vol.1, at 122ff. (2014). I use that version in some of my classes.

Brandon and I continued to do research and write—that is just part of academic life. He talked about us jointly writing a case study on Mark Kauffman's career that he could use for his business classes and perhaps get published in a professional journal. I laughed and said, "Not me; one paper on him is enough for me."

In October 2014, I missed my period. After two weeks, I bought a test kit and found I was pregnant. I did not want to tell Brandon or Mom. I thought about just quietly getting an abortion without telling anyone, but somehow that did not seem right. I talked to Mom. She said, "Why not talk to Brandon? What have you got to lose?"

"Did you talk to, ah, you know, my biological father?"

"No, but that was different."

Different how? But it was different. I was three times older than she had been, much more educated, with a good job and career ahead of me, and, I thought, a solid loving relationship with the father-to-be. Then I realized something: Mom was being the parent, maybe for the first time since I was nine or ten, and I was being the child, an adult child but still the child. I hugged her and cried for a long time. Did she know what I was crying about? We never talked about it, but I think she did. A mother would.

Brandon was kind of quiet when I told him I was pregnant. He held me close and said, "It's OK; it'll be OK." After a while he said, "Do you plan to have the baby? Keep it I mean."

"I don't know. I wasn't planning on this, you know." I had been on birth control, an IUD. We knew they are not 100% effective, but we hadn't worried about me getting pregnant.

"You sure? Maybe you've felt your biological clock is winding down."

"Brandon, come on. I wouldn't have done it on purpose without talking to you, without both of us agreeing that we were ready."

"Well, I don't know that I'm ready, but I'll do the right thing for you. If you want to keep the baby, we can get married."

"But I don't want you to feel that you got trapped, that this is the only reason we got married."

"It wouldn't be the only reason. I love you, you know."

"I love you too." And I thought the baby would bring us even closer together.

We got married the day before Thanksgiving. I didn't want Mom to dip into her housing down-payment fund for a big wedding. Brandon's family was on the east coast and he was not very close to them, so he thought they would not come anyway. It was a small wedding, just Mom, Dr. DeProulx, two couples from our bridge group and a few colleagues from the University, at a private wedding chapel in Seattle. Mom gave me away.

We went to Cabo San Lucas for a short honeymoon. We had to be back to teach classes on Monday. I had morning sickness. We tried to blame it on the water, but we drank only bottled water. We did learn, though, that if you swim in the ocean and then lie on the beach and get sand in your swimsuits, it's best to take a shower before you make love.

After the first couple of months, my pregnancy went smoothly. Looking back now, I realize that Brandon was starting to become somewhat distant, but I was madly in love and thought it was just that he was adjusting to the idea of becoming a father and of having to give up the quick trips and outdoor things we had enjoyed so much. I remembered Mark saying he could not relate to his unborn children, and I assumed Brandon would get into being a father like Mark had.

I was nearly four months pregnant when I got yet another letter from Mark:

Jan. 28, 2015

Dear Katy

Hi, there! It's me, Mark. I thought about sending you a Christmas card or letter, but I'd promised not to write for six months. I've been counting the days and my six months is up now. So, a belated Merry Christmas and Happy New Year.

It's been over a year since our last meeting. I miss you so much. I dream about you sometimes. I don't mean sexual dreams, nothing dirty, nothing like that. Well, OK, I've had some fantasies about sleeping with you, but I know that could never happen. You're younger than my daughter. I'm just saying, well, you know, guys think like that sometimes. It doesn't mean a thing.

What I'm trying to say is I'm very fond of you. Not in a way that is inappropriate. It's just that you were such a good listener. It felt so good to talk to you. It was good to write stuff down for you. And, of course, I'm lonely now.

I don't see any reason why we couldn't continue to have some kind of relationship. Maybe we could have coffee or lunch every month or so. Of course, I'd like for you to come visit me here. It's over a year until I get out and time goes so slowly now.

I love you very much. I'm looking forward to resuming our relationship whenever you can find the time to come here or I can come to you.

Love, Mark

I did not plan to resume a relationship with Mark and I certainly was not going to go down to FCI Sheridan see him. I did not show this letter to Brandon because I knew he would say it was more pathetic than the last one.

Brandon and I still played bridge on Wednesday nights and went to bridge tournaments. He got more and more aggressive, using all kinds of obscure conventions, taking more risks and looking totally disgusted if I made a mistake. In fact, though, he made more mistakes than I did, sometimes forgetting which cards had been played or which opposing player probably held various high cards. I did not say anything, though; I was trying to be the perfect bridge partner.

I tried hard to be a good wife. I kept the apartment clean and neat. I cooked healthy and wholesome meals and presented them the way the Andersons had taught me. I tried to be sensitive to Brandon's moods and wishes, making myself available to spend time with him if he wanted, leaving him alone when he seemed to want that, trying to be responsive when he wanted to make love, faking it sometimes when he did not put a lot of effort into it, initiating it sometimes when he seemed withdrawn, but never pressuring him when he wasn't interested. And it was not just about sex. I asked him about his classes, his students, his friends, the news, anything he was willing to talk about. I tried to be interested, cheerful, fun-loving, even when I did not feel like it. I came to see our marriage as a project. I was determined to succeed in this just as I had on many other projects over the years.

I worried that the baby might come before the end of Spring Quarter, but I got all the papers graded and grades sent in more than 48 hours before I went into labor.

Baby Claire was a joy but more work than I had expected. I said to Mom one day, "I'm exhausted. How did you do it? By yourself, at thirteen?"

She smiled and said, "You do what you have to, Honey." Mom helped a lot with the baby. Brandon tried to help but seemed uncomfortable and awkward with her. I remembered Mark saying he had a hard time relating to babies, so I assumed Brandon would become more comfortable and affectionate after Claire got bigger and developed more of a personality.

For the first few weeks, Claire slept in a bassinette in our bedroom, but we agreed that we should convert either Brandon's office or mine to a nursery. We decided to share space in what had been his office and make mine the nursery. It was not the same as each having our own space. He started spending more time at his office on campus, even during the summer which was the least busy time of year for us. I should have worried about that, but I was busy with the baby and preparing to teach new classes in the fall.

I got another letter from Mark:

July 28, 2015

Dear Katy

Hi, again! It's me, Mark. My six months is up. I hope time goes faster for you than it does for me.

I saw in the news that you were an expert witness in the sentencing hearing for that East Indian scammer, Brahamian Rao. From what I've read, he seems like a pretty slimy guy. Still, the press said a lot of the same things about me, so maybe he's OK.

It was good to see that you did get your PhD. I hope your dissertation turned out well.

What's going on with you now? I think about you all the time, but I still think of you as a graduate student. You must have moved on into a whole new phase of your life, which is great. I just wish I knew more about it. I might even have some good advice for you.

I looked over a draft version of that last letter I sent you and I'm embarrassed. I shouldn't have mentioned fantasies about you, especially sexual fantasies. I don't want you to get the wrong idea. I only want a Platonic relationship, warm and comfortable but not at all physical.

You and I somehow kind of got off on the wrong foot. I was a little hostile and you were a little suspicious. But we worked through all that and we came to have something very special, the kind of emotional intimacy that is rare and beautiful. Most people have that only a few times in their lives, and some people probably never have it. We should preserve and protect and nurture it. Of course, it's hard to do that just through letters, but it will be easier when we can spend time together.

Love, Mark

I left that letter lying on the kitchen counter and Brandon found it. "What's this crap," he said. "Is that guy still trying to harass you? And what was that about sexual fantasies?"

"Oh, he wrote something like that six months ago. I threw it away. He will give up eventually."

In September, just before Fall Quarter, we left the baby with Mom for the first time and went up to Whistler for a few days, mountain biking, drinking wine, enjoying some child-free time. But it was not the same as it had been the year before. We left earlier than planned. I missed Claire and Brandon seemed restless.

We had our first Christmas as parents. Claire was too small to understand what it was all about, but we made a big deal out of it with a tree, Santa hats for all three of us, lots of presents under the tree, lots of pictures.

We were trying to be good American parents but, frankly, neither of us had good role models for doing that.

Our lives had settled into the quarterly cycle of university life. As a student, of course I had known that each quarter starts slowly but the pace gradually picks up until the last frantic week when papers are due, exams are coming up, professors are rushing to make up for having gotten behind schedule. Now I found there is a somewhat similar same pattern for professors, except that the first couple of weeks seem a little stressful as you have get a feel for a new group of students, how much they know, how much they care about what you are trying to teach. Some classes just seem easier than others, but I was gaining experience and confidence as a professor.

By late January I had settled into the Winter Quarter classes and was feeling good about myself and my career. Then I got this letter from Mark:

January 28, 2016

Dear Katy

Hi, there! Me again. I hope you don't think that greeting is too flippant. I want to keep it light. I want you to smile when you think of me. Most of the times we met you seemed so serious, so intense, so I've tried to help you relax and lighten up.

Sometimes I think the reason you've been avoiding me these last couple of years is that you associate me with serious, sad, tragic things, like the collapse of my businesses and the destruction of my family and the sad and painful things in your life that we talked about. But our future should be merry and bright. It seems to me that you have achieved your goals and found your dream, and I will be starting a new life that, well, it won't be what I had before, but it still could be satisfying in other ways. At any rate, it will be better than being locked up in here. You know me. I'm the eternal optimist. So, I'm looking forward to the rest of my life and to developing a new and better relationship with you.

It won't be long now. I get out in a couple of weeks. I've dreamed about you meeting me at the gate. I'd love that, but you must be busy. You don't have to make the trip. When I get out, one of the first things I'll do is come see you at the UW or at your house. Please let me know what time and place would be best for you.

That's it for now. I still love you very much and I'm looking forward to seeing you soon, very soon.

Love, Mark

I showed it to Brandon. He said, "Jesus, Katy, that guy is a nut case. Is he going to stalk you? Do you think he's dangerous?"

"Well, I spent nearly three years trying to determine what mental illness or personality disorder he has, and I couldn't come up with anything. So, I do not think he is crazy or dangerous, but it is kind of creepy. I don't want to see him."

"No, I wouldn't expect you would."

For the next ten days I could not think of anything else. What should I do? What would be best for me and my family? How could I avoid Mark without hurting him too badly?

I called the assistant warden at FCI Sheridan to see how much time I had. "Can you tell me when Mark Kauffman will be released?"

"10:00 tomorrow."

"What happens then?"

"We put him on a bus for Seattle, his last place of residence before he was incarcerated."

God, I thought, I need more time. I hardly slept at all that night. I had a kind of panic attack after Brandon left the next morning. I can't be here. I packed a suitcase for Claire and me, and a big diaper bag, and called an Uber to get to the airport. "What airline?" the driver asked.

"I don't know. Just drop me off at Departures."

The driver dropped me off at Alaska. It seemed as good as any. We flew to Anchorage. I meant to call Brandon as soon as we got settled in a hotel.

We checked in to the Captain Cook hotel. Claire was fussy so I had to take care of her. I turned on the TV just to have some background noise. There was a picture of me. Mark had been arrested as a person of interest in the disappearance of Claire and me. Oh shit, I thought, I've really screwed this up now.

I called Brandon, upset, crying. He asked, "Are you OK? Where are you? What happened?"

"I'm OK. I'm in Alaska, in Anchorage, in a hotel up here."

"Jesus," he said. "The cops think he may have killed you and the baby."

"No, no. We're fine. Better tell the cops that. We'll be home in a day or so, but don't tell anybody where we are."

"You're sure you're OK? Anything I can do? I've been so scared. I love you, Katy, I really do."

By the time I got back home a couple of days later, Brandon had hired an attorney who had prepared papers for a restraining order to prohibit Mark Kauffman from communicating with me. I signed the papers at the airport. Brandon took me and Claire home. A paralegal took the papers to the courthouse and a judge signed the restraining order. We had agreed there would be no publicity about my whereabouts or return until after it had been served on Mark.

The next day I got this letter from Mark, handwritten on King County Jail stationary:

Mar. 28, 2016

Dear Katy

You won't believe this. Or maybe by the time you get this you'll know what happened. I'm sitting in the King County jail. This is so totally stupid, totally crazy. They think I may have kidnapped you and your baby, or maybe even killed you and her. That's just dumb. First, I would never hurt you or anyone you cared about. Second, I didn't even know you had a baby until they arrested me. I didn't know you were married either.

Now that I think about it, I don't know much of anything about you as an adult. I opened up to you so much; I told you things I'd never told anybody, even Cindy. Looking back, I realize our relationship was rather one sided. You opened up about your childhood and your "makeover" through FARRS, but you never told me a thing about your adult life. I thought I knew you pretty well but now I'm not so sure. Maybe you're a more private person than I realized. Maybe you never developed any feelings for me. All these months I've believed you did. I still hope so. Maybe that has something to do with your disappearance.

When I got out, I tried to rent a car but couldn't. My driver license is still good, but all my credit cards expired while I was in prison. The next day Julie took the bus to work and I borrowed her car. I drove to the university, found the psychology department, and asked for you. They had me sit in a lounge area, which seemed normal enough. But after about twenty minutes two security guards and a Seattle police officer came and told me I was under arrest. "What for?" I asked.

"Person of interest in the disappearance of Dr. K.T. Alvarez and her child."

"What? You've got to be kidding. I haven't seen her for, like, over two years. And I love her. I'd never hurt her."

The cop took me downtown where they booked me, fingerprinted me, gave me jail clothes, and locked me up.

I don't know what this is about. After I was arrested, I saw on TV that you and your child are missing. Where are you? What the hell is going on?

Love, Mark

Mark complied with the restraining order. I did not get any more letters from him.

There were stories in the news media about Mark stalking me, his arrest and my restraining order, and later about my dissertation and my relationship with him.

Jonathon Starke, then a freelance writer, published an article in May 2016 issue of Forbes magazine: "The Phoenix House Man and the Phoenix Lady". After decades as a reporter, his detective skills were well developed. He had found out a lot about me and my mother, but I give him credit for not including anything that might embarrass either of us. Rather, he focused on Mark's career, his downfall, and my conclusions that Mark did not exhibit persistent or pervasive evidence of any long-term mental illness or personality disorder.

The news media moved on to other things, as they always do, and my life returned to normal—as normal as life with a toddler can be. But then, in August 2016, someone knocked on my office door. I assumed it was a student or perhaps a colleague. I said, "Come in." Jonathon was about the last person I expected to see. I knew who he was; I had met with him several times and I had read his Forbes article. I said, "Ah, Jonathon, come in."

He came in, closed the door, and sat quietly for a little while. "Can we pray?" he asked.

"Jesus, I mean, oh shit. I don't know. I'm not sure I'd be comfortable with that."

"That's OK. I don't have to do it out loud and you could just meditate or something if you're more comfortable with that." He closed his eyes and clasped his hands. I assume he was praying. I wasn't meditating; my mind was racing. What could he want from me? After quite a while, he opened his eyes, looked at me and said, "You're wondering why I'm here, aren't you?" I nodded. "It's about Mark." I nodded again.

"Did he send you?"

"No. He doesn't know I want to see you. And he wouldn't send me because, ah, because of the court order."

"So, what do you want?"

"I can talk about that, of course, but first, do you want to know how Mark's doing?"

"Frankly, I didn't until you came. But, OK, what's going on?"

"He's been very depressed. His caregivers are doing everything they can to help him, make sure he is surrounded by love and, frankly, doesn't get a chance to hurt himself."

"Caregivers?"

"Well, not professional caregivers, but a group of family and friends who care about him a lot."

"What do you mean?"

"The biggest hero is his daughter, Julie. He lives with her. She works from home as much as she can to look after him and coordinate schedules for the others. Stephen spends a lot of time with him. Takes him out to plays, concerts, museums, movies, things like that, or just sits with him. His son, David, talks to him on the phone nearly every day, sometimes about AutoimuneX, sometimes about the news or weather or anything. His daughter-in-law calls too, and she flies up to spend time with him when he gets especially down. His former employees, Gretchen, Sharon, Eeko, Heinz all have turns visiting or talking on the phone. And Esther and me, of course. And Kevin. He's organizing a new charity to help convicts make the transition from prison to the outside. We all hope Mark will get into this and it will give him a new purpose, a new project, new people and new work to care about."

"Wow. And I suppose all of you blame me for his depression?"

"No, nobody does. Especially Mark. He wouldn't let anybody say that or feel that way. He's very protective of you. He says his illness comes from something inside him, not from anything you did."

"But, you know, he kept writing to me for, what, two years after I last saw him. He seemed so needy."

"Is that so bad, having somebody need you?"

"Jesus, Jonathon, for most of my life I've looked after my mother, propped her up, kept her from self-destructing. I just got out from under that. I don't need another person being dependent on me."

We both sat there for quite a while. Finally, I said, "It's a very sad situation, but I don't understand why you came to me. I still care about him some too, a little, I guess, maybe, but I'm not in a position to be any help. What do you want from me?"

"Several of us have talked about working together to write one more piece about Mark and what's happened since he was released from prison. I don't know if we would try to get it published—we certainly wouldn't publish it unless we thought that would help him. But by sharing what we know, maybe we can find ways to be of more help to him. Even if it doesn't help him directly, maybe we can help each other understand how to provide him a better support system."

"But what would that have to do with me?"

"Katy, you know more about Mark than any of us. You know some things that none of the rest of us do. And your professional training might help us figure out how it all fits together."

"I can't help but be suspicious, Jonathon. You've built a lot of your career around Mark. You've exploited your relationship with him before. The PI is dying; it's been on-line only for years now. Are you broke? Do you need to make some money by exploiting your relationship with Mark one more time? Or is this some plot to try to get me reconciled with him?"

"No, no, no. We want to do this because we care about Mark. We'd like your help behind the scenes, but you wouldn't have to talk to him or see him or communicate with him in any way. Of course, we would like to see you and Mark reconciled, happy together, but that would be up to you and way down the road from what we want now."

"I need some time to think about all this. I've got a husband and child. I'd need to make sure this wouldn't hurt them. And I've got a career, and students and colleagues to think about."

"OK, all good points. Can we both think about it? Can I come back in a week or so to talk again, and maybe come up with some ground rules that can work for everybody?"

"I don't want to talk about it anymore today, so that probably would be best."

I had serious doubts about the wisdom of cooperating with Jonathon on another story about Mark, even if there was no plan to publish it. Clearly, Jonathon had a deep respect and affection for Mark. I believed that he meant well, and the rest of Mark's family and friends did too, but there were so many ways this could go wrong.

To make a long story short, after several weeks I did agree to cooperate with Jonathon, but only on the condition that the resulting paper would not be published without my consent and, if I did agree to let it be published, I could take out anything that mentioned me or my mother.

Jonathon asked if he could see and copy the letters between Mark and me and my notes of our meetings while he was in prison. I refused because they included too much personal information about me and my mom. I did agree to share excerpts describing specific incidents that Jonathon or other "caregivers" remembered and asked about.

About a month or so into our collaboration, I said to Jonathon, "One thing puzzles me. Mark got very few visitors in prison, but now he is surrounded by friends and family all the time. Was it the four-hour drive that kept people away?

"No, not that. All of us would have been willing to drive down to see him any time."

"So, what was it, then?"

"Well, when people visited, they'd come back and report that he was OK, strong, upbeat or at least trying to stay upbeat. He'd ask about his family and friends. It was always clear that he still cared about us, but he didn't leave any room for people to express how much they cared about him. Nobody could get close to him. It was hard to visit when he wouldn't open up or let you express any sympathy."

"So that changed when he got out?"

"Yes. After he got your restraining order, he felt more isolated and couldn't cover it up anymore. Then he got so depressed that he had to accept our caring about him, or maybe just didn't have enough energy to fend us off anymore."

"That is so sad. He wanted more visitors when he was in prison. He didn't know he was driving all of you away."

The hardest part of our collaboration was when Jonathon asked why I fled to Alaska when Mark was released.

"I was scared, I guess."

"Why were you scared?"

"Well, he had written that he would come looking for me, like he would be stalking me."

"Were you afraid he might hurt you, physically hurt you?"

"No, he would never do that."

"What, then? Emotionally hurt you?"

"No, not on purpose. But I thought he would want to dig more into my childhood and my life. Like turning over rocks and looking at the slugs and spiders underneath. Or try to get me to look at my life differently."

"You mean he might try to take on a counseling role?"

"Yes, and I was not ready for that. Especially with him."

"Have you thought about counseling with anybody else?"

"Well, Mark told me I ought to do that, but I guess I'm not ready for that either, or afraid of it maybe."

"Were you afraid he might try to seduce you? You know, come on sexually?"

"No, he is too much of a gentleman. And anyway, I know how to stop that if I want."

"If you want. Were you afraid you might not want to?"

"I am married, happily married, and I have a kid. I would have stopped him. Even if I didn't want to, I would have stopped him."

"But you might have wanted to? Is that the problem?

"You know, we shared a lot of very personal things. Sometimes one form of intimacy ..."

"Morphs into another. I think I understand."

I met with Jonathon every week or so, sometimes alone and sometimes with one or more of the other "caregivers." Our project began to put a strain on my marriage or, more realistically, to make the strains more visible. Brandon became more cool and distant. When I asked about that, he said, "Look, you try so hard to be the perfect wife, but that puts pressure on me. I can't be the perfect husband; I can never measure up to your expectations. You've turned your Mark Kauffman into such an ideal, such a fantasy, I can't compete with him."

"It is not like that at all. I don't compare you to him or expect you to be like him."

"Maybe not, but it's like you think about him more than me, care about him more than me. It's like he's come between us. Even in bed, it's hard to tell if you remember it's me or you are having fantasies about him."

"Hold it there. I never slept with him and I don't want to. It's not like that at all. You're the only one I've ever been intimate with."

"Sexually, that may be true. But there's other forms of intimacy. Look, you're obsessed with him and his 'caregivers.' It's, ah, I don't know, like adultery without the fun part."

"Is that supposed to be a joke? It's not funny, not to me. I would never commit adultery, even if I wanted to, which I don't."

But it turned out that he had. And it had started when I was pregnant, long before I began meeting with Jonathon and the others. After I found out, I tried to talk to him about why he wanted other women and why he had not talked to me about that. He said, "It's complicated. We shouldn't have had the baby."

"Jesus, Brandon, it's way too late to feel that way. She's a year old. If we were going to abort, we would have had to do that more than eighteen months ago."

"No, I didn't mean that. It's just that, well, I guess I wasn't ready to settle down, give up all the fun stuff."

"You weren't ready to grow up? You are over thirty. Isn't it time?"

"Not for me. I'm not ready to accept the idea that I'll never be able to sleep with other women, that it will be just you, only you, the rest of my life."

"But Brandon, if you feel like our love life is not satisfying, we can work on that. I can learn, I can help on that."

"It's not you. It's me. I just don't want to be tied down."

Some of our friends knew he had been unfaithful, but nobody told me until I left him. Were they trying to protect me? It seemed odd that they would know and not tell me. But, then, at some level, I didn't want to know. It is like having someone you care about getting into drugs: there are warning signs, but you just don't want to know. Finally, I asked a friend from the bridge group, "You knew, didn't you?"

"Yes, I knew."

"When? When did you find out?"

"Well, it was there all along. He was sleeping with another woman when he started dating you, and that kept going on for quite a while, all the time until he started sleeping with you, and then he started again when you were pregnant."

"Why didn't you tell me? You could have warned me."

"Maybe I should have. But, you know, for a long time we didn't think he'd be able to seduce you. We thought you were just bridge partners and it would stay that way. But he seemed to take it as a challenge, like nobody had ever turned him down before and he needed to persist until you gave in. By the time we realized he was winning you over, it was too late to warn you."

Apparently, the chase was more important to him than the victory.

I tried to talk to Brandon about how I felt about his unfaithfulness. He said, "What century are you living in? Well, strike that. There never was a century where husbands really were monogamous. That's just a crazy romantic myth. It doesn't ever really happen."

"You're wrong, Brandon. Some husbands are faithful for decades."

"Name one."

"Well, Mark Kauffman for one."

"Oh, shit. Not him again. You know, one of the best things about the divorce is I won't ever have to hear his name again."

"Divorce?"

"Yeah, we're getting divorced, aren't we? Isn't that why you left? Or am I supposed to start it?"

I filed for divorce. He didn't contest it. I'd been so naïve. I know this has happened to thousands, millions, of young women, but I had been fooled. I was hurt and angry, very angry. I had tried to be the "perfect wife," and it had not turned out well. That got me thinking about what Mark had said. Was I too much of a perfectionist? Did I try too hard to be perfect in every way?

I had failed at marriage. I was not used to failing. I had thought off and on about hiring a counselor and decided now was the time to try it. At our first session, I said, "A very wise man told me once that I was a perfectionist, I tried too hard to be in control all the time, and I was ashamed of my history when I should have been proud of it."

She said, "Is that what you want to work on?"

"Yes, I think, and anything else that might help me."

We worked on changing how I thought about myself. Cognitive Behavioral Therapy they call it. It was helpful. I was tempted to write to Mark to tell him that, but I still had the restraining order against him and did not want him to think we might resume some kind of relationship.

I thought about a lot of things. If I had been dating all along, since my teens like most people, would I have been less vulnerable, less likely to fall for Brandon's charms, more likely to see through him? Maybe, maybe not. Lots of smart, mature, experienced women have fallen for people like him. Anyway, as Mark would say, what difference does it make? I needed to figure out how to go on.

Another thing I thought about was whether I ever would be able to love again. I had loved Brandon very much and gotten badly hurt. Should I avoid loving like that to protect myself from more hurts? Again, I thought about Mark. He was right: it's better to care about people than be afraid to. Caring about people is good. Even if it's scary.

One day, Jonathon, Dr. DeProulx and I met to talk about what we could do to comfort Mark and help him feel better. Jonathon said, "Losing Cindy really hurt him bad, but I think he is starting to get over that, maybe not ready to start dating yet but starting to think about whether he should try to develop relationships with other women. But he's afraid of the dating scene and doesn't know how to go about it. Do you think, Jackie, that you might go out with him a few times, not on a real date or as a potential girlfriend, but just to help him get used to being out in public with a woman again?"

"Well, I'd be willing to go out as part of a larger group but, you know, I'm in a committed relationship and I wouldn't want him to misunderstand that, to start getting fantasies that I might be available."

"How about you, Katy?"

"Good grief! He's old enough to be my father, or grandfather. He said so himself. And he has had fantasies about me, and he stalked me—that's why I had to get the restraining order."

"Well, you could make the restraining order go away. Just saying. You are available, aren't you?"

"Jonathon, I don't know what you are thinking, but I only agreed to help behind the scenes. I never agreed to meet him face to face."

"He adores you, Katy, he really does. I know you've got mixed feelings, but maybe there is some way for good to come …."

"My feelings aren't 'mixed'—I have been very clear. I don't want to see him.

Still, that got me thinking about what, if any, kind of relationship I might have with Mark.

By early March 2017, Jonathon had finished a draft of his paper, article, whatever it was. All the caregivers and I were given copies and we agreed to meet a week later at Jonathon and Esther's condo to discuss what, if anything, we should do with it.

When we met, I said, "Look, I don't think we should make any decision about this. It should be up to Mark. Let's give him a copy. Let him decide."

Everyone agreed. Jonathon and the others wanted to give it to him right away. I said, "No, there's something I want to do first. How about on his birthday, that's what, just ten days away?" We decided to give him a birthday party at his new apartment, at 7:00 on March 20. Julie and Stephen were in charge of making sure he was there.

I came about 7:30 when the party already was underway. The others knew I was coming but Mark did not; they all had promised to keep that secret. Of course, Mark was surprised to see me. I handed him a large envelope and said, "Happy birthday."

He opened the envelope, pulled out a legal document, started reading it, smiled, and then burst into tears. It was an order in the case of Katherine Teresa Alvarez v. Markus Kauffman, signed by the judge, quashing the restraining order and dismissing the suit. I came over and hugged him. By then I was crying and so were a lot of the others.

Jonathon gave Mark a copy of his draft article. "Bedtime reading," he said. "I hope you find it as moving as the rest of us do."

It was quite a party. There was a lot of crying and hugging, and later a lot of laughing.

By 10:00 or so, people started to drift out. By 11:00 only Mark and I were left. We sat across the room and looked at each other for a while. Then I came over, sat next to him on the couch, gave him a hug, and said, "Was it a happy birthday?"

"The happiest ever."

We hugged for a long time. Then I said, "Did anybody ever tell you that you are a kind and caring and lovable person?"

"Not lately." He thought about that for a while. Then he said, "No, that's wrong. People have been trying to tell me that. But coming from you, well, that's, ah, that's something very special."

I began to stroke his thigh. After a while, he very tentatively put a hand on my breast. Even through my blouse and bra, he probably could feel my nipple getting hard. "Are you OK?" he asked.

"Never better."

When we finished making love there were clothes all over the floor. We wiggled around to lie side by side on the couch, but it wasn't very comfortable. "We should move to the bed," I said, "but I better call the babysitter first."

He held me while I made the call. "Hi, it's me, Katy. I won't be coming home tonight. Can you take care of Claire until tomorrow?" She started to ask a question, but I cut her off: "We can talk about it tomorrow, Mom."

Jonathon's article was never published. We talked about changing the ending to cover Mark's birthday party and our reconciliation. "No," Jonathon said, "it's a very beautiful love story but it's your story and you should write it." So, I did, and this is it.

# # #

ACKNOWLEDGMENTS

Writing this book was a fun and challenging experience, but something I never could have finished it without help and encouragement from a lot of people. My friend, Bob Dockstader, struggled through several dreadful early drafts and provided helpful suggestions and encouragement. Then I hired a freelance editor, Amber Queresi, who provided a very helpful editorial assessment. It persuaded me to cut the word count by over a third and restructure the story. Then I hired another editor, Lindsay Means, who provided very helpful comments and suggestions on two later drafts. I found both editors through the Reedsy website, which I highly recommend as a source of help and information for new writers. The cover design is by Joleen Naylor. I found her through the Smashwords website, which also is a great resource.

Finally, I want to thank my wife, Carole, who patiently put up with my working on this book.

About the Author

I graduated from Shoreline High School in 1962, the University of Washington (B.A. English, 1966) and the Stanford Law School (J.D. 1969). At Stanford I was President of the Legal Aid Society and became interested in poverty law and other issues of the poor, but also interested in real estate, business and finance. After law school I went to work for Weyerhaeuser Company, expecting to work in those fields but quickly drifted into environmental and natural resources law. I retired in 2006. I wanted to try writing fiction for a long time, but this is the first I have written. If you have comments or questions about this book, please:

Follow me on Twitter: http://twitter.com/JanPauw3

Friend me on Facebook: http://facebook.com/Jan Pauw

Made in the USA
Monee, IL
03 November 2020

46540161R20225